RAVE REVIEWS
FOR THE NOVELS OF
MARIANNE WILLMAN

...ish

...JBLEDAY BOOK CLUB

The Enchanted Mirror

"Sweeping from the cold English winters to the blazing desert sands where intrigue, ancient secrets and grave dangers await the lovers, this fascinating blend of the mystical with a heated love triangle will keep readers glued to the pages. Ms. Willman's skill at crafting romances that merge paranormal elements and wonderful historical backdrops with engaging characters is remarkable."

—*Romantic Times*

"Will keep readers hooked until that final page."

—*Intrinsic Romance* magazine

"With THE ENCHANTED MIRROR, Willman excels at throwing every roadblock in the way of the hero and heroine, creating a nail-biting tale of romance and intrigue. Enchantment surrounds each page and turns a simple plot into a story rich in excitement and sensual lore. A loveless bride, a resolute villain, a stalwart lover...what more can you ask from a writer of renown?"

—*Reader to Reader Reviews*

Turn the page for more praise. . .

The Lost Bride

"A beautifully mystical journey of love, loss, and triumph."
—Nora Roberts

"A mysterious bride, a treasure hidden in plain sight, a brooding artist and a perfectly sensible woman—what more could you want in romance? A delicious atmosphere haunts this unique tale of dreams and redemption."
—Susan Wiggs

"Marianne Willman weaves enchantment into every page as we discover anew the course of true love never runs smoothly…well-drawn characters that tug at the heartstrings and warm the spirit."
—*Rendezvous*

"Wonderful! Willman's attention to detail is perfect and her characterizations flawless." —*Old Book Barn Gazette*

"Marianne Willman is well on her way to becoming a world-famous wordsmith." —*The Write Words*

"Marianne Willman brings the perfect touch of magic and illusion to her novel, infusing THE LOST BRIDE with myth, romance, and the ideal amount of suspense. She has crafted a Gothic romance for the '90s that satisfies the craving for the lush, chilling, hypnotic tales her fans desire."
—*Romantic Times*

The Mermaid's Song

"A lyrically woven tale that glows with romance, pulses with suspense, and shimmers with magic." —Nora Roberts

"It is impossible to resist the lure of THE MERMAID'S SONG. From beginning to end, this love story, entwined with passion, intrigue, and mystical charms, held me in its spell."
—Julie Garwood

ST. MARTIN'S PAPERBACKS TITLES
BY MARIANNE WILLMAN

The Enchanted Mirror
The Lost Bride
The Mermaid's Song

The
Wish

Marianne Willman

St. Martin's Paperbacks

NOTE: If you purchased this book without a cover you should be aware that this book is stolen property. It was reported as "unsold and destroyed" to the publisher, and neither the author nor the publisher has received any payment for this "stripped book."

THE WISH

Copyright © 2000 by Marianne Willman.

All rights reserved. No part of this book may be used or reproduced in any manner whatsoever without written permission except in the case of brief quotations embodied in critical articles or reviews. For information address St. Martin's Press, 175 Fifth Avenue, New York, NY 10010.

ISBN: 0-312-97577-5

Printed in the United States of America

St. Martin's Paperbacks edition / December 2000

St. Martin's Paperbacks are published by St. Martin's Press, 175 Fifth Avenue, New York, NY 10010.

10 9 8 7 6 5 4 3 2 1

The Wish

Prologue

It was a place where few visited, and none lingered.

Tortured stacks of weathered granite broke through the earth like ancient bones, and the land fell away sharply on either hand. The wind keened across the rugged heath, wild and desolate as the land itself.

In the thinning light of day, a shadow separated from the rocky foot of Giant's Tor. A woman, pale as candle wax, and stumbling in her haste. She was near collapse, her once-pretty face ravaged by fever and strain, her dark eyes wild with fear.

She was lost, confused by the ancient trackways that criss-crossed the open moor, and vanished far below into the secretive green valleys. Her serviceable dress of black twill was ruined, damp and splattered with dried muck. She had almost fallen into one of the watery bogs, hidden beneath a skim of seemingly solid vegetation. That had been a terrible moment!

Now she was so cold, so utterly bone-weary, that she didn't think she could go another yard. Her teeth chattered. It took enormous effort to set one foot before the other, to persevere against such great odds. Desperation gave her courage.

She must not think of herself, but only of the child.

An echo of distant thunder rolled across the moor, like the pound of pursuing hooves. The woman gasped, and struggled to rein in her galloping terror. Her ribs felt bruised from the pummeling of her heart. In her imagination she could almost hear the fierce snarling of the hounds, feel their savage fangs slice deep into her flesh. Panic drove her.

I must find shelter! And food!

But first she must get her bearings. Her memories of the area were vague and faulty. She realized that now. Oh, if only she'd thought this through more carefully before leaving! But there had been no time to do more than snatch up a few necessities. At least she'd recognized Stump Cross a while back.

Everything would have been different if only the horse hadn't shied and run off, smashing the gig to pieces! They'd have been safe by now. She touched the side of her ribs, bruised from a flailing hoof. Three days since the accident, and every breath still filled her lungs with cold fire. But it might have been so much worse! Another inch or two, and she would have been dead.

And then who would have saved the child?

The woman scanned the heath. There was no sign of human life. Ahead, the near-vertical moorland fell away sharply into steep-sided reeves, then narrow river valleys that widened and softened toward the distant sea. On a clear afternoon it was even possible to see the dancing silver-blue ribbons of light that marked the bay, thirteen miles away.

But things were not exactly as she had remembered. Either that, or she'd somehow missed the three standing stones that lined up with the grove where the old tree stood. The Druids' Oak, someone had named it. But others called it the Wishing Tree . . .

There must be another landmark. Some indication of which way to go. She shadowed her eyes against the flattening light. *Ah, yes!*

The landscape was deceiving! The vastness of the moors played tricks on the eye and mind: what she'd thought to be a distant meadow was actually a dark canopy of summer leaves, rising from the valley below. The thin finger of rock spearing up through them was not one of the strange granite tors, but the time-blackened steeple of the thirteenth-century church in Haycross Village.

Relief made her weak. She swayed and took a ragged breath, then turned slowly. There they were: three stones, cupped in a barren hollow. At this distance they looked like sheep, huddled against the coming night.

She pressed a trembling hand to her mouth. *Oh, thank God!*

But they were not safe yet. Darkness was not far off. The sun would set beyond the high tor with the abruptness of a blown-out lamp. The woman clasped her arms about her shoulders and shivered. There were treacherous bogs that looked like solid land, where straying sheep and lost men vanished. She would have to find shelter, and continue on at first light.

But first, the grove! The hour was at hand. Surely, oh surely, it lay somewhere just ahead . . .

Turning back toward Giant's Tor, she held up a warning hand to the small figure huddled there. Then, leaving the track, she skittered down through the bracken into the trees that grew thick along the ravine. In her state of anxiety time seemed to speed up. One moment she was in a dark tunnel, sharply inclined; the next in a wide clearing.

A jumbled wall of granite jutted up through the wild grasses. Inside the broken circle they formed, a massive oak stood alone, gnarled roots sunk deep into the loamy earth. Myriad flowers garlanded the base of the tree, in every hue of the rainbow, and its leafy crown rose high against the amethyst sky.

Joy rendered her giddy. She'd found it, after all!

Her ascent from the sheltered reeve was difficult. By the time she'd scrabbled up, the woman was at the edge of exhaustion. Fear spurred her on. As she reached the tor, wind moaned between the timeworn stone, snatching with eager fingers at her ruined skirts and disheveled hair. She brushed the loose strands from her face and reached into the looming shadows.

"Come," she said urgently. "Quickly, now."

A young girl slipped away from the base of the tor, the breeze whipping her Gypsy-black hair about her face. Her embroidered dress was rent by thorn and bramble, and stained with dirt and moss. She was trembling with fatigue.

"I wish to lie down," she said. "I cannot walk another step."

"No! We dare not. Can't you hear the baying of the hounds?"

"It is only the wind!"

"No! They are drawing near. Oh, do hurry!"

Reluctantly, the child edged closer to the woman, her only comfort in this alien place. She pushed a wisp of hair from her eyes. "We are lost, aren't we?"

"No. We are very close now, I promise you." Her voice turned cajoling. "Come, I will make you a garland of flowers! Which ones do you like best?"

The girl clutched the gold locket that hung from a soiled blue ribbon about her neck, fighting back tears. She had been promised a fair and a puppet show and all the marchpane she could eat; instead she'd been thrown into a ditch when the gig overturned, then forced to walk through mud and rain, and sleep beneath hedges and in cow byres.

No amount of artful coaxing could convince her that she was having an exciting adventure, like a storybook heroine. Even Cinderella had had her warm chimney corner.

The stony silence of the glade made her restive. Suddenly it was all too much: she was cold and hungry, and her violet eyes stung with tears.

"I want to go home!"

"Hush, my darling! They'll hear you."

The woman's frantic fear leapt to the girl. Her lower lip trembled but her limbs grew rigid, as if her body had turned as cold and hard as the granite of the mighty tors.

The woman held out her hand imperatively, and lowered her voice to a whisper. "Why do you hesitate? Come. I promise you can rest soon. And by morning we shall be safe and snug! Only a few more hours, my precious one."

The woman's voice soothed her, as it always had before. The girl did as she was bid, and followed the woman off the track and into the trees. But when they entered the clearing her eyes went wide with apprehension. The mossy ground absorbed the sound of their footsteps. Utter silence reined.

The hair at her nape prickled and gooseflesh rose on her arms, but not from growing cold. Although she couldn't articulate her feelings, they were a product of the strange stillness, the sense of immense power that might at any moment be unleashed. The very air shimmered with it.

Without warning, the upper limbs of the ancient oak stirred, and the leaves shivered green and black and silver. She tried to pull back.

"Oh! What is this place? It's horrid! I don't like it!"

"Hush! You mustn't say that." The woman's face grew beatific. "This is the place where wishes made in blood come true."

Still, a tremor ran through the woman. There was a primal presence here, something vast and sentient, and utterly indifferent to the intrusion of mere humans. Something that she could summon to her use, if she but dared.

She took a deep breath and sent her will winging out into the clearing, swift as a spear of light. She could feel the shock of its hitting home. Something that had been asleep and dreaming ancient dreams awakened.

"Wait," she told the girl. "Watch."

The air about them gathered. Thickened. While the last rays of sun slid through the notch in the rocks at the head of the ravine, the child closed her eyes. She was terribly afraid, but the woman beside her was comforted.

Any moment now . . .

Suddenly the sun dipped to the head of the narrow reeve. A path of hammered gold shimmered over the mossy ground, paving the way past the tips of the girl's worn-out slippers and over the carpet of beautiful flowers, to the base of the ancient oak. A burst of light almost blinded the woman. The shadowed gaps beneath the tree's coiled roots burned bright, with the brilliance of a thousand candles.

Throwing off the weakness that assailed her, the woman smiled and sighed in relief: *So, the legend is true, after all!*

And they had not been rebuffed, but welcomed.

She felt the girl sway, and looked down. *Poor child, she is almost asleep on her feet. But she must see this miracle for herself.* "Wake up! Oh, my darling, only *look*!"

The woman's fingers bit into the girl's arm. She gasped out a sob and opened her eyes. She felt as if she'd stepped into a fairyland. The flowers glowed like a rainbow tapestry at her feet. Weariness fell away like a cast-off cloak as she saw the golden path that stretched through them, and the dancing blaze of light beneath the tree. It seemed as if the clearing and everything in it must be consumed by the brilliance.

"Oh! What is it?"

The woman's voice was so soft she could scarcely hear it: "You will see!"

Although the girl held back at first, the beauty and magic of it drew her forward to the center of the clearing. When they reached the oak, she was dazzled by the glory of light, and even more afraid.

Then the sun shifted and she realized it was not a huge flame burning among the mammoth roots. It was a hollow space, domed with crystals, some as long as she was tall. Great spiky shapes, their bases white as milk and their tips as clear and shimmery as air—every one of them reflecting back the sun like a golden mirror.

It made her dizzy. She backed away.

"I want to go *home*!"

The woman gave her another shake. "Do not say that again!"

She pushed the girl down to her knees and knelt beside her. There was no time to explain. The hounds were closer. She must lure them away.

"You must hide, my darling. You'll be safe here, in this little hollow beneath the tree's roots. Do not venture out until I come for you."

The child balked in alarm. "I won't!"

"You must!"

"But . . . what shall I do . . . if you *don't* come back for me?"

A gray wave of illness shuddered through the woman's too-thin body. The very thought of it was overwhelming.

She gathered her wits. "Then you must go on without me. I have told you of Mrs. Redd, my old aunt. She will take you in."

The woman pointed to the green valley below. "If I do not return by morning, you must find the beck, and follow it until you come to the old stepping stones that form a bridge. Cross to the other side and follow the track."

Hunger and cold and fright rose up inside the exhausted child. "I can't," she cried. *"I won't!"*

The woman gripped the girl's shoulders and shook her until her teeth rattled. "You must!" They both burst into tears. Their arms twined round one another for comfort while they wept.

The woman dried their eyes and sighed, and the girl did, too. There was so much she didn't understand.

"Listen well! Eventually," the woman told her, "you will see the thatched roofs of the village to the right. Do not go there! Take the left track through the woods. It will be a fair distance. At its end you'll find a lovely cottage, with a tiled roof and a stone wall about it. That is our destination. You must say that I have sent you. My aunt will give you shelter."

She drew in a labored breath. "But I shall not fail you. I'll be back before nightfall." *God willing!*

"Can't you stay with me?"

"No." She cocked her head again, listening to the phantom dogs. "They are closing in!" She felt the brittle twigs beneath her feet, like shattered bones. "I must lead them away from you, my darling. You must be very brave while I am gone."

She didn't want to leave the girl alone, but they were in desperate need of food. If she could escape the hounds, there was an inn four miles across the heath as the crow flies. Surely she could beg their bread at the inn. But she would go alone.

Unpinning her brooch, with the brilliant blue stone, the woman pricked her hand with the sharp point of the pin. Then she affixed the jewel to the child's bodice, leaving a smear of blood on her shawl.

"This is your talisman, and my pledge that you will be safe. I must leave you now: the hounds are growing close."

"It is only the wind you hear!" the child protested.

But there was no sound but their voices in the clearing— no breeze, no cry of hounds. Nothing but the frantic beating of her heart.

The woman squeezed her finger where she'd pricked it with the sharp pin of the brooch. Three scarlet drops fell to the earth.

"I have made my sacrifice," she whispered. "Grant my wish. Do not let them find her!"

A strange breeze rose out of nowhere. The great, leafy limbs of the massive oak stirred restlessly. They shook in reproach, tossing like the waves of an angry sea, but the magic gathered in response to the woman's summons.

Without warning, she caught the girl's shoulders and shoved her, hard. The force of it sent the child sliding down a steep, mossy verge and in among the tangled roots. She was too surprised to even utter a single cry.

The great oak creaked and groaned, its thick leaves threshing the sky. Wild-eyed, the woman turned and fled up the ravine.

For some moments the child lay in the hollow beneath the tree, stunned and terrified as the elfin light burned around her. In the midst of the crystal forest, she clutched the locket on its blue ribbon for solace and felt the smooth blue stone of the brooch against her arm.

Gradually, fear turned to awe. The mossy ground beneath her was velvet-soft, and tiny golden flowers bloomed in the crannies between the crystals. Their sweet perfume filled the air, lulling her.

The girl discovered she could sit up without banging her head against the crystal spears. *It is like a fairy palace, the walls and ceiling all sparkly and bright.* And it was warm. Oh, she had been hungry and cold for so long! Days and days.

The light altered, dimmed. Gold faded to soothing mauve, to cool lavender and deep, hazy blue as she waited for the woman's return. Time passed and she remained alone.

Oddly, she was no longer afraid. She thought she heard music, like golden bells, lulling her gently. She imagined, without knowing why, that it was the flowers singing.

Peace filled her, and she curled up inside the hollow. Warmth seeped into her slender body, as if she were comforted again in her mother's arms.

Exhaustion overcame her, and she slept.

Lavender twilight faded to gray as the woman stared up at the sky. She was waiting for the clouds to part and the stars to come out. Could she still read their patterns, or had she lost that skill, living so long amid the bright lights and creeping fogs of London?

She remembered the skies above Dartmoor as being so low, so huge, it seemed that she could pluck the stars from the skies, like glittering apples of light.

But a thin gauzy layer of cloud floated between heaven and earth tonight, and the stars were only faint pinpricks.

Panic fluttered in her breast. *I should never have left the old trackway,* she thought. But she'd heard the sound of hooves and had run away, but it had only been one of the wild Dartmoor ponies. Somehow she'd gotten off course after that, and now she feared she wouldn't find her way back at all. *"I must!"* she whispered. *"I will!"*

By day the bald moors were disorienting in their vastness. By night they were a savage realm, filled with shadows and menace. She shivered with cold and fatigue. With fever and atavistic fears.

The wind soughed over the heath. It plucked at her garments, snatched her hair loose and whipped it, stinging, across her cheek. This was no place to linger. There were many bogs in this area. Places that looked solid, but were like vats of watery jam. She'd seen a dog swallowed up whole, without leaving a trace.

She must find the track, and quickly, before her strength failed her. At last she spied a light ahead, glimmering at the base of a deep swale. Plunging on with new hope, she passed the base of a low tor and came out into open ground. With every step her heart lightened. The inn was surely just ahead!

Cold water suddenly edged up over the sides of her ruined shoes. Then she felt the ground shudder beneath her feet. Heard the sickening squelch, felt the heavy suck of the bog that lay beneath the cover of bracken.

Her right shoe came off as she fought to free herself, and vanished without a ripple. She was sinking! She flailed her arms to keep her balance, but it was futile. Her left foot hit the ground and sank to the calf in the cold ooze. She was hopelessly mired. The more she struggled the deeper and faster she sank. The bog embraced her like a demon lover.

It was over quickly.

Bubbles rose to the surface, then ceased. There was nothing to show that she had ever been there. Nothing but the night and the moors, and the fitful sighing of the wind.

It was long past morning when the girl awakened, still alone. She forced herself to wait as long as possible, but the woman did not return. Somehow the child knew that she never would. Curling up in a ball, she wept bitterly. The hot tears fell, streaking her dirt-smudged cheeks.

After a time the warmth seeped out of her body. The hollow beneath the tree grew dark, the crystals frosted and cold. She knew she would find no more comfort there.

It was time to leave.

Drying her tears, she left her hiding place and followed the course of the rock-strewn stream. Fish flashed and leapt in the deeper pools. In places it was so clear she could have counted the pebbles lying on the bottom, had she wished. As she leaned forward, she was suddenly frightened by the face reflected up at her, all wild, tangled hair and huge eyes.

She shrieked and leapt away, not realizing for several seconds that the creature she'd seen was herself. Birds flew up from the trees, scolding.

"I must wash my face and bind up my hair," she said aloud, and was startled by the sound of her voice, so thin and hoarse.

Reaching to touch the locket that had been her birthday gift, her small fingers closed on the blue ribbon. Her heart turned over: the ribbon was there, but the locket was gone.

That was a cruel blow. It had been a gift from her father.

She touched the brooch pinned to her torn dress. The blue stone sparkled with inner lights. *The talisman. At least I still have it.*

She fought back a sob of panic, and went on. She walked and walked, but she was small and the way seemed endless. By late afternoon the last of the food was gone, but there were wild berries beside the bridge, and she filled her belly with them before crossing over. The sun was almost down when she reached the place where the tumbling beck joined the river. Not once, since abandoning her shelter, had she spied so much as the gable of a house, or heard the bark of a dog.

Her small body shook with exhaustion and hunger. She wanted to sit down on the mossy ground and weep her heart out; but she was too tired for tears. Too fearful of the coming night.

Lifting her head, she saw a faint light bloom in the distance. The village! No more than half a dozen buildings perhaps, but there would be food and warmth, and shelter. Then she saw it: a narrow track turning off to the left. It led into a stand of woods away from the friendly lights. For a moment she wavered.

Then she gathered her courage, and turned resolutely off the river path. She quickened her pace as she entered the trees once more, and shadows gathered round her. The light was failing fast, and her heart pounded wildly as she kept to the rutted track.

She found the gravel drive as the first stars bloomed in the rapidly darkening sky. *The cottage will be at its end,* she told herself. *I will be safe once I reach it.*

The way was hemmed in by black masses of rhododendrons, and briars and brambles encroached upon the edges of the drive. She scarcely felt the rough gravel beneath her worn slippers. When she saw the stone wall through the trees, she cried out in relief. Her ordeal was almost over.

The wall was backed by more towering rhododendrons, tarry black against the translucent sky, but the intricate wrought-iron gate stood ajar, as if welcoming her. She slipped through it, searching for a lighted window to guide her, and stumbled in her haste. She went sprawling forward, scraping her palms and knees. The girl was too excited to heed the stinging. The drive swept around a curve, and she followed it eagerly.

Only a little farther now!

The thought urged her on. When she reached the wide curve and rounded it, she stopped dead. Tremors racked her thin body and her teeth chattered with shock.

There was no lighted window. No hope of food and rest and safety. No lovely stone cottage. Nothing but charred timbers clawing at the starry sky, and the cold, gray scent of ash.

One

The barren, star-swept moors rose high in the distance, beyond the quiet village. The treetops danced like a restless, night-black sea. While the countryside slept, Haycross Manor glittered like a vision from another world, every window of its sprawling façade ablaze with golden light.

Inside, the grand house was filled with laughter and music, and the mellow glow of beeswax tapers in gilt and crystal sconces. The hour was advanced, the party half over, when the latecomer made his appearance. The new Earl of Ravenall paused in the ballroom doorway and regarded the dancers with remote detachment.

Only his eyes, blue as sapphires in a face bronzed by sun and wind, showed a flicker of emotion. Only his closest friends would have recognized it as anger.

His arrival caused quite a stir, and an audible murmur rippled through the glittering ballroom. Ravenall strolled coolly through the sea of bejeweled silks and satins, candlelight glinting from his thick, black hair. This was not his chosen world: he wished the waves of music were ocean waves, that the polished floor beneath his feet were weathered deck, and the numerous beeswax tapers scintillating stars.

The pretty young Duchess of Haycross, beautiful in white crêpe de chine and lace, watched her brother approach, and snapped her ivory fan closed. The diamonds at her throat and bosom flashed her indignation. She'd been anxiously awaiting his arrival all evening, praying that he would redeem his promise to her. For the past hour she'd been in an agony of despair.

She was suddenly struck by the thought that he might have planned it that way, to teach her a lesson.

"How like Justin!" she said beneath her breath. "Incorrigible!"

Despite that first moment of supreme pique, the duchess was incredibly relieved. His presence surely meant that his mission on her behalf had been successful! Oh, thank heaven! The smile she sent his way was more dazzling than the light of all the candles and glittering crystal in the ballroom.

Ravenall cut a dashing figure in his evening clothes. His presence added cachet to her small country ball, and her luring of him down to Devon would enhance her standing as a fashionable hostess for the coming London Season. Despite the dark whispers surrounding his past, Ravenall was the prime catch on the marriage mart. Noble blood and a substantial fortune made him exceedingly eligible.

That he was unwed, and had recently inherited the earldom from his late uncle, made him irresistible.

The young debutante beside the duchess, a toothy blonde in layers of spangled pink gauze, brightened perceptibly.

"Oh, your grace! Is *that* Ravenall?" She ignored the fierce blue eyes, his air of impatient hauteur. "He is quite striking! A dark angel!"

"Yes, Amanda." The duchess lowered her voice. "I'd advise you not to set your sights on him. My brother is proud as Lucifer, and with the devil's own temper. He wouldn't make a comfortable husband for you."

Rumors had swirled about Justin as long as she could remember. The duchess, of course, had still been in the schoolroom when some youthful folly had caused their father to pack him off to their uncle's estate in Jamaica. Daisey recalled that she had cried herself to sleep every night for a month and more, after Justin's exile from the bosom of the family. The entire household had been in an uproar. There had been shouts and whispers and tears, she remembered, and an epic quarrel between their already estranged parents.

Not that any of this past history altered Lady Haycross's fond opinion of her only brother, or outweighed an earldom, in the eyes of society. Or in the bright blue orbs of the pretty American heiress beside her.

Rosy color flushed Miss Bryce's fair cheeks as she watched Lord Ravenall cut a swath through the crowd. She was a very ambitious girl. Her elder sister had been at school with Lady

Haycross, and after a successful come-out, had settled for a mere baronet. *She* would not.

Miss Bryce had come to England, like so many of her wealthy compatriots, to obtain a titled husband. To snare such an illustrious title as the Countess of Ravenall would be a triumph indeed!

There was only one small problem: Lord Ravenall's banishment to the West Indies, an indiscreet affair that had ended badly, and rumors of a freewheeling, dissolute life had reached even *her* dainty, pearl-bedecked ears.

As Lady Haycross stepped forward eagerly, Miss Bryce turned to her chaperone, a turbaned dowager on her other side, and whispered behind her fan. "Is it true what they say of him?"

The dowager stiffened in shocked disapproval. "No, it is not! You are a young lady of quality, not a gossiping scullery maid, Amanda. If you cannot refrain from asking such a question, then your place is still in the schoolroom, and not among the ladies and gentlemen of the *ton!*"

Amanda's flush deepened. "I beg your pardon, godmamma! It was very wrong of me," she said quickly.

She smiled and watched in appreciation as Ravenall made his way through the throng. *How handsome he is, with his dark good looks and lithe frame! That face! Those moody sea-blue eyes. Even if it were true . . . much can surely be forgiven such a man!*

Although their reasons differed, the duchess agreed. Her brother was the only other surviving member of their immediate family, and she loved him dearly.

Other women watched his progress through the ballroom with great interest. Certainly no one would call Ravenall conventionally handsome. His jaw was too square, his features too strong to fit the accepted mode; yet there was something fascinating about his face. The sharply chiseled slant of his slashing cheekbones, the stern lines of his firm, sensual mouth, hinted at passion and command.

It was his eyes, however, that made the greatest impression. They were a startling, changeable blue against the sun-bronzed skin of an outdoorsman, and filled with cynicism and a reckless intelligence. Into the refined, civilized world of the ballroom, he brought an untamed element, like the gusting wind that heralds a storm sweeping in off the bay.

The young widows and matrons might be intrigued, and wonder what it would be like to have Ravenall for a lover; but the innocents, fresh from the schoolroom, found him more than a little intimidating. To more sophisticated title-hunters like Amanda, he was the means to an end.

The debutante's eyes sparkled: *Only think of how heads would turn if I returned to New York a countess! I would have a footman to follow me everywhere, and a fine lady's maid to look after my jewels and gowns. How my friends would stare!*

The duchess fluttered her fan to attract her brother's attention.

"He has seen you," Amanda exclaimed. A predatory look came into her eye. Lady Haycross gave a dainty sigh. Justin had an exceedingly low tolerance for fools and hangers-on. She only hoped he wouldn't give Amanda one of his icy setdowns when he took himself off toward the card room. Amanda was as headstrong as she was pretty and ambitious. *Ah well, she will learn soon enough.*

Heads turned as the earl strolled through the throng, bowing or exchanging a word of greeting with his acquaintances, until he reached their side. Ravenall bowed low over his sister's hand. "You see, Daisey, I am a man of my word."

"By arriving at almost the last minute!"

His sudden smile relieved the harsh cast of his countenance. "I never gave my word to be on time—only to attend. I redeem my promise."

The duchess would not be mollified so easily. She examined the scrape along his square jaw. "May I hope your opponent did you no further damage?"

He gave a bark of laughter. "Nothing so unrefined as a boxing match kept me from your side, Daisey. I was inspecting Ravenall Castle with my new agent, when one of the ramparts gave way. It set my departure back until late this afternoon."

She almost dropped her fan. "La! You've never come all this way today, Justin!"

His blue eyes danced with laughter. "Only for you, my dear."

She melted: how could she not? "You are a silver-tongued rogue!" she chided. "But one of these days you'll come to grief, traveling at such neck-or-nothing speed."

She introduced Amanda, who was almost bursting with impatience.

Lord Ravenall made another elegant bow. "Your servant, Miss Bryce."

Ravenall only stayed to make a few pleasantries. He didn't ask Amanda to dance, although the waltz was still in progress when he took himself off toward the cardroom. The disappointment of the young ladies and their hopeful mamas was palpable.

Miss Bryce was only more determined to attach him. After all, the party wouldn't break up for two more days. *There is still a chance for a clever girl to snare herself an earl.*

The earl had already dismissed her from his mind. He'd only come to please his sister, and intended to spend the rest of the evening in the card room. As Ravenall neared the door leading off to it, he was hailed by a stocky young man with curling chestnut hair. His face lit when he saw his cousin Andrew making his way toward him.

Though unalike in looks or temperament, the two men were the last of the Waverly line. Both had been orphaned young, and the two had always been close. Andrew had been in Jamaica in the wake of Ravenall's disastrous marriage. After the end of that sorry affair, their bond had grown even stronger.

"Well," Ravenall said with a smile, "this is quite a family reunion."

"You don't know the half of it. Bridgeforth is here, as well."

"The devil you say!"

"He was staying in the neighborhood, and Daisey couldn't exclude him, since he's a relation."

Ravenall's mouth thinned. "More's the pity!" He had no liking for Calvin Bridgeforth, and the sentiment was mutual. "When did you return from your mission in Vienna?"

"Ten days ago. I'm on leave while Lord Westmacott is honeymooning with his bride. I wouldn't have missed Daisey's ball for anything. Nor the chance to turn into an odious tuft-hunter, and drop casual comments of having spent a week at Haycross Manor."

He looked around the splendid room, with its gilded ceiling medallions and crystal chandeliers, its sense of history. Haycross Manor had been old when Drake had set out from Plymouth to fight the Spanish Armada. Andrew knew well that he would likely never have set foot within its walls if Ravenall's sister hadn't married the duke.

"Make the most of it," Ravenall told him, as if reading his mind. "There are men here who could further your career with just a word dropped into the right ear."

He glanced over at Amanda Bryce, who was watching them intently from behind her painted fan. "Look at all the eager debutantes hoping to snare a husband. Perhaps Daisey will play matchmaker between you and that hungry-looking heiress from Philadelphia."

Andrew grinned. "The only time she even looked at me was when she learned that I was related to *you,* coz. Damn your eyes, Justin! I don't know why the rest of us have even bothered to attend, when every beauty in the ballroom is bedazzled by you."

They moved past a tall branch of candles. Beneath Ravenall's thick dark lashes, his eyes glittered like sea ice. "Do you think so, Andrew? One year ago, I could have fallen dead at their daintily shod feet—and they would have stepped over mc without so much as a glance."

The younger man glanced at the earl in surprise. "You are in an odd humor to think so."

Ravenall's voice was light but mocking. "I have many sins, Andrew. Vanity is not one them. There is not a one of those eager beauties who cares a fig for me. As for their matchmaking mothers, before I was made an earl they were careful to whisk their daughters away from the dangers of entangling themselves with a man of my dangerous reputation."

"You are too severe. You've always had your share of flirts."

"Yes, dashing young matrons looking to cuckold their husbands. Not the type to entice me. And even the sweet young things who flirted behind their fans knew better than to set their caps for me."

Andrew's smile returned. "While no fault can be found with your bloodlines or your tailor, you must admit that your tongue is sharp, your humor ironic, and your temper legendary."

Ravenall smiled coolly. "And of course, I didn't have a

feather to fly with. Now that I've succeeded to my late uncle's dignities, they swarm around me like wasps to ripe fruit. I will not prove so easy for the picking."

"Can you blame them? The fair sex have a duty to their families to make the best marriage they can." Andrew tried to lighten his mood. "You know the saying," he joked. "A poor man makes a poor husband."

"Yes. And one who is suspected of murder in cold blood is an even worse choice!" Ravenall smiled wryly. "Of course everything is changed since my uncle succumbed to fever while sailing up the Nile, along with his son and heir."

Andrew pulled his cousin aside, into the shelter of an arrangement of potted palms. "Good Lord! What strange fancy has taken you since we last met, Justin? You have grown even more cynical."

Ravenall's voice was bitter: "Inheriting an earldom can change a man profoundly."

His cousin was bewildered. "I should think that wealth and ease and social position would have an opposite effect!"

"We both know I am no Prince Charming. It is the allure of my title that makes my company so sought after. The thought of becoming a countess, and of spending my considerable worldly goods on gowns, jewels, and gilded coaches, and of entertaining the *ton* in high style. It goes to their pretty, empty heads like champagne punch."

He swept a look of contempt over his shoulder, as he held the curtain of the alcove aside. "Make no bones about it: if my fortune vanished overnight, so would they."

"Oh? Perhaps I should be glad I'm the son of a country parson, with nothing but my charm to recommend me," Andrew said wryly.

"Perhaps you should, indeed. You'll know that any girl who throws her cap at you does it for love."

The young earl's face darkened. "When I first returned from Jamaica I was something of a pariah. The rumors were quite widespread. Now, of course, everything is changed. Even murder can be overlooked—if the man in question is an earl!"

"You are talking like a fool!"

"Do you think so? Then I will tell you that I overheard Lady Sarah Carstairs say those exact words not ten minutes ago."

Andrew was surprised. The beauteous Lady Sarah was a stunning brunette, truly a diamond of the first water. She had made her debut the previous season, but her father had turned down all offers for her hand thus far. He was said to be angling to make his only child a duchess, or a countess—and that she had set her glorious golden eyes on Ravenall.

Well, if that is so, Andrew thought, *she's blown her chances of becoming a countess to flinders. Justin will never forgive such an insult to his character.*

"She's a very foolish girl, then. I hope your heart is not bruised."

"Only my pride, Andrew," Ravenall said through gritted teeth. "Only my pride."

He put his hand on his cousin's shoulder. "Ignore the gossip, Justin. No one who knows you gives credence to those foul rumors."

Ravenall lifted an eyebrow. "Your loyalty does you credit. In fact, there were many occasions when I would have liked to throttle Véronique with my own two hands."

Andrew looked anxious. "That was in the past. And you should not say such things in public, Justin. You know what people are! As for Lady Sarah Carstairs, she is not the only accredited Beauty out this season, you know. There are dozens more from which to choose yourself a suitable wife."

Ravenall shrugged. "You may make an earl yet, Andrew! I sincerely doubt I'll ever wed again. My parents' marriage was a farce, mine a horror. An act of youthful folly, for which I've paid dearly. It's cheaper to mount an accommodating mistress than take a wife, you know—and in the long run, far more pleasant for all concerned."

"And I still say that you are a fool, Justin!" Andrew replied. "And I cannot think of a person less suited to step into your shoes than myself."

The earl stopped and glanced down into his cousin's guileless blue eyes. "You do not think it would make your life easier?"

Andrew gaped at him. "I do not. Has it done so for you?"

Ravenall's laughter was harsh. "It is a velvet-lined prison. Not the social duties—I could forgo them with pleasure. But the late earl's holdings are in a vast tangle. Clements, my man of business, is in despair. He says it will take years to sort them out and set things in order. I would far rather have spent those years at sea, than captaining a desk and a crew of ledgers!"

They'd reached the vestibule to the card room. Ravenall led the way with Andrew following. The door closed quietly behind the two men, shutting out the din of the overheated ballroom, and the outraged faces of matchmaking mamas and their eager young daughters.

A sigh rippled through the ballroom, like the murmur of turbulent waves against a rocky shore. Visions of diamond coronets and the wedding of the coming Season faded like mist on the moor.

But, they consoled themselves, there was still hope. Why, the Season hadn't even begun. And, of course, much could be forgiven such a man, if he would only cast his glance their way.

After all, he was a *very* great earl!

The strains of a waltz filled the air, lilting and gay. Perdita slipped into the old, unused musicians' gallery. It was the music that lured her down. Oh, how she loved the music! And someday, when she was older, she would put up her hair with fancy clips, dress in a spangled white gown, and spin round and round in her partner's arms until dawn.

But for now she could only watch. And dream.

The carved railing was polished until the dark wood shone, and draped with wine-red silk. Peering between the folds, Perdita could view the ballroom below. It glittered and twinkled like a jeweled music box. The beauty of it held her spellbound. She especially loved the ceiling, with its myriad gold-leafed stars.

Holding her breath, she took it all in: beeswax candles gleaming in branched sconces against the gold-brocade walls; shimmering crystal chandeliers, scattering light on the dancers; men in black and white evening dress, all as handsome as princes; and the ladies!—their elaborate coiffures done up with sparkling diamond clips and colorful feathered plumes, circles of blazing jewels or ropes of lustrous pearls wound round their creamy throats. The air rustled with the sweep of their elegant gowns, in shimmering shades of precious stones:

topaz and peridot, emerald and sapphire, and deep, rich, ruby, the color of blood . . .

A thump shattered Perdita's dream. Her eyes blinked open to the dark slant of rough-hewn beams, and unfinished boards overhead. She was on her pallet in the small space beneath the eaves of the Stag and Crown, where she and Sukey, the other serving girl at the old inn, slept. Her heart hammered painfully while the last fragments of glorious dream-turned-nightmare slipped away.

Her first thought was that the smugglers had returned to hide their wares in the inn's secret cellar. She'd been warned never to venture belowstairs, or to look out her window when the moon was dark.

While she caught her breath, a faint gray glow came in through the chinks in the walls and the shutters at the unglazed casement. Then she remembered that the landlord was dead and buried these past two years, and the smugglers came no more. Mrs. Croggins, the landlord's widow, had been too greedy to suit them. Since then the place had fallen into disrepair, but Perdita slept the better for it.

The light permeating the room turned to a lovely, luminous tint of lavender, outlining the square window. This was usually her favorite moment of the day, when she felt safe from the nightmares that tormented her, cocooned and protected in layers of shimmery, predawn light.

But the dream she'd been abruptly wakened from had been vivid and colorful, so unlike the others that haunted her nights, its loss left her bereft. In those others—they were always the same—everything was somber and filled with deep foreboding: a dark house with endless rooms, one leading to another, and ceilings so high they were always in shadow; people all dressed in black, speaking in stern whispers.

Night, and the sound of a woman weeping.

There were times when those dreams seemed so ominous, and so real, that she was relieved to awaken in her tiny room beneath the eaves, with Sukey snoring on the pallet next to her.

Of course, it didn't take long on those occasions for reality to intrude. A servant's life at the Stag and Crown, on the wilds of Dartmoor, was not an easy one. Although there were few overnight guests these days, the ancient inn sat near the place where two old roads met. The biweekly coach stopped for fresh horses and box lunches, there were commercial travelers and a busy local custom in the taproom, and Perdita was up before the sun, and rarely abed before the witching hour.

Her reverie was interrupted by the cock's crow, signaling dawn and the start of the long day. Rising, she slipped off the patched nightshift that was far too large, and put on her every-day dress. The faded fabric hung from her shoulders. It had belonged to Sukey, before the other girl had grown too buxom to fit inside it without bursting the seams.

With a deft movement, Perdita twisted up her cloud of night-black hair, and fixed it in place with a pair of broken-toothed combs. There was still no movement from the other pallet. Leaning down in the dimness, she reached to grasp Sukey's shoulder and shake her awake. Her hand closed on emptiness.

Perdita was concerned. The other girl hadn't returned from her tryst over the stables with one of the lads. Sukey had never stayed out until sunrise before—and if Mrs. Croggins learned of it, there'd be the devil to pay!

A scuffle on the shed roof outside the window was fol-lowed by a soft, insistent rap on the shutters. She went to open them, banging her head on the rafters, and swore beneath her breath. As she wrenched the shutters open Sukey poked her head inside. That explained the thump that had wakened Per-dita.

"Help me in! Quick," Sukey whispered, "afore the old bawd hears me."

The window was narrow and Sukey a healthy country lass. Her ample hips caught and stuck. It was a struggle, but with Perdita tugging hard, they made it. Sukey plopped to the pallet like a ripe apple hitting the ground.

"*Oof!* That was close!"

"Clumsy goose! You might have hurt yourself."

Sukey smiled wickedly. "More like a *stuffed* goose."

That shocked Perdita. "Oh, Sukey! You're a great fool to take the chance," she scolded.

The landlady was a robust woman, hard and sour as a green apple. Both girls still bore bruises from the last time she'd taken her broom to their backs. "What if Mrs. Croggins heard you? '*Catch you out after dark, you silly slut, and I'll peel your hide, I will!*' "

Sukey grinned up at her. "How do you do that? Make your voice just like *hers?*"

"I don't know. And don't try and turn me off so easily. Nothing," Perdita said, "not even a kiss from bonny Rafe Black, is worth the risk of another hard beating." Not to mention an unwanted pregnancy.

"Stuff old Croggins!" Sukey looked sly in the pale light. "'Twasn't Rafe," she said, and held out her hand.

Silver gleamed in her palm.

"'Twas the gent what took the private room. He's coming back next week, from Plymouth. He's going to buy me a bonnet and a muslin dress trimmed with ribbons, and take me up to London with him."

Perdita didn't say a word: she couldn't. She felt a gulf open between them, wide and empty as the moors that rose so high beyond the village.

Sukey glanced sullenly at her friend's shocked face. "Don't look at me that way. So what if he doesn't? There'll likely be others. At least I got two shillings and a ribbon for my hair from him, which is more than Rafe ever gave me. A few more under my mattress and I'll take *myself* off to town."

Perdita was suddenly near tears. Sukey's older sister had thought the same. May had returned, gin-raddled and broken, a gaunt and silent creature, with a dry cough, and dulled eyes. Six months later, she'd been dead.

"You cannot mean you would leave your family! Not after what happened to May. Only think of your mother, Sukey."

"She wouldn't miss me. Only the odd coin that I bring home." The other girl's pretty face grew hard. "She's got no more sense of mothering than a cow with a weaned calf. I'll look out for myself from now on."

A shiver ran through Perdita. Sukey had started off along that same dark road as her sister, and would likely end up the same way, cast off and ruined, her fine plans all trampled in the dust. Perdita couldn't bear to think of it.

"You mustn't!" she said. "It's pure folly. You'll only live to regret it."

"Don't try and come the parson's daughter over me: I don't give a care what you say." Sukey shrugged and tossed her sunny curls. "Any road, you're just jealous, you are."

She lifted her chin and stared hard at Perdita. "What's gone is gone for good, and no sense crying over spilled milk! As you'll find out soon enough, one day. And you'll come to learn it's better to give yourself for some silver, than it is for free."

With a sullen shrug she knelt down, and shoved her coins into the chink in the worn floorboards. Rafe was a lusty lad, but shiftless, and only the youngest son. He'd never amount to much, would Rafe Black. Not unless he dug up one of the treasures the Old Ones were said to have buried up on Giant's Tor.

Sukey slipped on her mended apron, stiff with grease and the broth from yesterday's soup. She had many plans, and drudging her life away at the inn wasn't one of them. Someday soon she'd have pretty dresses edged with lace and ribbon, and fine feathered bonnets. Gold earrings and proper shoes, with tiny buttons up the sides. The images in her mind dazzled her like sunbeams.

The sooner she shook the dust of Haycross Village from her clogs, the happier she'd be.

"You could come with me," she said, eyeing Perdita up and down. "Might happen the merchant has a friend who'd take to you," she said grudgingly. "You could do worse."

Perdita shook her head. "No, Sukey. I'll not go that road. Nor should you!"

"Think you're better than me," the other girl sniffed, "with your fancy talk and book reading. One day you'll wish you hadn't such fine notions!"

"No matter how hard life is here, or how many beatings Mrs. Croggins gives out, I will never sell myself to any man."

The other girl gave her a shrewd stare. "Maybe not for money," she said with a shrug.

"Not for anything!"

Sukey's eyes narrowed. "Happen girls like us don't have much choice. Where's the difference in marrying some skinny-shanked old farmer or ham-fisted drover, and warming his bones in bed, all for the sake of marriage lines and a roof over your head?"

"I won't do that, either," Perdita said quietly. "I'll pay back Mrs. Croggins and go to the hiring fair next year. I'll take any honest work that's offered. But I will never sell myself."

"Ah, so high-and-mighty!" Sukey said harshly. "Mark my words: for all your fine airs, you can't reckon what you'll do, if someone offers you the right prize."

Perdita turned away and hurried down the narrow, twisting stairs, with Sukey's laughter following her.

After starting the kitchen fire, Perdita started the stew that would simmer on the hearth all day. Her thoughts were knotted up with Sukey's plans and fear for the other girl. She couldn't understand it.

If I had a family, I would never leave them, Perdita told herself. *I would sleep in the chimney corner and count myself lucky to see my mother's face every day. To know there was one place on this earth where I truly belonged.*

She scrubbed down the worn wooden table, where Sukey had left congealing grease from the night before, and began chopping vegetables for a stew. Not that she'd ever have a taste of it herself. The landlady was mean with food, and thought bread and cheese sufficient for her serving girls.

She sighed and began scrubbing turnips. She had certainly come down in the world since her arrival at the Stag and Crown. Three years ago, instead of that cold pallet beneath the eaves, her worn hand-me-down garments, she'd had a snug room at Moor Cottage, two serviceable dresses with crisp white aprons, and a narrow blue ribbon to bind up her hair. She'd gone to bed with a full belly and slept on clean sheets in a real bed. Life had been good.

Perhaps there had even been a time when it had been better. A time when the people and places in her dream had been her true world. Perdita doubted that she would ever know, and the knowledge of it was a hollow ache inside her.

Seven years ago, Perdita had been found wandering the narrow lanes above a small country village, half-starved and delirious with fever. Miss Barnstable, the reclusive spinster who owned Moor Cottage, had taken her in. Waking up in a narrow bed beneath Miss Barnstable's roof, with the kindly woman reading beside her, was Perdita's earliest true memory.

She'd opened her eyes to the sight of a slender, elderly woman perched on a straight-backed chair with a book bound in red leather on her lap.

"Ah! Awake at last, I see. Are you hungry, girl? I am Miss Barnstable. I'll ring for Gladys to bring up a tray, while you tell me who you are and how you came to be wandering about on your own."

But Perdita had had nothing to tell Miss Barnstable. Not even her name. Her past was as blank and dense as the heavy mists that made the moors so treacherous.

"Then I shall call you Perdita. It is an old name, and means 'little lost one,' " Miss Barnstable told her. "In time, I am sure, we shall unravel the mystery and restore you to your home."

But time passed and no one came to seek Perdita. Miss Barnstable raised inquiries in the village, but no one knew anything of the young girl or her history. The spinster guessed right from the start that there was somethng different about Perdita. Over the long years of her life, other children had been found, lost or abandoned or orphaned when times were hard; but none had been dressed in garments that had once been of the very best. None had known how to read. And, of course, there was that silver brooch with the unusual blue stone.

On the fourth day, Perdita felt well enough to get up from the bed and tiptoe downstairs. The parlor was empty, and she followed the sounds of voices to the small whitewashed kitchen. Gladys, the stout, no-nonsense maid-of-all-work was peeling onions into a blue pottery bowl, and Perdita realized that the two women had been discussing her.

"You can't be too careful, miss," Gladys warned in dire tones. "With that dark hair, she might be one of them tinkers what come through now and again in their painted wagons."

"She's no Gypsy's child," Miss Barnstable said crisply. "It's plain that she's sprung from quality. You have only to listen to her speak to know that. And the dress and shoes she was wearing when I found her were once lovely. Someone paid dearly for them."

"Mayhap she's some gentleman's by-blow, like poor Nell Otis," Gladys clucked, "cast out to fend for herself when her father took a new wife."

Miss Barnstable nodded. "I have come to a similar conclusion, Gladys. Otherwise someone would have come seeking word of her. Poor child! Well, I am pleased that she is bright, and can read and do ciphers. I will see what I may teach her, so that one day she may go out into the world and earn her bread. Meanwhile, she can help you with the household chores and the gardening, and read to me of an evening while I sit over my needlework."

And so Perdita's future had been settled over a bowl of peeled onions. As soon as she was well enough, she settled into Miss Barnstable's small but comfortable home. Her position fell oddly, somewhere between servant and lady's maid, and companion-in-training.

For four quiet years Perdita lived with the spinster and Gladys high above Edgecombe-in-the-Moor, sweeping floors and polishing furniture by day and learning to cook. In the evenings she would read aloud to the increasingly frail Miss Barnstable, and later yet brush out her long, faded red hair each night and fix it into two plaits. Every morning she would bind it up in a smooth coronet atop the spinster's head, and fix it with ivory pins.

Life was safe, if unexciting, and Perdita was warm and fed and had her place in their tidy little universe.

Then everything had changed. While Perdita was out weeding the kitchen garden and Gladys preparing a roast chicken, Miss Barnstable quietly passed away at her embroidery. If not for that terrible day, Perdita sighed, she would still be at Moor Cottage, sharing a room with Gladys.

The spinster's odious nephew inherited Miss Barnstable's meager estate, and there was trouble with them from the first day when he brought his wife and son to live at Moor Cottage. Gladys went off to live with her sister in Cornwall, and young Mr. Barnstable had proved to be no gentleman. Perdita had escaped with her virtue intact, and very little but the clothes on her back.

She'd hidden in the cow byre, and made her way down to Edgecoombe-in-the-Moor near the end of market day, and crept into a cart to sleep. When she'd awakened, it had been in the stableyard of the Stag and Crown, miles from anywhere at all, on the old moor track. And that had been that.

Ah, well, she told herself now, chopping carrots for the stewpot. *What can't be cured, must be endured.*

But as Perdita worked, fragments of this morning's dream still whispered in her head. She wondered if the splendid ballroom, the beautiful music and elegant dancing couples, were from stories she'd heard, or something she'd read to Miss Barnstable. Or if they sprang from her own vivid imagination. All she knew was that when she was under their spell, they seemed far more real to her than anything she experienced while awake. In her heart of hearts, she wanted them to be real. Memories of whatever her life had been before she'd been found by Miss Barnstable.

Memories of a time and place where I belonged!

Perdita sighed and finished chopping the last of the vegetables. After putting turnips, carrots, and onions to simmer, she realized that Sukey still hadn't come down. And at any moment the landlady might make her appearance.

"Drat the girl, she's fallen asleep! Mrs. Croggins will beat us both!"

Wiping her hands on a damp cloth, Perdita slipped out of her shoes and tiptoed upstairs. Sukey was sprawled on her pallet, her hair in a wild tangle, as she snored softly. There were sounds of movement from the room beneath the attic.

Perdita bent down and shook her. "Sukey! Wake up! Quickly. I hear someone stirring."

Sukey awoke with a start. "Go back down. I'll be right along." She gave Perdita a shove toward the door and sat up, rubbing her eyes.

"Make sure you don't fall back to sleep!"

"Be off with you. I'll be down in a winking."

As she descended the worn old stairs, Perdita prayed that the landlady hadn't heard them talking. Pausing, she listened on the landing, but heard no sounds from Mrs. Croggins's door. Perdita hurried on.

When she was halfway between the attic and the next floor, a figure moved in the darkness of the stairs: Sam Bailey, the man who was courting their widowed—and much older—landlady.

Perdita hesitated. She didn't like Sam. He was a handsome, thickset man. Ox-strong, Mrs. Croggins said, with a shock of flaxen hair and eyes as gray and chill as a January sky. And he had no business creeping up the back stairs in the thick shadows.

He leered up at her and she paused, wondering if she should retreat. Although he'd never touched her, he had a way of watching Perdita that made her skin crawl. As if he were stripping away her dress and shift with his hard, cold stare.

While she hesitated, a little flame grew in his eyes, turning them hot and hungry. Sam moved to the corner of the landing as if to step out of the way. Instead, as Perdita tried to brush by, he caught her about the waist and spun her into the dark corner instead. A miasma of ale and unwashed flesh radiated from him. His hands grabbed her breasts in a bruising grip as he leaned against her.

"Let me go!"

Panic choked the words in her throat. She could hardly breathe. Perdita tried to push against his chest, to no avail. His body pressed against hers, hips grinding. She recoiled in revulsion, but could not escape. There was nowhere to go.

He put his weight against her, pinning her limbs beneath his. Her breath came out in a rush. She couldn't move, almost couldn't breathe.

He didn't say a word as he fumbled at her breast with his dirty hands, while the other yanked her skirts up her bare legs. The utter silence, the unexpected violence of his attack, was like something from a nightmare, and she struggled futilely to free herself. Gasping in a breath, she opened her mouth to cry out.

He released his cruel grip on her breast and slapped his palm over her mouth. *"Shut your face!"* he growled.

Perdita tasted blood.

His hand slid up her thighs, digging into her flesh. *"Don't struggle,"* he warned, *"and it will go easier on you."*

He fumbled with his own garments, keeping his weight pinned on her. Spreading his legs on either side of hers, he jerked his loins back to thrust. Desperation gave her strength and she took advantage of his distraction. Perdita's broken-nailed fingers gouged at his eye, and her slender knee came up swiftly between his legs, the way Sukey had shown her once.

Her attacker doubled over, with a long outrush of air, cursing as he gasped for breath.

At his groan of pain, there was a muffled sound in the best bedchamber overhead. The landlady was awake and stirring. The door of her bedchamber on the floor above opened. "Samuel?" Mrs. Croggins murmured.

"Aye," he called up to her. "Get back in bed, my bonny

lass, and I'll give you a quick, hard ride to start the day off right."

Perdita heard the landlady giggle and shut the door. She'd manged to get herself out of the corner, but Sam's bulk still blocked her way. As she tried to dart around him, he recovered enough to grab her arm and give her a vicious shake. Hot pain shot up her arm. Her teeth rattled and she stumbled back against the wall. Before she could duck his hand swept out and delivered a blow to the side of her face. Her head reeled with it.

"I've no time to teach you your lesson now," he growled. His hot gaze raked her body, lingered on her breasts. "But harken well, you haughty strumpet! The day is coming when I'll be master here, when everything beneath this roof belongs to me—including *you*."

"That day will never come!"

He smiled unpleasantly. "Aye, it will. I'll be off this morning, but I'll be back at the Stag and Crown before month's end. Then we'll finish up this little business between us. You have Sam Bailey's word on that!"

Perdita ran down the rest of the way, heart pounding so fiercely she thought it might burst. She went out through the kitchen door and into the yard, taking great gulps of clean, fresh morning air. The yard was deserted, the stablelads still asleep. The sky to the east was slatted with clouds in cool lavender and fiery rose. *Rain before nightfall.*

The narrowness of her escape shook Perdita badly. She wanted to run from the stableyard, to run out into the road, to run and run until she put the Stag and Crown and Sam Bailey behind her, forever.

Instead she filled a bucket at the pump, and dabbed at her bleeding mouth with the moistened hem of her apron. She wouldn't get far. Not without careful planning. While she pumped the water, Perdita could hear the dull thudding of Mrs. Croggins's bed against the wall of her bedchamber above, as Sam Bailey labored away.

It made her sick. She bent over as a wave of nausea gripped her. She could still smell his fetid breath, feel his brutal hands upon her naked flesh. She couldn't bear to be touched by him again.

It took real effort to make herself go back inside the inn.

Once Sam got Mrs. Croggins to marry him, Perdita wouldn't have another moment of safety at the Stag and Crown. She had told Sukey that she'd never sell herself to any man, and that horrid, filthy animal had almost taken her there on the stairs, like a savage beast rutting in the dark! Her entire body shook with reaction.

Hurrying through the kitchen and into the taproom, she tried to light the wood already laid there, but her hands were shaking too badly to strike a spark in the tinderbox. She leaned her head against her knee and tried to steady her nerves. It did no good. It was only a matter of time before Sam made good his threats.

She couldn't let that happen!

Panic blurred her judgment. *Perhaps Sukey has the right of it. Better to give myself to a man who would treat me kindly, than suffer the same fate at the filthy hands of Sam Bailey.*

No! Every sense revolted. Perdita sighed. *There must be a better way!*

There had to be. She didn't know what to do, where to go. Oh, if only Miss Barnstable hadn't succumbed to her weak heart, and left everything to her odious nephew, how very different these last few years would have been!

How much more hopeful the future.

Then Perdita's violet eyes brightened: the annual hiring fair was held in Oakleycoombe at month's end. It would take days for her to reach the town, but surely her effort would be rewarded. People came from all around, bearing implements of their trade, in search of employment. Men would be there with carpenter's aprons and hammers, or groom's whips, or pieces of mended harness to show their trade. There would be other women, as well—cooks with ladles and caps, laundresses with wooden tubs and maids with mops and aprons, all seeking new employers in hopes of bettering themselves.

And she would not be the only runaway servant there, mingling with the crowds the annual event drew.

Perdita heaved a great sigh. Yes, the hiring fair would be her means of escape. Her speech was good, her person tidy, even if her garments were worn and patched. Someone was sure to take her on as a scullery girl, or maid-of-all-work. She could be both safe and useful, in a household of high-minded spinsters or beneath the roof of some soft-spoken, elderly widow.

And, she thought, *if I can't attend the fair honestly, having earned my freedom, at least I will go there with my head held high, and my virtue intact.*

The getting there would be the difficulty. It was a good two days' walk along the moor road, but she daren't chance it. Cross-country along the edge of a wooded combe would get her halfway there. The rest would be open moorland. A shiver of apprehension shook her. The rain and mists could be disorienting, the cold nights lethal. And then there were the patches of solid-looking heath that were in reality perilous bogs . . .

Perdita pushed those last thoughts from her mind. Giving the flint a strong strike, she watched in satisfaction as a spark leapt into the tinderbox, igniting the tinder. It was only a moment's work to light the kindling in the great stone cooking hearth. A spark just as fierce burned in her breast. She would lay her plans carefully, be prepared as best she could for any eventuality.

If only she had a few coins!

Then she remembered her brooch. The one with the blue stone, which had been pinned to her frock when Miss Barnstable had found her wandering about in her delirium. Where it had come from was a mystery. At present it resided in Perdita's secret hiding place, in the stillroom.

Sam Bailey's absence would give her a few days' grace. There were horses in the stable, but two problems prevented her from stealing one. The first was that horse thieves were hung when they were caught, as she would surely be. The more mundane reason was that she couldn't ride.

Perdita had a great fear of the huge beasts, with the strong, yellow teeth and flailing hooves. She had no idea why, only that it had been there as long as she could remember.

She sighed. There was no use even considering it. She'd never make it out of the stableyard. But somehow, some way, she'd get down to Haycross Village on market day, and trade the brooch for whatever she could get. Surely that could pay her fare to Plymouth or even farther afield. Excitement and determination filled her.

I will make good my escape, and find a new life.

It gave her a pang to think of parting with the brooch: the small piece of jewelry in its silver setting was the only clue she had toward solving the riddle of her past. But now her hand was forced. Although Sam Bailey was a cruel and wicked man, crossing the moor on her own filled her with foreboding. Every year someone vanished, never to be seen again by mortal eyes.

A shudder ran up her spine, but Perdita quelled it: she would rather end up in a bog, than as Sam Bailey's whore.

Two

Despite the sideboards groaning beneath silver domes of hot food, and bewigged footmen at their places, the cheerful Breakfast Room at Haycross Manor was nearly empty. The few guests present were all men: the ladies of the house party, after dancing half the night away, would spend most of the day in their rooms, recuperating.

Lord Haycross, a courtly man of sixty years, sipped his coffee. "I didn't hear a soul stirring abovestairs. If I see Lady Haycross before afternoon tea, I shall be greatly amazed."

Andrew Waverly, having just polished off the last rasher of bacon, helped himself to a second portion of everything that was offered. Sunlight poured through the tall windows, glazing the yellow silk wall hangings, and winking back from the polished silverplate. He looked up as his cousin entered.

"There you are, Justin. This is the most excellent ham. You must have some."

Lord Ravenall, dressed in buckskins and jacket for his return journey, took some scrambled eggs and joined their host at the table. The duke eyed his brother-in-law in surprise.

"Surely you don't intend to fly back to Ravenall Castle with the same speed with which you came here!"

"I intend to get a good start before the weather changes. There's a squall brewing out at sea."

"Then stay another day, and help me keep these restless young cubs out of mischief," Haycross said, with a smile at his young guests.

Justin expressed his regrets. "Duty recalls me, sir. There is still much to do in settling my late uncle's estate."

The duke understood: the late earl's holdings were extensive, but had been poorly maintained. From what he'd heard, it would take a good deal of work to untangle the snarls. He

sincerely hoped that Ravenall was equal to the task. He didn't
know his brother-in-law well, but had a liking for him. Surely
his darling Daisey's brother could not be so bad as rumors
claimed.

Haycross began proposing various excursions for his young
guests. Andrew put down his fork and glanced out the window
opposite.

Beyond the steep, wooded sides of the Dart River valley,
the humps of the moor rose, stark and desolate against the
bright blue sky. The shadows of the high clouds sweeping in
from the south flew swift across the bracken. They gave the
illusion that the landscape quivered, like some ancient beast
twitching in its sleep.

"Is it true that the sea can be viewed from Giant's Tor?"
Andrew asked. It was his first visit to the West Country, and
he was eager to explore.

Lord Haycross nodded. "Thirteen miles from the top of the
tor to the bay, on a clear day. But if you're wise, you'll take
a groom along if you venture into the uplands. We wouldn't
want you to vanish into one of the bogs, never to be seen
again."

Justin laughed at the look of surprise on his cousin's face.
"The moors are wild and beautiful, but they are indeed treacherous. It's said there is more rainfall on Dartmoor than any-
place else in the whole of England. There are hidden bogs
waiting to trap the unwary—or the foolish. Calvin Bridgeforth
lost a prime horse there in his youth—and almost lost his life,
as well."

"Now you're bamming me," Andrew exclaimed. Calvin
Bridgeforth, a minor aristocrat vaguely related to both Andrew
and Ravenall, was fastidious to a fault.

"Oh, it's quite true," the duke told him. "A farmer had to
pull him out with a cart horse. He lost his hat and both his
boots to the bog. The poor fellow was so coated with ooze his
own mother would not have recognized him."

"By Jove, I would have paid admission to see that!"

A sudden silence fell over the Breakfast Room: Bridgeforth
himself had entered in time to hear the last part of the discussion.

He was a tall man in his mid-thirties, who cultivated a
dandified air; only those who had not seen him fencing at the

academy he frequented in London would have been fooled by it. Bridgeforth was all muscle and sinew beneath his well-tailored jacket, and he had the reflexes of a snake.

"Certainly I have no wish to visit the moors again. Dartmoor is no place for a civilized gentleman," he said languidly. "In any case, it looks to rain by afternoon."

The duke rubbed his chin. "There are some interesting sights in the vicinity. If any of you young bucks have an interest in antiquities, there are stone foundations at the base of the downs that go back to prehistoric times. Closer in are the remains of a thirteenth-century church in the village, if you like mossy, time-blackened ruins. A few of the headstones in the churchyard go back to the Conqueror."

Bridgeforth dug into his dish of deviled kidneys and fixed Andrew with a jaundiced eye. "I believe a curiosity such as the haunted grove would be more likely to catch Waverly's interest."

"Ah," Lord Haycross said. "You are speaking of the Druids' Oak."

Andrew set down his fork. "The Druids' Oak? Intriguing!"

"It's the only surviving remnant of an ancient grove—haunted, some say, by the ghosts of the ancient order. Others claim it goes back even deeper into the mists of time, and that the fairy folk took refuge beneath it when the church bells made them flee the land above. According to legend, flowers bloom around it, even in the coldest months, and its great roots are carved of ice and fire."

Ravenall lifted his eyebrows. "I have heard of it, but thought it a fairy tale."

The duke smiled reminiscently. "I remember looking for it as a boy. It's also called the Wishing Tree, and locals say wishes made there come true, if they're pledged in blood. It is said to be the oldest oak in all of Britain. But it has a darker side, and a violent history, as well."

Seeing his audience caught, Haycross settled back in his chair and related the story. "When the Romans invaded, they slaughtered the Druids who worshiped there, and tried to destroy the sacred grove. But though the legionnaires tried their best, those massive trunks proved hard as iron. Their leader vowed that he would cut the largest one down himself, or die trying."

The duke paused for effect. "The intrepid captain attacked the tree with brutal force. He took one swing of his axe against the oak's great trunk. It bounced back as if it had struck stone—and his own axe blade struck him dead on the spot."

Haycross sat back, pleased with the effect on his audience. "They say the gash in the bark is still there. No one has ever dared try to cut it down since."

"By Jove!" Andrew exclaimed. "I should like to see this marvel!"

"Have you seen it yourself, duke?" another member of the party asked.

"When I was sixteen, I rode up there with my cronies. We did find it, although it was difficult to locate, but we arrived at the wrong time of day. Sunrise, sunset, or high noon are when its magic is said to be most potent. All we saw was an enormous oak, but I must say there was a strange atmosphere to the place. We all felt it. We made our wishes quickly and departed—and then got hopelessly lost for hours on the way back to Haycross, in the midst of a drenching downpour."

"Did you never go back?"

The duke shook his head. "Soon afterward I became much more interested in horse-racing, cockfights, and flourishing my bunches of fives, with the other young bucks of my set. The boyish urge to go trudging over the tors and through bogs lost its luster."

Bridgeforth gave a delicate shudder. "Dartmoor! An eerie place. And not one I'd care to visit again myself."

Andrew's imagination was fired. He was eager to ride out immediately. "Is it very far, sir?"

"A good morning's ride. Perhaps a party could be made up for tomorrow, if anyone cares to go."

Since there was a race meet set for the following afternoon, none of the others seemed particularly enthusiastic. "It is," Bridgeforth said in bored accents, "only an oak, after all, and hardly worth a drenching."

But Andrew was not so easily discouraged. "I say, you must put off your departure another day, Justin, and ride up with me. You know your way across the moors, and I am not afraid of a little rain."

Ravenall smiled.

Was I ever that young and eager? he wondered. If so, he couldn't recall it.

"I'd stay but my man of business is down from London to settle the rest of the estate with me." Andrew's face fell. He looked like a small boy who'd just been told he couldn't have a pony.

"So it is duty that calls you away," Calvin Bridgeforth said with mock sympathy. "Ah, the plight of the noble landowner! Now, if you were in my shoes, Ravenall, or those of young Andrew here, you'd be free to follow your fancies instead of the dictates of your weighty affairs. How very tiresome for you."

A muscle ticked at Justin's jaw. "I take my responsibilities to my tenants, and to my future heirs, very seriously." Turning away from Bridgeforth, he addressed the duke. "How far is it to this oak, Haycross?"

"Twelve miles as the crow flies. Considerably longer by carriage. There's a deep reeve above Haycross Village that cuts far back into the moors. The Druids' Oak is somewhere at its head, west of the ancient stone known as Stump Cross."

"Rid yourself of that long face, Andrew." Ravenall finished his coffee. "I suppose I can put off my affairs for one day. Come back with me to Ravenall Castle. We'll detour a bit and view this wonder on our way."

His cousin grinned. "Capital!"

"When you visit the Druids' Oak," the duke said, "you must not forget to make your wish."

Bridgeforth pushed the deviled kidneys aside. He disliked Ravenall, and despised Andrew. "It is easy to guess young Waverly's: surely to capture the heart of a wealthy heiress." He smiled coldly. "Dudley Drew is still looking for a husband for his darling daughter."

A hush fell over the Breakfast Room. Dudley Drew was a wealthy vulgarian, who schemed to buy his way into society. His daughter was a querulous girl, with boiled-gooseberry eyes and a voice so hard it could scrape barnacles off a rock. Both were set on her marrying into the aristocracy, if not the nobility. Thus far there had been no takers. Not even the gazetted fortune hunters could bring themselves up to scratch for such a miserable alliance.

It was difficult, but Ravenall reined in his temper. Old habits might die hard, but the days when he fought his cousin's battles were long over. He watched with eyes opaque as stone.

Andrew flushed. It was common knowledge that his pockets were to let. His father's estate had been small, and he had two young sisters who depended upon him to provide for them. His jaw squared. He would not let Bridgeforth's breach of etiquette goad him into causing a scene.

"Are you saying that wealth is what you would rate most highly in a bride, Bridgeforth? For myself, I would rate virtue, intelligence, and a happy disposition far higher on my list."

Angry color flooded Bridgeforth's face. He hadn't expected the young cub to give him such a public set-down. A wiser man would have let the matter drop but Bridgeforth couldn't leave well enough alone. He had seen the first shaft go home, and nocked another arrow.

"If you go to see this oak," he said suavely, "you must stop for luncheon at the old inn above the valley. The Stag and something or other—"

"The Stag and Crown! I recall it from when I was a boy," Lord Haycross said, trying to smooth over the incident.

Bridgeforth nodded. "They used to set out a spread of hearty country fare, for the locals. Not up to your standards, duke, or mine," Bridgeforth drawled. "I am sure, however, that Waverly will enjoy it."

A gasp went round the room, and then a dangerous silence followed. The duke glowered.

Justin was afraid for a moment that Andrew would land a sharp right to Bridgeforth's smirking face. By God, he was damned tempted to do so himself! But that would not only be interfering in his younger cousin's business, it would be a great insult to their host.

He forestalled Andrew's reply with a sharp look, and showed his teeth to Bridgeforth. "You might come with us, Calvin," he said silkily. "That is, *if* the duke has a horse to spare."

Bridgeforth turned an ugly shade of red. "I prefer the company here," he snapped.

The duke, a man of exquisite politeness, eyed Bridgeforth calmly. "Indeed? How very unfortunate for you."

The ugly color leached from Bridgeforth's sharp countenance. "I understand you, sir."

Every other man present also understood: Bridgeforth had crossed the line. He would not be invited back to Haycross Manor.

He rose abruptly and made a curt bow. Silence held sway until he exited.

When he was gone, the room seemed brighter, as if the sun had come out from behind a cloud. The clink of knife and fork on porcelain resumed.

The duke took another cup of coffee, and changed the subject. "I believe you'll be glad you took the time to visit the Druid's Oak. Tell me—what shall be *your* wish, Ravenall?"

Justin glanced out at the sky, where towering clouds were piling up in the distance, as thick as Devon cream. "At the moment, Haycross, I have only one: that the weather will hold off until we reach the Stag and Crown."

Ravenall stood at the edge of the terrace wall, exulting in the brewing storm. Wild winds snatched at his cloak and tousled his hair, and the sky beneath the towering thunderheads was like polished sterling. If he closed his eyes, he could almost imagine himself at sea again.

For a moment the longing to be free of all responsibilities except for his ship and crew was so strong that he ached with it. He had never asked for titles and estates: if he could have wished away the earldom and all that came with it, he would have done so without regret.

Lightning shattered the sky and thunder rolled ominously. The Duchess of Haycross opened the door that led from the terrace into the Music Room and stuck her pretty head out.

"Justin! Come inside before you are struck!"

He turned, reluctantly, and strode back to the shelter of the manor. The first drops came spattering down as he stepped inside. The Music Room was a beautiful chamber done in crimson and white, the perfect setting for the golden looks of Lady Haycross. The lamps had been lit against the storm's darkness, and warm light shimmered on her sophisticated ivory tea dress.

"There," the duchess said, watching the downpour beyond the windows. "You would have been drenched, if not for me. I was sorting through my music, and looked up, startled to see someone foolhardy enough to be out in such weather!"

He laughed down at her. "I've been out in far worse, Daisey, and come through without a scratch. But I must admit that I'm delighted to enjoy your hospitality another night. And I've been looking for an opportunity to deliver these into your hands."

Reaching into his pocket, he pulled out a small velvet bag tied up with gold strings. "My commission is completed. Here are your earrings."

She took the pouch and poured the contents into her palm. The diamonds were large and of excellent quality, although their cut and settings were heavy and old-fashioned.

The duchess smiled. "Oh, *dearest* of brothers!"

"Easy enough to say, when you have only one—most *indiscreet* of sisters."

"I will not let your scolding put me out of charity with you." She held up one of the expensive baubles. "Thank heaven! I never thought I'd be so glad to see these ugly earrings again! I've been in such a quake that Haycross would discover what I'd done."

"What in God's name were you thinking, when you pledged them to cover your debts?"

"I wasn't thinking at all! Or rather, only of how angry Haycross would be, when he discovered I'd lost my quarter's allowance in one night at the gaming tables. I'd never tried anything more than silver loo before, and I got lost in the excitement of it. When I came to my senses and realized what I'd done, I was appalled!"

"As well you should have been!"

She placed her hand over Ravenall's, and her face was suddenly serious. "If ever I can return a favor to you, Justin, you have only to ask! I give you my word on it."

He smiled wryly. "I'd rather you give me your word that you'll never wager the Haycross family heirlooms again."

She eyed the earrings jaundicedly. "I found them in the bottom of my jewelry chest. So positively barbaric-looking! I wouldn't have worn them to anything but a masquerade. Who would have guessed such ugly things were part of the Haycross heirlooms?"

"Anyone familiar with the older portraits in your gallery," Ravenall said severely; but there was laughter in his eyes. "My dearest girl, I trust you'll never be so foolish in future."

"Oh, no! Indeed, I have decided that I will not try my hand at cards again. I have no talent for it," she said ingenuously.

Ravenall laughed. "Haycross has my sincere sympathy."

"Ah, no. He says that I am a perfect wife to him," Daisey said, tucking the velvet pouch into her bodice. "Which is why I particularly didn't want to disappoint him in my character. But I meant what I said, Justin: if ever you have need of a favor in return, you have only to ask and it is yours."

"I'll remember your promise, Daisey—if ever I have the urge to pawn the Ravenall jewels."

She dimpled. "You would never do so. You have too much respect for your consequence. You have always loved Ravenall Castle, haven't you?"

"Above all things but you."

"Charming!" She stood on tiptoe to kiss his cheek. "I will settle up with you at the next quarter."

"No, by God, you won't!" Ravenall grimaced. "I am not a moneylender."

"Oh, no! I didn't mean to insult you!"

"You gave a very good imitation then, for an amateur." He glanced at the stack of sheet music on the table beside her. "Opera? Good Lord!"

"You needn't sound so horrified," she laughed. "I know I can't carry a tune in a basket. It is Miss Bryce who has promised to sing for us."

Silver rain lashed the windows and the wind shook them in their frames. Justin studied the downpour. "I wonder if it is too late to make my escape?" he said ruefully. "I believe I should prefer to take my chances out there."

"Terrible man! Miss Bryce is thought to have a very sweet and superior voice."

"By whom—Miss Bryce?"

The duchess shook her head. "I didn't realize that you were such a connoisseur of opera, Justin." She gave him a roguish glance. "You'll be delighted to know that Mrs. Hofflemeister, the famous soprano, has agreed to entertain at a musical evening when we return to London. I shall be sure to send you a card of invitation."

Little lights danced in his eyes. "My dear sister, I most sincerely regret that another engagement prevents me from accepting your kind invitation."

"That is too bad of you!" The duchess laughed. "I have not even told you when she is to perform."

"Whenever it is," he said suavely, "I shall make certain to have another engagement."

His sister tilted her head and gave a mock sigh. "Is there no hope of civilizing you?"

"None at all, my dear Daisey."

"I know what would do the trick. You are in need of a wife."

The laughter died in his eyes. "Disabuse yourself of that notion. The unfortunate affair in Jamaica was sufficient to last me a lifetime!"

The duchess bit her lip. "My foolish tongue!"

He was silent a moment. He'd thought he was free of beautiful, wanton Véronique, but even here in England, she still had the power to torment him. He wondered if he would ever be truly free of her. And if there would ever be a time when he thought of her without his hands knotting at his sides, without tasting the bitterness of a curse on his lips.

He realized that his sister was distressed, and turned the subject by picking up a miniature in a gold and enamel frame from among several on a side table. The ink and watercolor rendering showed a wide-eyed, much younger version of the duchess, arm in arm with another girl.

"How charming! I've never seen this before."

"No. It used to be in our mother's sitting room." Lady Haycross sighed. "That is Catherine, our older sister." She'd died of summer fever, when Daisy and Ravenall were still in the schoolroom.

Ravenall was surprised. "I thought this was you in the painting!"

"In that outmoded gown?" she laughed. Then her face grew serious. "That is Serena Mannington, Catherine's best friend. They were presented at the same Drawing Room in their first Season."

Ravenall looked at Catherine's portrait, surprised at how much she resembled Daisey. "I'd quite forgotten what she looked like. You favor her, but are much prettier, Daisey."

She pinked with pleasure. "Do you think so?" Catherine had been an acknowledged beauty. "Serena was beautiful, wasn't she? A diamond of the first water."

He turned his scrutiny toward the other girl: dark hair, oval face, straight nose, and thickly lashed light eyes. "No. I should rather call her pretty, in a candy-box sort of way. Who did you say she is?"

"Serena Mannington." Daisey frowned. " Mama did not like her. She said that Serena had 'great charm, some beauty, and no real opinions of her own on any subject—all shining ringlets and wide blue eyes, combined with that sort of girlish naïveté that men find so incredibly appealing.' "

Ravenall shot her a look. "Acquit me! I prefer a woman with intelligence and character. Past mistakes to the contrary."

Daisey didn't know quite what to say. Her brother rarely spoke of his sojourn in Jamaica. She had been a girl of ten at the time, and knew little about the circumstances—only that the beautiful and willful Véronique had played him false.

Many members of the *ton* believed the stories of his jealousy and violence to be true. Daisey was not among them. Justin had never been anything but kind to her. She had missed him dreadfully during the years of his exile. Her eyes searched his.

"Are you truly still so bitter? I would hate to think of you going through life alone! And you must have an heir to Ravenall one day."

"I already have one in Andrew." He gave a careless shrug. "He may succeed me, with my very good wishes."

The duchess shook her head. "Andrew is not cut out for it."

Ravenall laughed ruefully. "Neither am I, Daisey. Neither am I."

The duchess took the miniature from him and stared down at the two girls captured in the prime of their youth. "Poor Serena!"

He set the miniature down. "Why do you call her that? Did she not marry well, despite her charms?"

Daisey glanced at the portrait and her face grew pensive. "Quite the contrary. Her husband was rich as Croesus, and it was a love match from the start. Almost an obsession. But it ended badly . . ."

"I can understand that completely!" he said.

"Not all marriages are unhappy, Justin."

She put her hand on his sleeve. "Haycross was not my first

choice for a husband, but my father gave me to him in marriage. I wept for three days—such a little fool as I was!"

Her eyes misted a little. "Although I did not love him, I liked and respected him. Love—real love—came later. I must tell you that I am completely content. Indeed, I swear that I could not have found a better husband had I searched the whole world over."

He smiled down at her warmly. "Are you, Daisey? Then I am glad."

She glanced at the miniature, her face pensive. "Serena was less fortunate. She died young, and her husband shortly after. It was a terrible tragedy. And then their young daughter vanished with her nurse . . ."

The door to the connecting salon opened, and Andrew Waverly came through. He had a thin book in his hand. "I say, Justin, there's a bit in here about the Druids' Oak that Haycross found for me in his library. Quite interesting! Oh!"

He spied his hostess belatedly. "Hullo, Daisey! The duke was just asking after you. He was wondering if you might like to ride out with us as far as the Druids' Oak, and take your nuncheon at an old inn on Dartmoor before turning back."

Daisey looked horrified. "I must tell you, my dear cousin, that I would look forward to an early morning expedition over the moors in the same way that you and Justin would do of a musical evening with Mrs. Hofflemeister!"

Andrew grimaced and laughed. "Then I may safely assume you will not be accompanying us tomorrow morning, Daisey?"

"Indeed you may!"

Ravenall kissed her cheek. "I'm off, then. I promised this young scamp, and Standhope, a game of billiards." He paused at the door, unable to resist teasing her a little. "I hope you won't regret your decision, Daisey. The moors are a beautiful example of raw nature at its best. It promises to be a rare adventure."

Lightning flared, and shadows flitted about the room. The duchess waved a beringed hand at the large floral arrangement on the mantelpiece.

"I prefer my adventures in comfort." Her dimples peeped out and she gave him a saucy look. "Nature in the raw is all well and good, Justin—however, I much prefer it in a crystal vase!"

Ravenall kissed his fingers to her, and the two cousins exited the room, laughing.

The door closed softly behind him, and Daisey sighed. The Ravenall line was an ancient one, and filled with scandals and violence. She had heard all the tales growing up. Legends were woven around rumors that their great-great-grandfather, whom Justin so greatly resembled, had been a pirate. Some even claimed he was the infamous smuggler known as "Black Roger," who had evaded capture for twenty years, and was never brought to justice.

The rest of their family tree bristled with assorted heroes and villains, including the notorious second earl, who was said to have married and murdered two heiresses, each within a year of their wedding day.

Perhaps that is where the rumors about Justin's past have their root, she thought. But at times, when he looked so fierce and bitter, it was enough to make anyone wonder, just a little.

Even, she finally admitted, herself.

The sky, so gray a few hours earlier, was a deep, crystalline blue. Perdita sang to herself as she cracked eggs into a thick stoneware bowl, in the kitchen of the Stag and Crown:

> *O, her hair was black as the blackest night,*
> *And her heart was blacker still.*
> *I have never met such a fair, cruel maid,*
> *And I doubt that I ever will . . .*

The door to the taproom burst open and Sukey came in with a tray. "Move your arse," she said as she brushed past, "or Missus Croggins will show you 'cruel'!"

Perdita laughed. "Not in as bonny a mood as she's in today."

It was early still, but the shabby Stag and Crown was busy as a hive of bees. A coach had lost a wheel, causing several unhappy travelers to break their journey with an unplanned stop at the inn.

"Like old times, it is," the landlady had declared. "And not the usual travelers, either, but persons of *quality*." She'd breathed out the last word as if it were a prayer. It was certainly the answer to her own private invocations.

Delirious at such unexpected bounty, Mrs. Croggins was waiting upon the guests in the private parlor, while the others kicked their heels in the taproom, over tankards of her best home brew.

Sukey grabbed up a wet cloth and wiped off her tray. "Missus says to get hopping on those fancy wafers right away. The inn's bursting as full as it can hold, and everyone wanting their bit *now*!"

There had been a strain between the two girls since Sukey had let the traveling merchant tumble her for a handful of coins. As she stirred flour, water, and eggs into a thin batter, Perdita tried to ease it. Sukey had often talked of trying for a position at Haycross Manor.

"There was another grand party at Haycross Manor last night," Perdita said. "The house looked like a fairy rath, or something from a dream—all the great windows glowing gold across the valley! I've never seen the like."

"Oh, and did the duchess invite you? Did you wear your satin gown and glass slippers?"

Perdita ignored Sukey's barbs. "No. I stood on the chair in Mrs. Croggins's bedchamber, and looked out the casement."

Sukey goggled. The high-backed, heavily carved chair was the landlady's pride and joy, bought by her at a bailiff's auction.

"You never dared! Mistress will have your hide if she finds you've been standing on it."

Perdita smiled. That was better. They were allies once more. "Ah, but you see, I did dare. And Lord, how it creaked!" Her blue eyes shone with excitement. "Oh, Sukey, you should have seen it!"

"I'd rather see you stir your stumps before old Croggins comes and thumps you one on the noggin!"

Mrs. Croggins was a robust woman, with an arm like an axletree. The last time the landlady had boxed Perdita's ears, they'd rung for hours.

There was little time for further talk as the two went about their chores. While Perdita heated the lard in a deep skillet, she thought again of the ball at the great house across the valley. Surely that was the source of her strange and wonderful dream this morning. But oh! It had seemed so real!

In the light of day it was hard to reconcile the warm, glowing image of Haycross Manor in its splendor with the cold reality of the Stag and Crown: low beams, ceilings between them black with centuries of smoke. Plaster falling from the walls, the whole place smelling of spilled ale and the damp.

Hot though it was, at least the kitchen smelled good. The pullets were turning on the spits and game pies baking in the oven, their succulent juices bubbling up through the slotted crusts. The rich aroma of meat and pastry made her mouth water. There'd be none for Perdita or Sukey, but there'd be bread and drippings later. Her stomach rumbled and she tried to turn her imagination away from the tempting foods so lovingly prepared for other mouths.

From the open casement she spied the steeple of St. Michael's Church in Haycross Village, a needle of dark stone thrusting up through the trees in the valley below. Beyond it, the windows of the manor winked silver and gold.

"Oh, Sukey," she sighed again. "I truly wish you could have seen the manor across the valley last night! So beautiful, all lit up like a fairy castle!"

"You'd best keep your eyes on your chores. Haycross and fancy balls aren't for the likes of us."

"Well, if 'a cat may look at a queen,' I don't see why we cannot look at Haycross Manor, and dream of handsome lords and ladies in silk gowns."

Sukey threw down the heavy brush she had been using to scour the cookpots. There was a time when she eagerly waited for night, when Perdita would whisper fairy tales to her beneath the eaves. Now it only exasperated her.

"Dreams and wishes and fairy godmothers!" She picked up a heavy pot of water and set it on the hook to boil. Their exchange of words earlier still rankled. "Those books you read before you came here did you no good, filling your head with a lot of fine, fanciful ideas. All they'll fetch you is a clout from the mistress for lollygagging."

But even as she protested, she felt uncomfortable. It was true that Haycross Manor and fancy balls had nothing to do with her—but Perdita *was* different somehow. The way she talked, the way she carried herself. Even her name, although Mrs. Croggins always called her "Polly."

"*Polly,*" the mistress always said, "*is a good, plain name for a serving wench.*"

Sukey agreed. But it was no name for someone like Perdita, all fine features and slender limbs—exactly like a sleek little colt that had somehow wandered into the cow byre.

Which, Sukey suspected, was one of the reasons that Mrs. Croggins kept her hidden away in the kitchen, instead of in the taproom, where she might draw more custom: the landlady had taken Perdita in as a young girl, and given her a roof over her head. In return, Perdita had to work off her accumulated debt. An elopement with some passing tradesman or lusty farm lad didn't fit into Mrs. Croggins's plans.

Not, Sukey amended, *that she's likely to, with her nose in the air.*

"Here, you'd best watch that lard before it catches fire. If you've any brains left over from your daydreams, you'll start frying up those batter-wafers that the mistress is wanting."

Perdita sighed. Sukey was right. Mrs. Croggins was desperate to make a good impression on the delayed travelers, in hopes of improving custom. The batter was ready, the lard in the pan hot and sizzling. She lifted the wood-handled iron piece, with its lacy pattern at the other end. Like the upholstered chair in the best bedchamber, it had come from the bailiff's sale held to settle the accumulated debts against a gentleman's estate.

None of them had ever used the wafer iron before, but Perdita followed her mistress's careful instructions: dip the iron, with its flat snowflake-shaped end into the sturdy stoneware bowl, coat it with batter, and plunge it into the hot oil in the skillet. Then pull it out, quick as you please, and carefully flick the delicate, golden-brown wafer onto the stone slab to cool.

It was a delicate task, and she burned the first five wafers before she got it right. The hot grease spattered her apron and stung her face. When Perdita finally had the hang of making the wafers, her thoughts curved back to last evening's ball at Haycross Manor. Three days earlier she had watched—from the same carved chair—the parade of traveling coaches and chaises and luggage carriages sweep up the mansion's avenue across the valley from the inn.

"What do you suppose the guests dined upon last night at Haycross Manor?" she asked suddenly. "Shaved ham and rare roast beef? Swan with pearls and hummingbirds' tongues?"

Sukey stopped in mid-action: "What nonsense are you talking?"

Grinning, Perdita kept on with her task. "It's from one of the Arabian tales I read when I lived with Miss Barnstable. On the whole, I'd much prefer not to eat anything rare or beautiful. But oh! how I would love to wear colorful silks and satins and lace as fine as cobweb, instead of this drab homespun or rough wool that chafes my skin!"

"Well, you'd freeze your arse when winter comes," Sukey said flatly.

Perdita wasn't listening. She imagined herself at Haycross Manor, bowing to a handsome partner as the music struck up. Her hair would be swept up and pinned with diamond stars, like the pictures in Miss Barnstable's pattern books, and she would wear a gown of fine silk dressed with silver ribbon, to match her eyes . . .

While she was rapt in her gilded daydreams, Mrs. Croggins hurried along the passage to the kitchen, lost in her own. Oh, she would put on a dinner to remember! One taste of those plump pullets dressed with onion and savory, and the dainty wafers, drizzled with honey and her carefully hoarded spices, and the custom would flock to her doors!

She envisioned the strongbox hidden in the floorboards of her chamber filled to the brim with coins of glittering gold. *No. Too small.* Perhaps a larger box, banded with iron. *Yes. And so many gold coins it would take hours to count them all!*

She entered the kitchen and stopped short, arms akimbo. Fate had given her the opportunity to make her fortune—and there was that dratted girl, staring off into space, when she should be hard at work.

"Polly!"

At the landlady's bark of outrage, Perdita jumped. "Oh!"

Scenes of bejeweled ladies and candlelit ballrooms vanished. The smell of burning batter assailed her. Perdita saw that the wafer was turning black around the edges, and tried to peel it away. Mrs. Croggins gave her a clout to the ear, and the hot dough flew from the iron. It landed on Perdita's wrist, stinging like a live coal.

Her breath hissed in at the searing pain. Tears smarted in her eyes, and she bit her lip. She forced herself to peel the hot wafer of dough away from her skin. It left a bright red mark shaped like a six-pointed star, just above her wrist. Blisters formed as she stared at it.

"She's burned herself," Sukey said in horror.

"Serves her right," Mrs. Croggins snapped, and boxed Perdita's ears again. She gave Sukey a slap for good measure. "Get back to work, you lazy slatterns!"

When she was gone, Sukey hurried to the butter crock and took a small dab to spread over the burn on Perdita's arm.

"Do you think it will scar?"

"Not if you keep it greased up, like. And you must blow on it three times, and whisper, 'Burn, burn, go away! Cool, cool, cold.' "

Perdita blew on the burn and repeated the charm. "It's not good. It still hurts like the devil!"

"Hush! You'll get your ears boxed again if the missus hears you cursing."

"That's not cursing," Perdita said, tears of pain still sparkling on her thick lashes. "If I said, 'May Mrs. Croggins's sharp tongue turn to a scaly serpent and sink its fangs into her red, pointed beak,' now *that* would be cursing."

Sukey winced and looked over her shoulder. "Oh, Perdita! Mind your tongue for once. The missus wouldn't need much excuse to give you a proper beating again!"

Placing her arms akimbo, Perdita cocked her head in the way Mrs. Croggins did when she was in a rage. " '*Lazy sluts! Useless strumpets! Stir your stumps, or I'll peel your hide in strips, I will!*' "

"Ooh, you sound as like her as can be," Sukey said with a nervous glance at the door. "Fair sets my teeth on edge, so it does! How do you do it?"

Perdita took her gift of mimicry for granted. She shrugged. "A parrot's trick, nothing more."

To Sukey it was just another thing that set Perdita apart from the rest of them. She dried her work-roughened hands on her apron, jealousies forgotten, and searched for the right words.

"I'm thick as a plank, not clever like you—but if you could forget about Miss Barnstable and those fancy stories you learned to read . . . Oh, if only you could be more like me— not think so much—there'd be far less grief in store for you!"

Perdita shook her head. "I can't change myself," she said softly. "It is the way I am."

Sukey sighed. "Stubborn is more like it!"

But Perdita shook her head. "Even if I could change myself, I wouldn't do it."

Couldn't do it.

The other girl grew cross. "Someday you'll wish you had, sure as mist on the moor!"

She went back to scrubbing out the pots with sand and a bristle brush, frowning. She liked Perdita, but she didn't understand her. The girl was out of place at the Stag and Crown, no doubt about it.

Sukey searched her mind for a comparison. Perdita was like a bit of clear, glittery quartz, shining bright at the bottom of a stream bed, among all the common gray pebbles. Mrs. Croggins might change her name to Polly, but to change Perdita herself was impossible.

It would be like trying to catch moonbeams in a sieve.

She finished her task and set the last pot aside. "Have you brought in the water?"

There was no answer. Perdita was staring out the window at the rugged face of Dartmoor, the great hump of Giant's Tor against a fathomless blue sky. Her eyes were dreamy.

Somewhere, beyond the primitive sweep of land, lay a world far different from the one where she and Sukey dwelled. Bustling cities filled with people and music, with books and laughter. With adventure and romance.

Someday soon, she vowed, *I will be a part of it.*

Three

"Damn it, Justin, you'll overturn us!"

"I didn't take you to be such a chicken-heart, Andrew!" Ravenall's eyes glinted wickedly. "You said you wanted to see this legendary oak tree—and so you shall!"

Andrew hung on tightly as Ravenall's chaise took the moor track at a clipping pace. Sunlight glazed a graying sky and swift clouds blew in from the direction of the sea, heavy with the threat of rain. The green valley and the steep slopes of the lower moor were already lost in mist.

They'd left late, due to a problem with one of the vehicle's straps, and were trying to outrun the weather. It was a wildly exhilarating and fierce landscape, far removed in every way from the neat Devon thatch-and-whitewashed cottages of Haycross Village. Here and there great towers of broken stone— the Dartmoor "tors"—rose up; but the centuries-old track was straight and level before them, and the yellow and black carriage flew along the open moor.

A grumble of thunder echoed from behind. "Shall we outrace the storm?" Andrew was growing increasingly uneasy. "The lightning must be fierce in such a stark, exposed place."

Ravenall cast an experienced eye at the sky. "This storm is all bluster, and will blow itself out quickly. We'll reach the Stag and Crown before it breaks. By the time we've had our nuncheon, the sun will be out, the horses rested, and we'll be on our way, no worse for wear."

A distant drum roll of thunder came on the heels of his words, and the sheep grazing on the upthrust of land to the left raised their heads and began milling about.

Another, closer crack of thunder shattered the air, but Ravenall kept his hands steady on the reins. The horses pricked their ears but felt the steady hand of their master on the reins, and were reassured. Manes tossing, nostrils wide, the spirited steeds covered the track eagerly.

Ravenall felt the same sense of adventure as his purebred team. Only Andrew seemed worried. He glanced over his shoulder. "We'll be caught in the cloudburst!"

"Not us!" Ravenall told his cousin. "The Stag and Crown is just ahead."

That didn't seem possible. Behind them was nothing but heath and bracken and great granite boulders that shouldered their way out of the moorland. In the distance, beyond the sweeping rise, an immense tor thrust up into the cloudswept sky, its tilted layers of granite looking like blocks stacked by a mad colossus. The carriage wheels clattered over a stretch of broken stone, and Andrew muttered beneath his breath.

"I warned you that I'd travel fast," his cousin said. "I intend to be at Ravenall tonight—and in London the following evening."

Andrew grimaced. "I thought you were making a joke."

The earl raised a dark brow. "I never joke about anything that matters. I have to meet my banker in London. There are 'grave matters' which he wishes to discuss with me as soon as possible."

Andrew was startled. "Good God, what can he possibly mean?"

"That is exactly what I intend to discover," Ravenall said curtly.

A shaggy Dartmoor pony ambled across the track ahead, then bolted as the carriage approached. Ravenall feather-edged the track along a tumble of boulders and Andrew grabbed his hat. "Well, damn your eyes, it matters more to me to arrive in one piece than to sit down to soup on time!"

"You're fickle," Ravenall laughed. "Your enthusiasm blows hot and cold. Not half an hour ago, you were grumbling about the emptiness of your stomach."

"That was before you turned it inside out!" Andrew shot his cousin a darkling look. Despite the duke's assurance that they would be safe enough if they kept to the moor track, his doubts were growing. "I am not accustomed to haring across the countryside at such a reckless pace."

Justin groaned. "I begin to wish I hadn't brought you along. Am I to listen to your complaints all the way to the castle?"

Andrew made a wry face. "I am sorry I ever professed an interest in the Druids' Oak."

Ravenall grimaced. "What? After all this, you don't wish to see it?"

"I would rather see a roof over our heads before the clouds open!" Despite his mutterings, he had complete faith in his cousin's handling of the ribbons. That brush past the boulders had been timed to the inch. There had never been any danger. Had there been, Andrew was certain that Justin would have welcomed it.

"You miss the sea, don't you?"

"More than I can say. Although the *Raven* is a solace to me."

"There are times when I believe that you would trade the earldom away, if you could."

"There are times," Ravenall admitted, "that I would indeed."

"Madness!"

"Life as a peer of the realm is more comfortable, certainly. But the responsibilities are heavy. There are times when I long to stand before the mast with the wind billowing the canvas, the ship leaping like a dolphin beneath my feet—and nothing before me but the wide blue horizon."

Andrew laughed. "How is it that we two come of the same ancestral line? Unless our grandmother played our grandfather false, there is no explaining it. Enough to provide dowries for my sisters and myself with a snug cottage, a comfortable carriage, and a library of good books is the sum of my ambitions at the moment."

Ravenall glanced over at his cousin, and his eyes gleamed in the odd light of the advancing storm. "Have you no sense of adventure in your soul? No curiosity as to what would happen if we took another fork in the road, or left the safe, well-trodden path?"

"I know exactly what we would find: bad roads, indifferent food, and damp beds. I'll leave the adventuring to you, Justin. If you're lucky, perhaps we'll meet up with highwaymen upon a deserted stretch of road."

Ravenall threw back his head and laughed. "Bring them on. Although it would be a poor sort of villain who would hope to make his fortune by his pistols in this godforsaken place."

He brought them round another tower of rock with easy skill. Thunder rumbled and Andrew glanced behind them uneasily. "The storm will be upon us at any minute."

"You have been at sea with me aboard the *Raven* many a time. Even when the weather turned wild, did you not trust me to bring you safely to shore?"

"I did. You are in your element at sea."

"Well, I can read the weather here, as well as I can upon the water. Not a drop of rain will so much as wilt the set of your cravat."

Andrew smiled. "I shall hold you to your promise! But your groom and valet will be drenched, following behind in the other carriage."

Ravenall lifted an eyebrow. "They would, had I not instructed them to hold off leaving Haycross until this afternoon."

Andrew heard the rising wind, and shot a look at the massing clouds that gathered behind him. "Is there nothing that catches you unprepared?"

"I've been caught short many a time, but never for lack of planning! The sea taught me that."

His eyes deepened to the fathomless blue of the deep-water oceans he loved so well. "A man with no knowledge of where he is and where he wants to go in life will soon find himself adrift. I learned early on to keep myself shipshape and ready for anything—so that if the wind shifts in my favor, I can take advantage of it. And if a squall blows up, I can trim my sails, and still bring myself about!"

Not five minutes later, they reined in at the squat stone cross by the roadside. Their track across the moor continued on, while two others branched away to the left, and at sharply diverging angles. Andrew unfolded the map the duke had drawn for them on a sheet of paper.

"Devil take it! Haycross said nothing about *two* tracks. How are we to know which one leads to the Druids' Oak?"

"By reckoning our position the same way we do at sea. The inn should be northeast of us."

Ravenall scanned the heath, with its steep rises and ancient undulations. "There!" A peaked roof and red and yellow sign outlined in black were visible beyond a tor off to the left.

Andrew was taken aback by its appearance. "A mean place!"

"Mean and rough, but there isn't much that can be done to spoil smoked ham, a round of cheese, a loaf of bread, and a good tankard of home-brewed. Now hang on to your hat. I vowed I'd get you there before the rain moved in—and I mean to keep my word!"

Mrs. Croggins spied them as she hurried in from the kitchen garden: two gentlemen in a fine chaise, racing the coming storm—and heading straight to her door. Oh! the luck of it! Wiping her hands upon her apron, she rushed inside, shouting for Perdita and Sukey.

"Make haste! Make haste!"

The girls came running out of the kitchen, sure some accident had befallen. Instead they found the landlady stripping off her dirty apron. "Sukey, fetch me a clean apron! Perdita, sweep out the private parlor. Make sure there are no cobwebs or mice droppings to be seen!"

Her plain face was transformed by a beatific smile. She couldn't believe her good fortune, all in the same day. She jerked her head toward the open window. "Here's a carriage driving up the road with two gentlemen. Someone wanting their midday dinner and a tankard to drown the spark in their throats."

Sukey muttered something beneath her breath. "This is my half-day to go home," she said.

Perdita felt her companion's disappointment, mixed with a wistful tinge of longing. *Home!* Such a simple word, yet the things it conveyed to her—family, affection, belonging—were so complex. She wished with all her might that she had a home to go to, family to surround her. One place where she truly belonged.

Mrs. Croggins stiffened. It was even better than she'd thought. "Two young lords," she said in awe, "in a spanking carriage with yellow wheels. Oh, they'll have plenty of blunt to drop at the Stag and Crown, they will!"

While Perdita ran for the broom, Sukey gawked out the door. Sure enough, even from this distance, she could tell they were fine gentlemen driving up to the Stag and Crown. She'd never seen such a fancy vehicle, and the passengers' hats and

driving cloaks, the way they held themselves, made their im-
minent arrival as rapturous and unexpected as the appearance
of angels from heaven.

Here was the opportunity of a lifetime, dropped into her
lap. If they were generous with their wallets it would be well
worth her staying.

Sukey glanced up at the sky. "Rain!" she commanded beneath her breath. *"Rain!"*

Mrs. Croggins gave her a quick thump on the ear. "Rain it
will, but only if we can keep them here long enough. Stir your
stumps, girl, and get me that apron. Then help Perdita in the
parlor. They'll be here before we know it!"

Taking the apron from Sukey, the landlady put on the clean
one, and hurried out to the stableyard. "Jed? Jed! Get in here
and start a fire in the parlor. Will, run out front. There's gentlemen coming."

Sukey had vanished. Perdita swept the floor in the parlor
and dusted down the few cobwebs that had formed. Otherwise
the room was clean, the table and chairs polished only yesterday. She made sure the lampwicks were clean and trimmed
and hurried out. Mrs. Croggins came bustling in from the
kitchen, and clouted her on the shoulder.

"Stop standing around, girl! Go up and prepare the private
bedchamber. The gentlemen will want to freshen up before
they tuck into a meal."

Perdita stared at her. "Private bedchamber . . . ?"

"My bedchamber, you little ninny! Hurry now. Fresh linens
and clean water in the jug!"

"What shall I do with your things, Mrs. Croggins?"

"Carry them up to your place beneath the eaves for now."

Ducking another thump from the landlady, Perdita hurried
up the stairs. She opened the door and stopped in dismay. It
was Sukey's job to tend to the room each day after the landlady came downstairs. The bedchamber was a disaster, with
the counterpane on the floor, the sheets in a pile, and the washbasin unemptied. The remains of cold chicken and a heel of
bread were on the table beneath the window.

Racing against time, Perdita gathered up the soiled linens
and got the spare set from the clothespress, along with Mrs.
Croggins's best feather bed and the white-work quilt from the
chest. As she worked she could hear the approach of the car-

riage wheels, the sound of voices from below. There wasn't enough time to carry off the remains of Sam Bailey's late-night picnic.

With a quick glance out the side window to see that the landlady wasn't down there, Perdita pitched the meaty chicken carcass out. The stable cats would make short work of it. Lifting the heavy stoneware pitcher from the dresser, she tossed the water out the window, as well.

A sharp oath came in response.

"What the devil!"

She froze. Peering down past the ivy, Perdita spied a gentleman in a fine hat and driving cloak, both splotched with water from the jug. For several seconds shock held her immobile. He raised his head at her gasp of dismay, revealing a harsh, scowling countenance, and the most piercing pair of blue eyes she had ever seen.

Rounding the corner, Ravenall had been brought up short by the sudden, brief downpour from the open casement above. Andrew had escaped, but he'd taken the brunt of it. Water dripped from the brim of his hat and spattered the wide shoulders of his driving cape.

Perdita was transfixed by his icy blue gaze and affronted air. He was so elegant, so patently out of place at the Stag and Crown, that it was almost comical. And so darkly handsome that he took her breath away. She doubted he would see the humor of the situation, and popped back inside the window, clanging the pitcher against the sill.

"Only a pitcher of water. Console yourself." Andrew grinned. "It might have been worse." He looked up. "By Jove, what a pretty girl!"

Ravenall glanced up again at the open casement. An oval face was framed by the opening. He had an impression of a graceful figure in a faded dress, of lustrous black hair and thickly lashed violet eyes.

Frowning, Ravenall ducked his tall frame through the inn's low door and led the way inside. The inn was dark, with the smoke of three centuries on the ceiling, and stone walls that had not seen whitewash in almost as long. Scents of ale and roasting meat wafted through the open door to the taproom.

"Ah," Andrew said appreciatively, "it smells as if they've killed the fatted calf in our honor."

"More like the stringy sow," Ravenall muttered darkly. He glanced up the staircase, all shadows and worn treads. The inn was shabbier than he'd expected.

"That girl at the window!" Andrew exclaimed. "What in heaven's name is a female so delicately fashioned doing at a ramshackle place such as this?"

"Pouring water on me, damn her impudence!"

There wasn't time for further exchange. Mrs. Croggins came scurrying out to greet them in her best apron, bowing and scraping so low her beaky nose looked in danger of touching the floor.

"My lords, welcome! You honor my humble establishment. Come in, come in, before the storm blows up! The best bedchamber is above if you wish to refresh yourselves, and the private parlor is here, on the right. We'll serve you up proper, my lords. It will not be what you are used to, but I pride myself on setting a good table: smoked ham and black pudding, and jugged hare. I'll send a lad to wring the neck of my plump goose and—"

Justin raised a hand. "Spare your fowl, my good woman. If you have bread, cheese, and ham, with tankards of home-brewed, we shall be well content."

The landlady looked properly horrified. "Ah, no. 'Twouldn't be fitting for fine lords such as yourself."

"But I assure you, it is exactly what we should like!"

At that exact moment Perdita came lightly down the stairs. Too late to flee to the kitchen! Her stomach fluttered like a field of butterflies.

The gentleman was hatless now, and even more elegant at close range. His eyes met hers in recognition.

Mrs. Croggins took in the water stains on his driving coat. She glanced in puzzlement out the open door. Although clouds were sweeping in, not so much as a drop had fallen in the inn's yard. "You've encountered rain, my lord?"

Perdita felt the blood drain from her face. The air grew thick and tense as the stranger's eyes held hers, like the moment of sudden stillness before a storm. *Now I am in for it!* She opened her mouth to confess.

"A most unexpected shower," Ravenall said shortly. "Nothing that signifies."

Perdita almost fainted with relief. He seemed aware of her

predicament, and an odd little smile played over his lips. An infinitesimal nod of his head directed her to make her escape while the landlady's back was turned to her.

She blushed deeply. It was a gentlemanly thing to do, and made her agonizingly aware of her mended dress and crumpled apron, of the wisps of hair that had come loose at her nape. Not even the meanest servant in his household would look so bedraggled.

With a quick curtsy, she retreated toward the scullery. Perdita found Sukey leaning up against the chopping block and grinning like a jack-o'-lantern on All Hallows' Eve. Wiping her hands on her apron, she tiptoed to the door and peeked out for a view of the newcomers.

"Did you ever see the like? Why, it would take a twelve-month of custom before old Croggins could pay the price of his coat sleeve! And that emerald ring upon his finger..." She shook her head in awe.

Perdita hadn't noticed my lord's ring, nor the quality of his coat. It was the wide shoulders beneath it, his elegant air, and striking angular face that had captured her interest. And his eyes! Not the pale tint of her faded dress, but the hot, intense blue of a summer's day. One glance from them and she'd been stricken mute.

She found her tongue now. "Sukey...I...he—" She broke off in confusion. Better not to say anything to the other girl about what she'd done. "Ah ... don't let the mistress catch you staring," she warned. "She'll take it out on our backs."

"Pooh. A cat may look at a queen, you said, so we may look at a lord if we like! It will be worth it, whatever the cost." A calculating gleam came into her eye. "Mayhap they'll decide to break their journey and overnight here ... and one of them might take a liking to me."

"Oh, Sukey! You would not!"

The other girl lifted her chin defiantly. "And why not? What is the difference in lying with Rafe for a few kisses and a ribbon for my hair, or with one of those handsome lords who'll give me a purse full of coins and treat me like a lady, besides? They're alike enough to be brothers, aren't they?"

"We're not of their world." Perdita's violet eyes were shadowed. She picked up a knife and began slicing ham from the bone. "There is no guarantee that a fine lord such as those two will treat you any better than the worst ruffian who frequents the taproom."

Sukey shrugged. "I'd take either one, if they'd have me. A lass must get her fun where she can. Although," she reflected, "the taller of the two has a cruel set to his mouth, to my way of thinking."

She carved thick wedges of cheese onto the platter. "And you'd best not be so hard to please. You'll sing another song when you're a rheumaticky old lady, still carrying slops for Mrs. Croggins, with the mark of her stick across your back."

She sent Perdita a mocking glance. "Or when Sam Bailey takes you for a ride beneath the sheets."

Perdita dropped her own knife with a clatter. Sukey laughed sourly. "Aye, I've seen how he looks at you, like he's a wolf and you're just the tempting bit he'd like to sink his teeth into."

"Don't joke about him!" Perdita said, fighting the fear and panic warring in her chest. "Or about playing the strumpet with those two gentlemen, so you can feather your nest with a few measly coins."

"What's a quick tumble to me?" Sukey flounced her yellow curls. "No skin off my nose, if you get my meaning. What's gone is gone. And I'll have something to jingle in my pocket when I'm done."

Her jaw squared. "We're not getting any younger, either of us. A girl has to look out for herself: if my bonny merchant fails me, well, there are plenty of strapping lads who'll take me to wife with my silver coins, and not scruple to ask how I came by them."

Before Perdita could reply, Mrs. Croggins came into the room and cuffed the other girl. "Lower your voice, you shameless slut! I'll settle with the two of you later," she said furiously. "Now there's work to be done. Sukey, go tell Jed to kill the goose, and start the plucking of the carcass."

Ignoring the bustle their arrival had incurred, Ravenall and his cousin took their ease in the inn's private parlor. It was a dark room, meanly furnished. A worn wooden table, one bench, and two rustic chairs. Two small windows, with thick roundels of glass, let in little light. Ravenall made a sound of disgust.

"Without the flames in the hearth and the lighted oil lamp,

it would be difficult to see one another across the table. I'll be glad to set out after the rain passes."

"And I. It's a long way to Oakhampton." Andrew grinned. "Although if that pretty little maid at the window waits upon us, instead of that dragon of a landlady, I'd be more inclined to linger."

"Yes." Ravenall pulled out a chair, straddled it, and leaned his chin on his hands. The image of that delicate oval face, those dark-fringed violet eyes, lingered in his mind. It had been a long time since he'd felt such a strong tug of interest over a woman, however lovely.

"Who would suspect to find such a fetching little thing within these wretched walls?" he said, almost to himself.

Andrew grinned. "Remember: I saw her first, cousin."

Ravenall didn't appreciate his joke. "We're neither of us the sort to cavort with serving wenches at a public inn," he snapped. "Although I do admit she is a little beauty."

"Yes. A veritable diamond. Not from the village," his cousin reflected. "They're sturdier stock hereabouts, it seems. Although if her mother had half her beauty, it is little wonder some gentleman dallied here a while."

"It certainly wouldn't be anything new," the earl said. "You know what an old rogue our great-grandfather was! He sowed his wild oats with abandon. They say that half the children in the county had the Ravenall nose in his day."

Andrew choked on his ale. "A fearsome sight!"

His cousin raised an eyebrow. "I happen to think it is a very fine nose."

"Yes, since yours is a much smaller replica of his." Andrew glanced at the doorway. "There are times when I think it would be very convenient to have been born without a conscience."

Justin sprawled back in his chair, keeping one eye on the doorway. He also wanted another look at that black-haired girl, but she seemed to have vanished. It was a bouncing girl with guinea-gold curls who brought them their ale.

"Here you are, my lords. The best that the Stag and Crown has to offer." Sukey shot a sideways look at Ravenall and gave him a sultry smile. "In the way of spirits, that is."

It was gone in an instant, but Sukey had seen the way his eyes darkened, the sudden quirk at the corners of his mouth.

A warm glow began in the pit of her stomach and spread out through her limbs. She sucked in a breath.

He was a knowing one, all right. He'd be fierce in bed, he would, know just how to please a girl, if he wanted. And generous with his coins after. She'd be a fool not to try her luck with him.

She put her hands on her curvaceous hips. "I'm Sukey. If there's anything more you'd be wanting, my lord . . . ?"

"We have," Ravenall said coolly, "all that we require."

"Ah, but you might think of something else that you'd want."

With a swish of her skirts and a flash of a smile over her shoulder, she exited the room. She hovered just outside for a bit: to her keen disappointment, neither gentleman called her back.

Lightning flashed at the window, and the room darkened as the rain came pelting down. It was as short as it was fierce. By the time Ravenall and his cousin had finished their meal it was gone, leaving a clear-washed sky and rapidly vanishing ground mist. There was no reason to linger over their half-empty tankards.

If they were disappointed that the landlady herself waited upon them, neither gentleman showed it. But Ravenall caught himself hoping for a glimpse of the lovely girl with the wide violet eyes. She intrigued him in spite of himself. He wondered if she were married: on the whole, he doubted it. There was a dewy freshness to her, an air of innocence at odds with her surroundings. Perhaps she dreamed of some strapping young lad from one of the outlying farms.

Mrs. Croggins came back with a tray covered with a clean cloth. The hapless goose was still being plucked by one of the lads, but her fine guests had supped well on roast chicken and dumplings, and smoked ham served with wedges of cheese. The landlady smiled and whipped off the cloth to display fresh scones served with bramble jam and Devon cream.

Andrew groaned. "I thought I could not eat another bite, but I am tempted out of all reason."

"Our Polly has a light hand," Mrs. Croggins said.

Polly, Ravenall thought. *The name doesn't suit the girl. It should be something airy and as delicate as she. Rosalind, or*

Alinor. He realized the conversation had gone on without him.

Andrew had asked about the Druids' Oak. "Oh, aye!" Mrs. Croggins nodded. "The Wishing Tree, my granny called it. If you make one true wish, 'tis said it will be granted."

"So, you have actually seen it?"

"Oh, a fine, splendid tree it is, my lord. Why, I daresay its trunk is wider than this room!"

Ravenall arched an eyebrow. Her voice held the ring of truth. "My friend and I wish to see this marvel. We've been told that it is difficult to find."

"*Very* difficult," the landlady added, "unless your lordships are given good directions by some like me, as has *been* there."

Taking the hint, Ravenall dropped a coin into her ready hand. "And was your wish granted?"

A strange expression rippled over the landlady's features. "Well, my lord, I can't exactly say. I wished to wed Hugh Croggins, a Dartmoor man who'd gone and went to sea. And so I did, when he came home. Eleven years we were wed, God rest his soul."

Andrew was impressed. "Then your wish was granted!"

Mrs. Croggins sighed. "I suppose so, in a manner of speaking. But not a day's peace came from it, from the moment our vows were said, to the day I buried him. A fine set-up man, Hugh was, strong as an oak. Good-natured and easy in his ways—until the drink was in him. Then he was something else altogether!"

"A mixed blessing," Andrew said.

"You might say that." She nodded vigorously. "Drunk as a wheelbarrow, he was, when he stumbled out in front of a carriage. A terrible accident," she said darkly. "They had to shoot the horses!"

Andrew choked on his ale, and didn't dare meet his cousin's eye.

"Terrible, indeed," Ravenall drawled. "I imagine that Mr. Croggins would agree."

"And so he would, my lord, had he survived the collision." She smiled suddenly. "But I have the Stag and Crown, which is more than I ever hoped for as a girl, so it all ended well enough, as you can see."

She dipped a curtsy and bustled out of the parlor to refill their tankards. Ravenall exchanged a wry glance with his cousin. "Such wifely grief! One hopes that the late Mr. Croggins finds the present circumstances as much to *his* satisfaction, as they are to hers!"

He took a quaff of ale and frowned. "You see why I have no particular urge to take a wife and carry on the name. The more I see of the fair sex, the less I find to enchant. In their book, the males of our species, regardless of their station in life, have only one purpose: to set up the female in comfort—and then, if they have any sensibility at all, to cock up their toes, leaving behind a wealthy young widow."

"What a gloomy philosophy, Justin!" Andrew finished his own ale. "It is all the product of your disappointment in Lady Sarah Carstairs' character. Silly chit! She may be beautiful, I'll grant you that. But she is not worth breaking your heart over."

"My heart was not involved. Nor hers."

Ravenall brooded. Was it so much to ask, that a woman would love him for himself? He shrugged. "The only thing wounded was my damnable pride."

"If you had less pride you'd be the happier for it," Andrew responded with a grin.

"If I had less pride I wouldn't be a Ravenall!"

"True enough." Andrew's face grew solemn. "One day you will find a worthy and beautiful young woman who will fall head over heels for you, and not care if you are prince or pauper."

Ravenall raised his tankard in a toast. "When—and *if*—I find such a paragon," he vowed, "I shall marry her out of hand."

Perdita stood at the scullery window. She had overheard every word about the ancient oak as she lingered outside the parlor. *Druids' Oak! Wishing Tree!* The very names were magical, like something out of one of Miss Barnstable's storybooks.

She could see it clearly in her mind's eye. A clearing in the forest-crowned valley. The gnarled oak, awesome in its ancient majesty. Branches stretching up and up into the sky, lobed leaves whispering softly in the wind.

The rest seemed a bit farfetched. If she tried—very, very hard—she could almost see its legendary roots carved of ice and fire.

Almost.

The gauzy vision thinned and vanished: it was too much of a stretch, even for her vivid imagination.

"Polly!"

She jumped at the voice, but it was too late to escape. Mrs. Croggins came up behind her and boxed her ear. The landlady's face was as red as a hen's wattle.

"Stupid girl! I heard what you did! Barty saw you toss the water out the window. It's lucky for you those two fine gentlemen didn't ride off again."

"I didn't know that anyone was beneath the window!"

Mrs. Croggins stood with her arms akimbo, her face suffused with color. "Next time, look first! If you'd lost the chance for them to loosen their pursestrings here, I'd have taken a strap to your hide." Her eyes narrowed. "And I may yet, if you don't hurry with that water!"

She raised her hand, but Perdita was too quick this time. Catching up the bucket, she slipped past Sukey, out through the door into the side yard.

While Andrew went out to the stables, Mrs. Croggins tried to dissuade Ravenall from leaving. "It will pour again within the hour, my lord," she prophesied falsely. "You would be wise to stay the night."

Ravenall's mouth twisted in a humorless smile. "Do you take us for a pair of city-bred dandies, unable to read the sky? The next storm will not come this far inland today. It will blow itself out before it reaches Dartmoor."

The landlady was desperate to keep them. Such fine gentlemen! So distinguished and condescending—and so ready to lay down their blunt! Through the open window of the parlor, she saw Perdita fetching water from the well. Inspiration struck. She quashed what few qualms she had.

Opening the casement further, Mrs. Croggins nodded in Perdita's direction. "There are other reasons than weather that might delay a gentleman's journey."

Ravenall followed her gaze to the stableyard. An apple-cheeked boy was dismounting from a farm cart; but it wasn't the youth who caught his attention. It was the violet-eyed girl.

She stood by the well, graceful as a willow in the afternoon sunlight. Her slender figure showed to advantage despite her shabby garments, and she looked fresh as a new rose against the unkempt walls of the stable. A dark flush settled over Ravenall's cheekbones. His fingers tightened about the handle of his whip.

He stared down at the landlady, his face inscrutable. "Do I understand you correctly? Are you offering us the use of that girl for our pleasure?"

"Aye," she said eagerly, lowering her voice. She knew that some men took added pleasure in deflowering the innocent. "She is a virgin, my lord, I swear it."

Visions of gold blinded her to the cold blaze of anger in his eyes. "And you've already seen the other bonny lass," she went on avidly. "Sukey, that is. A fine, bouncing girl. One of more experience, if you get my meaning. I'm sure as she would please your young friend."

Ravenall's whip raked the tankards from the tables and onto the floor. The clatter brought Sukey running from the kitchen, to hover in the doorway with a hand to her mouth.

A fierce scowl marred Ravenall's countenance. "You unscrupulous old bawd! You should be horsewhipped where you stand!"

Mrs. Croggins's mouth drooped in astonishment. She jumped out of his way as he pushed past her.

Perdita heard the commotion and looked up as Ravenall burst out into the stableyard. His eyes were hard, a ring of white around his firm lips. There was something dangerous in the set of his wide shoulders, the tension of his lithe frame as he crossed the cobbles. She set the bucket down on the edge of the well, heart thumping wildly as he approached.

Ravenall saw the sudden leap of fear in her eyes, the quiver of her soft mouth. What in God's name was such a tender blossom doing in this midden heap—and how much longer would she stay fresh and innocent?

"What is your position at this inn?" he asked abruptly. "Is that old beldam any relation to you?"

"No, my lord." Perdita was bewildered. "I am a scullery maid, in service to Mrs. Croggins."

"Your mistress does not have your best interests at heart," he said curtly. "My advice is to leave this place at once, and seek safer employment at Haycross Manor."

"I do not understand you, my lord."

He regarded her with a wry smile. "No, I don't suppose

you do. And that is exactly the problem. Although," he added, "I imagine you've seen and heard enough to solve the riddle, if you put your mind to it. This place is not exactly a nunnery!"

She stared up at him with those wide violet eyes. Ravenall wanted to shake her. "Listen well: you mean as little to that greedy shrew as the goose whose neck she ordered wrung," he said brutally. "A commodity, to be bought and sold."

Perdita's face went red, then blanched as she felt the blood drain from her. Mrs. Croggins had tried to bargain away her innocence to him. Her eyes shone darker violet with humiliation and fear.

Ravenall watched the dawn of comprehension. "I see you *do* understand." His heart was filled with anger, and with pity. "Fortunately for you," he added softy, "there were no takers today!"

Perdita was dizzy, as if the ground had dropped away beneath her, and she was falling through a rush of air.

While she stared at him in shock, Ravenall saw Mrs. Croggins standing in the doorway. The look he sent her was so black she darted back inside the shadows.

He turned to block her view, and withdrew a small pouch, heavy with coins, from inside his coat. He set it down on the stone ledge of the well, where the wooden bucket shielded it from prying eyes. Taking Perdita's hand, he placed it on the pouch. Her skin was roughened but her bones delicate beneath his broad palm. Ravenall cursed beneath his breath when he felt the fine tremors that shook her.

"Take this purse and keep it hidden," he said quietly. "Its contents should prove sufficient to get you well away from this place."

Without waiting for a reply, he strode across the yard to where his chaise stood waiting. Perdita stared after him in mute amazement. She could still feel the warmth of his hand on her skin, the tingle it had ignited in her blood. No man, except Sam Bailey, had ever touched her before. She couldn't bear to think of them in the same breath.

Her fingers closed over the bag and she felt the heavy coins shift. This fine lord—this handsome stranger—had changed her life forever with a single gesture. She was overwhelmed with surprise and gratitude.

Ravenall mounted his chaise and took the reins, calling for
Andrew to join him. Perdita plucked up the purse, and slipped
it into her commodious pocket. It swung against her leg with
a satisfying weight. She prayed the rattle of the iron-banded
bucket would offset the subtle chink of coins as she hurried
across the inn yard. Her heart was pounding even more loudly,
or so it seemed to her.

"My lord . . . !" she called, but her voice went unheard as
the stablelad stepped away from the horses' heads. The chaise
sprang away.

She watched it rattle over the cobbles and out to the road,
carrying the two men away from the Stag and Crown, and out
of her life.

I will never forget you! she vowed. *Every night I will remember you in my prayers.* She sent her pledge winging after
him on the wind.

Mrs. Croggins came out into the inn yard, her face dark
with anger. She'd offended the fine lords, and they would not
be back again. She looked for the nearest servant to vent her
wrath upon, and Jed was the unfortunate one. The landlady
boxed his ears soundly.

"Get back to work, you idle fool!"

Perdita didn't want to be next. As the lad slunk away, she
rushed inside, scarcely able to catch her breath, stunned at her
unexpected good fortune.

Ravenall was still brooding over the episode twenty minutes
later, as the chaise rolled along the ancient track through the
bracken. The way went arrow-straight across the land, worn
down by centuries of foot traffic. The heath had soaked up the
rain, pouring it into swift-running streams, and deceptive bogs.

"That poor young girl! Lovely and unspoiled, despite her
surroundings. Like a rose blooming in a midden pile!"

Andrew raised his eyebrows. "You seem to be quite taken
with her."

It was true that Ravenall couldn't get her out of his mind.
"She's quite beautiful, I must admit."

He shook his head, and sunlight gleamed over his thick,
dark hair. "There was a time when I was a fool for beauty,
but that time is past. No, it is her circumstances that gnaw at

me. To leave such a delicate creature behind in so sordid a place is hard for me to stomach."

"There is nothing else you could have done," Andrew pointed out reasonably. "You couldn't very well kidnap the girl and carry her off in a two-man chaise."

"Perhaps," Ravenall said fiercely, "I should have tried."

He couldn't shake off the anger. *That girl! Those luminous eyes, innocent but shadowed—no, perhaps* haunted *was a better description.*

His gut clenched again, remembering her sudden pallor, her stunned expression, when she understood that her mistress had tried to sell her to him.

"By God, there must be something more I could have done!"

"Your conscience does you credit, Justin. But only think! Human nature is suspicious. Once it was learned that she had been seen bundled in the chaise with us—and believe me, even in this empty-seeming countryside, someone would surely have seen her—she would never be hired in any honest household in the county. This way is best. Her safety is secured, thanks to your gentlemanly actions."

"Acquit me of sainthood!" Ravenall frowned. "My boots cost more than all that was in that purse!"

His cousin shrugged. "It is all relative. To her, you must agree, it is a fortune. Enough to secure her freedom and perhaps provide a dowry. You cannot ride all over England like a knight errant, rescuing girls from what is, after all, a common enough fate for someone in her station in life."

"No, I can't. *Damn it to hell!*" Ravenall's face was grim. "Though it may be a 'common enough fate,' that does not make it right!"

"If you mean to go all moralistic on me and preach sermons from here to the castle," Andrew said, in an attempt at lightness, "I shall leap out and take my chances with the bogs."

That made Ravenall laugh. "You've spent too much of your life with your nose between the pages of a book, my dear cousin. You'd never make it as far as Stump Cross!"

There was nothing for Andrew to do but grin and agree. "The life of an adventurer has never appealed to me. Bridgeforth and I must take after our great-grandmother's side of the

family. It is you who has inherited the old rogue's derring-
do."

"But not, I hope," Ravenall said suavely, "his famous
nose."

He changed the subject and the chaise bowled along, but
the clouds seemed to be gaining on them. Their darkness echoed his mood. He'd spent years in the West Indies, and knew
there was something very wrong with a world where men and
women were sold into slavery. Somehow he hadn't expected
to find the same tragic conditions in England, masquerading
under another name.

The wind rushed in from the sea and the horses sensed the
coming storm. Ravenall knew it would blow itself out before
it reached the high moors, but he was as anxious as his team
to be well under way. He noticed that Andrew seemed increasingly nervy and on edge.

"Are you sure you wish to stop and look for this magical
tree?"

Andrew struggled to hide his disappointment. "Not if you
feel we should press on," he said lightly.

Ravenall shrugged. "We have already come this far, it
makes no difference to me. To the Druids' Oak, then."

When they reached the thickly wooded combe that cut deep
into the moor, he slackened the pace. "Our landmarks should
be visible shortly," he said. "Three standing stones, and the
foundations of some early Briton huts."

It was Andrew who spied the stones first. Although they
were man-sized, their location was in a small dip in the land,
making them easy to overlook from the road. Five minutes
later they left the chaise and approached the stones on foot.
The granite slabs leaned in toward one another, as if huddled
in conversation: legend claimed they were three women, who
had stopped to gossip on the way to church one Sunday, and
been turned to stone for their impiety.

"Although where a church is in all this vast expanse is more
than I can tell," Andrew said.

Ravenall didn't answer. He'd gone ahead, leading the way
over rough granite ribs, to the head of the combe. The descent
looked almost vertical, till he spotted the leafy ravine. It was
so well hidden he'd almost gone past it.

"There's the trail," he said. "A rough climb. I only hope it is worth the effort."

The way was thick with trees. Velvety green moss and scaly gray lichens hugged the rough brown bark, and blackberry bushes, their fruit long gone, sprawled through the few open spaces. Brambles plucked at his riding breeches and the branches slapped at his shoulders as he strode through. From behind he could hear Andrew cursing good-naturedly.

Abruptly, the ravine widened into a narrow gorge. Ravenall followed it down, and came out into a clearing that overlooked a sharp drop-off. Unlike the boggy moorland, the ground here was hard as flint. He examined his surroundings. It was unnatural, this wide-open space ringed by woods. And in the center, alone and majestic, just as Haycross had told them, stood the great oak.

There was an utter stillness to the place that was unsettling. No sound of birdsong, no rustle of creatures in the brush. The silence was so profound he imagined he could hear the beating of his own heart.

"By God!" Andrew said, joining him. "The legends are true! This is indeed an eerie setting."

Ravenall laughed. "I doubt there is the slightest danger, as long as you don't wield an axe."

It *was* an amazing sight. He'd never seen an oak so ancient and gnarled. It covered a vast area. The leafy limbs bowed low, protecting the expanse between its outer perimeter and the massive trunk. Ravenall strode toward the tree.

"It takes little imagination to envision Druids here, chanting and harvesting mistletoe from those great branches, with a golden sickle."

He left the sunny glade and ventured beneath the overhanging limbs with lively curiosity. Plunged suddenly in emerald gloom, he checked his stride. A primal shiver ran up his spine. There was an uncanny atmosphere to the place—a sense of ancient, living presence in the shifting light, the arcane whispering of leaves.

Andrew stepped just inside the branches, but went no further. "Egad, it's dark as a cave in here! I can't see a thing."

"There is nothing *to* see," Ravenall said. "Unless one is a botanist. Oak leaves on the branches, and moldering acorns underfoot. As for magic, I must disappoint you. The roots are plain bark."

Andrew didn't look crestfallen. "It is still a capital tree! Surely the oldest in all of England."

"Yes, it is rather awe-inspiring."

Ravenall consulted his pocket watch. "At least we have not lost more than two hours in this little side trip."

"You are in a great hurry. What is it that draws you back to the castle in such haste?"

Again a shadow crossed Ravenall's lean face. "Nothing to which I look forward with any great enthusiasm, I assure you."

Andrew frowned. The late earl had been a bad steward to his inheritance: he'd neglected his lands and tenants, and spent lavishly on gaming, fast horses, and faster women. Justin was made of different stuff. The only thing he loved as much as Ravenall Castle was the sea.

The angle of the sun changed. Blinding light blazed from the base of the tree, chasing the shadows back. Both men shielded their eyes. It was Andrew who backed slowly away, Ravenall who went forward.

Once out of the direct path of the light, his eyes adjusted. He moved sideways until he reached the gnarled surface roots, and looked down. The hollow beneath the tree seemed filled with flame. It took him a few seconds to sort out the illusion.

"Nothing to fear here," he announced. "But I have found your roots carved of fire and ice."

"Have you, by Jove?"

"Indeed." Ravenall leaned down to peer beneath the tangled mass, to the great pocket of quartz crystals beneath a section of the oak. "And quite an impressive sight they are!"

With the sun hitting them obliquely, the enormous crystals appeared to be lit from within. Some glowed red like embers, others molten gold. At the edges of the cavity, still others were clear as ice, with rainbows captured in their hearts. Ravenall had never seen anything like it. He marveled at the differing shapes and sizes. Many of the crystals were six-pointed, while a few were as flat and smooth on their ends as polished mirror.

He leaned forward and almost lost his balance. Putting his hand out to right himself, he felt a sharp stab of pain.

"Devil take it!" The razor-sharp edge of a broken crystal had sliced his palm. The gash bled freely, great gouts of blood splashing red as rubies, over the glittering crystals. Cursing, he reached for his handkerchief and wadded it up to stem the flow.

While Ravenall was binding his wound, Andrew joined him. "Well," he said lightly, "you have made the blood sacrifice. Now you must make your wish. What shall it be?"

"What more can I want than I already have?" Ravenall's face darkened. "I would be guilty of the sin of greed if I wished for anything at all."

"There must be something you lack, Justin!"

On the heels of his cousin's words a wind sprang up, shaking the leaves of the giant oak. The air grew still and thick and rich as honey, as if the entire glade were trapped in amber. Ravenall froze in place. He heard Andrew's voice as if from far away.

"You must make your wish . . ."

And he felt it then, welling up inside him, spreading out like a flood from a burst dam. A loneliness so deep and pervasive that it shattered him.

He felt dizzy. The clearing shimmered and blurred. Vanished into dense blackness, filled with the buzzing of tiny, golden bees. The sound changed to a great, rushing roar, as Ravenall looked deep into his soul. A black void opened beneath him. He felt like Dante, staring down through the nine levels of hell.

Ravenall was overpowered by a sense of desolation. By the urge to fling himself out and into that terrible chasm. By the need to obliterate the pain that pierced his breast. So tempting to tip over and let himself drop off the edge of the world . . .

It rose up and engulfed him.

"No!" The cry was ripped from him. He fought back the darkness with all his might. The rushing ebbed, altered, became the soft thrum of blood at his temples. His vision cleared and the ancient oak came into focus.

Only the pain remained.

He knew then what it was he lacked, and what his one, true wish must be: "Grant me this," he whispered softly. "That a woman—just once—would love me for myself alone."

Once again the great branches stirred and tossed like a wind-lashed sea. The air grew cold and thin, the light an odd golden-green. Everything shimmered darkly.

A shiver passed through Ravenall. It was as if he were viewing the oak from beneath the water. He felt the weight of it pressing him down, trapping his breath within his chest. He blinked, and everything became clear again. The stillness of the clearing held a sense of something ancient and remote. And he realized that Andrew had seen and heard nothing of his anguish.

"Let us quit this place," he said quietly. "We are trespassers here."

The two men turned as one and left the grove in silence.

Ravenall stopped at the top, to glance over the ravine. The view was fantastic. He could see the other side of the reeve in the distance, and another stretch of open moor beyond. But looking down he saw nothing but a forest of green. The legendary Druid's Oak was invisible from his vantage point.

Ravenall joined Andrew at the carriage. "That didn't take as long as I'd feared. We'll reach the castle before sundown." He was eager to be on his way.

The horses were restive as he approached, as if his unease had communicated itself to them. The matched bays were high-spirited. They snorted and chuffed, but he stood at their heads and spoke to them softly, gentling them with his voice. Under his mastery the team settled down, reassured.

Andrew had stopped and was searching along the ravine. "My fob! I've lost it."

Ravenall spied the small gold seal where it had fallen on the stony ground. "Behind your left boot."

He walked back and was swinging himself up into the vehicle when disaster struck without warning: out of a sky so clear it might have been made of azure glass, there came a sharp crack of thunder.

The frightened horses shrieked, then plunged and thrashed between the traces. Amid flailing hooves, the chaise lurched forward. Ravenall held the reins with all his strength, but there was no controlling the team, even for someone of his skill.

Ears back, eyes rolling, the horses bolted in desperate panic.

The chaise's wheels rumbled over the uneven ground, then foundered and wedged among the granite boulders hidden by the heath. The carriage slowed, but Ravenall pitched forward. In an instant he was flung from the runaway vehicle.

But not thrown clear: the whipping reins caught his arm,

and a piece of decorative brass along the vehicle's side snagged his coat. Stunned by the fall, dragged over the heath at astonishing speed, Ravenall was powerless to extricate himself. Brambles ripped at his garments, tore at his flesh, as the vehicle hurtled onward, drawn by the terror of the team.

Grit clogged his throat and stung his eyes. His body bounced and twisted. He heard the snap of bone, felt the shock of it through his frame. Curiously, there was no pain—not in the least. Time slowed down with a startling clarity, as if every second were carved in crystal. Ravenall felt no fear, only a cold and numbing disbelief.

He was exquisitely aware of every detail: Andrew's cry of horror, the frantic, churning hooves; the creak and groan of protesting wood and leather; the sight and pungent scent of late wildflowers, their golden petals and silvery leaves crushed beneath rumbling wheels; the soft heath that gave beneath his weight; and the rough, ribbed granite that bruised him to the bone.

Even the merlin soaring so gracefully, wheeling in a swift arc against the deep blue dome of sky.

Then time sped up. In the blink of an eye, the laboring beasts and wildly careening vehicle reached the edge of the precipice. With terrible shrieks, the horses plunged over the edge, and the chaise tumbled after them. Ravenall could do nothing to free himself; but the reins broke loose at last.

Momentum and gravity acted together. He felt an instant of shock and incredulity. There was no time for more.

Suddenly he found himself flung away into space, arcing out high above the steep valley. It was the most amazing sensation, he thought with odd detachment. He saw the sky and clouds, the flight of birds across the valley. The rock-ringed clearing and the great Druid's Oak, its branches reaching up to him like gnarled hands.

The next moment he was falling, plummeting down toward the earth like a fallen god, through the rush of silver-bright air.

Four

"Aren't those plum tarts done yet?" Sukey hissed, as she swung into the kitchen with a heavy tray in her hands.

Perdita pulled the last tart from the oven. Dark red juices bubbled up between the latticework of flaky crust. "Piping hot and almost ready to be served. They must just set up a bit."

The other girl put the tray down and wiped her forehead with the hem of her apron. She'd been running all afternoon: the Stag and Crown was filled with the market day regulars, returning from Haycross Village after successful selling and bartering.

She sent Perdita an assessing glance. "I saw you out by the well with that fine lord, Polly. He looked mad as fire." She lowered her voice. "If you turned him down, then you're the biggest fool in Devon! I'd have let him tumble me without a second thought."

"It wasn't like that," Perdita said with a flare of anger. She cut the flaky crusts into wedges, ready to dish up the moment they cooled. "He was angry with Mrs. Croggins . . ."

She didn't have time for more, as the landlady burst through the door. "Stir your stumps, you lazy strumpets! Polly, slice another plate of ham. Sukey, get back in the taproom and help Jed."

She was off in a whirlwind of greed and activity. Except for the time years before, when some free traders had hidden several casks of smuggled French brandy at the inn, and were captured before they could return for them, the Stag and Crown had never had such a profitable day in its entire history. She still wondered if it had been her late husband who'd turned the free traders in to the Inland Revenue, so that he might keep the casks, and sell the brandy himself.

Sharp as a knife, Hugh Croggins had been, with ever a keen

eye to increasing his profit! The landlady hurried out with Sukey right behind her.

Taking up the knife, Perdita began carving thick slices from the smoked ham. The soft leather bag of coins swung against her leg with a betraying jingle. It was a goodly sum. Perdita could tell by the heft of the pouch, by the soft clink of the coins. Silver coins, rather than coppers, she was sure! But there had been no time to open the pouch, much less hide it away.

I shall never forget his generosity, she vowed silently. Nor the man himself, with his dashing air and fierce blue eyes. Her heart gave a little flutter as his image floated in her mind's eye. He was the most handsome and intriguing man she'd ever met. Perdita lost no time in endowing him with every heroic virtue. It gave her a pang to know their paths would never cross again.

She finished her task and gave the roast on the spit another turn. It was another hour before things quieted down enough for Perdita to escape to the stillroom. The bag was wrapped with leather strings, and her fingers were clumsy with excitement. With her back to the closed door, she undid the purse strings, and gasped. Gold glittered softly among the silver florins and shillings. Crowns and half-crowns, and—yes!—precious sovereigns, gleaming bright as the sun. Her future suddenly shone as golden.

She took one out and held it in her trembling palm. He'd given her the purse as easily as she threw a crust of her bread to the birds. Did these coins—a small fortune to her—mean no more to him than that?

No matter! The wonderful thing is that I am now free! Or will be, when I pay off my debt to Mrs. Croggins.

And for that, she surely had sufficient means.

Her heart skipped a joyful beat. The stranger's gesture had lifted her up in the world.

Perdita's hands shook as she counted the coins. It would more than repay Mrs. Croggins for her keep, and plenty left over for herself. There was enough to purchase a seat on the stage, or even the mail coach, to whichever town she chose. Enough to furnish her with lodgings when she reached her destination, and some decent garments to help in her search for employment: a plain round gown and warm shawl, a serviceable bonnet and sturdy half-boots, and she would make a quite presentable figure.

I might even find a place in some genteel household, she thought giddily. *Or even a tearoom or shop.*

But for that she would need a note of recommendation. For a moment her hopes were dashed.

Why, I could write it myself! she thought suddenly. Mrs. Croggins had pen and paper up in her room, where she did her accounts. Perdita threw back her head and laughed softly. No one would suspect her letter of recommendation wasn't genuine! *Why, who would even guess that I have been taught to read and write?*

Smiling, she bent down beneath the stillroom sink. There was a loose stone down near the floor where she hid her treasures. The silver brooch with the blue stone gleamed dully as she lifted it out.

She counted out half the coins and wrapped them in a clean cheese cloth. After slipping them in her pocket, she put the pouch with the other half into the hole in the thick wall, then tried to replace the stone. There wasn't enough room for it all. Something must come out.

She would have to find another secure hiding place for the rest of it. Then she remembered a loose board near her pallet beneath the eaves. She could pry it up and hide it there.

Adding more coins to those in her pocket, she tried again. Still too much for the small chink in the wall. She took out the brooch, glad she wouldn't have to part with it. Perhaps one day it would provide a clue to her past.

Since there was no place for it now, she reached down her bodice, and pinned the brooch to the inside of her shift. The blue stone was cool at first, then warmed against her skin, familiar and comforting.

Gratitude to the man who'd given her her freedom overwhelmed Perdita. Once a girl was sold for money, her descent was swift and sure. But his warning of Mrs. Croggins's intentions would have been useless without this precious handful of silver and gold. It had made all the difference.

She took a deep breath and sat back on her heels. Between Mrs. Croggins and Sam Bailey, she must make her move quickly. The sooner she was away from the Stag and Crown, the better.

Footsteps on the kitchen flags roused her from her happy daydreams. Rising, Perdita was very aware of the soft clink of the remaining coins from her pocket. A shadow fell across her from the doorway. Perdita's heart hammered. Sukey stood there, frowning.

"There's a clerk wanting some supper and the lads from Beck Farm come in, and the missus calling for her tea. She's up in her room, counting out this afternoon's profit."

"Here's ham and cheese and a piece of tart for the clerk. I'll see to her tea." That would give her a chance to talk privately with Mrs. Croggins, about buying her freedom.

Sukey nodded. She had high hopes of the clerk, but very little where her mistress was concerned.

Perdita prepared a tray for the landlady and mounted the stairs. Mrs. Croggins was doing her accounts at the small desk beneath the windows. She could add and subtract simple sums and used symbols to represent items and those who owed her payment. With many a blotch of ink, the pen scratched over the paper slowly, while she pursed her thin lips.

After setting the tray upon the side table, Perdita hovered, gathering her courage. "If I might have a word with you, mistress?"

Mrs. Croggins looked up, scowling. "Yes? What is it, Polly?"

Perdita licked her lips and felt how dry her mouth was. "I have come to pay off my debt." It could not be much, since she had worked every day for her keep.

"Have you lost your wits, girl?"

"If you please, Mrs. Croggins, I am in earnest. I wish to repay you and seek other employment." Perdita lifted her chin. "If you will only tell me the sum of my debt to you, I will pay it now!"

The landlady's scowl changed to astonished laughter. The girl didn't have a farthing to her name. "A pound, for your keep!"

Feeling for the coins in her pocket, Perdita retrieved a sovereign.

Mrs. Croggins goggled at it. She looked from Perdita back to the piece of gold, gleaming in her outstretched hand. Her face grew red. She jumped up, hand raised to deliver a blow.

"Ungrateful wench! You have stolen this from the customers! Oh, we shall be ruined when word gets out of thieving at the Stag and Crown!"

"No! I swear!" Perdita ducked nimbly away. "It was the fine lord . . . he gave it to me."

"What?" The landlady stared. That toplofty young lord had turned down her offer of taking the girl for his pleasure, yet had given Polly his gold? It made no sense at all: but that was the Quality for you. There was ever an odd kick in their gallop.

A quick, darting movement and she snatched the gold from Perdita's hand. Her eyes narrowed. She'd had a good deal of experience in assessing just how much blunt a customer carried on his person. The way Perdita's hand hovered near her pocket, the way the dress hung down on that side, told her there was more to be had.

"A pound a year is what you owe me. Three pounds in all."

Perdita's heart sank.

She placed two more sovereigns on the table beside the first. It gave her quite a pang.

Mrs. Croggins smirked. There was more where those had come from, she'd be bound. "And the clothes I've put on your back," the landlady said acidly. "Another pound for those."

Perdita bit her lip and counted out four half-crowns.

The landlady licked her lips. "If you think that is enough to repay me, you are well out! Every dish you've ever broke is added to your debt, as well. What else have you?"

Perdita was on to her game. "You must tell me first the entire sum of my debt to you, mistress."

"I will tell you this, you little strumpet! You are my servant, and anything you had from that gentleman beneath my roof belongs to me!"

With a sudden movement, she reached out and grabbed the edge of Perdita's pocket. The worn fabric ripped, spilling the other coins onto the floorboards. Mrs. Croggins smiled. "Not quite enough to purchase your bond," she said cruelly. "But I will take it on account."

"Liar!" Perdita cried. "You cannot take it all!"

The landlady pushed her out of the room. "Can—and will! Now get back to your chores, or you'll feel the broom about your shoulders!"

Perdita's lids came down to hide the flare of defiance in her eyes. Turning away, she went back down the steep stairs.

She was shaking with anger. Despite what old Croggins said, she'd repaid her debt, and more.

At the first opportunity, Perdita decided, she'd slip away from the inn, make her way down to the village—and never look back. Thank God she had the rest safely hidden away. That, and the precious brooch with the blue stone, pinned inside her dress.

She was surprised to find her face wet with tears and wiped them hastily. Suddenly there was a great commotion from the stableyard. Shouts and exclamations, and a few sharp oaths. Perhaps a fight had broken out. Perdita raced to the landing and looked out the window.

A strange scene met her eyes: an exhausted, wild-eyed horse lumbered into the yard, in the westering light, drawing a makeshift litter of splintered wood bound with strips of leather. The poor beast's hide was scraped raw, and the man who walked before it, holding the bridle, was pale as death beneath the bloody scratches on his face.

There was more blood on his jacket, but she realized it wasn't his. There was another man in far worse shape, strapped to the litter. Dark hair tumbled across a pallid brow, and his head was turned to the side. Whether he was dead or alive, she couldn't tell.

"Mrs. Croggins! Sukey!" Perdita ran down the last steps and out into the yard.

Her heart kicked over, then started up like a runaway horse. It was only when she reached the injured man's side that she recognized him: the fine lord who had given her the purse of coins.

His profile was beautiful, and a lock of dark hair fell like a thick skein of silk across his marble forehead. *How much younger he looks, without that fierce scowl,* she thought numbly.

But his skin was ashen, his lips bloodless, and he appeared almost beyond the reach of human aid. Her heart was wrung with pity.

"Jed! Bartholomew! Bring him into the parlor, at once. No, you fools," she cried as they bent to remove the straps. "Carry him on the board!"

The other man stumbled. Perdita caught him and almost

crumpled under his weight. His face was so white she feared he would faint.

"You'll have a glass of Mrs. Croggins's best brandy, and Jed will ride down to Haycross Village and fetch help," she said, assisting him inside. They followed the others into the private parlor. Jed and Bartholomew set the makeshift litter down. There was no sound, not the slightest movement from the man bound to it.

The stablelads were at a loss. "What shall I do, then?" Jed asked.

"Go to Haycross Manor, at once," Andrew gasped hoarsely. He collapsed on the settle inside the door, his skin gray beneath the grime and sweat. "Tell them that Ravenall is dead!"

Jed and Bart crossed themselves hastily. Mrs. Croggins took off her apron, and started to lay it over the stricken man's face.

"Wait!" Perdita pushed past her and knelt down beside the litter.

The man's face had an odd, translucent look, like beeswax. His nostrils and mouth were rimmed in white, his lips pallid. Blood had congealed along the right side of his face and matted his dark hair. She opened his collar and felt for the pulse at his throat.

Reaching gently among his disordered locks, she found the hard lump at the back of his head. When she withdrew her hand, it was bloody. Her world blurred through a mist of tears.

But she remembered the intensity of his blue eyes, the force of his presence. She could not believe that a man so strong and vital was gone.

Ah, no!

Touching his throat lightly, she felt a thready pulse beneath her fingertips. Relief shivered through her, and her breath came with a throaty catch.

"He is alive!"

Perdita brought fresh cloth she'd torn into strips for bandages, up to Mrs. Croggins's bedchamber. It was not yet sunset, but the curtains had been drawn against the light. A single lamp burned on the bedside table, casting shadows over the man upon the bed. He lay still and white beneath the quilt.

Perdita paused in the doorway. She'd never seen a naked

man before. His physique was taut and well-muscled. Holding her breath, she watched his bare chest, motionless beneath the sheet. A shiver, a sigh, and it rose again raggedly.

He was not dead yet, but close to it, she feared.

While she hovered in the background, Lord Haycross and Andrew Waverly stood at the foot of the bed, watching Dr. Crawleigh examine his patient. The physician was a stocky man, neatly dressed in the black frock coat of his profession, and his blunt hands were quick and sure.

"This is a sorry day," the duke murmured. "Something must have frightened the horses, to make them run mad. I wish to heaven I had never spoken of that damnable legend."

"You, sir!" Andrew said in a broken voice. His gray eyes were dark with misery. "It is I who wished to see the Druids' Oak. If not for me, my cousin would have been miles away. Any blame must be mine."

"Don't be a young fool," Haycross said gruffly. "No one ever made Ravenall do anything he didn't wish to do."

Slipping in behind them, Perdita set the linen strips down on the table. The fire had burned low, and she laid another log in the grate. The flames caught and licked at the wood eagerly, casting a false glow of health upon the unconscious man. How beautiful he was!

The doctor bound another strip of cloth around the splint on Ravenall's leg.

"Well, man?" Haycross demanded.

"There is nothing more I can do for him, Your Grace. He is young and strong. I can soothe his abrasions, ease his sprains, and tape his ribs. But it is the injuries we cannot see that are the worst."

"Will he live?" Andrew asked numbly.

"I cannot say."

Perdita bit her lip. It seemed very cruel. Only a few hours earlier the earl had handed her a purse of coins and gone on his way. She had envied him. Envied his wealth and ease and freedom from care. And now he lay immobile, every privilege of rank and status brought level.

The Duke of Haycross was anguished for his wife. Poor little Daisey had gone out for a day's sailing on the river with some members of their house party, and didn't know yet of her brother's accident. He dreaded telling her. "I should like to remove him to the manor," he said.

"I would not advise it at this time, Your Grace," Dr. Crawleigh replied.

"Damn it, man, he'll be much more comfortable at Haycross than beneath the roof of this ramshackle place."

The doctor bristled slightly. "If it were only the broken collarbone and ribs, I would say you might carry him off with no great harm: but the jarring to his brain was severe. I am experienced in such cases, Your Grace. I fear that any further jolting might prove disastrous. Of course, if he ever awakens—"

"If?" The word was torn from Perdita.

The men turned to her, as astonished at her interruption as they would have been if the bedpost had spoken. Perdita flushed in the firelight. She was a mere serving wench. It was not her place to interrupt the conversations of her betters.

Dr. Crawleigh turned back to his patient. "We shall say *when* Lord Ravenall awakens. Well, there is little I can do here now. I will return in the morning." He frowned at Perdita. "And you, girl, will stay with him through the night."

"Yes, sir."

"Keep him warm, and try and give him ten drops of my willow bark elixir when he becomes feverish—as I have no doubt he will. If there is any other change in his condition, you must send for me at once."

He put his instruments back into his bag. "I will call upon you tomorrow, if it pleases Your Grace, and let you know how the earl is faring."

The duke had to be satisfied with that. "Good, good. I'll send his valet back in my carriage, with everything he needs." Haycross touched Andrew's arm. "Come, Waverly. I'll convey you back to the manor."

"Thank you, sir, but I believe I will remain here with my cousin."

"Very commendable. But unnecessary. And," he added, looking about the cramped room, with its low ceiling and rustic furnishing, "damnably uncomfortable!"

"I should prefer it, sir," Andrew said with quiet firmness. "I wish to be with Justin, should he need me."

"As you wish."

The three men went out, leaving Perdita alone with the injured man. *The Earl of Ravenall! A weighty title for so young a man.*

In her ignorance she had thought that earls and dukes and princes were blessed with everything the world had to give. It seemed that fate struck down rich and poor alike. The handsome earl's gold could buy him tender care, but it could not restore his health or save his life. It hung in the balance now. She imagined that she could feel it, a tentative quiver in the air, as if he were deciding whether the struggle was worth the pain.

Brushing the hair back from his forehead, she looked down at him in pity. A bandage swathed half his head and the right side of his face. Fresh blood seeped along the edges of dried, crusted areas, but the doctor had warned her not to disturb his handiwork. Beads of sweat stood out on his pale brow.

Folding a piece of linen, she dabbed at his forehead. It was a curious moment. She couldn't recall ever being so close to any man in her life.

Except, of course, for Sam Bailey. A shiver ran through her. The very thought of Sam sickened her. She had meant to be well away before he returned. Her plan had been to slip away from the inn before dawn, and be on her way. It was still the wise thing to do. And yet . . . Perdita sighed. *You cannot abandon him now,* she told herself sternly. She must stay as long as Lord Ravenall had need of her.

But, oh! If only he would awaken from his deep sleep. If only those blue eyes would open, filled again with life and intelligence, and his strength and vigor return.

But as the hours passed, Ravenall neither moved, nor murmured. The clock ticked the monotonous minutes and hours away, while Perdita kept her vigil. Her gaze swept over his chiseled face, the pulse beating at his throat, the sculpted muscles of his wide shoulders and broad chest.

He was strong, as Dr. Crawleigh had said. That surely would weigh in his favor. And his chin and jaw were surely those of a stubborn and determined character. That would surely see him through the predicted crisis.

Again she wiped the beads of sweat from his brow. There were dark smudges beneath his eyes, and the hollows beneath his cheekbones. The fever would be on him by morning, raging like a storm. She tried to pour some willow bark elixir between his lips, but it dribbled out.

She refused to despair. Time was in his favor, and hers, as well. It might be many weeks before Sam returned. By then she would be far away. As for the handsome young Earl of Ravenall, he would either be recovering safely at Haycross Manor, or else he would be—

No! Unthinkable! Perdita blotted the word from her mind. She could not bear it if he died.

She touched his face tenderly. He was warm beneath the pallor of his skin. Perhaps it was merely the fever, but she felt as if he had responded in some subtle way to her touch.

"I will not let you die," she whispered with sudden fierceness.

Ravenall gave a great sigh and turned his head toward her. She could almost imagine that he smiled.

Perdita heard the sound of carriage wheels. Dr. Crawleigh must have returned.

She wrung out a fresh cloth to cool Ravenall's fevered body. Her hand followed the contour of his jaw and throat, over the hard muscles of his shoulders and the furred vee of his chest. As Mrs. Croggins had said—several times—he was a splendid specimen of a man!

He had been to sea, Mr. Waverly had told her, and was a noted horseman, as well. That would explain his manly form; it didn't explain the strange sensations that shot through her when she looked at Ravenall's naked body, or the heat that rose inside her chest when her bare skin touched his. She'd been tempted to peek beneath the sheets, but propriety had won out over curiosity.

So far.

Footsteps on the stairs roused her from her thoughts. Barty came up to Ravenall's chamber with a fresh can of cool water, all agog at being let into Mrs. Croggins's private room.

"So this is where Her Highness and that bastard Bailey do the deed," he snickered.

"Hush, Barty! You'll wake my lord."

The lad gave a startled look. "Think you he'll be waking at all? There's hard wagering on it in the stables, Polly."

"Shhhh! If you disturb his rest, they'll be wagering on how

many times I boxed your ears instead," Perdita said briskly. "Now fill up the pitcher and be on your way!"

He grinned at that. If it was Sukey now, there'd be somat to consider in that threat. Polly was another matter. The lads were all in awe of her. Although they dreamed their secret dreams of her, among the straw of the stable loft. There were some lasses who had a certain something about them, as kept a lad in his place.

Barty poured some water into the china pitcher, and set the can down, running a hand through his shock of blond hair. "There's a gentleman belowstairs what's demanding a room," he said by afterthought, "and Mrs. Croggins nowhere to be found."

Perdita hesitated. She could hear raised voices from below. "Stay with him, Barty. I'll attend to it."

She hurried down the stairs and found a severe-looking man eyeing the place with disdain. Sukey stood wringing her apron in agitation, rendered speechless, for once, by the man's haughty bearing.

"Oh, Polly! Thank goodness. I don't know what to do," she said, with a beseeching glance at Perdita.

"I will take care of it." Perdita addressed the newcomer: "May I be of service, sir?"

He looked her up and down with the same twitch of his thin nose. He hadn't expected such good speech of her, dressed as she was. "You may show me up to the bedchamber without any further delay!"

"Alas, there is no room to be had, sir. They are all taken."

He lifted his thin eyebrows. "To his lordship's chamber! Set up a truckle bed for me, if you have not already done so."

Awareness dawned. "Ah, you are Lord Ravenall's man?" She was amazed that a servant would be dressed with such elegance.

"His valet, Danes. If you will be so kind as to take me up to him?"

"Of course, sir. Please follow me, and one of the lads will bring up your trunk and valise."

Danes was somewhat mollified by Perdita's soft voice and pleasant manner. Perhaps the rest of the place was not as shabby as the entry had hinted. He followed her up the crooked stairs and that notion was soon disabused. When he saw the small size of the "best" chamber he made a moue of disgust.

Then he spied his master lying still beneath the sheets, and paled.

Perdita spoke quietly. "I have given him a draught for pain and fever, sir, as Dr. Crawleigh ordered. My lord was bathed after his wounds were dressed. I was about to sponge him down again, for his skin is very warm."

"Hmmph!" The valet was more shaken than he'd expected to be. The duke had said it was "rather a bad situation," but Danes hadn't expected anything like this. He couldn't remember ever seeing his lordship so still in all the many years he'd known him.

Pretending to blow his nose in his fine linen handkerchief, he wiped his eyes instead. Once recovered, he examined everything. The room was clean, the linens fresh, if coarse, and his master looked properly cared for. His somber countenance lightened a little.

"You appear to be a young person of some good sense. I will bar everyone else who toils here from entering the chamber."

Perdita didn't know whether to laugh or take offense. *I would like to see anyone bar Mrs. Croggins from the room,* she thought. Then she noticed the implacable look in the valet's eye. If she had to place a wager on either the landlady or the valet, she would have to put her money on Mr. Danes.

"If there is anything at all that you require, sir, you have only to ask. If it is in my power, I shall obtain it for you."

"You are the landlord's daughter, I presume?"

"No, sir. I am but one of the serving wenches. It is Mrs. Croggins who owns the inn."

He scrutinized her closely. She was a puzzle, and he couldn't quite see where she fit. But, at the moment, that failed to hold his interest. "I've brought bed linens from Haycross. After his lordship is sponged down they must be put on, and his lordship's own nightshirt."

"Not the nightshirt," Perdita said firmly. "It will only keep in the fever. I have some experience with such matters, sir. He will do best with only the linen sheet for now."

Danes nodded. "Very well."

"Mr. Waverly is in the private parlor if you wish to speak

with him. Meanwhile, I'll unpack and change the bed linens."

Danes drew himself up with dignity. "I will attend to his lordship personally, until he is well enough to be taken down to the manor. In the meantime, you need only fetch and carry. You may set up a truckle bed for me in here."

Perdita smiled. "There is scarcely room to move about now, Mr. Danes, and you must rest sometime. If you do not, how can you render him your best care?"

She saw the truth of this sink in. "There is a storage room next to this. Very small, but adequate for a bed and washstand. I'll have the lads clear it out, so you might have a place to sleep that is close by. And I shall sit up with his lordship by night."

The valet struggled with his reservations, but gave up. She seemed superior to her drab surroundings, and his instincts told him she could be trusted. And she was right, of course.

"Very well. I will allow you to keep night vigil beside his lordship, but you must give me your word that you will call me the moment there is any change." He swallowed. "For good or for ill."

With a truce declared, Perdita left Danes alone with his master, and went below to make arrangements for his stay.

The household was soon in an uproar, with this new arrival. Barty and Jed didn't even grumble when Perdita told them to move everything out of the tiny storeroom, or Sukey complain when she was told to scrub it down. The lads went up the staircase in high good humor: "There will be coins a-plenty, afore this is done!"

Sukey was unsure of having so many gentlemen in the house. "Mr. Waverly is genteel. But that Mr. Danes! So scornful and full of himself, as his lordship's man is," she exclaimed, "I didn't know which way to turn! I wish he had stayed away!"

"Do you?" Perdita asked. "I must say that I'm happy he is here!"

She fixed a tray for Danes, selecting a plump chicken breast, smoked ham, a wedge of pale cheese, and the fruit pie she'd baked earlier, and carried it up herself.

When she entered the chamber, the valet had already put on the spanking white linens, with a richly embroidered crest centered on the top sheet and pillowcase. The stitches were so fine they might have been set by fairies, and the white fabric had the velvety softness of a rose petal. Not even Miss Barnstable had had anything so fine.

Perdita smiled in relief. Lord Ravenall would get the best of care now. And she would still have the care of him by night. For some reason, that gave her immense comfort.

It was the following morning that Lady Haycross came, holding back tears, to visit her brother. Perdita was in the kitchen when the carriage with the ducal crest arrived. A few minutes later a woman in an elegant outfit of blue trimmed in yellow, went up the worn steps, supported by the duke. Perdita had only a glimpse of her from the back.

Mrs. Croggins sent up refreshments, including her best ham, and a plate of fried batter-wafers drizzled with honey. The trays came back untouched. Lady Haycross stayed for the better part of the afternoon, and then left, weeping softly.

"He'll come about, Daisey," she heard Mr. Waverly say as he escorted the duke and duchess back to their vehicle.

Although Perdita craned her head, she didn't get a good look at the duchess. Neither did Sukey, but she'd had a glimpse of her as she'd left the inn. "Did you ever see such a fine bonnet?" she exclaimed. "Oh, how I long for one like it!"

Mrs. Croggins gave her a clout for her trouble. "It would take you twenty years on your back, you lazy strumpet, to earn enough to purchase one half so fine! Now shut your face, before you disturb his lordship!"

Perdita only wished she might. For twenty-four hours Lord Ravenall lay as if he were dead, only the rise and fall of his chest disturbing the fine linens. The low-pitched brangling between Sukey and the landlady was so abrasive and continuous that Perdita was glad to escape them for a few hours of rest.

She splashed her face with cold water before taking over the midnight watch for Mr. Danes. "His lordship is in a violent fever," the valet said ominously. "I've given him another draught of willow bark."

After reassuring Mr. Danes that she would wake him at the slightest need, he retired to the tiny storage cupboard. Perdita began sponging Ravenall's lean body with a cool cloth. He was so warm she almost despaired. *He is all sinewy strength,* she told herself, as her fingers brushed his wide shoulders. *He will not die!*

She heard a creak behind her, and turned around. Sukey had sneaked into the chamber. "Oh, he's a handsome fellow. Arms to wrap about a woman and hug her close. And that chest!"

The other girl reached out and ran her fingers sensuously through the dark hair that matted his chest. "Here's a man I could fancy," she said. "What's he like beneath that sheet?"

She started to pull back the linens, but Perdita grasped her wrist. "You'd better leave, before Mr. Danes hears you. Or Mrs. Croggins!"

"Pooh, I'm not afraid of either of them." Wrenching Perdita's restraining hand away, she peeked under the covers. "Like a bull!" she said. "I knew it, the first time I saw him and those long fingers of his. You know what they say about a man's fingers . . ."

Perdita didn't, but she wouldn't give Sukey the satisfaction. Once the other girl finally left, however, she struggled with her curiosity.

He had long, shapely fingers.

Just when her conscience and modesty had won the day, the inevitable happened. He groaned, and threw off his covers. Perdita stared, blushed, and stared again. *Oh, yes. Like a bull.*

She hastily pulled the sheet back over his lower limbs.

After that it was difficult to keep her thoughts from straying from him, to the ways of a man with a maid. Growing up in the country, as she had, Perdita knew all about it. Or thought she did. What the fuss was about, all for a few seconds of joining, was more than she could fathom. But something that had been asleep inside her wakened, like a dormant seed sprouting in the spring-warmed earth. It stirred, unfurled, and left her with a strange yearning for which she had no name.

She was relieved when dawn came, and Mr. Danes returned.

Ravenall had stayed restless all through the long hours, and Dr. Crawleigh came the following day, to visit his distinguished patient.

"I'd have been here sooner, but the sexton fell into an open grave he was digging, and broke both his legs!" he said, setting down his leather bag. "Drunk as a wheelbarrow, of course."

He examined Ravenall while Perdita and the valet hovered anxiously. Crawleigh appeared satisfied. "He seems to be in a less deep state of unconsciousness. A very good sign. However, he is not out of the woods. I predict the crisis will come in the next forty-eight hours."

He turned to Perdita. "I've a young village woman in hard labor. I expect the midwife can handle it, but I've promised to look in. His lordship is in good hands between your ministrations and those of Mr. Danes. But you must send one of the lads for me immediately, if there is any change."

With Danes's help, Perdita bathed Ravenall's heated body with lavender water, and placed cool cloths upon his head all through the day. She felt a sense of tenderness toward him, this stranger who'd tried to better her life, and now lay injured beneath the same roof as she.

"You must not worry," Dr. Crawleigh said as he left them. "His lordship has the constitution of a bull."

Perdita bit her lip and had to turn her head away so neither of the men could see her face. *Oh, yes. Indeed!*

It was a long day, with Ravenall tossing and turning. By evening Danes decided to give his master a draught of poppy juice. "He'll sleep well now," he told Perdita. "It would be best if you rested yourself, before you take up the night watch."

She bit her lip. "But he is still so feverish!"

The valet drew himself up with dignity. He was willing to let Perdita share in the nursing of his lordship, but he was not going to let her oversee his master's care. That responsibility belonged to him.

"If you do not rest, I will not let you keep vigil," he announced sternly. "It wouldn't do if you fell asleep!"

"I would never do so," she protested, but the valet was adamant. "I am counting on you, miss. A bite to eat and a few hours of rest are what I advise."

She was so surprised that he'd dignified her with that title, that she ceased to argue. "Very well. But only for a little while." She went out, sure she wouldn't be able to sleep a wink at such an early hour. Why, the sun was hardly down!

After she left, the valet smiled. A most dedicated and superior sort of serving girl! One he could trust, not like that slattern Sukey, or the old harridan, Mrs. Croggins.

He wondered where she had come from and how she'd ended up at the Stag and Crown, but would never condescend to ask. Gossiping with the lower servants was beneath the dignity of a gentleman's gentleman.

Perdita found a slice of cold meat pie that had gone untouched, and slipped out into the side yard of the inn to eat it away from the landlady's watchful eye. The cool blue shadows lured her along the walk and into kitchen garden. The few rows left of late vegetables were dark mounds and twisting tendrils along the ground. It was a safe, known place, unlike the barren moorland, but she was drawn toward the wicket gate that led to the path beyond.

The moon was up, brilliant and gold as a new-minted sovereign, the air was gossamer soft, and unusually warm. The trees stirred in the slight breeze, whispering their arcane secrets. Suddenly she felt as feverish as her patient, lying beneath his fine sheet upstairs in the best room.

Perdita rested her hand on the gate and looked down the narrow lane. Moonlight paved a path of gold dust along it. She'd never ventured here by night before, and now she wondered why she hadn't. It was a fascinating world, utterly different from the one she knew by day. Mysterious and beckoning. A night bird called softly, and was answered in kind. Her restlessness grew.

Most people lived and died in the constricted worlds of the farms and villages where they were born and raised. Certainly her own had narrowed to the Stag and Crown, clinging tenaciously to the edge of the moors like a flea on a horse's flank. And yet there was an entire, fascinating world out there, of which she knew next to nothing. She'd had glimpses of it between the pages of Miss Barnstable's books, and long ago she'd yearned to explore it. Over time those yearnings had become dim, fading away, like hazy memories of long-ago dreams.

Suddenly Perdita was terrified of losing them. Of growing old and bent inside the grimy, grease-slicked walls of the inn. Of dying inch by inch, day by day, knowing that she'd never really lived.

A sigh rippled through her. It was the coming of Lord Ravenall into her life that stirred up this discontent, this restless panic, along with her old longings for romance and adventure.

Fighting it, she stayed by the gate and admired the wild, gold and black night. What right had she to dream of such things? She, a poor serving wench, without even a name of her own!

The temptation to fling off the past was too strong. Opening the gate, she passed through and out into the narrow lane, almost tripping on a garden implement one of the lads had forgotten to put away. The urge to run free, to run toward something wonderful instead of away from something bleak, surged through her veins.

The moors, a tarnished bronze in the moonlight, rose just beyond a little section of woods. They swooped up at such a stark angle it was difficult to judge their true height. She imagined that the great humps were the coils of a mighty dragon, the spiky tors like jagged scales and fins and grasping claws. Perdita felt for just a moment as if she'd stepped out of her drab life and into a fairy tale. The magic of the night surrounded her.

Then she heard the cries, and her heart froze solid in her chest. At first she thought they were the sounds of an animal caught by a predator: a rabbit in the jaws of a fox. Then she realized they were a child's muffled cries, coming from the copse at the foot of the moors.

She didn't think of the dangers to herself. The child was injured somehow—attacked?—and in pain. Reaching back, she snatched up the gardening tool and ran fleetly down the path toward the copse.

The sounds of violent thrashing came from the right, and she followed the broken path through the trees, her heart thumping like a cracked cartwheel. There was a small clearing among the trees, and she stopped dead at what she saw.

A young woman lay on a blanket spread on the ground, her naked body aglow in the mellow light, and her hair spread out like a gleaming shawl. But her gasps were of pleasure, not fear. Her naked flesh gleamed, and she cupped her full breasts in her own hands, as if she were offering them to the moon.

But it was a man to whom the woman was offering herself.

The muscles of his bare back knotted as he leaned over and covered them with his hands, his mouth. Then he slid down her length and buried his face in the valley between her legs.

Perdita was so stunned she couldn't move. This wasn't what she'd expected to find.

It wasn't the act of their lovemaking that shocked her. The mating of creatures was no mystery: but this was something different. Something frightening and wonderful. The man was worshiping the woman with his own body, like a suppliant offering homage to his goddess. Then he became the god, and his partner the needy one. The woman cried out again, a sharp cry softening to a moan of sensual pleasure, as her partner shifted fluidly, sliding into her with a fierce thrust of his loins.

Shame and embarrassment flooded Perdita, and something else that sang along her veins and warmed her blood. A yearning to be held and worshiped and loved. To join with someone so utterly and completely.

So wantonly.

She turned and fled. Their soft cries followed her through the night, mingling with the sigh of the wind, the whisper of the arching trees.

She ran back up the lane to the wicket gate. She didn't stop until she was safely past the kitchen garden and reached the back door of the inn, trembling and out of breath. Of course she'd guessed the lovers' identities: Sukey and Rafe, arching against each other with wild abandon. She laughed shakily. *Sukey will box my ears if she thinks that I have been spying on her!* But those few seconds of unwitting trespass had shaken Perdita profoundly. For a moment she envied the other girl.

What would it be like, to be loved by a man? To feel strong arms embrace her, and the touch of another's warm flesh against her own?

She shook the thought off, confused by the way it made her feel. By the images of Lord Ravenall's lean and naked body.

I must go back before I am discovered out here!

Slipping inside, Perdita closed the door and turned to find the landlady scowling down at her.

"What are you doing sneaking out at this time of night?" Mrs. Croggins asked, cuffing Perdita on the shoulder.

"Just . . . just a breath of air, that's all!"

"Little fool! Don't you know better than to wander about in the dark?" Her face was red with anger. "I've already got that slut Sukey out whoring—don't try to tell me it isn't true," she said hotly.

The landlady's face was so stern that Perdita winced and braced herself for another clout. It never fell. The landlady's raised hand dropped. She shrugged suddenly and turned away.

"Stop your gaping, girl, and go lie down. Mr. Danes said he'd ordered you off to catch a few winks. I'll not have you nodding off tonight, while you're supposed to be watching his lordship!"

Grateful for the reprieve, Perdita hurried upstairs to her place beneath the eaves. Her shoulder ached and would be bruised by morning.

She stripped off her gown and lay down in her shift. She was overtired but that wasn't what had her heart bounding and her body quivering. No, it was the memory of the two lovers entwined so passionately in the copse.

Perdita realized that she'd willfully blinded herself to the magnetism that drew female to male, woman to man. The abandonment to pure joy and pleasure she'd seen in the other girl's face had been as unknown to her as the far side of the moon. The need to hold and be held, to love and be loved in return, was so strong, so basic an urge that it astonished her. Her refusal to recognize it in herself had been shield and weapon, like a hedgehog's prickly coat.

The episode tonight had caused her to shed that protective skin.

Rafe loved Sukey. She'd seen that in her brief glimpse of his face. Loved her and lusted for her with earnest passion and awkward tenderness. Sukey was a fool to play him false. Love like Rafe's would surely never come her way again.

Perdita stared up into the shadows. Had anyone ever loved *her*? In all her memory she could not recall a single instance of it. Not one loving smile, nor one tender touch. Not even a cool hand, or a mother's light kiss upon her brow.

The magnitude of her loss was overwhelming. Turning her face away from the moonlight streaming through the half-open shutters, she wept.

The ballroom glittered and glowed, all gold and crystal and silk. Perdita stood in the musicians' gallery high above the dancers, wishing she could join them. A sound from behind the curtained alcove startled her and she turned away from the colorful scene below. As she did so, she heard the whisper of satin around her, caught the dazzle of diamonds on her wrist.

Stepping out of the gallery, she found herself in a dark corridor. Silver light fell at infrequent intervals from the tall windows, but did little to lighten the gloom. Heart racing, she glided to the grand, sweeping staircase. The pier glass at the head of the stairs reflected her pale image.

She was no longer a child, but a woman grown.

The music called to her, lured her down the white marble stairs, although the hall below was nothing but moonlight and shadows. The moment her slippers touched the floor, she began to move with the strains of the waltz. Arms outflung, she spun around and around until she was giddy. The great unlit chandelier above sparkled like icicles, and she laughed softly. There was nothing but the gleam of crystals, the music, and herself, whirling faster and faster . . .

She turned and was suddenly up against something solid. And warm. Two arms closed around her shoulders, and she looked up into Lord Ravenall's face. The bandage was gone, his face unmarred and incredibly handsome. The moon's glow silvered his high cheekbones, his sculpted mouth, and his eyes burned bluer than flame. But it was his smile that stole her breath away. Secret. Seductive.

"I've been waiting for you," she whispered.

She surrendered willingly to his embrace, to the shelter of his wide chest and strong arms. He pulled her so close she could feel her heart fluttering against the steady beating of his own. "I know."

Swooping her into the dance, they circled the wide hall, which changed to an empty ballroom. Around and around they went, and faster and faster. His eyes never left hers. She couldn't have torn her own gaze away, if she'd wanted to. And she didn't in the least. She wanted this magical moment to go on and on forever.

They danced across the floor and out the open doors to a wide terrace. Across velvety lawns and down a wide walkway that narrowed to a small lane, barred by a wicket gate.

"Will you come with me?" Ravenall whispered, and she nodded. "Oh, yes!"

Then they were in a wooded copse, floating on moonbeams. The music stopped, but she thought she could still hear the *notes spinning in her head. Ravenall's hands were on her bare shoulders, kneading them sensuously. They moved lower, cupped her breasts, and his mouth was on hers, hot and demanding. His nearness, his strength, and the answering sensations in her body stilled the final notes of the waltz.*

There was nothing but the two of them, and the longing that shook her.

Lightly, so lightly, he brushed the gauzy gown from her shoulders, slid it down and away. He kissed the curve of her throat, and the cool moonlight rippled through her. His hand caressed her bare breasts, brought the tips erect and tingling, until her body burned for him, melted with heat and pleasure.

She arched her back for his questing mouth, and shivered. Her body arced against him taut as a silver bow. Then he drew her down, and they were on the moss beneath the spreading tree, his body covering her nakedness.

Sliding her hands up his bare chest, she delighted in the splendor of sinew and muscle, the rough delight of the crisp mat of hair as his chest brushed her over her breasts. His hands slid down her thighs, parting them gently. She felt as if she were floating up, like little motes of moonlight, higher and higher into the black velvet sky.

"Love me," she whispered, in a voice almost choked with tears. She was trembling with need.

Instead he rose up over her, grasped her shoulder and shook her violently. Light flared harshly behind her closed lids . . .

Five

Sukey stood over her, shaking Perdita's shoulder. "Get up! Come on, you stupid cow!"

Perdita sat up so abruptly she knocked her head on the low beam. "Ow! Give over, Sukey!"

"Get up, I say! That toffee-nosed Mr. Danes asked me to fetch you. He saw me creeping up the stairs and called out so sharplike, I thought he'd wake the old bawd. Then I'd have been in for it!" Sukey grinned in the wavering glow of the rushlight. "But she was snoring away when I slipped past her door."

Perdita was suddenly, and fully, awake. "How long have I been asleep?"

"'Tis well after midnight."

Throwing her dress on, Perdita smoothed her hair and knotted it at her nape. She'd never had an erotic dream before, and her body felt languid, her emotions very confused.

She didn't dare meet Sukey's eyes, afraid the other girl would see all the guilty secrets in her own.

The other girl didn't notice. Sukey pulled off her garment to reveal a grass-stained shift, and rolled up in the threadbare blanket. In less time than it took for Perdita to pour water into the chipped basin, Sukey was snoring contentedly.

The cold water dashed away the cobwebs from Perdita's thoughts, but could not banish the image of Sukey and Rafe in a tangle of limbs and passion, nor the searing memory of her dreams.

As she went down the creaking steps, the touch of her dream-lover still tingled over her skin, and she felt her cheeks flush with heat. She was mortified: how would she ever be able to look at Lord Ravenall again, without embarrassment?

She paused before opening the door to his chamber to

gather her wits, and went inside. "I am so sorry, Mr. Danes . . ."

The valet made soothing noises when he saw her distress. "No need to have yourself in a fret. His lordship is resting quietly, as you see." He smoothed the sheets over Ravenall. "I instructed the landlady not to disturb you earlier. You've worn yourself thin as a rail, looking after him. There's a dish on the side table for you, from the kitchen."

With assurances that she would awaken Danes if he were needed, Perdita sped him on his way. She nibbled on cold pie and a piece of roasted chicken, glad to be alone again.

There was no way she could avoid looking at Ravenall. He was, after all, in her care. And no way, she discovered to her dismay, that she could avoid smoothing a lock of tumbled hair from his forehead, or touching his warm hand with her fingertips. It sent her pulse racing.

The princes in Miss Barnstable's storybooks had always been beautiful and fair, but she preferred his dark, sternly chiseled features. The way his long, dark lashes lay upon his cheek, the firm curve of his mouth, even the shadows beneath his eyes and the new hollow under his strong cheekbones held some arcane power over her.

Perdita reached out and placed the back of her hand against his jaw. *Wake up. Wake up and look at me, and see me as I am. Yearning for you. For you!*

As he stirred slightly, she was filled with awe and great tenderness. And touched with fear.

Oh, what have I done? Perdita thought, heart pounding. But she knew. She had crossed over an invisible line tonight. She was falling in love with him—a nobleman who was as high above her station in life as the sun was from the earth.

It was both foolish and doomed. A girlish fancy based on little more than his elegant person, his former kindness to her, and his intriguing face.

She shook her head and sighed. No matter how she tried to rationalize it, it was too late. She had fallen deeply under his spell.

A vast and terrible longing swept through her, and she trembled with it. He would live—please God!—or he would die. Either way, his path and hers were forever separate. Once he left the Stag and Crown she would never see him again.

The knowledge of it broke her heart.

The shadows jumped around the room, startling her. Mrs. Croggins had entered, carrying a candle. "How does my lord fare?"

"There is no change, mistress."

On the whole, Mrs. Croggins was well pleased.

Two gentlemen staying at the inn for an extended period was an unexpected gift of Providence. That one was a nobleman was almost more good fortune than she could bear. Weaving plans of greed and ambition put her in a happy mood.

Thank the heavens that the harvest was in: she had been able to hire the two younger daughters from Beck Farm to come in daily for the duration. Let them toil in the kitchen and taproom with Sukey, and fetch trays and water up to their guests.

But Perdita she would reserve to wait upon her noble guest. And surely that would lead to something that would fill her hands with gold. She felt it in her bones!

She stood beside the bed and appraised her unexpected guest: Dark hair, falling across his noble brow, aristocratic cheekbones, and a fine, chiseled nose; a deep chest, wide shoulders and muscular arms. He'd be strong and lusty in bed!

"In my younger days . . ." she sighed, and shook her head.

As the landlady leaned down for a closer look, hot wax fell from her tilted candle. Perdita swept her hand to catch it. The tallow dripped across her arm, and over the dark red brand from the hot batter iron. It stung only a moment on her unharmed skin, but burned like flame upon the star-shaped mark.

She hissed in a breath and peeled the cooling wax away.

"I'll send Sukey up with some grease to put on it," Mrs. Croggins said, surprising Perdita. "You'll not want it to scar." She set the candle down beside the lamp.

" 'Tis true he is an earl, you know. Rich as Croesus," she added dreamily. Her face creased in a beatific smile. "To think I've had a duke and an earl beneath my roof at the very same time! I never thought I'd live to see it!"

"Nor I."

Perdita instantly regretted her wry tone, as the landlady whipped around to face her. She ducked out of habit, but this time there was no hand raised to box her ears. Instead the other woman was staring at her.

"He must have seen something in you to like," Mrs. Crog-gins said with an odd measure of respect. "You're a clever girl, Polly. If he recovers he'll be grateful. There's many a man has taken up with the woman who nursed him back from the grave. You could do worse in life than warm his bed."

"If there is any thought at all in his head at present," Perdita said curtly, "I am sure that would be the last one."

A tiny light gleamed in the landlady's eyes. *So, little Polly is not indifferent to him. Well, and why should she be? There's been naught but stableboys and old men to please her young eye at the Stag and Crown.*

"If you've any sense, my girl, you'll see that you exert yourself to keep him here, if he recovers from his injuries. You just slip between the sheets once he's awake and warm his bed, and I've no doubt he'll linger a while. And when he leaves, he'll be generous to you."

Perdita lifted her chin, eyes bright with anger. "I won't sell myself to any man."

The landlady's fingers dug into Perdita's shoulder pain-fully. "Listen to me, you little fool. You're still a maid, but that's something you can't hold on to much longer. Some man will take you, willing or no! The thing is to make it happen to your advantage."

"I won't!"

For a moment she thought she saw something like pity in the older woman's eyes. Then it was gone. Mrs. Croggins placed her arms akimbo. "You think you're better than the rest of us, because you can talk so la-de-da, and were in service to the gentry. Well, for all your fine airs, you'll end up the same as the rest of us, scrabbling to keep food in your belly and a roof over your head."

Her mouth drew down. "I'll tell you this: better to lose your maidenhead to one who is a gentleman! And better in a clean bed among good sheets, than on a dirty barn floor, like hap-pened to me!"

Her eyes clouded. "I went in service to a farmer's wife when I was just a girl. There were too many hungry mouths to feed, and my ma was glad to find me a good place. I went to milk the cow of a fine summer evening. It was warm, as I recall. Two farm laborers were hiding in the stalls. They knocked me down and stuffed straw in my mouth and had their way with me. I didn't know what was happening to me, I tell you, and a painful thing it was! Worse, nine months later, when I delivered a stillborn lad."

Perdita stared at her in horror. She'd only known the landlady as a lewd-mouthed, grizzled harpy. She'd never imagined Mrs. Croggins as either young or innocent. Or what a dark and frightening road she'd wandered, before fetching up years later as the landlady at the Stag and Crown.

"How terrible! I am so sorry!"

Mrs. Croggins brushed at her dress, as if ridding herself of invisible bits of dirt and straw clinging to her soul, from that long-ago day. "What's done is done. An egg that's broken can't be made whole again."

"But surely those men were punished . . ."

"Hah! 'Twas I who got a belt across my legs, for spilling the milk in the dirt." Mrs. Croggins shrugged. "And not a farthing to show for it when it was over. Let that be a lesson to you, girl! Choose your own fate. A man like his lordship will show his gratitude, I'll be bound."

She paused. "If, that is, he lives."

Perdita was devastated to hear her fears put into words. Her mouth trembled and her vision blurred behind a veil of tears.

He will live, she vowed silently. *He must!*

Ravenall was adrift, helpless in the inky sea. The cold pulled him down like a stone. At first there was no sound. Then he heard it: a voice, as soft and seductive as a mermaid's song, luring him up through shifting layers of black and gray. The plaintive notes strung out like wavery stars in his mind:

> *Oh, who will comb your pretty fair hair*
> *When I am gone, when I am gone,*
> *And who will shoe your bonny little feet,*
> *When I am dead and gone . . .*

He struggled against the numbing chill, fought with the last of his strength to break the icy grip of the waves. The warmth of the soft voice gave him strength. He burst upward through the raging darkness, toward a dazzling light.

The light burst and splintered, showering down around him. Ravenall awakened to pain and an intolerable red glare. Clos-

ing his eyes, he tried to lift his head and the resulting agony
was so swift and punishing he groaned, and almost passed out.
White-hot swords lanced his chest, spitted his brain. When it
subsided to a slightly more tolerable level, he was still aware
of the ruddy light glaring through his closed eyelids, bright as
the flames of hell.

He must have made some sound. Instantly a cool hand was
laid upon his brow. A gentle voice murmured soothing words,
and something bitter was pressed between his lips. He swallowed, too weak to protest. *Laudanum. Who would have
thought the devil so considerate?*

The opium rounded the sharp, spiky edges of his torment.
His sluggish awareness shredded like weak fabric and he
drifted away to a place where there was no thought, only deep,
unremitting pain. It was as relentless as the winter sea, beating
against the high cliffs at Ravenall Castle. He tried to move
away from the pain, but it was too strong. It gathered its forces
and rose up like a tidal wave. There was no way to escape its
onslaught. Black agony smashed into him, sweeping him away
on its roaring currents.

Perdita sat beside the bed while Ravenall slept. The house was
settling down for the night. She rose and pulled open the curtain at the single window. The moon was wrapped in clouds,
and the air smelled of coming rain. She could barely make out
the humped shape of Giant's Tor, rising in the distance. It
vanished as she watched, lost in swirls of fog.

She went back to her vigil and waited until she was sure
everyone was asleep. A light was always kept burning in Lord
Ravenall's chamber, and she'd decided to take advantage of
it. Cautiously she removed the treasure she'd smuggled in earlier, and had tucked beneath his mattress. Until tonight, she'd
kept it hidden beneath the floorboard under her pallet, afraid
that Mrs. Croggins would confiscate it.

Perdita's fingertips caressed it gently. It was a thin green
book that Miss Barnstable had given her long ago: *West Country Tales.*

Her heart pounded as she opened the slender volume, and
she felt sick with anxiety. What if she no longer knew how to
read?

Her hands trembled as she turned past the flyleaf to the first page. The print was so fine, so small it made her eyes ache. At first it was almost like looking at faint designs. Then the swirls and curlicues sorted themselves into individual letters, and finally into words. She could almost taste them on her tongue, as if they were ripe summer berries.

Within minutes she was lost in the epic ballads and tales of dashing knights and maidens fair. Of harps that sang, and women who turned themselves into bonny black swans, of changelings and of fairy raths hidden away beneath the hollow green hills.

And of the ancient oak where fairies lived beneath its arching roots. Where any mortal brave enough might make one true wish for the price of three drops of blood, and have that wish granted—for good or for ill.

Perdita was startled when she came to that last poem, and she read it again. It sounded very like the Druid's Oak that Lord Ravenall had inquired about the day of his tragic accident. She sighed, and wondered if he'd ever found it.

And if he'd wished unwisely. In the old tales there was always a hidden twist, a penalty for those who were not wary enough to turn the magic to their own advantage.

Perdita leaned her cheek on her hand, and wondered what she would ask for if she could find the magical oak tree, and make *her* one, true wish. Perhaps she would wish to know her history, and why she'd been abandoned as a child. Little good it would do her now, though. And the tale might not be one she'd like to hear.

She remembered her dreams of the beautiful ballroom, the swirling dancers in their silks and satins. Perhaps she would wish instead for wealth and position, although they couldn't guarantee happiness. Lord Ravenall's sorry state was proof of that!

A sound from the bed had her instantly alert. She looked over at Ravenall, lying so still beneath the quilt. Had he tried to speak?

Slipping the book beneath the linen chest, she rose and went to his side. There was no change. In the hours of keeping her vigil, she had memorized every line of his face, every line and angle of cheekbone and temple and jaw. The strong arms and well-formed hands, the smooth muscles of his chest, beneath their mat of hair. The way his hair fell across his brow.

She could remember his eyes clearly, a bright and piercing blue, although he hadn't once opened them.

The dark lashes lay against his cheek, a contrast to the layers of soft linen and ointment that covered one side of his face. *He has gone from having everything the world can offer, to almost nothing. At least I still have my wits and my health!* She knew then what her one true wish would be if she had to make it there and then: that he recover. She would not allow herself to think beyond that.

There was not much of the night left to her. She took her chair and tried to read, but found she could not concentrate. The heat of the fire was making her drowsy and hot.

Danes was fast asleep, like the rest of the house. Perdita poured cool water into the basin and stripped off her dress. Standing in her thin chemise, she wrung out a cloth and bathed her face and throat, her smooth white arms. The shock of the water refreshed her, and she let the moisture evaporate from her skin, cooling it.

Ravenall opened his eyes.

He had no idea as to where he was or what had happened to him. It didn't seem to matter. Not even the pain, which had been transmuted to a curious numbness.

Then he saw her. A sylph, in a flowing shift, shaking out her cloud of long, dark hair and then plaiting it with quick, delicate hands. How beautiful she was, he thought with strange detachment. Those arms like pale ivory. The supple line of her back and neck as she dressed her hair. The firm upthrust of rounded breasts as she turned and the firelight shone through her thin garment. They would fill his hands with their softness. His mouth with their sweetness.

He had been slipping in and out of dreams, barely able to lift his eyelids, but each time the girl had always been there. Sometimes standing at the window, other times sitting in the chair beside the bed looking down at something in her lap. Candlelight shone on her glossy hair as she stood before the stone basin and dried her fair skin.

He frowned, wondering what she was doing in the room alone with him.

But as he watched her he was aware that something was amiss with him. There was no arousal in his body, only appreciation of her grace and beauty in his mind.

The effort of thinking had fatigued him profoundly. His mind grew muzzy. Ravenall tried to fight it. He didn't know where he was. It puzzled him in a vague sort of way. Was he even in England?

If he were not so very tired, he would sort this mystery out, he told himself.

His vision narrowed. He saw nothing but the girl, now. She filled up his entire view. And she seemed to be retreating, growing smaller, as if he were viewing her through the wrong end of a spyglass. The sensation was very odd. The rest of the room was blotted out, leaving only that dimming circle of light that held her. Even that began to vanish rapidly, and he felt himself being pulled through the darkness at a great, rushing speed.

Ravenall knew then, with a curious sense of detached surprise, that he was dying.

Perdita pulled her dress back over her head and folded the cloth over the end of the washstand. Where she had been hot before she now felt cold.

There was a chill in the room, a sudden restlessness. A gathering of shadows in the corners that she found ominous.

She placed another quilt over Ravenall, then threw more wood upon the fire. The flames leapt high, but still the room seemed darker by the minute. *A trick of the eye,* she told herself. *It is only that I am a little tired.*

The shadows crept in, hovering near the bed. A violent shiver passed through her. After a moment, Perdita picked up the taper, and lit the lamp on the mantelpiece, as well. Then she took Ravenall's hand and gripped it tightly.

Ravenall dreamed:

He had fallen from the castle's parapet, into the wintry moat. The gray water closed over him. He struggled up, reaching for something with which to save himself. A tree grew on the bank of the moat, an ancient oak with a canopy of crystal leaves, and roots of icy fire. He reached out for one, and recoiled. His skin was seared.

He went under again, swallowing great gulps of brackish water. As he watched, the water ripples overhead turned trans-

lucent, and coalesced into a thick sheet. He was trapped beneath the rapidly forming ice.

He could not breathe. It was agony to try. Pushing up and up with all his might, he tried to breach heavy ice. It was slick and gray now. Opaque. Despair came, but was overwhelmed by anger. I will not die this way, he cried, and the burning cold water filled his mouth.

Again and again he forced himself against it, pummeling the frozen surface with his bruised hands. It was no use. He was drowning in the fierce cold of the moat. His limbs weighed heavy as stone, dragging him inexorably to the bottom.

No! He would not give up so easily. Kicking at the weeds that clung to his ankles, he gave one last surge of effort. Once again the wall of deadly cold barred his escape. He hammered and pounded against it in bleak despair. Then, just as his strength was ebbing, the ice fractured into silvery sheets, shattered into thousands of brilliant crystal shards.

A hand reached out to him. He grasped it with all his strength. Suddenly he burst upward through the grayness, and into the clear, golden light . . .

Ravenall heard a soft rustle, and realized it was raining, a low, steady murmur against the thatch. Jamaica? No, it was too cold, and he heard the crackle of a fire leaping in a hearth. Someone was holding his hand tightly.

A woman, from the sound of her light breathing. His pulse sped up erratically. "Do not leave me," she said huskily. "You cannot leave me! I will not let you go!"

Véronique?

But, no. That was impossible. He remembered that now.

It came back to him in terrible detail: her head flung back over the arm of the pale blue settee; her fair, unbound hair stirring like sea grass in the breeze from the open window; the wine-colored stains spreading slowly across her white lace gown, seeping down into the satin cushions.

Then the sound of the door to her dressing room opening. Véronique's maid standing there, her face stark with horror.

The bright red blood upon his shaking hands.

He moaned and tossed wildly, but was entangled in something that wrapped itself around his legs. Flailing with his arm, he felt it strike flesh, heard a sharp cry. A man's shout.

Something wet and bitter was pressed against his lips. Ravenall had to swallow the draught or choke. Strong arms held him down while the bitterness flowed along his veins, cold as regret.

This time he didn't fight the blackness that rose up to engulf him. Anything was better than remembering . . .

The next time Ravenall awoke, he was much more aware of his surroundings. He was in a low room, meanly furnished, with dark smoke stains on the ceiling and marks of old damp on the wall. The chamber was filled with soft lavender light. He seemed immersed in it, floating in air.

He turned his head.

A girl—no, a young woman—sat beside the bed. Her face was turned to look at the fire in the hearth, her profile lovely, with a straight nose and determined chin. She was dressed like a serving wench, in worn and shapeless garb, but her carriage was graceful and her figure slender. There was a curious mark, like a small red flower, just above her wristbone.

She held, to his surprise, a small, leather-bound volume open on her lap. He blinked and tried to focus. It appeared to be a book of poetry. *I am still dreaming,* Ravenall told himself. *Serving girls do not read poetry.*

He didn't recall falling back to sleep; but when he opened his eyes again, the sun was up and a blue patch of sky showed through the narrow window. Beyond the casement all was sere and brown, an open, sweeping landscape as different from the lush green Caribbean island as London was from Istanbul.

He stirred and groaned. Perdita jumped up at once and came to stand beside him. "You are awake at last, my lord!"

"Aye," he said rustily, "and hurting like the devil."

"I'll fetch you a draught Dr. Crawleigh made up for you."

"No!" He lay back against the pillows and closed his eyes. Even that brief exertion had tired him out. His tongue felt thick as an old boot sole. "What is this place? How came I to be here?"

"The Stag and Crown Inn, my lord. On Dartmoor. You were brought back here by your friend, Mr. Waverly, after your accident." She saw the frown between his eyes. "You were thrown from your carriage."

For just an instant Ravenall had an image of terrible speed, flying hooves, and then . . . nothing at all. The fractured pieces

of memory had gone by too swiftly for his drugged mind to
grasp.

"Here, my lord." Perdita held a vial to his lips, with a dark
fluid inside.

He caught her wrist. "Wait a bit." Ravenall tried to remember more. It was no use, he decided. Everything was a blank.

She pulled back a little and he realized that his fingers encircled her wrist. Her bones were delicately made, her hand
shapely, if roughened from her work. Ravenall frowned, as
something she'd said hit him.

" 'Awake at last,' you said? How long have I been here?"

"It has been four days since you were brought to the inn,
my lord." Perdita waited till her words sunk in.

"Is it so?" He scowled in an attempt at concentration. "I
have no memory of it. Nor of how I came to be on Dartmoor."

The last thing he recalled for certain was walking on the
parapet of Ravenall Castle, looking out over the choppy gray
waters of the Channel. The image steadied. Bits and pieces
came back, coalesced into a scene that seemed almost like
something he remembered from a picture book.

Someone had been walking beside him. Ah, yes. Oliver
Clements, his agent, who with his ailing father had served the
previous earl. Ravenall struggled to catch the memory as it
took shape. They'd been inspecting the estate together. He and
Clements had climbed up the Watch Tower.

He'd clapped his hand on Clements' shoulder, pointing out
where his yacht, the *Raven*, rode at anchor in the shadow of
the granite headland. The poor man had suddenly lost his balance and stumbled against the stone. The low wall, which had
stood since the time of the Black Prince, had given way like
crumbling sand.

It was only his quick reflexes that had saved the other man,
and possibly himself, as well. He'd grasped an iron ring in the
wall and by some miracle he'd managed to keep the other man
from pitching forward over the sheer vertical drop to the cliffs
below. *Clements would surely have been killed.*

"Do you mean Mr. Waverly, my lord?"

"I didn't know I'd spoken aloud." Ravenall was shocked
at the weakness of his voice. His tongue felt thick and clumsy.

Once again the girl tried to give him the laudanum. He
waved it away. "I need to think. My brain seems to be clearing

very slowly." He rubbed his temples. "Waverly! Where is he now?"

"Out for a walk on the moor." She saw the flash of concern in Ravenall's eyes and smiled. "He has promised not to go out of sight of the inn," she said.

"Not wanting to end up in a bog, I take it. Very wise of him. Well, give me some of your poppy juice, then. My head is throbbing like the devil!"

He thought he only closed his eyes a moment, but when he opened them he blinked. The girl was sitting in the chair but her hair looked different. It was tied back with a faded blue ribbon.

"Has Mr. Waverly returned from his walk?" he asked, puzzled to hear the thickness of his voice.

"Mr. Waverly went to Haycross Manor this morning, my lord. He has not returned."

Ravenall lay still for some moments, digesting the unpleasant news. Then he tried to sit up. Pain wrapped itself around him like steel claws, and he fell back against the pillows.

The girl was beside him instantly, her face pale with concern. She hesitated to awaken Danes, who had just gone to lie down for an hour. "I have drops the doctor ordered, my lord. They will give you ease."

Ravenall fought back the agony by sheer willpower. Beads of perspiration stood out upon his brow. "I would rather have my wits," he said between gritted teeth.

He became aware of other things: there was a splint on his lower leg, and his ribs felt bruised and battered. One side of his face felt odd. Reaching up, he touched the heavy gauze dressing that covered it.

"It must be quite bad."

"I do not know, my lord," she said soothingly. "Dr. Crawleigh has always changed the dressing himself."

It wasn't exactly a lie. When he'd been brought to the Stag and Crown, his face had been so bloodied and bruised she couldn't judge the nature of the wound. But she'd overheard Dr. Crawleigh tell Mr. Waverly that it was a very grievous injury.

The pain rasped at Ravenall, wearing him down. He refused to surrender to it. One week of his life was gone forever, but he would not willingly lose more. He turned his attention to his companion. The girl perplexed him. Her speech lacked the thickness he associated with Devon, and her features were vaguely familiar.

An interesting puzzle, he thought, *but well beyond my present capabilities.*

Perdita wrung out a cloth and sponged off his face. When her sleeve rode up he saw the mark above her wrist like a small star. That, too, was familiar.

"You have a gentle touch," he told her.

"Thank you, my lord."

She was nervous. To be in such proximity to him now that he was awake, was almost overwhelming. To have him clasp her hand in his strong fingers, while he lay naked beneath the bed linen, seemed so intimate that she trembled. She prayed he wouldn't notice.

"Where were you born? Not Devon," he said with authority.

"Devon is all I remember, my lord."

He was about to pursue the matter, when the sounds of an arriving carriage, of a voice from belowstairs, drifted up to them. Perdita turned quickly. Dr. Crawleigh came up the stairs, with Danes and Mrs. Croggins in his train. He broke into a smile when he saw his patient awake and alert.

"Well, my lord, this is a happy day!"

"For you perhaps, sir," Ravenall muttered. "I must say that I find it rather a painful one. But it seems that I must be a most fortunate man . . ."

"You are, indeed," Crawleigh agreed. He changed the crusted bandages on his patient's leg. "Except for the broken ribs and collarbone, a crack in one of your leg bones, and that knock on the head, it is mostly cuts and deep abrasions. You're young and fit, however. A few weeks' rest and you'll be almost as good as new."

"What of my face?" Ravenall touched the stiff bandage on his cheek and winced at the pain.

"I'll not bother changing that until you are back at Haycross," Crawleigh said smoothly.

Before Ravenall could ask further, Andrew Waverly came bounding up the stairs. "By Jove, it's good to see you awake, Justin!" he exclaimed, beaming. "Daisey will be over the moon! She has come every day to see you."

Ravenall shook his head. "I don't remember it at all."

"Well, she'll remind you every chance she gets, if I know my cousin! I'll send a note down to Haycross by one of the stablelads. The duke promised to send his personal traveling coach to convey you to the manor in the utmost comfort, the moment you awakened."

Ravenall looked up at the low-beamed ceiling and the plaster cracks that jagged across it like lightning bolts. "Certainly it will be more comfortable for everyone."

Crawleigh put away his instruments. "I prescribe a good dose of laudanum for you, my lord, to keep the pain at bay during the travail of getting you down the stairs and back to Haycross. It will not be pleasant."

Taking the bottle from Perdita, he stood over Ravenall. "Drink up, my lord. You'll feel better presently. And if the weather holds, you'll be back at Haycross Manor before supper."

Perdita stood hidden behind the doctor's bulk, and sighed in dismay. She'd been waiting for days for him to awaken, and now he was to be snatched away from her care, without any warning.

"Surely another day or two . . ." she began.

"In this cramped, damp hole? No," Crawleigh said emphatically. "The sooner my lord is safely ensconced at the manor, with warm sheets and good food, the more rapidly he will recover."

Perdita looked back at the bed. Ravenall's eyes were closed once more.

Although Perdita hoped for one glance, one smile, before they set out, her wish wasn't fulfilled. Ravenall was in a drugged sleep when they carried him down and settled him inside the commodious coach. No one at the Stag and Crown had ever seen such an elegant vehicle, with velvet squabs and the ducal crest carved on the doors. Andrew thanked her personally for her care of the earl, as did Danes.

The valet got up into the coach and settled a pillow gently behind Ravenall's head. The doctor mounted his gray, and the cavalcade set off. Mrs. Croggins watched mournfully as they drove away.

Perdita felt as if her heart were breaking. She went back to her chores in the kitchen, and when Sukey asked why her eyes were reddened, she blamed it on the smoke from the fire.

Six

A cold rain rattled the casements and pelted the window glass as the storm closed in on Haycross Manor. A fire leapt in the hearth of the sitting room, chasing shadows over the richly papered walls.

While his man of business waited in silence, Ravenall stood in the window embrasure, staring out at the wild, elemental fury. Except for the slight limp, which would soon be gone, he was as strong as he had ever been before the accident. Everything else, however, had changed.

The heavy, dark clouds and lashing winds suited his mood, which was far bleaker than the weather.

"How bad is it, Clements?"

The other man, seated at the mahogany desk, raised a hand to his immaculate cravat and pretended to straighten it. Clements was only a few years Ravenall's senior, a handsome fellow, with light eyes and curling dark hair; but so precise in voice and mannerisms that he seemed older than his years.

This was the moment Clements had been dreading. Firelight reflected from his spectacles as he carefully adjusted the pen across the sterling silver antlers of the elk's-head ink stand. Once satisfied that it was settled properly, he folded his hands.

"From my preliminary calculations—very preliminary I must add—"

A crash of lightning made him jump. Ravenall didn't even blink. Clements marveled at his apparent calm: few men, narrowly escaping death, would have been so focused on the business at hand. Especially such a bad business.

"The fifth earl, from whom you inherited the estate, had no interest in it, other than its revenues. I would not wish to say anything that could be misconstrued, my lord. Nor do I wish to presume . . ."

He fiddled again with the pen. "This is very difficult! Had my father been in better health and of a more forward-putting nature—"

"I sent for you to tell me exactly how matters stand. You needn't bother to wrap it up in fine linen! I am aware that my affairs are in serious disarray." Clements cleared his throat. "There *were* a series of unanticipated drains against the estate's coffers—"

"It is common knowledge that my uncle was a gamester," Ravenall interjected brusquely, "with neither the luck nor the skill for it! Do not prolong the agony by trying to spare me. Out with it, man!"

Clement's sigh echoed through the chamber. "It is very bad, my lord." He named a sum of outstanding debts.

Ravenall was incredulous. "My uncle was profligate with his inheritance, but surely even he could not have spent the half of it!"

The agent was silent. Ravenall's voice, flat and emotionless now, drowned out the chattering rain. "Tell me the worst."

"If not for your untimely accident, my lord, we might have brought it off. It would have taken careful planning, but in time the damage wrought by the late earl might have been repaired. But when word of it got out, your creditors . . . that is to say, the *estate*'s creditors—"

"Damn your eyes! Say it!"

Clements could not meet that intense blue gaze. He looked away. "The demesne lands are mortgaged to the hilt. There is no way to repay the notes that have been called due, my lord. My attempts to secure further credit were unsuccessful."

Silence reigned inside. Beyond the glass, the winds howled with all the fierce anger that Ravenall felt within his breast. A vein throbbed at his temple. When he turned to face the desk, his lips were white, his eyes like ice.

Ruined! Generations of proud heritage, reduced to dust by one man's greed and stupidity!

Aloud he said simply: "The castle?"

Clements stared in fascination. He had never seen such hot rage held in check by cold effort of will. He looked down at his hands.

"It is in need of repair, as you know. If the estate lands are sold off, and some of the foreign investments come through, you might keep it, my lord, but only under the very strictest of economies."

"Will I be able to discharge all my debts?"

"I believe so, my lord. In time."

Ravenall's rigid stance eased a bit. He leaned his boot against the fender. "Ah. That is all that matters."

The agent felt a stab of pity for his employer, along with a baffled admiration. Ravenall had lost almost everything he held most dear, yet his main concern was for his good name. A proud man, in the best sense of the word. That pride would see him through the worst of what was still to come.

"You will survive this, my lord."

"Yes."

A knot burst in the hearth, sending a great shower of sparks up the chimney. The earl turned away from the window. Firelight danced over the sharp planes of Ravenall's cheekbones and aquiline nose.

Clements gasped: he hadn't been told the half of it.

The flames gilded the savage scars that slashed across Ravenall's right cheek and temple. The earl smiled frostily. "As you can see, I have survived far worse."

They listened to the wind sing its savage tune. Ravenall turned and paced the room. "What was your father thinking, to have let my uncle speculate so wildly? Could you not convince him it was a fool's game?"

"My lord," Clements protested, "you know what he was! My father could not convince him, nor I. Please believe that I did everything that was in my power; I could no more rein in the previous earl than I could fly!"

A cannonade of thunder shook the air. Ravenall turned back to the window. "You will tell me what I must do. The truth, with the gloves off."

"It is a delicate matter." Clements folded his hands. "If you could bring yourself to consider such a thing . . . You might stave them off and salvage something through marriage to some wealthy merchant's daughter . . ."

The expression on his face made it plain he thought this was doubtful, given the circumstances.

"Marriage, especially one of convenience, does not tempt

me." Ravenall eyed the other man in bitter amusement. Firelight played on his ruined face. His long fingers traced the scar.

"Moreover, I doubt you could find an heiress to consider *me*, my title notwithstanding. You, who have known me all my life, cannot look me in the face. Even if some poor girl were to be coerced into marriage with me by an ambitious family, pride would prevent me from forcing myself upon a cringing bride. Not even to save Ravenall Castle!"

"Many a nobleman in your position has been forced to make the sacrifice, my lord. You needn't concern yourself that you would have to take part in any settlement discussions. I would, of course, take care of all the arrangements."

The wind howled, and drafts stirred through the chamber. Ravenall struggled with his pride and his anger. He kicked a fallen log in the fireplace with his booted foot, and glowing ash danced up like fiery moths.

"Damn it, man! There must be some other alternative."

Like his father before him, Clements had grown up in the shadow of Ravenall Castle. As a young man he had enjoyed the pursuits and education of a gentleman, and he'd been carefully groomed to take over as agent to the sixth earl one day.

He shook his head sadly. "No other way that I know of, my lord."

Ravenall turned back to the window. The storm was in full intensity now. Sheets of rain assaulted the casements, obscuring the view. In his mind he could see Ravenall Castle clearly: on a night such as this, the sea at the cliff base would be whipped to a white fury by the savage wind, the villagers tucked warm inside their stone cottages with shutters drawn against the night.

Within a few hours, though, it would be morning, and the gale blown out. The bay would be a sparkling sapphire, the air washed clean beneath a fair blue sky. As if the dangerous storm and crashing waves had never been.

If only, he thought, *my own circumstances could change back as easily.*

To see Ravenall Castle and its estates fall into a stranger's hands would be more than he could endure. His glance fell on one of the leather portfolios he'd found among the papers sent from Ravenall.

"There is an odd matter I came across. What of this girl, over whom my uncle was appointed guardian?" Ravenall moved stiffly toward the table and pulled a thin packet from one of the folders. "I found the notice of her father's death, along with a copy of his will. Since it does not specify *which* Earl of Ravenall, I take it I am guardian to this orphaned brat?"

Clements was startled. "I know nothing of any guardianship, my lord."

He took the packet from Ravenall and glanced through it. For a few minutes there was no sound but the rustling of papers and the hammer of rain against the windows.

"This must have been misfiled years ago." Clements glanced up. "By Jove, I do remember my father speaking of this Hexham heiress."

Ravenall frowned. "An heiress, you say?"

"Yes. I recall the story now. It is most affecting. The daughter of Sir Christopher Hexham of Hexham Court. He and his wife died not many days apart, when their only daughter was ten or eleven years old. The one of a sudden illness, and the other of grief."

Ravenall kicked a log with the toe of his boot. "Touching. A fairy tale, in fact."

Clements laughed uneasily. "How very like your late uncle you sounded just then, if you will allow me to say so."

"Do you think so?" Ravenall's eyes grew hard. "Let me assure you that I am a different man, entirely."

"I am glad to hear it, my lord." Light winked off his spectacles as he nodded approvingly.

"Tell me more of this fairy tale," Ravenall ordered.

"Hexham's grandfather was a nabob who made his fortune in the East India trade. He was raised to the peerage for service to the Crown, and purchased a fine estate in Sussex. He became a man of great influence in the county, and his lands and investments prospered. His son and grandson were educated as gentlemen. By the time Christopher Hexham met his untimely end, the estate had grown to ten times its original size."

Ravenall had gone very still. He regarded his agent from beneath raised brows. "You begin to interest me, Clements."

Clements shrugged. "If matters had turned out differently it might have benefited you enormously, my lord. The entire estate was left to Hexham's only child, a daughter, and the only surviving heir of the blood. The Earl of Ravenall was named her guardian in Hexham's will, with the revenues from the estates reserved to him until her marriage, or her twenty-fifth year."

"The devil you say! Where is this ward of mine?" Ravenall said abruptly.

Lamplight shone on Clement's profile. He sighed. "That is the mystery, my lord. Pauline Hexham vanished from Lyme Regis with her nursemaid nearly seven years ago. Nothing has been heard of her since. Without proof of her existence or demise, the estate has been in limbo. If nothing is discovered it will soon revert to the Crown."

A sudden light of excitement came into his eyes. "And therein, my lord, may be your hope of salvaging your estates! If Hexham Court and its lands were to be sold, my lord, and the investments called in, they would be enough to pay off all your debts. With careful management, you might yet bring yourself about."

Ravenall rubbed his jaw. "A fine guardian I should be, if I were to sell off my ward's estates to repair my fortune!"

"You would not be the first to do so."

"No," the earl snapped. "But I would hope that I would be the last!"

The flash of anger in Ravenall's eyes warned the estate agent that he'd trespassed. He tugged at his shirt collar. "Times change, my lord, and we must all change with them."

Ravenall's eyebrows met in a straight line. He seemed to be missing a piece of the puzzle. He rubbed the place between them with his long fingers, as if to clear his mind.

Six weeks had passed since his accident, and his broken ribs and leg had healed. Soon the savage scar on his right cheek would be the only souvenir of this sorry episode; but at the moment the cogs of his brain seemed to be turning rather slowly. "I don't quite comprehend your meaning, Clements. Perhaps it is the lateness of the hour. You are saying that, in order to save Ravenall Castle, I must find this long-lost girl and . . ."

Clements leaned forward in his chair, light blue eyes shining. "Oh, no, my lord! That is the beauty of it. You needn't find Pauline Hexham at all. You must merely prove her *dead*."

*   *   *

"Sukey? Is that you?" Perdita's voice was dry and ragged.

There was no answer in response. She'd been sure she'd heard footsteps on the stairs, but perhaps it was only the sound of the heavy rain against the thatch. Sukey had slipped away early to meet a man, and Perdita was so near-delirious she had no reckoning of the time.

Her teeth chattered like hail, and great shivers wracked her body, but she felt so hot she thought her sleeping pallet might ignite from the fiery heat of her skin. She was desperate for a drink of water, but too weak to rise up and fetch it from belowstairs. She couldn't remember ever being so ill before. Drawing on all her reserves, she crawled to the rude shutters and flung them wide. Storm clouds rode the night, backlit by the hidden moon, and the wind whipped off the moors, keening like a lost soul on All Hallows' Eve.

Gusts of cold air swirled through the room as she knelt at the open casement. She thought she heard the sound of a horse and rider, but who would dare brave the moors on a night such as this?

Perhaps it was one of the haunts that Sukey told her roamed the wilds of Dartmoor. The legendary highwayman, shot down with his pockets full of gold, or the weary ghost of some traveler who'd fallen in a bog years ago, still seeking to find its way home.

On a night like this, anything was possible.

Lifting her face to the icy rain, Perdita opened her mouth and let the drops fall on her tongue. She almost expected them to sizzle against her heated flesh. She let the rain stream over her, slicking her dark hair against her temples and bathing her face and throat.

Her illness had been coming on for several days. At first she thought it was only low spirits after the departure of Lord Ravenall and his party. Then one of the stablelads had been stricken with it, and Mrs. Croggins had taken to her bed for an entire day, something none of them could recall happening ever before. Perhaps one of the passengers on the coach to Oakleycombe had spread the infection.

The storm grew so fierce she had to shut the window. Lightning flared and thunder cracked overhead. Huddled in misery, Perdita fell at last into an uneasy slumber . . .

It was hot in the ballroom. She felt as if she were melting, along with the wax tapers in their gilded sconces. Her damp gown clung to her and hindered her movements. She looked for a doorway to the terrace, hoping to slip away before she was noticed.

A woman stood in a shadowed corner, almost hidden in the folds of her velvet cloak. Her blue eyes were lit with a feverish glow. "Hurry," she said. "Follow me. I will save you."

"Save me from what?"

"Hurry, my darling. They mustn't find you!"

Hesitating just briefly, she followed the woman from the room. The door opened and she found herself alone in a deserted copse. From somewhere hidden in the darkness, she could hear two lovers whispering. Silence, a laugh cut short, and then the sounds of their lovemaking.

She turned and hurried away. But where was the house and the lovely ballroom? There was nothing but star-swept moor, beautiful yet vaguely menacing. Suddenly a figure loomed up before her. She recognized him at once, despite the bandage covering his face like a mask.

"Lord Ravenall!" she exclaimed in relief. He held his arms out and she ran toward him.

"I was so afraid," she told him. "So lost!"

"Never fear," he said, and his voice was strange and rough. "I have you now!"

He caught her to him and tipped his head back to laugh. The mask slipped. It was not Ravenall's darkly handsome face revealed in the starlight, but that of Sam Bailey. "You won't escape me now, my girl!"

Perdita woke up in a panic. Her fever had broken during the night, and her damp shift clung to her. A hand was over her mouth, muffling it. She was weak, but twisted away and fell against the low wall with a violent thud. She couldn't believe her eyes: Sam Bailey in the flesh.

"Damn you, girl," Sam said, "are you trying to wake the house?"

"Don't touch me!" Perdita snatched up the kitchen knife she'd kept hidden on the beam beside her pallet. "Come nearer, and I'll slit your gizzard."

He laughed, low in his throat. "I'm not one of your tame barnyard chickens, little fool. Ah, no. I'm cock-of-the-walk here. And you'll do as I say."

Perdita brandished the knife. Her hand was so sweaty she almost dropped it. "You'll be no rooster, but a capon if you come much closer!"

The pale glow of a rushlight came from the doorway. The landlady stood there in her shift. "What in the name of God is going on?" Mrs. Croggins said, brushing the grizzled hair back from her loosened plait.

"Ah, there you are, my love. I didn't wish to awaken you. I was trying to get this lazy slattern up to fix me a meal and fetch up a pan of hot water for bathing."

Mrs. Croggins eyed him suspiciously. "I'm awake now. Go to my room before you wake the house. You, girl! Go fix a tray for Mr. Bailey. And Sukey, fetch some hot water to my room at once."

She turned and went out without noticing that there was nothing but a rolled-up shift beneath Sukey's blanket. Sam followed her, but took a moment to look back at Perdita. "I've quite a healthy appetite," he said with a leer. "It takes a good deal to satisfy it!"

When they were gone, Perdita pulled on her dress with shaking hands, and stumbled down to the kitchen. She felt less feverish now, but she was sick with dread: Sam Bailey was back at the inn, far too early, and she hadn't made good her escape. She was so weak from the effects of her illness, she didn't know what to do, and couldn't think clearly.

It took her a moment to realize that the fire in the kitchen hearth was completely out. Sukey was supposed to have banked it and washed up before she left, but the worn wooden table was cluttered with unwashed tankards and pots. Perdita touched the side of the kettle gingerly. Cold as a stone.

It wasn't like Sukey to leave her chores untended, and certainly she'd never let the hearth fire go out before. *Either one would fetch her a beating! Why would she take such a chance?* A sudden suspicion chilled her.

Perdita roused Jed to start the fire, and slipped back upstairs with a rushlight. As she ducked beneath the low door, the flickering flame illumined their sleeping space and the empty peg that had held Sukey's best dress. Even her thin blanket was gone.

She has only slipped away to meet Rafe in the copse, Perdita told herself.

But the small covered basket where Sukey had kept her ribbons and fairings was missing, too. Another suspicion struck her.

Perdita was sick with fear. She felt as if she were still dreaming, and prayed it was so. But the stone flags were cool beneath her bare feet as she went past Jed sleepily laying a new fire, and made her way into the stillroom.

One glance was all she needed. The faint light illumined the small space, with its stone sink and rows of labeled bottles on wooden shelves—and the gaping hole beneath the sink, where the loose stone had been pulled out. Kneeling down, she thrust her hand inside. Despair struck her like a blow: her secret hiding place was empty.

Sukey had run off, taking Perdita's precious pouch of coins with her.

The Duchess of Haycross sat before the pianoforte in the Music Room, her fingers dancing lightly over the keys. The pale gold of her ruched silk dress was matched by the sunbeams shafting through the tall windows.

She was intent on mastering a new piece, and had almost succeeded. The rippling notes filled the elegant room, until a shadow fell across her. She glanced up smiling, and saw Ravenall standing there. The music faltered, and died on a discordant note.

This was the first time she'd seen his face unbandaged.

"Justin! I thought you'd gone out for a stroll."

"I'm just back now. The music lured me here."

Ravenall smiled wryly and touched his ruined face. The jagged lightning bolt of livid flesh stood out against his skin, still puffy and raw. There were deep lines of strain etched in his face, and his blue eyes were shadowed.

"Have I frightened away your muse, Daisey?"

She rose in a rustle of ivory silk, stricken. "I was merely surprised. I thought myself alone."

He turned his head so only his good side was exposed to her. "Tactful as ever, my dear."

The duchess went to him and took his hand in hers. It was an act of love and courage. This was the first time she'd seen him with all the bandages removed. His handsome face was hideously marred. She couldn't bear to see him so grievously wounded, and stifled the sob that rose within her breast.

"It is not so very bad," she lied. "It will fade with time, Justin. And you will still set hearts a-flutter."

He smiled wryly. "But not in the way I'd once hoped."

He saw he'd distressed her. Ravenall's eyes warmed with affection. "You needn't pretend with me, Daisey. The house-maids flee at my approach. Even my own valet cannot look me in the face without flinching."

"I think it is fear of offending you. Let me have a good look, then, and get over the awkwardness."

He did as she bade him. His sister forced herself to examine his face, but could not steel herself to touch the puckered scar. Her face was white as rice powder, and her blue eyes swam with tears.

"Does it pain you greatly, Justin?"

"Not in the least."

What pained him was the thought of losing Ravenall Castle.

Her eyes searched his. "You are leaving tomorrow, Hay-cross told me. Do you think it wise?"

He shook his head in regret. "Not only wise, but urgent. There are matters that must be attended to immediately."

She touched his sleeve. "But should you make the journey so soon? Are you sure you are up to it?"

"Physically, yes." Ravenall caught sight of his face in the mirror and gave a twisted smile. "Everything is intact, except my vanity. I can't believe I couldn't control my team. It's a great mortification to me."

"You're a proud man, but the least vain that I know," the duchess laughed. Cocking her head, she smiled up at him. "I think that is one of your greatest attractions."

"If so, I'm sure it is my only one."

Something caught his eye. Idly, he picked up a gold en-ameled frame from the others on a side table, and frowned down at it at the portrait of Catherine, their late sister whom Daisey so resembled, and her schoolgirl friend.

This time it was the friend who suddenly drew his interest. She looked strangely familiar in an unsettling way. Dark eyes, straight little nose, rosebud mouth, soft brown hair arranged in an outmoded style. There was something about the shape of her face and set of her eyes.

"This girl who died young," he said slowly. "What was her name?"

"Serena Mannington. Serena Hexham, later. She married Sir Christopher Hexham in her first season."

"Hexham?" Ravenall shot his sister a look of disbelief. "Not the mother of the missing heiress?"

"Oh, you know the tragic story, then?" His intensity surprised her.

"Only a little." His expression was unreadable. "Merely that both she and her husband died, and their child vanished shortly after."

He noticed the duchess's hesitation. "I do not wish you to think I ask out of idle curiosity, Daisey. Christopher Hexham's will named the Earl of Ravenall as his daughter's guardian. He meant my uncle, of course, but by unfortunate wording, that duty has passed on to me. If the girl is alive, it is my duty to find her. For her own sake." His mouth turned grim. "And for mine, as well."

"Ah, yes. Poor little Pauline." Lady Haycross took the portrait from him and her face grew pensive. "Then I will tell you everything that I know, which is precious little. I was still in the schoolroom then."

She went to the window and looked out across the terrace. The view was a sweeping one of well-groomed parkland with a winding river, and the steep moors beyond; but it was the past that the duchess was seeing.

"Have you ever known two people so involved with one another that they became each other's entire universe? It was like that with Serena and Kit Hexham, so Haycross told me. They went everywhere together—most unfashionable of them! And not even the birth of their daughter altered their attachment. Indeed, I believe the poor creature had more love and attention from her nurse than both her parents combined. They preferred town life to living at Hexham Court; however, they traveled extensively, leaving their daughter in care of the servants for months at a time."

"In fact," Ravenall said wryly, "exactly the kind of lonely upbringing we had ourselves."

His sister looked surprised. "I always thought that you were happy out on the water in your little sailboat. Why, you hated to come back to shore!"

"Yes. The sea was my comfort and salvation." His gaze grew distant. "Then and later, the sea kept me sane."

He is thinking of Véronique, again. Daisey shivered. *When will he ever be free of her?*

"Tell me of the girl and her disappearance," Ravenall said with a brisk change of mood. "Everything you can recall."

"There is little enough that I know." The duchess closed the piano. "When their daughter was ten or eleven, Serena suffered a bout of influenza and was very low afterward. Her husband took a house in Lyme Regis, hoping the sea air would restore her spirits. Alas, he also succumbed, and both were dead within the week. The household was in an uproar, as you can imagine. Then, before they were even laid to rest, the girl was taken by her nurse for an airing the morning of the funeral. They never returned."

"They couldn't have vanished into thin air!" Ravenall frowned. "A thorough search was made of the grounds?"

"Yes, and inquiries in Lyme Regis. It was in the newspapers, I do know that. Ah, but you'd already left for Jamaica, I recall."

The irony of it struck Ravenall forcefully. If the girl hadn't disappeared, she would most likely have been brought up by his uncle, at Ravenall Castle. He mulled the mystery over. "This nurse—had she been with the family long?"

"Oh, yes. Since Pauline's birth in London. The constable believed she'd abducted the girl for ransom, but no note was ever received. The other servants claimed the nurse was most sincerely attached to the girl. Indeed, she was very upset at the thought of being parted from her."

"There is the answer, then! She must have taken the girl back to London with her."

"Indeed, a young woman with a female child had booked seats in Lyme Regis, on the London stage. But when the stage was intercepted, it proved to be a case of mistaken identity."

Ravenall looked at her sharply. "They were sure she was not the girl in question?"

"Quite sure. Like every member of that lineage, Pauline Hexham had the family birthmark. The 'mark of the Hexhams' it is called: a small, six-rayed star." She sighed. "The child on the stage to London had no such mark."

Ravenall went completely still. His recollections of the time immediately after the accident were distorted and blurred, like images seen through a pane of rippled glass. But when Daisey described the birthmark, that clouded window suddenly opened.

He was back in a tiny room beneath the roof of the Stag and Crown. He could see it clearly. A soft-voiced serving girl, lovely despite her worn and shapeless dress of drab brown homespun. *Polly.* Yes, that was her name.

He remembered a slender but work-roughened hand holding up a cool cloth to bathe his aching head, or offer a quaff of some vile-tasting potion. If he concentrated he could feel the gentleness of that hand as it brushed his cheek. He recalled the same hand by candlelight, slowly turning the pages of a worn leather volume.

Most importantly, he remembered the odd, star-shaped mark, just above the girl's wristbone.

Could there be a connection between the serving wench and the missing heiress? It seemed farfetched, but excitement burned in his veins. Could she be the answer to an old mystery, and the solution to his own terrible dilemma?

Ravenall shook his head, afraid to believe, yet the gods of coincidence had always played a large part in his life. A few years ago he'd been the black sheep of the family, banished to the West Indies: today he was an earl.

He could have laughed aloud. So many random threads, yet woven together they formed a pattern. If Andrew hadn't wanted to visit the Druid's Oak, his near-fatal accident would not have occurred—and he would never have seen the girl with the star-shaped birthmark in an obscure inn on the forlorn fringes of Dartmoor.

He took up the photograph of Serena Hexham again, and tilted it to the light. If the hair were darker, the eyes violet instead of pale blue, and filled with a good deal more intelligence . . . Yes, it was possible. But only just.

Still, Lyme Regis was not all that great a distance from Dartmoor. If the nursemaid had fled in the direction opposite to London . . . if she perhaps had roots in Devon . . . friends or family in the area. He willed his voice to be calm.

"Dearest Daisey! I don't suppose that you might know the name of the girl's nurse?"

"Why, yes. It was Redd. Agnes Redd."

Ravenall was pleased. Redd was a familiar surname on Dartmoor. He felt in his bones that his hunch was right: the nurse hadn't headed for London, she'd taken the child to Devon.

The duchess clapped her hands together. Justin almost looked, Daisey thought, like the adventurous youth she remembered. Her eyes sparkled with excitement. "And you intend to find her! Oh, yes, I see that you mean to do so!"

Her face sobered. "But only think, Justin . . . so much time has passed, without a sign of her!"

A slow smile transformed his features. Despite Clements's suggestion, a living heiress would be of more use to him than a dead one.

"Do you believe in miracles, Daisey?"

"Of course." She laughed lightly. "And in fate, and destiny, and all the little coincidences that rule our lives."

"So do I," Ravenall said. He took her hand and kissed it lightly. "Then I shall do my best to pull off a miracle. Tell me, if I find this missing girl—if she is alive and well—would you do everything in your power to help her assume her place in the world?"

"What a peculiar question! But of course I would, Justin."

"Even," Ravenall said carefully, "if she has not been brought up with the advantages and education befitting her station in life?"

For the first time Daisey looked doubtful. "I would of course do what I could to sponsor her, you know that. But if the poor child has been living barefoot among the Gypsies— or worse, selling her wares in Covent Garden—then there is little that even I could do to establish her in society!"

"If my hunch is right, I promise you the situation will not be quite so dire. But you will have your work cut out for you."

He rubbed his hand along his jaw. Since his disastrous meeting with Clements, his mind had been turning over the story of the lost heiress, looking for some way to solve his problems. It had seemed futile. Financially, his lot would be better if he could prove that little Pauline Hexham was dead. But it was difficult to prove someone dead without a body. It could take many months, and the vultures were swooping in eagerly, ready to pick the bones of the former Ravenall fortune. It would be much quicker to fend off his creditors with a live heiress in hand.

Ravenall felt the spark of hope fan into flames of excitement. He'd always been one to take a risk. Fate had handed him a plum, but whether it was good fruit or bad, he'd yet to discover.

This could prove to be the biggest gamble of his life. His smile widened. After all, what did he have to lose?

"If Pauline Hexham is alive, I mean to find her and restore her to her rightful position," he promised. "It may take me a day or two to set things in train, and then I'll be off. If I succeed in my quest, I'll rely on you to support me."

"Of course." Lady Haycross was alarmed by the flicker of cold determination in his eye. "But must you set out so soon? You are not recovered entirely from the effects of your mishap."

His mouth turned up wryly. "Nothing will ensure my good health more than finding Miss Hexham."

"Is it wise?"

"My dear girl, it is imperative!"

Daisey tucked her hand in his. "Well, then, I wish that your search will prosper, Justin, and that Dame Fortune will smile upon you."

"It may be that she already has." Ravenall's face was enigmatic. He kissed his sister's dainty, beringed hand and took himself off.

The duchess was left alone in the Music Room with her memories, and a good deal of unsatisfied curiosity.

Seven

Darkness had fallen like a cloak over Dartmoor. The wind carried the scent of the heath, the furtive sounds of small creatures creeping out of burrows and crannies. Inside the Stag and Crown the smells of ale and onions mingled with sweat and wood smoke.

Perdita stood just outside the inn's side door, looking up at the stars. Wishing with all her might that, by some miracle, Sukey would return and give her back her stolen coins. Her safety, and her future.

Knowing it would never happen.

She would have to make her escape from the Stag and Crown the hard way. Only a sennight left until the hiring fair. Perdita pulled her shawl close against the night air. There was no way she could hold Sam Bailey off that long. He'd almost cornered her twice since his return last night. Although she was still weak from the illness she'd suffered, she realized that she had no choice: she must set out before first light.

Her plan was to go over the moors along the ancient trackways, then cut down a wooded reeve toward the river. She hoped to find work on one of the outlying farms until the hiring fair, and then—a new life!

She heard the door from the taproom to the corridor swing open, and jumped. Perdita opened the kitchen door, expecting to face the landlady's wrath.

Meg, the new girl from Beck Farm, laughed merrily. "'Tis only me. You needn't worry about old Croggins. She'll be too busy to bother to clout us this night."

"She's never too busy for that!"

But Meg's face creased in a wide smile. "She is now that her lover's come back from his travels. I took him up a pint, and plate of ham and cheese, while you stepped out to fetch the firewood. They're going at it upstairs now, sixteen to the dozen. They'll knock a hole in the wall afore they're through."

Meg leaned over the thick plank table, picking at the gravy-dribbled crust of a cold game pie. "Who can blame him? Word in the taproom is they mean to marry. The missus is rolling in gilt since those swells were here, and custom has picked up with the new stage coming through each week. He could do worse."

"But *we* could do far better." Perdita forced down a wave of nausea.

Her back was to Meg, but something in her voice alerted the other girl. "He seemed a pleasant enough fellow to me. Do you think he'd be a hard master?"

"Old Nick himself would be better than Sam Bailey." She hesitated. "Has he ever . . . bothered you in any way, Meg?"

"Lord, no. My six brothers would rend him limb from limb."

Perdita had no family to protect her from Sam. And if she spoke of it to the landlady, she'd only stir up more trouble for herself. It was best to keep quiet and make good her escape.

"You look pale as cheese. Have you got the fever still?"

"No." Perdita's hands shook as she finished her task. "Only a touch of headache."

"Aye, it's not so long since you were knocked off your pins. No wonder, waiting on his lordship as you did, day and night." Meg lowered her voice. "And not so much as a farthing did Old Croggins share with us, from the handsome gift Mr. Waverly gave her for all our hard work! You run along. I'll see that everything's set for the night before my brother takes me home."

"Thank you, Meg!" Perdita tried not to let her relief show in her voice.

The moon was near full. If she set forth now, while everyone was sleeping, she could be miles away by morning, before anyone missed her at all.

She'd squirreled away a few items in a space beneath the eaves: the old woolen shawl Sukey hadn't taken with her, a muffler with a great rent in it that had been abandoned by a traveling merchant, and the worn-out socks that Jed had been using to buff the harness in the tackroom. The latter would serve her as mittens during the cold night walk. With a stone bottle of ale, a rind of cheese, and the ends of the bread loaf, she'd have plenty to fill her stomach.

It was agony waiting until she was certain the house had settled down for the night. When she was sure not even a mouse was abroad in the woodwork, she crept silently down the stairs. No squeaky stair, no bold voice, challenged her.

By keeping to the verge of the track at first, she could make good time in the moonlight, slipping in and out of the shadows. Once daylight came, she would take the shortcut across the reeve and come out on the far side, catching the moor track there. As long as she didn't wander from the ancient foot paths, she could avoid the bogs.

If anyone came after her, they would surely take the main road into Haycross, expecting her to have taken the most direct route. She would be miles away in the opposite direction by the time they realized she hadn't.

There were two slices of game pie and the remains of a chicken in the larder, and a few apples in the root cellar. She put them all into a net bag, checked inside her bodice to make sure the brooch with the blue stone was securely pinned inside, and let herself out into the side yard.

The moon hid behind a black cloud edged in silver, and the wind blew keen. Drawing the shawl around herself tightly, Perdita moved swift and silent as a doe past the stables and through the kitchen garden.

As she pushed the gate open, the hinges groaned protestingly. She froze, listening for any sign that she'd been heard; but there was nothing except the wind singing through the treetops.

With a quick prayer for her safe escape, and a silent plea to guard her on her journey, she vanished into the copse.

She had never seen anything so godforsaken as the moors by night. The wild vastness, the stark tors filled her with terrible uneasiness. Only her fear of Sam Bailey kept Perdita from running back to the Stag and Crown. Although she rested frequently, she was exhausted when the sky began to lighten— and nowhere near the reeve that was her goal.

"It shouldn't have taken this long to reach it," she said shakily. Her own voice startled her. She turned around slowly to get her bearings, and caught the gleam of granite thrusting high into the night. It rose up sharply, like an island in a dark sea. Her heart fell. She didn't know where she was at all! It was a miracle she hadn't stumbled into a bog.

She fought back tears of weariness and frustration. The moor track ran up and away, over the barrens. And once the sun rose, and she passed that long tor, she'd be visible for miles upon the open moorland.

I should have taken my chances on the road! she thought in dismay. *I'd be safe across the reeve, in the woods on the other side of the valley.*

Closing her eyes, she prayed for something to tell her her location. When she opened them the sun was just coming up, hitting the moorland at an odd angle. Every stone and boulder stood out in sharp relief, littering the ground as far as she could see.

Something glittered like gold a few yards ahead. Perdita picked it up. Not gold, but a piece of gilded brass stamped with an insignia. With a start, she recognized the crest it bore. It matched the emerald signet ring Lord Ravenall had worn.

Perdita looked about. She must be near the place where he had suffered his accident. If she could find the tracks, perhaps it would help her get her bearings.

Yes! There, a few yards ahead, were the terrible scars of the runaway horses' hooves, the straight lines of the carriage wheels cutting deep into the heath. Unable to resist the urge, she followed them to the edge of the ravine. The view over the valley was not just out, but down, straight toward the tangled tree branches far below. It made her dizzy.

Perdita imagined Lord Ravenall's horror as he went plunging over the lip of the ravine, and she shivered in the dawn light. It was a miracle that he had survived at all.

For several long moments, she stood there. Wisdom told her to hurry around the top of the reeve and be on her way; instinct urged her in another direction entirely. A strange obstinacy formed inside her. She wouldn't leave until she saw the Druids' Oak and made her wish.

Scrambling down the zigzag path buried in the bracken, she finally reached the clearing. She was hot and breathless, despite the cool air. It was like standing in cold water. Perdita felt frozen to the marrow.

The oak tree drew her eye. It was ancient, and immense. She'd never realized one could grow so large! It was no wonder that legends had sprung up about it. And even now, so late in the year, the ground beneath it was covered with a tangle of blossoms and flowering vines.

While she was staring up at the towering crown, the uppermost branches dipped and swayed. The leaves caught the light, shimmering silver and green and gold. Perdita cocked her head and listened. A soft murmur filled the air like the echo of fairy voices.

She pushed through the brambles and felt a thorn snag her palm.

The hair prickled at the nape of her neck. Every sense urged her to run. Instead, wiping her scratched and bleeding hand upon her skirt, she approached the tree. The atmosphere was so charged she expected that anything could happen.

Would happen, if only she had the courage to ask.

"I . . . I don't know what to wish for," she said desperately. "I have so very many wishes."

Was it safe to ask for more than one? In the old fairy tales, greedy wishes were punished. But she wasn't asking for wealth or power. Perdita folded her hands tightly. A drop of blood fell from her scraped hand.

"I used to wish for . . . for excitement, and splendid adventures! Like the heroines in fairy tales. But now . . . now I want only to find a safe haven . . . to uncover my past . . ." She hesitated, unaware, as the second drop of blood flowed from her fingertip to the ground.

The leaves sighed, and the bell-like voices murmured. Gathering her courage, she said what she had never dared to admit before, even to herself. "To be *loved.*"

Waiting, breath held trapped within her chest, she prayed for a sign.

There was none.

A rabbit suddenly bounded out of the space beneath the roots, eyed her with surprising boldness, and sped away. Perdita let the air escape from her lungs in a long sigh and blinked away a sheen of tears. She had hoped for an omen. Something—anything.

How foolish of me to have believed it even for a moment, she thought in discouragement.

Perdita turned to make her way back up through the thickly wooded ravine. It had been a waste of her time, and she hoped she wouldn't regret it. But for those few minutes she'd forgotten about Sam Bailey and the danger she was trying to escape.

The third drop of blood fell softly to the ground.

She was suddenly aware of the stinging of her scraped hand, and bound it swiftly with her handkerchief. Perdita turned her back to the oak and left the clearing, but the echoes of her fervent wishes still whispered through the ancient glade. She had already reached the moor when the sun poured like liquid fire over the edge of the ravine behind her. Unseen by any but woodland creatures, the great oak shimmered gold and black in the brilliant flare of light.

A ripple of movement shuddered over the highest limbs of the Druids' Oak. Branches tossed like waves. The smallest twigs stretched up and up to meet the sun's rays, like the hands of delicate supplicants.

Or perhaps fairies.

The clearing exploded with elfin light. The glassy quartz spears hidden in the cavern beneath the tree reflected the morning sun on their flat, shiny planes and threw it back like a thousand mirrors. The sunbeams were shattered into ten thousand glittering pieces. The crystals beneath the ancient roots blazed blindingly, like sun-struck ice.

Like fire.

Eight

Two riders crested a wild stretch of heath and reined in, insignificant beneath the vast sweep of fathomless blue sky. Andrew turned to his cousin anxiously.

"The last time we came this way, it did not end happily. I wish you would turn back."

Ravenall smiled grimly. "I want to see the place where I ruined my reputation as a capital whip."

"Are you sure you really wish to do this, Justin?"

The young earl's mouth thinned. "I've spent the days of my recuperation thinking about it. I have to know. Perhaps it's only my damnable pride. But I cannot imagine how I lost control of the team, and then failed to regain it."

He scanned the horizon, where the height of the distant tors was so distorted they appeared to be small clusters of jumbled rock. Sheep milled about on a hillside, like errant clouds.

He had no memory of the accident itself. The first moment he could consciously recall, was waking up at the inn with the pretty serving girl reading beside his bed. Everything in between was gone.

Something teased at the edge of his thoughts. He frowned, trying to force some further collection. It was no use: it ended there, as neatly as severed rope. "What happened next?"

"We had just come up from the clearing and were making our way toward the chaise. I looked up, and stopped to watch a hawk wheeling in the sky." Andrew had gone over and over the events in his mind.

"There was a sudden crack of thunder. I heard a horse scream and you gave a shout. I turned just in time to see the chaise set off behind the runaway team. You were fighting to control them. The next thing I knew you were thrown out, being dragged along behind them, toward the precipice."

Ravenall's eyes were hooded. "Let us examine the wreckage."

"Surely you don't mean to climb down toward the clearing!"

"That's why I asked Jack to meet us there. I want no further accidents."

Nudging his black gelding into a trot, Ravenall headed toward the scene of his accident. A third man, a leathery redhead with keen green eyes, awaited them beside Giant's Tor, his horse and wagon nearby.

"I've spied out the lay of the land, and set up a rope line," he told them. "Nothing much left of the poor beast after three weeks. Nor the chaise, either. 'Tis not a pretty sight, my lord."

"I don't expect it to be, Jack. I want you two to keep watch, while I work my way down."

"Not with those healing ribs and collarbone," the red-haired man said firmly. "If you'll pardon me for saying so, my lord."

Without waiting for so much as a by-your-leave, he grabbed the rope he'd secured, and went down over the edge of the precipice. Ravenall cursed, but there was nothing he could do to stop him.

It was a goodly wait before Jack tugged on the line.

"Haul with me!" Ravenall told his cousin, and the two of them pulled on the rope. Andrew expected to find a leather sling filled with harness and trappings on the end of it. There was more, and it was the dull gleam of bone and equine teeth that floored him.

"What the devil!"

Ravenall untangled part of the animal's jawbone from the harness when Jack came up and over the side of the ravine. Except for some shredded sinews, the scavengers had picked the bone almost clean. He examined the relic in grim satisfaction. "I should have guessed. At least my pride is intact. I'm relieved to know it wasn't due to any carelessness on my part that the team bolted."

Jack nodded. "Is that what you were expecting to find, my lord?"

Andrew knelt down beside his cousin, as Ravenall turned the grisly thing in his hands. "I don't understand!"

"That wasn't thunder you heard," Ravenall said roughly. "Not in a cloudless blue sky. You can see where the missile sheared off the gilded brass boss of the harness here. It wasn't the fall that shattered the poor beast's jawbone, but this lead ball imbedded in it."

"Good God! It must have been a careless hunter, or some fool boy playing with firearms. I cannot imagine anyone would purposely aim at the horses!"

"Perhaps," Ravenall said slowly, "the horse was not the intended target."

"By God!" Andrew's lips went white. "You can't mean that someone tried to murder you, Justin!"

Leaving the jawbone among the withered grasses, Ravenall rose and dusted off his hands. "Far be it from me to shatter your illusions, Andrew; but not everyone loves me as well as you do."

"I cannot think it! Why, who would want you dead?"

Ravenall smiled coolly. "At least a dozen people, I daresay!"

He rubbed the tips of his fingers over the knotted scar on his cheek. His eyes were deep as lapis. "Who succeeds me if I die without issue, Andrew?"

His cousin looked startled. "Why, I do!"

"And think—who is next in line?"

"Bridgeforth! I see where you are going with this, Justin." The young man's blue eyes were fierce.

"Calvin has no love for either of us, and a great desire to raise himself up in the world. He could have rid himself of both of us at one blow, and succeeded to the earldom."

"But . . . you cannot seriously believe that he would do something so dastardly!"

"I am only saying that it is a possibility. Perhaps I do him an injustice." Ravenall wrapped the spent bullet in his handkerchief and placed it in his pocket. "But I would give a coach wheel to know where Calvin Bridgeforth was at the time of my accident."

Something is wrong with the sun, Perdita thought. *It should be at my back. How did it get before me?* Somehow the vastness of the land with its steep swales and unreadable features had disoriented her.

Goose bumps stood out on her arms. She stood in a world that was primitive and unforgiving, a wild landscape that seemed to move, to breathe, as the wind blew over the heath. That seemed incredibly empty, and yet alive.

And she was hopelessly lost.

Perdita bit her lip and turned back toward the sun. It had seemed simple enough to leave the valley and cross the moorland above, using the odd shapes of the tors as her guides; but she had come to realize they changed with the light. Had she come this way before? From one angle a jumble of stones was on the horizon, and from another it was down in a hollow.

She sat against a worn outcrop of rough gray granite that burst up through the bracken like stained and broken teeth. The sky pressed down upon her like a weight. Perdita took out a piece of game pie and nibbled at the edges. Hunger was sharp in her belly, but she had to make the food last as long as possible.

She was on the crest of a steep rise, and the ground stretched, deceptively level, all the way to the base of a jagged tor. There was bogland in between, hidden under the skim of green foliage. She'd certainly strayed from the path she'd planned to take.

Should she double back, or forge ahead? "Ah, if only I knew what to do!"

Closing her eyes, she prayed for an omen. When she opened them, she saw a small, mouselike creature run out from a crevice among the boulders. The wind ruffled her skirts and the tiny rodent froze in place. The lure of the food she carried was too strong for it to overcome. It stopped to watch her, eyes like tiny jet beads, pink nose quivering eagerly.

"Little beggar! Are you hungry? Here."

Strewing crumbs of bread, she watched as it hesitated, then darted in for the precious morsels. A quick nibble, a flick of its furry tail, and it whisked across the heath toward its burrow.

Too late, alas. A swift shadow passed over the moor, then a silent dive and the creature was snatched up by a fierce-eyed hawk. A squeak of terror, a fan of wings, and the bird flew away with its meal.

It seemed like a sign: she must avoid the open moor.

It would cost precious time to retrace her steps, but it was safer in the long run. Then she saw how she could take a shortcut. It would mean slithering down a steep ravine, crossing the flashing stream that ran through it, then struggling up the other side.

Half an hour later she was stepping carefully from stone to stone across the narrowest part of the stream. The water flashed silver where sunlight struck the gentle pools, or rushed deep and clear over the shadowed stream bed. She'd taken off her shoes for better footing and to keep them dry, and the cold rock made her bare feet ache. By the time she reached the bank they were numb and red.

For a despairing moment she wondered if she would ever be safe and warm again. *No time for repining,* she scolded herself sternly. She put her shoes on and trudged through the bare briars and dried brown grasses.

The sides of the bank were slick with moss and damp. She grasped at a sapling to pull herself up and the earth began to crumble beneath her. She shrieked. Just as she was about to go sliding down in a hail of dirt and stones, a strong hand reached down and grasped her wrist.

Stones as big as hams went hurtling past her, but that warm hand kept her from following. Another gripped her other arm and she was hauled bodily up to the top of the ravine. A glimpse of blue sky, then she was facedown, clutching gratefully at the earth. Safe!

"Oh, thank you! Thank you!" she mumbled, brushing the clinging leaf mold away from her lashes.

"No need to thank me," her rescuer said. "Leastways, not with words."

Perdita gasped and twisted in his grasp. Sam Bailey stood over her menacingly. She couldn't believe her misfortune.

He smelled of stale sweat and ale. His eyes were hot with anger and something more. "A merry chase you've led me. But now it's over and done."

"How . . . how did you find me?"

He threw back his head and laughed. "How far did you think you'd gone, you silly widgeon?" He pointed his meaty hand off to the right. "See that old track running beyond the tor? The three ridges yonder, and that faint line of trees?"

She shaded her eyes against the glare. The ground rose in wrinkled folds as far as the eyes could see. Here and there weathered outcrops of granite thrust up, like bones of a gigantic beast. If she strained her eyes she could make out the shape of bare treetops peeking up above the last rounded shelf of land.

"The track leads past Giant's Tor beyond the first ridge," Sam told her. "And a few miles beyond is the Stag and Crown." He laughed. "You've gone a great circle, lass. Another few minutes and you'd have been back where you started."

Perdita felt sick. It had all been for naught. She tried to rise on trembling limbs. Sam barred the way with his sturdy bulk.

"I'll be heading back, then," she said nervously. "Mrs. Croggins will be wanting me hard at work."

As she tried to push past him, Sam grabbed her arm and whirled her around so quickly she lost her footing. "All in good time," he said huskily. "But first I'll be wanting something else."

"No! Take your hands off me."

He twisted her left arm up behind her back. She gasped with pain. "You're in no position to give orders," he said, with a cruel laugh. "I'm the one that says what's what. The sooner you learn that, the better."

Pulling her back against his chest, he pawed at her breast, laughing as she writhed and tried to free herself. "Don't like that, do you? Well, you'll learn soon enough, Just like Sukey did! And a prime student she was."

Sam jerked her arms up so high behind her back that she almost passed out from the jolt of agony in her shoulder. He forced her to her knees and rolled her over onto her back. Perdita closed her eyes, summoning up her strength. As Sam straddled her, she brought her knee up with all the force she could muster. With a yowl of anger and mingled pain, he staggered sideways and fell heavily.

She was on her feet in seconds. She didn't know how long he would remain down, but delivered a sharp kick to his ribs to gain her more time. At the same time he twisted to his side, and her foot instead connected with his nose. Perdita felt the crunch of bone, saw the sudden gout of blood down his unshaven face, and fought a wave of nausea.

It didn't stop Sam. Cursing, he lunged for her, just missing her ankle. She turned and began running toward the misshapen rocks of the nearest tor. The weird humps and broken stone offered protection that might turn out to be false: instead of a hiding place, it might prove nothing more than a trap.

She had little choice: at least there she might hide from view while she found something to use as a weapon.

She could hear Sam crashing after her. Blind with fear, she stumbled over the rough terrain, more intent on the pursuer behind than the way ahead. She could hear the thud of his booted feet, hear his heavy breathing, as he gained on her. Perdita summoned every bit of strength and energy, racing across the heath, through thorny shrubs that snagged her skirts and stung her legs.

Only another yard or two. Almost there!

Turning her head to see how much ground he'd gained, Perdita tripped over the knobby knuckles of rock extending from the base of the tor, and went sprawling. Sam was on her before she hit the ground.

The wind was knocked out of her. Perdita lay on the stony heath, gasping for breath. His weight pinned her down completely.

"Don't move," Sam said into her ear.

She felt the cold of a steel blade against the angle of her jaw, and cried out at the prick of the sharpened point against her flesh. Any more pressure and it would break the skin, bite into the vulnerable place where her pulse pounded now with sickening force.

"Not a blink or a twitch, or you'll feel more of *this*!"

She was afraid to breathe. "For the love of God," she said hoarsely, "I would rather die!"

His laughter was low against her ear. "Dead or alive," he said fiercely. "It's your choice. It doesn't matter a whit to me."

She knew in that awful moment that he'd never live to let her tell the tale. She didn't want to die, didn't want her life to end so sordidly, like a quivering rabbit caught in a raptor's talons. Perdita said a swift and heartfelt prayer for deliverance, despairing that there was any chance of it being answered.

Sam laughed again, sensing victory. He slid one hand up her leg, while keeping the knife pressed against her flesh with the other. "And now . . ." he said.

A gunshot shattered the air. Sam cursed and rolled off Perdita. She rolled away and scrabbled to her knees. Three riders came thundering toward them across the moors.

Another shot rang out, and Sam grunted and clasped his

shoulder. Blood welled up from between his fingers, staining his shirt. He was stunned only a moment, then moved so quickly he had her around the waist from behind, before she knew what was happening. Using her as a shield, he dragged her with him, into the shadows of the great tor.

The jumble of granite surrounded more than an acre of moor, like the curtain wall of a ruined castle. Inside were a series of broken terraces, where rain had gouged deep furrows. Soon the ground proved too uneven and his bleeding too profuse for Sam to pull her along with him. Without warning he shoved Perdita away, hard, and loped off toward the tallest rocks.

She fell awkwardly and lay dazed on the heath, listening to the confusion of hoofbeats and shouts. As she gulped in great breaths to fill her burning lungs, a pair of polished boots filled her vision.

"Come! You are safe, now."

The voice was harsh, but familiar. She took the gloved hand held out to her, and was hauled upright by a strong arm. The man kept his face slightly averted, but she saw the cruel scar that marred his lean cheek.

She would have known him anywhere. *"Lord Ravenall!"*

Her heart gave a little leap. The last time she saw him he'd been thin and pale as they loaded him into Lord Haycross's traveling coach. To see him so strong and fit again amazed her. Only that blazing scar and the shadows beneath his dark-fringed eyes gave evidence of his terrible ordeal. She saw that he still held a pistol in his other hand.

Ravenall watched Sam stumble over one of the rough granite knobs protruding from the heath. Jack pointed out the trail of blood leading back to the tor.

"Winged him, by God!"

"Yes. He'll not get far. Flush him out, Jack. I'll handle it from there."

"Yes, my lord." The other man loped over the ground like a greyhound.

Perdita gathered her scattered wits. She had dreamed that, one day, she and Lord Ravenall would meet again; certainly she hadn't expected the circumstances to be so humiliating. She couldn't tell from the stern set of his features if he remembered her at all.

She touched the cut beneath the angle of her jaw. Her hand came away streaked with blood. "Oh!"

Ravenall examined the cut, and made a pad of his own handkerchief to press against her wound. "It's not deep. A scratch, only, I assure you. It will not leave a scar."

That was the last thing on her mind. "He meant to kill me." Her voice shook.

"Yes." Ravenall had seen the expression in the man's eyes as he struggled with the girl. "But you are safe now. Do you know this man?"

"Yes, my lord. Sam Bailey, a commercial traveler from the north. He puts up at the inn where I'm employed, when he is on Dartmoor." A shudder wracked her. "Mrs. Croggins—the landlady—is going to marry him, they say."

Ravenall lifted his brows. "That poses a problem, doesn't it?"

Andrew joined them, leading his horse by the reins. "Why, it is Polly, the serving girl who nursed you at the Stag and Crown!"

Ravenall, of course, had recognized her at once. The situation was ironic. They'd planned to take refreshment at the Stag and Crown, after this excursion to the accident site. To his companions it would be hearty fare at a country inn, and nothing more. His own motive, however, had been twofold: to personally thank those who had cared for him so well—and to take stock of this serving girl, and make sure his memory and wishful thinking hadn't deceived him. She was every bit as delicate and lovely as he recalled.

He favored her with a bow. "My belated thanks for your kind offices on my behalf."

She smiled at him tremulously. "As to thanks, it is I who am in debt to you, my lord. You have saved my life."

Ravenall saw the gratitude shining in her eyes. And the fear. "A life for a life, then. Our debts have canceled one another."

Perdita was shaking violently. Her hair had come loose, tumbling over her shoulders in a rich cascade. Ravenall removed his driving cloak and threw it around her shoulders. He handed her his silver brandy flask.

"Drink this. It will chase away the chill."

As she raised the flask, her sleeve fell back. Ravenall's gaze brushed over her arm, and he had a quick glimpse of a small red mark, like a six-pointed star. Then her sleeve covered it once more.

He rubbed a hand along his jaw. He'd have to change his plans. They mustn't be seen together after this incident. "Andrew, I regret that I have to rescind my invitation to the castle. I have a boon to ask of you."

"Name it!"

"I wish you to go to Bath."

"What on earth . . . ?"

"Yes. I'll explain later. But first," Ravenall said in a warning tone, "you'll see this poor girl back to the Stag and Crown."

The brandy warmed her blood, curling in the pit of her stomach. Perdita shook her head. "I cannot, my lord! Not now . . ."

"For fear of this man? This . . . Sam Bailey, is it?"

She tried to control the trembling of her mouth. "Yes, my lord."

"Return to the inn," he said, his face severe, "and go on about your business as usual. Say nothing to anyone of what has happened here today. Do you understand me?"

"Yes, my lord. But . . ."

The blue eyes looking down at her turned cold and gray as stone. Ravenall's face was stern, and remote as a statue. "You have my pledge that he will never harm you again."

Perdita wanted so desperately to believe him! "I do not see how you can prevent it."

"That is my business. You have the word of a Ravenall on it!"

A shout from among the rocks alerted them that the groom had spied his quarry. "Good man!" Ravenall said with satisfaction. "Jack has him at bay."

Andrew dismounted, agitated. "Give me your pistol, Justin. I may have need of it."

"Damn your insolence!" Ravenall snapped. "Do you think I'd have sent Jack in alone, if I thought he couldn't handle the challenge?"

His cousin colored. "Of course not! But the man looked a cruel brute. A cornered animal, wounded or not, is the most dangerous."

"Allay your fears! I put all my dependence on Jack. He'll bring the villain back to meet my justice."

Perdita's eyes widened. There was a cold ring of steel to his last words. "My lord, what do you intend to do to him?"

He raised his eyebrows. "Does it matter?"

"No." She took a shuddering breath. "Not to me!"

"Then I think," Ravenall said grimly, "it is really better that you not know."

Nine

Perdita scrubbed the stoneware platter with a hog bristle brush, lost between fatigue and curiosity. She dipped the basin in the rinse water. The hour was late, the Stag and Crown quiet—and Sam Bailey had not been seen at the inn since early in the day.

His absence hadn't been noted until he failed to return for his supper. Had Sam escaped his pursuer, only to die of his injuries? Or was he holed up among the tors somewhere, biding his time?

Or, she wondered for the hundredth time, had Lord Ravenall made good his promise to her? And if so—how? A shiver danced up and down her back.

The scullery door opened behind her suddenly. She gasped and the heavy platter dropped from her hands. It shattered on the stone-flagged floor. The sound was shocking in the small room, but almost drowned out by the drumming of the blood in her ears.

"You're jumpy as a scalded cat," Meg exclaimed.

"I . . . I thought you'd already gone up to bed."

The other girl stooped to help Perdita pick up the pieces. She shook her head. "We'd best get rid of this afore the missus sees it. She's like to give you a hiding you won't forget! Worked herself into a tizzy, she has, with her man gone off today, without a word to her."

Perdita couldn't look at Meg. She was afraid her knowledge of Sam's disappearance would somehow be visible in her eyes for all to see. She reached for the dust broom. "Has there been no word at all?"

Meg shook her head. "Mrs. Croggins thinks he's gone off sniffing after a woman somewhere. Jealous old thing." She leaned closer. " 'Tis my belief he's dead up on the moors."

"Ow!" Perdita drew her hand back from a jagged piece of crockery and sucked at the cut on her thumb. "Why do you say that?"

"Stands to reason." Meg rose and dusted off her hands. "If he took off, why did he leave all his things behind?"

Perdita's heart thudded so hard she was surprised the other girl couldn't hear it. "Then . . . you suspect foul play?"

"Lord love you, no." She gave a snort of disdain. "Men like Sam Bailey don't die easily. He was rough-and-tumble. But he wasn't a *Dartmoor* man. He'd no business to be straying off the tracks! I'm thinking that he got hisself lost and stumbled off into a bog—likely he'll never be found. Any road, Jed and some others will go out searching at first light. If Sam Bailey's still alive, they'll find him and bring him back."

Meg saw that Perdita was trembling. "Don't mind me. I was just talking to hear myself talk. Why, chances are, Mrs. Croggins won't notice the platter gone, so much crockery as she has. If she does, I'll tell her it was well before my time here, that it must have been that hoyden Sukey that broke it afore she ran off."

She scooped up the last of it. "There now, you've cut yourself! Bind it up, and don't worrit your head. I'll whisk these pieces out to the midden heap in my apron."

Perdita smiled weakly, and thanked her. The broken platter was the least of her worries.

Finishing her chores as quickly as she could, she went up to her place beneath the eaves. Pulling the blanket over herself, Perdita stared up into the night gloom, exhausted but wide awake. Lord Ravenall had sworn that Sam would never bother her again, that she was safe. She only wished she knew what measures he'd taken to ensure it.

A cold breath brushed along her spine. *Perhaps it is just as well I do not!*

Whatever happened to Sam, it was something he brought down upon himself. It was only after she tossed for an hour or two that Perdita realized it wasn't his ultimate fate that bothered her, as much as Lord Ravenall's part in it.

If, she told herself, *he did have a part in it.*

While she tended to him after the accident, she had somehow embodied Ravenall with all the best qualities of a storybook hero. A wounded prince or knight.

After he'd been taken back to Haycross, she'd daydreamed about him constantly. She'd imagined him a superior being, untarnished by the sordid flaws of the Sam Baileys of the world. Yet on the moor, she had seen another man entirely. One who chilled her blood.

Worst of all, she finally realized, was that she hoped and prayed he'd disposed of Sam Bailey, by whatever means necessary.

The thought of him dead, his body dumped in a bog or hidden among the rocky tors, filled her with great relief. It shocked her to realize it. It was like peering into a looking glass, and seeing a red-fanged creature staring back instead of her own, familiar face.

And she didn't care one whit. Not as long as she was safe.

Perdita woke up, terrified and disoriented. She'd been dreaming that she was lost on the moors in a thick fog, with Sam Bailey gaining on her.

It was Mrs. Croggins's rough hand that shook Perdita's shoulder in a hard grasp, her voice that whispered so severely in the feeble light.

The wax from her tallow candle dripped down on Perdita's arm, stinging. The pain chased back the nightmare. Meg snored softly on the pallet beside her.

"Get up, you lazy slattern, and shake a leg! Hurry, girl!" The landlady caught Perdita's dress from its peg and threw it to her. "Put this on and come with me."

She stumbled up, unnerved by the landlady's urgency. It was chill in the unheated space, and so dark she couldn't gauge what time of night it was. She threw her plain brown dress on over her shift, and pulled on her stockings.

As she reached for her shawl on its peg, she caught her plait of hair on a nail. Her hair came loose and fell over her shoulders in a cloud. She tried to pull it back, but the older woman stopped her.

"Leave it be. Come along!"

Perdita slipped into her shoes and followed Mrs. Croggins out of the attic room and down the steps. "What's wrong? Is someone stricken ill? Has there been an accident?" *Or had*

*Sam Bailey somehow escaped from whatever fate Lord Rav-
enall had planned for him?*

The panic that overcame Perdita had her almost mindless
with fear.

"Hush, before you wake the house!"

Mrs. Croggins led the way along the hall to her own bedchamber. Perdita wondered, fearfully, what awaited her on the
far side of the door; but instead of throwing it open, the landlady stopped and gave a soft rap with her knuckles. A deep,
masculine voice bade them enter.

Perdita was wide awake now. "What is this?" she cried and
tried to wrest away from Mrs. Croggins's hold on her arm.

"You'll know soon enough!" Her companion pushed the
door open and shoved Perdita across the threshold. "Inside you
go! Quickly! And if there are any complaints in the morning,"
she said in a low voice, "be sure you'll have me to answer
to!"

The door closed firmly behind her. No lamps were lit, but
a fire burned low in the grate. She glanced around apprehen-
sively. A gentleman's hat and driving cape were tossed across
the foot of the empty bed.

"Old Croggins will do anything for gold," Sukey had said
once. *"Why, she'd sell either one of us to the devil and never
turn a hair."*

Perdita turned to flee the room, and heard a sharp click as
the bolt was slid home behind her. A man stood behind her
with his hand on the latch. Her heart, which had been racketing
along like a steam engine, gave a sudden lurch. It started up
with a painful thump at twice the speed.

He was fashionably dressed, with a gleaming cravat and
polished boots. Because of his fine garments it took a moment
before she placed him: then Perdita recognized Lord Ravenall's groom—the one called Jack—and shrank away.

"Easy now," he said, in a soft Irish brogue, as if she were
a mare to gentle. "I mean you no ill, lass. And I'm not the
one who's sent for you."

He nodded into the deeper shadows of the room. Only then
did she realize there was someone else present. Tall, lean, and
elegantly dressed in riding clothes. An aristocrat in every inch.
He didn't say anything, just examined her thoroughly.

Perdita was as terrified as she had been in her dream: it

was after midnight, and she was locked in a bedchamber with two unknown men, with the consent of her mistress. The doors were stout oak. Even if she raised a cry, no one beneath this roof would come to her aid. She must depend on her own wits and courage.

Reaching out, she grasped the brass-headed walking cane propped beside the door. "Do not come any nearer," she said, edging away.

"You may put down your weapon." Ravenall stepped out into the center of the room. "I haven't come to offer you violence, my girl. In fact, quite the opposite."

This is only another nightmare, Perdita thought wildly. *If I try, very hard, I can awaken myself.*

But her senses told her it was real enough. She could feel the heat from the fire, hear the popping of the dry wood. She was aware of the thinness of her dress, of the way the cool air had brought her nipples erect. Perdita crossed her arms over her breasts.

Ravenall was aware of it in the same moment. In the firelight, with her body outlined beneath the thin fabric and her hair tumbled about her shoulders, she was very beautiful. Eminently desirable. That was a complication.

He frowned. He must not think of her as a woman: she was merely the means to an end. He nodded to his companion.

"You've done your part, Jack. Leave us now. We'll rendezvous later."

While Perdita watched in astonishment, the groom went to the window, opened the casement, and climbed over the sill. "Good luck to you both," he said, and disappeared into the night.

"I *am* dreaming," Perdita said firmly.

"I assure you that it's all quite real." Ravenall reached out the casement, drew in the rope the groom had used to lower himself, and shut the window. "That is better. Now we can be private."

He glanced over at the mark just above her slender wristbone. It could change both their lives.

Perdita's voice shook. "What do you want of me?"

"Far more than you expect, I'll wager." Firelight leapt and danced across his features, making them difficult to read.

"Once before the landlady offered to sell you to me for a

handful of coins." He moved so the light shifted, and Perdita could see his scarred face. "Now," he said dryly, tracing his index finger along his scarred cheek, "your price has apparently doubled."

She stiffened. "I am no whore, but an honest serving wench. If you desire food or drink, I can fetch up ham or cold chicken from the larder and ale to quench your thirst. My gratitude to you does not extend further. If you have other cravings, sir, they must go unfulfilled."

Ravenall laughed, surprising them both. "You're very frank."

"I am a virtuous maid, my lord. And I am very tired." She shook her head. "If you seek amusement of another sort, you must seek elsewhere."

Firelight reflected from his blue irises. "Don't be too hasty in your judgment. You will be well paid for your services."

Perdita clenched her hands at her sides. "Do you think me coy and greedy, my lord? Or merely ungrateful? You came to my rescue, not once but twice. But I think that you are not the knight in shining armor I imagined you to be."

"I am not," he agreed with a cool smile. "But you really know nothing at all about me." His forehead furrowed. "Why the devil didn't you flee this place long ago?"

"I would have done so," she said sharply, "if not for your accident. I felt I owed it to you to stay until you were out of danger. And while I tended to you, my lord, another girl stole the coins and ran off with them."

He relaxed and moved closer. "Most unfortunate. But perhaps your services will be rewarded tonight. Hear me out. I believe it will prove well worth its while."

Her throat was dry, and she swallowed around the lump in it. "I am not anyone's chattel to trade or sell. I have paid for my room and board here by dint of my drudgery. And I will not be bought or sold!"

"Ah, but perhaps you can be persuaded."

He let his gaze linger on her mouth. And a pretty little mouth it was, he thought, soft and pink and ripe for kissing.

He was a man well-versed in pleasuring a woman. Ravenall let his mouth turn up slowly in a warm, seductive smile. Let his eyes show admiration and appreciation of her abundant feminine charms. Imagined, just for a moment, what would happen if he closed the gap between them, and drew her soft body against the hardness of his own.

Perdita's knees felt weak. No man had ever looked at her in exactly that way before, as if she were not merely an object of lust, but something rare and precious. Almost as if he were caressing her with his gaze.

Heat sparked in her without warning. She was unprepared for the intensity of her reaction, for the need that surfaced, raw and hungry. It seemed as if he were caught in the same spell. She felt it in the air between them, thrumming like the pounding of her heart.

"Come here," he said softly.

Perdita moved jerkily, like a marionette. She would have refused an order; that air of quiet command held her in its thrall. With her heart pounding beneath her dress, she did as she was told, and stopped in front of him.

She had seen him act with kindness; she had seen him remote and sinister. Which was the real man? Looking up into his face, so beautiful on one side, so terribly scarred on the other. Was it a reflection of his soul?

She searched his eyes for a clue. They were unusual, shadowed yet luminous, like an April sky, just before the rain. Perdita held her breath. She was aware of the silence of the house, the lateness of the hour. Of his height, the breadth of his shoulders beneath his jacket, the steely determination in that firm jaw and mouth. She felt a flush rise up from her breasts to mantle her throat and cheeks. She was intensely aware of his masculinity. Suddenly she was aware of her own sexuality burning at her core. It was like a banked fire, ready to flare up at the least provocation.

Ravenall read the doubts in her face, and the knowledge of her vulnerability. Still she stood her ground. "You have courage," he said with approval.

She lifted her chin and lied. "Courage is not the same as foolhardiness. There is nothing you can offer that will cause me to change my mind!"

He turned his face away. Perdita spoke quickly. "I do not consider your scar, my lord. It is my principles that compel me. I have seen where that sorry road leads."

"Then you will not lie with me either for gratitude, or for money," he said slowly.

Something crackled in the air between them, as hot and fierce as the flames dancing in the hearth. Perdita's breath snagged in her breast. Something had changed, she didn't know what. But she had the oddest feeling that he had been testing her in some way. That there was more to come.

As he stepped forward, she moved back, placing the chair between them. An inadequate shield, she knew, but it made her feel better.

Ravenall regarded her intently. "So shy, my dear?"

Her mouth went dry and she felt a strange quickening inside her, a lazy heat that spiraled up from the pit of her stomach and flowed out along her limbs.

He watched in satisfaction. A delicate flush covered her throat and put roses in her cheeks. Ravenall was a man of the world, experienced with women. He could gauge to the inch exactly how much flattery or seduction she could handle.

"And yet just now," he said smoothly, "I felt a tug of attraction between us. Can you deny it?"

She didn't even try. What use was it when she knew it was written on her face? He looked deep into her eyes, and she was dazzled by his intensity. She was too young and inexperienced to play his game.

"What," he said silkily, "if I asked you instead to spend the night with me of your own free will—because it is what you and I both wish. What then?"

Silence spun out, cocooning them in intimacy that was palpably sensual. For the barest of moments she, who had never been held, nor been caressed in all her memory, faltered and wondered what it would be like to spend the night in the strong arms of this intriguing stranger.

The thought of it was dizzying. To kiss and be kissed, to lie flesh to flesh and know that, for a few hours, the terrible loneliness that plagued her might vanish. That she would be initiated in the arts of womanhood by a man who she sensed was a skilled and ardent lover.

But in the morning she would be just another girl who'd exchanged her maidenhead for a charming smile and a few hours of false tenderness. Another Sukey in the making.

Perdita drew in a ragged breath. "I would still wish you good-night, my lord," she said softly.

He changed before her eyes, and the seductive smile vanished as if it never was. "Clever girl!"

Ravenall was pleased. She had passed an important test. Although, for just a moment, he had wondered if *he* would do so. If she had agreed, could he have fought the temptation? The dark flush that spread across his features was visible even in the dim light.

Perdita stepped back until she felt the door behind her. "Forgive me if I have angered you, my lord. May I retire now?"

"No," he said firmly. "In fact, you will be staying all the longer. Your refusal pleases me. I am not here in the role of ravisher." She didn't quite believe him, he could tell. Ravenall laughed softly.

"What would you say if I told you that I have the ability to transform your existence from one of drudgery, to a life of ease—in fact, of great luxury?"

Perdita lifted her chin. "At the very least, I would think you had drunk too much ale, my lord."

"And at the worst?"

"That you are a raving lunatic." She dipped a tiny curtsy. "My lord."

"I salute your candor."

Her state of undress was distracting, and he saw she was chilled. Ravenall plucked a garment up from the chair. It was a cloak of rich wool. "Wrap yourself in this before you catch your death."

Perdita took the warm garment he handed her, rather than let it fall to the floor, but didn't put it on. He seemed to find that amusing. Taking the jug, he poured amber liquid into a mug and offered it to her.

She kept her place and refused to don the cloak. "What a suspicious girl you are! It is only cider," he said impatiently. "Sit down!"

She took the chair.

"Excellent. The last thing I want is hysterics."

He draped the cloak over her and she felt the chill ease. "What . . . what did you do with—"

"The man upon the moors? Are you still concerned?"

"Yes, my lord."

Ravenall shrugged. "You need worry about him no longer.

I told you I would dispose of him, and I have," he said firmly. "However, there are more Sam Baileys in your future, if you remain at the Stag and Crown. It is inevitable, you know."

The truth of his words rattled her. She'd escaped Sam's clutches, but there would be others. Serving wenches were considered fair game.

Perdita took a drink of cider to ease her dry throat. It filled her mouth with the taste of apples and autumn, and her heart with the wild yearning that came with the turning of the leaves, or the first warm winds of spring.

He took up his tankard of ale and watched her face carefully. There'd been a glimmer of something in her eyes, yet he couldn't read it. She'd learned to school her features well.

"The landlady calls you 'Polly,' " he said. "Is that your true name?"

"No, sir. I am a foundling, and my true name is unknown. The lady who took me in named me Perdita."

"Ah!" He was surprised. And pleased. His hooded lids dropped to hide his reaction. "Do you know what it means?"

"No, sir."

" *'Little lost one.' "* He cocked his head and examined her. "Your speech is good, with only a hint of Devon in it. I doubt you were raised on Dartmoor. What is your history?"

Perdita sighed. "I have no memory of my childhood, my lord." *Only strange and troubling dreams.*

Ravenall nodded. That fit with what Jack had learned earlier from Mrs. Croggins—and with the story of the missing heiress, as well. "Continue."

"As a young girl, I was found wandering alone on the moors early one morning, delirious with hunger and fever. When I awakened I knew nothing—not even my name. Miss Barnstable, a kindly spinster, took me in and nursed me back to health." Her eyes grew misty with remembrance. "She was very kind. When no one claimed me, she kept me on as her companion and maidservant. It was she who named me."

"And why did you not stay under her protection?"

Her face clouded. She bit her lip. "I would have remained with her, sir. She died suddenly . . . her nephew—"

She stopped and took another swallow of cider and spilled some from the trembling of her hands. Best not to go into that. "Her nephew," she resumed shakily, "turned me out of the house without a character. I walked and walked until I came to a market town, where I hid in a farmer's cart. It didn't stop until it reached this inn near nightfall. I sought honest work of Mrs. Croggins, and have been here ever since."

"That explains your speech," he said, almost to himself. "There is only the slightest veneer of Devon in it. But it poses other questions."

There was a long silence. She felt as if he were sifting through her words, trying to sort them out into a pattern of his own making. Perdita waited while he took a turn about the room. When he spoke his voice was low, intense.

"If I had the power to grant you a wish—what would it be?"

Perdita didn't hesitate. "To know who I am, and how I came to be abandoned. And if I have any family still living, to leave this place and go to them!"

Ravenall tossed back his ale. She had passed another, crucial test. "It might be in my power to grant your wish. Because, you see, I believe that I know more about you than you know yourself."

He watched that sink in. "And it is possible that I already know the answers to all your questions."

Her head buzzed and Perdita felt as if she might faint. "You know my true name, sir? And my history?"

"Perhaps. Give me your hand."

She hesitated and he caught his reflection in the polished brass of the candle holder. For a moment he'd forgotten the picture he must present, with his ruined face. It was no wonder that she felt repulsed by it. There were days when he could scarcely bear to look at it himself.

"You have no reason to fear me," he said harshly.

She realized she'd offended him, and was mortified. She held her hand out.

Ravenall took it carefully. It was delicate and well-formed, though chapped and rough from work. With a little care, it could quite easily pass for the hand of a lady. He pushed up the sleeve of her shift.

The star was very distinct, and matched the description he'd read. Ravenall frowned. He'd never seen a birthmark with such precise margins. His thoughts were racing as he ran his thumb over the mark.

Perdita couldn't sort out the feelings that poured through her. His nearness clouded her thinking, and his touch sent sparks of mingled pleasure and apprehension through her. She jerked her hand back, and pulled herself free. She could see the red imprint of his long fingers on her wrist, feel the tingling warmth of them on her skin. Ravenall said nothing, but leaned back in his chair, deep in thought. He was used to trimming his sails according to which way the wind blew. He'd taken bigger risks before. And certainly there was more than the basic raw material to work with here.

He scrutinized Perdita, trying to imagine her patched shift as a fashionable gown, her tumbled hair—glorious hair!—dressed becomingly. The girl was clever and quick, and had an innate grace to her carriage and gestures.

But time was short. Even with the help of Fanny Fitzmorris, it would be difficult. He wondered if he could really pull it off.

He wondered too if he had inherited the same faulty gambling instincts as his late uncle. Only a fool would place his entire fortune on the turn of a card. And yet, if it were to be the *right* card . . .

The moment of decision had come. He threw caution to the winds. *Everyone has their price.*

God knew, he had his.

Reaching into his pocket, he drew out a thin book bound in green morocco and handed it to her. He'd sent Jack haring down to Hexham Court to retrieve it after Daisy had told him Serena's story. "Open it."

Perdita took it, but when it fell open she saw it was actually a traveling case with a pair of portraits. One of an aristocratic woman, exquisitely dressed, with a dreamy expression and a necklace of glowing gray pearls. The other a pampered young girl with blue ribbons in her glossy brown hair, and a fluffy white cat on her lap.

"They are very beautiful," she said hesitantly. "Your wife and daughter, sir?"

He was taken aback. "Certainly not! Their garments should tell you these likenesses were painted many years ago."

"You must excuse me," she said stiffly. "I do not move in fashionable circles." She tried to hand the case back to him.

"No. Keep it a moment." He folded his hands. "I shall tell you a story."

His voice was as soft and low as the crackle of flames in the hearth.

"Once upon a time there was a little girl, pampered and much loved. She had a young nursemaid who'd cared for her since birth. Her mother fell ill, and her father hired a house outside Lyme Regis, hoping the air would restore her health. Both parents succumbed to an outbreak of influenza within days of one another."

Perdita bit her lip. "A sad story, my lord."

"Yes. And it is only half-told. After their deaths, the child was left to the wardship of a guardian who didn't wish to be burdened with a young girl. There was talk of sending her away to a boarding school in Kent."

"Poor thing! To suffer such loss and be wrested away from everything she knew!"

"Yes," Ravenall replied. "Evidently the nursemaid felt the same. She couldn't bear the thought of being riven from the child she had cared for since birth."

He'd not only talked to the constabulary in Lyme Regis, he'd been fortunate enough to locate the Hexhams' former housekeeper and hear the tale from her own lips. "While the matter was being decided, the nurse vanished with her young charge. The authorities believed they went to London, where the nurse had been hired. I believe she headed to Dartmoor with the child, possibly to relatives, when they met with some sort of accident."

Perdita was trembling with hope. Could it be? She raised her eyes to Ravenall. He held her gaze steadily. "I judge you to be the same age as the missing child would be at present."

Perdita couldn't breathe. She felt as if her heart had expanded and contracted so rapidly her chest might burst. If what he said was true, then she had a name and a place in the world. But she had nothing else. No mother or father. No family to gather her to its loving bosom. The knowledge was shattering. It took great effort to hold back her tears.

Ravenall observed her closely. Her skin had gone white, but now was suffused with color. "Look at the portraits again, then look in the mirror! Do you not see the resemblance?"

She was too moved to speak. Oh, how she wanted to claim

this beautiful woman, this secure past, for her own! She examined the miniatures, then her reflection in the mirror over the bureau. The coloring was different; but the faces in the portraits, like hers, were oval, with determined chins and small, straight noses. And surely there was a similar shape to the up-tilted blue eyes.

But there was not the slightest sense of recognition in her mind or heart.

Ravenall grew impatient. "For almost seven years, the girl in the portrait was believed to be dead. But what if she were only lost? What if her memory of the past had been wiped out by illness or accident?

"That girl does not belong in this godforsaken place. She has a place in society, and a home. A very lovely one, I might add."

Perdita felt dizzy with excitement "What reason do you have to believe that I might be this missing girl, my lord?"

Ravenall's eyes glittered in the darkness. Now they had come to the crucial moment. "Every reason, once I saw that mark above your wrist! It is very distinctive."

She gazed at him blankly. "I do not understand you."

He took her hand and pushed the sleeve up to expose the mark above her wrist. "Every blood member of the family in question carries a birthmark of a certain star-like pattern somewhere upon themselves. The missing heiress had that star-shaped birthmark—as do you."

Perdita's heart tumbled. *The burn scar from the wafer iron! He thinks it is a birthmark!*

Ravenall leaned closer.

"Do you understand what I am telling you? The girl I seek does not belong at the Stag and Crown, laboring as a serving wench. She has a name and a home and a history. And a considerable fortune! There is a new life waiting for her to claim, one filled with ease and all the luxuries that life has to offer."

"But . . ." Perdita stopped herself before the fatal words were spoken.

The prize he held out before her, glittering with hope and promise, was beyond her wildest imaginings. With a few words—a few lies—she could escape the Stag and Crown and the bleak future that was her likely lot. She could change her life completely. The temptation was overwhelming.

All she had to do was step into a dead girl's shoes.

She raised her eyes to him. "You seem very certain, my lord."

He smiled. "You bear a good resemblance to both mother and child. You have the birthmark that proves your heritage. Do you lack the courage to claim it?"

Perdita was in shock. To have so much offered, but at such a price! It was wonderful and incredibly cruel. She took a shaky breath. "You say both parents died and there is no family. What is your part in this story, sir?"

Ravenall locked his gaze with hers. "Merely one of guardian. It would be my task to prepare you for your entry into society, and see that you take your rightful place."

Perdita's emotions warred with her conscience. The struggle was severe. He was offering her things she had never dared to dream.

The girl has been missing almost seven years, a tempting voice whispered in her head. *Surely she has indeed gone to her rest long ago. What harm would there be in taking her place?*

He saw the emotions flicker over her face: hope, surprise, calculation, fear. And longing so naked he wanted to turn his face away. Instead he pushed her further.

"You have nothing to lose by trusting me," he pointed out, "and a world to gain." He let that sink in.

Her voice was small and quiet. "What do you expect of me, my lord?"

"Nothing difficult. Only that you forget this place, this meager existence! Trade hard work for a life of comfort and leisure. Learn to be a young lady of elegance and fashion."

She sucked in a tiny breath and his eyes glittered like sapphires. She was caught now, he knew it! "Think! Instead of these mended, hand-me-down garments, you would wear beautiful gowns and own wonderful jewels. Learn to dance and make pleasant conversation. Ride in the park in a fine carriage, and attend plays and parties, and flirt with eligible gentlemen. Surely," he added wryly, "not a daunting task."

"It sounds like a fairy tale," she said. Anything too good to be true usually was. No, something was amiss.

"I do not understand one thing, my lord: why such secrecy?" she challenged. "If you think I am this missing heiress, surely you could ride up to the door and claim me by daylight."

Ravenall's face was a mask in the dim light of the fire. Yes, she was clever. That was all to the good—unless she proved too clever for her best interest. But that was a hurdle he'd jump when he came to it.

"To protect your reputation, of course. Do you think society would readily accept a girl who has worked as a common tavern wench into their exalted ranks? No, the fewer who know your past, the better. That is why you must come away with me. Now!"

"Tonight?"

Perdita stared up at his beautiful, ruined face. Was there really any alternative? Any woman with no prospects of marriage faced an uncertain life. One who was poor, and with no relations in the world, could expect only drudgery and a sad end.

She weighed the risk she would be taking, placing everything she valued—her very life—in this stranger's hands. In return, though, he was offering her a future so safe, so bright, it dazzled her to everything else.

She closed her eyes and made one last effort to resist temptation. It was too hard a task. "My lord, will this . . . birthmark . . . be enough to prove my identity? I have no recollection of my past."

"You need only prove it to me," he told her.

He cannot know what he is offering me, she told herself. *An identity. A home. A past.* Everything that mattered most to her.

And the ease and luxury she'd never aspired to, except in dreams.

He held the lure of it out to her, as if it were a golden apple from some fairy tale. And like fairy fruit, it exacted a payment. It would be difficult to live with the terrible lies—but only a fool would refuse. She was not a fool.

"I . . . I have this!" Perdita fumbled inside her shift and took out the brooch she'd pinned there. Since Sukcy had stolen her coins she'd kept it always on her person. "I was wearing it when Miss Barnstable found me."

While she watched nervously, Ravenall turned the brooch

over and over in his long fingers. The blue stone caught the candlelight, glowing like his eyes. "A pretty bauble. A shame there are no initials or maker's marks by which to trace it."

He handed it back to Perdita, and regarded her straightly. "Even if your mind cannot remember, surely somewhere deep in your heart, the memory of your mother is buried. Gaze upon these portraits," he said, "and tell me not what you see, but what you feel. Is there a pang, however distant, of recognition?"

He saw the trembling of her hands, heard her breathing quicken. He lowered his voice. "Do you believe that the woman in this portrait is your mother?"

Perdita stared down at the miniature in desperate confusion. How she wished that she could claim this woman, this family, as her own! The longing was so strong, the need to anchor herself somewhere so intense, she was shaking with reaction.

And all because I burned myself with the wafer iron. Perdita tried to sort out her disordered thoughts.

Lord Ravenall's words spoken earlier echoed in her mind: *". . . there are more Sam Baileys in your future, if you remain at the Stag and Crown. It is inevitable, you know."* Perdita imagined her future, and saw its bleakness. If she did not seize this chance that fate offered, she was indeed a fool.

Meeting Ravenall gaze for gaze, she cast her scruples to the winds.

"Yes," she said, only slightly appalled at how easily the lie tripped from her tongue. "I do believe it."

"Excellent." Ravenall took the traveling case from her hand and bowed over her. She wished that she could see his face, read his eyes.

But he turned away. "I require no other evidence than that, and the mark you bear. I accept you as the missing heiress—and there is no one who will dare challenge me. Not," he added, "once they see the birthmark upon your wrist."

It had been so easy, it left Perdita weak. One lie, and her life was about to change completely and forever. She thought of the missing girl, whose identity she was borrowing.

No. Not borrowing—stealing! a small internal voice said.

"What is her . . ." Perdita swallowed. "What is *my* name?"

"I will reveal everything to you eventually. But this is neither the time, nor the place."

She stood her ground. "But I wish to know it now, sir."

"You do not trust me," he said quietly, and took her hands in his, pulling her to her feet. The cloak slipped from her shoulders and her heart pounded so wildly it shook her slender frame. He laughed, softly. "But you *will* come away with me."

Perdita could only nod.

Ravenall's mouth twisted cynically. Had there ever been any doubt, once she realized exactly what it was he offered her?

Still, his relief made him grateful to her. He lifted her work-roughened hands to his lips and kissed her fingertips lightly. "Good girl! You will not regret it."

The moment his warm mouth touched her hands a jolt went through Perdita, from the crown of her head to the soles of her naked feet. He drew her like lodestone drew iron filings. The attraction was alarming to her.

She was alone in the world and very vulnerable—and he was, she thought with a catch in her throat, a very dangerous man.

Ten

"Quickly, now!"

Ravenall slipped out the stillroom door and gestured for Perdita to follow. She tucked her hair in the hood of the dark wool cloak he'd given her, and obeyed his summons.

Black clouds held a thin slice of moon captive, and the inn yard was all ink and shadow. He paused, listening intently. A shiver ran up Perdita's back. He seemed mysterious, his scarred face sinister, in the faint light.

This is madness, she thought, with a bright surge of panic.

"Come!" he whispered, holding out his hand to her. She stepped out into the cold air and moved with him alongside the kitchen wall. A cat, dozing nearby, sprang awake with a hiss and snarl. Its eyes flashed like gold sovereigns, before it vanished into the night.

His warm breath ruffled her skin. "I'll slip around the back of the stable. Not a sound or a movement until I signal you. Then hurry softly after me. I'll meet you beyond the outbuildings."

Perdita caught at his arm. "But . . . the road is not that way!"

"Don't be a fool! Do you expect me to announce your departure by waking the household? That would set the cat among the pigeons!"

Something rustled alongside the barn, and he held up his hand for silence. Only a mouse.

Ravenall smiled, but when he looked down at her, he saw the fear in her widened pupils. "It's best that no one know exactly when—or how—you came to leave the inn. I've a carriage waiting on the track beyond the trees."

He frowned at her hesitation, sapphire eyes gleaming in the faint starshine. "I'll not carry you off unwillingly! Commit to me now—or return to your warm bed and forget this ever happened."

Perdita was still more than a little afraid of him. She was, however, far more afraid of the bleak future that awaited her beneath Mrs. Croggins's roof.

"I have no warm bed," she told him with a sigh. "I will come with you. You need not fear I'll lose heart."

"Good girl!" He lifted her chin with his fingertip and smiled down at her.

His glance held hers. Something shimmered in the air, and heat rose up inside her in bright, hot sparks. Without meaning to, she swayed a little toward him. "Oh!" Her hair had tangled in the clasp of his cloak, and he worked to free it with his long fingers. His touch tingled from her scalp to her toes.

Perdita was the first to look away.

The temperature had dropped considerably since sunset. Frost nipped the crisp autumn air, and her breath made little icy puffs before her.

"Wait for my signal," he said again, and vanished beyond the angles of the old inn's walls.

A gust of wind caught her cloak, swirling it out behind her. As she drew it closer she was immediately swathed in warmth and the scent of sandalwood. She wondered how she knew that exotic scent.

A dizzying sense of déjà vu came over her, and fractured images tumbled through her mind: *Night. Stars. Hunger and cold. A swirling red cloak that looked like dried blood in the darkness.*

The moment passed as quickly as it came, leaving her feeling dizzy and slightly disoriented. She felt terribly vulnerable and alone.

Perdita rubbed her temples. She didn't know if the images that sometimes filled her mind were memories of books she'd read aloud to Miss Barnstable, or remnants of dreams. Perhaps the one she'd just experienced was a phantasm, born of fear and fatigue, and the lateness of the hour.

Just as she began to wonder where her companion had disappeared to, Ravenall stepped out and motioned for her to follow. Swift as a shadow she covered the ground between them but almost stumbled on the uneven cobbles near the stable. He had vanished once more into the night. She turned, jerkily, wondering what to do.

A hand clapped over her mouth, a strong arm wound round her, and she was pulled back against a hard chest. Ravenall's voice was low in her ear.

"Not a sound."

At first the wild beating of her heart drowned out everything else. Then she heard it: someone stirring in the stables. One of the stablelads came out, adjusted his trews sleepily, and sent a glittering stream arcing out against the wall in the starlight. Bladder emptied, he stumbled back into the warmth of the stables once more.

Perdita realized that she was shaking. Her companion released her, then took her cold fingers in his gloved hands and held them briefly. As her anxious gaze met his, her heart, racing so boldly, seemed suddenly to stand still.

He gave her a reassuring nod, and drew her into the pooled blackness at the corner of the inn's angled walls. They moved past the dark buildings at the back of the yard, and through the low board gate in the wall. She waited for its characteristic rusty groan. There wasn't a sound, and the gate swung to on newly oiled hinges.

Perdita realized he'd planned this out very carefully. Had he been so sure of her, then? She shook her head. Of course he had.

He hurried her along the edge of a copse and into a dark clearing. The stars and silhouetted branches formed a canopy of black lace overhead, sparked with diamonds.

She stopped, suddenly. "I . . . I have to go back!"

"What, has your courage failed you?"

"My book . . . it is still hidden beneath the eaves!" She couldn't bear the thought of leaving that precious volume behind.

Ravenall took her face between his hands. Her very real distress touched him. "I promise you that you will have more books than you can hope to ever read! Hundreds of them."

She searched his face. Was it even possible? "But it was a gift from Miss Barnstable. *West Country Tales*."

"I will get you a copy of it. Come, my girl, I'm offering you something far more than a collection of stories in a worn binding. Surely that is worth the sacrifice."

She nodded and sighed, but it was very difficult. It was the last thing she had to connect her with the kindly woman who had taken her in.

"I promise I shall make it up to you. We'd best continue on our way. It's a brisk walk," he told her. "But you will soon be rewarded."

Swallowing her sorrow, she followed him along the ancient footpath that led up into the hills, and then across an empty tract of land and through a small wood a goodly distance away. Her thin half-boots, hand-me-downs from Mrs. Croggins, were no match for the frost, and her toes tingled with cold. The air smelled of damp earth and turning leaves, and the distant smoke of cozy village fires. Perdita imagined the inhabitants snuggled deep beneath their quilts and feather beds, and wondered how long it would be before she slept.

After several minutes of walking in silence, they broke through a line of trees and came out on the verge of the road. The sky was now covered over with velvet clouds.

There was a faint glow up ahead, from a half-shuttered lantern. Even in the dim light Perdita could make out the wink and glint of burnished brass.

Ravenall guided her to a waiting carriage. The coachman mounted the box and the horses shifted and gave muffled snorts. A groom stood at the team's head, and two outriders waited a short distance away.

Now that it all proved real, Perdita hung back, heart hammering. Her companion put his hand on her shoulder. "Don't let your courage fail you now," he said brusquely. "We are only at the beginning of our journey."

The beginning. Yes!

She let him assist her to mount the step into the dark interior of the vehicle, but Ravenall made no attempt to follow after her. As he lifted a lantern, relief washed through Perdita. She was not alone.

A trim young woman, with brown eyes and a spine as stiff as iron, sat in the far corner of the carriage beneath a warm throw. Perdita thought she looked eminently respectable, from the tips of her toes to the crown of her fashionable bonnet.

The woman scrutinized the new arrival in the lantern light with sharp interest in her dark eyes and, Perdita thought, a good deal of misgiving. "So, my lord" she said coolly, "this is the object of our mysterious journey!"

Ravenall grinned. "Indeed she is, Mrs. Fitzmorris. Take good care of her!"

The woman nodded. "I shall do my best, my lord." From her tone, she thought it extremely doubtful.

Laughing softly, Ravenall retrieved his cloak and started to close the door.

"But . . . aren't you coming with us?" Perdita was dismayed.

"I ride ahead. Mrs. Fitzmorris will see to your comfort."

He handed her another fur throw from the seat opposite. "This will keep you snug and warm." Then he shut the door firmly.

Perdita let the soft throw enfold her. It was warm, but light as air. Her fingers caressed it nervously. This clandestine adventure was certainly not at all the thing to involve a true lady, yet there was nothing havey-cavey–looking about the other woman.

Outside the carriage, Lord Ravenall was giving instructions. She listened as they prepared for departure. *"Stand away!"*

The team pulled away at quick pace, despite the darkness. The carriage rolled forward with gathering speed.

"He must be mad to travel so swiftly on a dark night," Perdita exclaimed.

"You'll soon become accustomed to it," her companion said. "Ravenall always travels as if the devil himself were after him. Accustom yourself to it. We've quite a way to go, Miss Hexham!"

Miss Hexham!

Hearing herself called by that strange name was startling. No one had ever called her "miss" before, except for Danes, his lordship's valet. Perdita fought the growing realization that everything was now completely different—and totally out of her control.

"Where are we going?" she asked nervously.

"For a very long ride," Mrs. Fitzmorris answered briskly. "I intend to sleep until we reach our destination. I would advise you to do the same."

Her coldness disconcerted Perdita. "But . . . where *are* we going?"

"Didn't his lordship tell you? Well, he must have his reasons. I'm sure he'll explain everything—in his own good time." Tucking the thick robe around her shoulders, Mrs. Fitzmorris closed her eyes again.

Perdita didn't think the other woman was really asleep. She couldn't tell in the darkness. One thing she did know, was that her companion was ill-pleased with her part in the entire affair.

Pulling back the curtain, Perdita could see nothing but vauge black silhouettes of hills and trees flashing by. The carriage was well sprung. The sound of the wheels, the rhythm of the hooves, lulled Perdita's senses, but she was far too excited to sleep. She leaned back against the luxurious squabs and tried to figure out in which direction they were heading. It proved impossible without the moon to guide her, and it had long disappeared behind the massing clouds.

From the dark silhouettes beyond the window, she was aware of the change in terrain from the open sky and moorland, to a compact, compressed landscape. She felt closed in, not just by the padded walls of the vehicle, but by the thick trees that lined the dark road, the knowledge that the roads they traveled were hemmed in by the steep walls of the winding river valleys.

By the decision she had made in not telling Lord Ravenall that it was the scar from a burn, and not a birthmark that marred her skin.

But the missing girl vanished almost seven years ago, and her family is all gone, as well, Perdita rationalized. *If she were alive, she'd have claimed her inheritance by now. I am taking nothing from her. And I must save myself!* But no matter how she tried to convince herself, the guilt remained.

The carriage swung abruptly right, and she grabbed the strap again to keep her balance. At times their path widened to a proper road, at others it narrowed until it was no more than a tree-hung lane, as the carriage took her far away from the only life she remembered.

From the way she was jostled to and fro, Perdita deduced that they were not on one of the ancient tracks that spanned the bleak moors, or the Roman roads that crossed England, since both ran straight as an arrow's flight.

It didn't really matter, as long as it was away from the Stag and Crown. Her relief grew with every passing mile. *Safe!*

Safe! Safe! sang the jingle of the harness and the rumble of wheels and hooves.

She felt as if she were caught up in a strange dream, or wondrous fairy tale. She ran her bare hand over the rich velvet of the cushions. How unreal it all seemed—quite like Cinderella, dashing away to the ball in her splendid pumpkin carriage.

I only hope, she thought fervently, *that I can play my part well. That midnight does not come too soon—and that this story has a happy ending.*

But as they raced through the darkness, Perdita sensed that the future might prove to be as dark and twisting as the roads they'd left behind.

Ravenall led the way through the night, with outriders guarding the coach. Taking the side roads and skirting the villages, the small cavalcade left forest and farm behind; but because of the darkness they had to sacrifice some speed until they reached the coast.

One of the outriders, a red-haired, loose-limbed man, rode forward to join him. He noticed the grim lines of exhaustion around Ravenall's mouth.

"Sure and we should have stopped an hour ago, my lord!"

"Are you angry with me, Jack?" Ravenall laughed at his friend. "That's the only time you are so formal with me in private."

"Times change, my lord. Now that you're a peer of the realm, as they say."

"Damn it, you hardheaded Irishman, we've shared too many adventures in the West Indies and the China Sea for me to come cock-lofty with an old comrade! You saved my groats more than once."

"And you saved my life off Cape Hope, aye, and again in Melbourne. You're looking peaky, my lord. Nay, downright seedy! We should stop at the White Hart and rest the horses, while you and the ladies have a rest yourselves."

In the light of the carriage lamps, a golden spark lit Ravenall's blue eyes. "Ah, I understand at last! Your concern is not for me or the ladies, but the horses!"

An answering gleam shone in the other man's eye. "In part.

But 'tis said only fools or brigands ride abroad at such an hour."

"I am neither. Merely desperate."

"You must be, to have embarked on this chuckleheaded scheme!"

"A wise man cuts his coat to suit his cloth."

"There's surely other ways to bring yourself about." Jack rubbed a gloved hand over his jaw. "With your experience at sea, you could easily have gone free-trading instead, like your great-grandfather before you. You told me long ago that the Ravenall fortune was founded in boatloads of brandy and silks, brought over from France."

Ravenall grimaced. "Don't tempt me, Jack. I've no notion to create a scandal by ending my career on the gallows!"

"Fear of scandal's never stopped you before."

"Ah, but I've never been an earl before, you see. In any case, it would take too long to get everything set up, fetch the brandy and store the goods hidden away from the excisemen until I could get it off my hands." Ravenall's mouth thinned. "I need something surer and infinitely quicker, to stay my creditors from calling in my debts. The girl will serve my purpose nicely."

They had come out into the open. There was just a flicker of regret in the earl's heart as he turned away from the road that would lead them to a comfortable inn, in the small village of Crancoombe. It was still too close for safety.

"I am sorry to disappoint you, Jack, but we'll press on to the George as planned. The more miles we put between the girl and that wretched inn, the better for all concerned."

"Aye, Capt—" Jack grimaced. "Aye, my lord."

"My name is Justin! Damn it, man! There was a time when you called me friend, before anything else."

"I still do . . . my lord."

Ravenall saw the stubborn set of his old friend's jaw. "Let us make a pact. If I can pull this off, I'll set you up in Ireland with that horse-breeding farm you long for. Then I'll call you 'Squire Malone,' and you can 'my lord' me as much as you please!"

The Irishman shot him a guileless look. "Yes . . . *my lord.*"

Laughing softly, Ravenall urged his horse to an easy canter, leading the way through the night.

They rode on until the sky began to lighten in the east. A thin streak of gold shone to the east and gossamer mist rose off the land, wrapping around the trees and clothing the distant village in a strange silver glow.

Ravenall reined in suddenly.

The carriage slowed as it pulled abreast with him. "What's amiss?"

"Nothing." The wind ruffled his hair as he took in a deep breath. Some of the tension left his body. "We're almost there. I can smell the sea."

"You've seawater for blood, I swear."

Ravenall didn't hear him. Urging his horse forward, he rode on.

Jack Malone shook his head. Where this mad escapade would end, he wasn't sure. There would surely be squalls ahead—even a hurricane or two; but he'd sailed round the world with his old comrade, and Ravenall had always brought them safely home to port.

The sky was changing rapidly when they neared the cliffs. The breeze blew in soft gusts, carrying the tang of the sea. Jack pulled his muffler tighter, but Ravenall spurred his mount and rode off ahead, eager for his first sight of the water.

His heart lifted. There it was spread out below, a vast pewter gleam in the gathering light. The waves surged up the strand, flashing like molten silver.

Seabirds launched themselves into the air, skimming over the endlessly changeable face of the Channel. Dawn conjured her ancient magic, infusing sky and sea with the iridescent grays and blues and pinks of a mollusk shell. Some of the weariness lifted from him.

He'd embarked on a mad adventure, but he would bring himself about, just as he had so many times at sea. Time and again, when it looked as though all were lost, he'd won the day. All it took was a little luck—and the courage to risk everything.

An odd smile played at the corners of his firm mouth. Perhaps he had more in common with his uncle, the late earl, than he'd imagined. They were both gamblers, it seemed, and reckless to boot!

Ravenall glanced back over his shoulder, at the carriage trundling up the road. The first part of his plan was almost completed now. The most challenging task still lay ahead. If swooping down on the Stag and Crown, and making off with the girl, had been like a swift raid on a single ship, the next stage would be more like a pitched battle on the high seas. Ravenall's jaw squared. He would succeed, flags flying, or go down in the attempt.

He would save Ravenall Castle, no matter what the cost.

To himself or anyone else.

Scanning the long line of cliffs, he spied a sleek yacht resting at anchor. He knew its lines as well as he did the contours of his own face. *More so these days,* he thought, running a gloved fingertip over his scarred cheek. There were still times when he caught a glimpse of his face, unexpectedly reflected in a window or a piece of polished silverplate, and suffered a shock at the sight of it.

The carriage rolled to a stop beside him. He saw Perdita's face at the window, pale with fatigue and anxiety. He hardened his heart against the quick stab of sympathy. He must remember that she had chosen to come away with him of her own free will. That she would gain immeasurably.

And he must never forget that she was only a tool, to be used by him to achieve his goal.

Jack rode up and joined him. "And so it begins."

A muscle ticked in Ravenall's jaw. He stared out over the water, now steel-blue shot with flame. His expression was as unfathomable. "It begins, yes. But where it ends . . ."

Jack turned in the saddle, frowning. Something wasn't quite right. Even the horses sensed it, and grew restive. Then he saw the dark glow in Ravenall's eyes. *He's in one of his wild moods. Oh, he's reined it in, but there's no fooling me!*

"Tell me straight-out: are you convinced this girl is truly the missing heiress?"

Ravenall's teeth gleamed in a wicked smile. "What does that matter? It is not I who must be convinced, but society."

"Sure and that's true enough, my lord," Jack said wryly, "but 'tis not what I asked."

"She is no typical serving wench, you must admit. She can read and cipher. All she lacks is polish, and exposure to the world at large."

"But her world has been a rough tavern, not a fine drawing

room! Are you mad enough to think that no one will notice her lack of accomplishments?"

The wind ruffled Ravenall's dark hair, and his voice turned wry. "If she can learn to dance and flirt and utter empty pleasantries, she'll be as accomplished as most of the young ladies making their come-out in society. And," he added, "she is the right age and bears a star-shaped mark upon her left wrist. No one can refute that."

Jack was silent a moment. Then he shook his head. "She's a fine-looking little filly, but I'll tell you this: I wouldn't back an untried mare in a horse race, without being sure of its dam and its sire."

Again, that wolf flash of teeth. "At the moment I have only one concern: that she will be able to carry off her part in this Pygmalion farce upon which we now embark." Ravenall looked suddenly grim. "God help us both, if she fails!"

Something in his voice brought Jack up short. "Devil take it, Justin! Then you are *not* convinced of her identity!"

"If she is not Pauline Hexham," Ravenall said, "she is a most accomplished liar." He smiled. "Either way will serve my purpose."

Perdita awakened suddenly. The carriage swayed, turned, then came to a rolling stop. The horses snorted and there was much stamping of hooves, followed by raised voices. For a horrid moment she thought they were under attack by highwaymen.

Then she looked out the window and blinked. The streaky dawn light was muted by the high walls of an elegant building. They had pulled into the yard of an inn, but it was as unlike the Stag and Crown as a palace to a pigsty.

It was a long, galleried two-story construction of whitewashed stone with shining brass lamps, freshly painted trim, and sparkling diamond-paned windows. Even at such an early hour, the place bustled with excitement and activity. Liveried ostlers bustled out from the stableyard, ready to tend the horses. Several gentlemen were leaving on horseback, and a footman with powdered hair helped a well-dressed lady and her maid into an elegant closed carriage.

Mrs. Fitzmorris awakened, made a sound like a surprised kitten, and clutched at her bonnet to straighten it. The door opened abruptly and the steps were put down. Ravenall stood ready to hand them from the vehicle.

"Come, ladies. A hearty breakfast awaits you after your journey."

She hesitated. While she was glad of her warm, hooded cloak that hid her worn gown, there was little she could do to hide her scuffed, hand-me-down boots. Wiggling her toes, she saw the edge of her stocking peep out where the sole was loose from the dilapidated top.

Before she had time to worry further, Ravenall whisked them toward the door. She tried not to gape. "What place is this, my lord?"

"The George, a busy posting house on the road between Sidmouth Road and Lyme Regis, where our coming and going will be of no note to anyone but ourselves. More importantly—it is the place where a tavern wench from Dartmoor begins the process of transformation into Miss Hexham of Hexham Court!"

Ravenall read the doubts written on her face. "Trust me. I will see that you have all the help you need to succeed."

As she stepped to the cobblestones, he leaned down and lowered his voice. "Keep the strings of your cloak tightly fastened and the hood up until we're inside. From this moment on, however, you must forget everything you know. You will be given a new history. And I would advise you, until the veneer of Dartmoor is removed from your speech, to speak in public as little as possible."

She nodded mutely, and stepped away. After assisting Mrs. Fitzmorris down, he led them inside. Ravenall spoke to the manservant who came out to greet them. "Ah, yes," she heard the man say, as he bowed low. "Everything is ready for your party, my lord."

He escorted them into a private parlor with several chairs arranged around the gleaming table, and some wing chairs pulled up before the hearth. "Warm yourselves by the fire and I'll have the refreshments sent right in."

Perdita shook her head in wonder at the luxury of it all. There were beeswax tapers in the glass-covered lamps, and plump cushions on the chairs and window seat, and prints of famous hunts hanging on the green-papered walls.

After the servant left, Mrs. Fitzmorris examined them, but

Perdita went to the fire and enjoyed the welcome warmth of it. "Mrs. Croggins would never have wasted fuel on an empty room," she said beneath her breath.

Ravenall gave her a sharp look. "You know nothing of Mrs. Croggins. The Stag and Crown does not exist in your memory. You are a clean slate, Miss Hexham, and I will write your history for you."

"Yes, my lord."

A short time later a knobby maidservant of indeterminate age appeared, with a tankard of ale for Ravenall, a pot of chocolate for the ladies, and several crystal jars of jam that glowed like jewels. She was followed by another carrying a covered dish that proved to hold scrambled eggs, deviled kidneys, and a platter filled with slices of thick bread and cheese, succulent roast fowl, and smoked ham.

"Will there be anything else, my lord?"

Mrs. Fitzmorris stepped forward. Now that they were at the George she was back in her element, and ready to take charge of domestic matters. "Have cans of hot water heated for the bath in Miss Hexham's chamber, and there are clean sheets to be put on the beds in the small trunk. And, if you please, prepare a pan of coals to warm the bed."

The maid wasn't the least bit offended. Members of The Quality often brought their own linens, even though there was no fear of damp sheets at the George. "Yes, madam. Everything will be ready in a twinkling."

Mrs. Fitzmorris frowned. "I believe I shall go up and see that everything is properly disposed, and the sheets warmed. It would not do for Miss Hexham to take a chill! I will take a little tea and toast in my chamber after."

Perdita almost laughed aloud. No one had ever worried about her sleeping on damp sheets at the Stag and Crown. A bed was luxury enough!

When they were alone Ravenall pulled out a chair. "You may lower your hood, Miss Hexham, and apply yourself to the food. I particularly recommend the ham. The George is known for it."

His voice was so nonchalant she relaxed a little. He watched her with a slight frown between his brows. He knew she was hungry, from the way her eyes had grown so large when she'd seen the modest spread. Poor thing, what must her life have been at that squalid inn?

And how would she make the adjustment to her new life? Everything hinged upon it. Ravenall wondered if he'd bitten off more than he could chew, in attempting to turn her into a lady of quality. If she was up to the task.

He only hoped that he was.

Belatedly he realized that she was waiting for him to begin eating. "Ladies first," he told her, and placed a slice of ham and half a chicken breast upon her plate, along with a generous helping of eggs.

Perdita was ravenous and the scents of the food were tantalizing. She tried not to wolf the food down too quickly. But oh! She was so very hungry!

The sweet-bitter tang of the marmalade, the lush flavor and silky texture of the chocolate brought a tiny moan to her lips. Had she ever tasted either before? If so, she had no memory of it.

Perdita was awed by the amount of food set out for such a small party. She was so famished and delighted that she thought she might clean the entre platter herself.

Ravenall frowned. It was plain she'd gone hungry many a time.

When she was full and content, yet another maid in a sprigged dress with a crisp white apron and a lace-edged cap came to lead her away.

Perdita examined her surroundings, trying not to gawk. The sitting room was far grander than anything she'd seen, except in her dreams. The coffered ceilings were high and white, and the windows hung with blue brocade that matched the color of the papered walls. There was even a small desk, fitted out with a blotter, a stationery box, and two crystal inkwells in a silver inkstand.

There was no sign of Mrs. Fitzmorris, but the door on the right was open to another room, where her voice could be heard issuing brisk orders. The maid led Perdita past the sofa and chairs and to another door on the opposite side. "Your chamber, miss."

The bedroom was almost as large as the parlor, and a cheery fire leapt in this room's hearth too. Leather trunks were stacked in one corner. Brushes with silver backs were set out on the bureau. And—joy of joys!—beneath a pale blue tester dripping with white lace, the carved walnut four-poster was larger than the entire tiny attic space where she'd slept the last few years. The feather bed atop it was deep and fluffy as a cloud in high summer, the embroidered lawn wrapper and night rail laid out upon it, as fine as morning mist.

Perdita sighed in happiness. The last of her lingering doubts were fast disappearing.

While she was admiring her lavish surroundings, two buxom girls arrived with cans of hot water and poured them into the copper bath behind a delicately painted screen.

"Shall I help you remove your garments, miss?" one of the hovering chambermaids asked.

Perdita froze. Was this something that was expected of her? She supposed it was. She clearly remembered that Gladys had always helped dear Miss Barnstable with her buttons and corset. But she didn't dare let anyone see the tattered garments she had on, hidden beneath her cloak.

"No! I mean, I will manage myself."

"Very well, miss. Ring if you should be wanting anything."

A bar of lavender soap was produced and a thick drying towel. After a quick check around the room, the chambermaids departed. Although Perdita was tired, nothing in the world, at this moment, could possibly be more seductive to her than the thought of a hot bath in the enormous copper tub.

At Miss Barnstable's, it had been sponge baths with hot water fresh from the hob for every day, and the hip bath twice a month before the kitchen fire. At the Stag and Crown it had been icy water in a bucket from the pump, whenever she could find a few minutes of time. She could have danced with delight. *Oh, to feel clean and fresh again!*

Perdita removed her cloak and draped it over a chair. Her clothes, which had looked woefully shabby before, now looked like cleaning rags in need of a good wash. They were disgusting. Far too awful to leave on one of the velvet-cushioned chairs or the immaculate bed. Stepping out of them hastily, she tossed them on the floor, to one side of the stone hearth.

Steam rose from the water of the polished copper tub and she stepped over the rim and into the scented water. A small cotton bag, tied with a blue ribbon, floated and then sank beside her thigh. Picking it up, Perdita squeezed the wet out and held it to her nose. Lavender and rose petals and something she didn't recognize. She felt like a princess.

It was a moment of pure, sensual bliss: the warm water lapped at her waist and she sank lower, until it just covered the tips of her breasts. The scent of the lavender was so relaxing she could have stayed there till the bath went cold; but the thought of the comfortable bed with the soft linens and downy comforter waiting for her was an even more potent lure. She wouldn't linger too long.

The creamy soap lathered, releasing a rich bloom of lavender scent, as she skimmed it over her skin. It made her think of drowsy, warm days, with the hum of bees threading through the purple blossoms. Of sunlight on dappled leaves. She closed her eyes . . .

It was summer, and bright birdsong came through the open windows. She tiptoed past Cook's broad back, and darted into the pantry. It was the work of a minute to fill the pockets of her white pinafore with heels of bread and the tiny bit of stale cake that were to go into a bread pudding later in the week. If she was seen before she escaped out the door to the kitchen garden, she would get a good scolding; but Cook was busy preparing for the dinner party, and hadn't seen her take them.

The other servants were all a-twitter, and an extra girl had been hired just to slice the vegetables and scale the fish. A mound of them gleamed silver and blue against the white wrapping paper. She slipped past them, with their round, glistening eyes, and hurried out into the sunshine.

Once she passed the neat rows of vegetables, she hurried through the gate to the dovecote, and out to the meadow beyond. She wasn't supposed to be there, which only added to her glee. Chaffinches cocked their heads in the hedges, and the sparrows sang. A colorful butterfly, yellow as its namesake, flitted across the garden beds. After an erratic flight, it came to rest on a spear of fragrant lavender.

Lifting her hand, she held her breath and willed it to come to her. If only she wished hard enough, it would happen. And it did.

The tiny creature alighted on her index finger, and folded its dainty wings. It was a magical moment, filled with joy and wonder . . .

Perdita woke with a start. The garden vanished as the dream faded. She'd never had that dream before. How real it had seemed!

If she closed her eyes, she could see the gleaming fish in the cool shadows of the kitchen, smell the lavender in the garden, and feel the fairy touch of the butterfly upon her skin.

She wondered if it could be a memory, a bit of her past jogged loose.

Then she suddenly realized that the scented water had cooled. Perdita wondered how long she'd dozed in the bath.

She sniffed. Something was burning. Fears of dropped tapers, or hot coals on the carpet—of her threadbare garments left beside the hearth!—had her scrambling up in a hurry.

She rose from the hip bath and peered over the screen. She reached for the drying cloth—and knocked the folding screen over instead. Perdita froze in place.

There was no fire in the room except in the hearth, and it was her discarded clothing burning merrily there. Ravenall was standing before it, busily feeding strips of Perdita's torn shift into the flames. The fabric blackened and curled as she watched. Bits of ash rose up the flue on the draft, like dusky moths rising.

"What are you doing? My clothes . . . !"

Ravenall turned at that exact moment. He felt the blood rush from his head to his loins. She stood in the copper tub, with water cascading off her skin. The drops beading looked like golden spangles in the firelight. In those few, long seconds of surprise he took in the shapely curve of her breasts, the delicate span of her waist, and the womanly flare of her hips.

She felt his hot gaze on her. A shiver danced over her skin, as if it were his strong, shapely hands that grazed her flesh instead. She crossed her arms over her breasts, feeling the heat rush to her skin. Ravenall snatched up the fallen cloth and handed it to her, averting his face; but not before she saw the astonishment in his eyes replaced by a dark flush of desire that colored his cheeks.

"Cover yourself," he said brusquely, and righted the screen. Righting the screen, he turned quickly back to his task of feeding her garments into the fire, but he was not as controlled as he appeared.

He was a connoisseur of beautiful women, and had known that she would have a remarkable figure beneath her shabby clothing. But he had not been prepared to see it revealed, and so stunningly. Her breasts were perfect, tip-tilted and as round and white as globe flowers, and the soft line of her hips and thighs enough to drive a man mad.

As he reached in too close, a flame nipped at his fingers, but even that could not burn away the image of her that was seared now in his memory. He had no doubt at all that it would return to haunt him in the days and nights ahead.

Perdita was mortified, and all her fingers seemed to have turned into thumbs. She almost dropped the towel. Shivering violently, more from reaction than cold, she pulled it around her without stepping out of the tub first. The edge of the hem floated in the water as she splashed out of it, then clung to her legs in wet folds as she stood dripping on the floor.

"My clothes . . ." she said again.

"You won't be needing them."

Fear shook her. She snatched up the embroidered gown laid out upon the spread, and hastily donned it. The fabric was soft as a whisper. It settled over her head easily enough, but stuck to her wet breasts and back and to her slim flanks. Perdita prayed he wouldn't turn around while she wrestled with it. Then she realized he could see her just as easily in the oval mirror above the mantelpiece. Their eyes met in the looking glass and her heart stuttered and skipped a beat.

She put the wrapper on, as well, and did up the matching pearl buttons—glad the width of the bed was between herself and Ravenall. He came forward.

"Not another step closer, my lord!" Her hand closed on a heavy brass candlestick.

"Calm yourself, Miss Hexham. I am not in the habit of visiting unmarried women at their baths. I heard voices from Mrs. Fitzmorris's room, and thought you were in the chamber with her, or I should never have intruded here."

He fixed her with a tight smile. "In future, turn the key in the lock, Miss Hexham. It might spare us both a good deal of embarrassment!"

Ravenall left without a backward glance. Perdita locked the

door behind him with a satisfying click, but she could not lock away the heat, the aching need that surged through her. She understood now what had drawn Sukey out the attic window to meet Rafe in the starry glade. She knew then that Ravenall had power over her in ways she had never suspected.

What would it be like to be his lover?

She stood there trembling, long after he was gone.

Eleven

"The crowning touch, Miss Hexham!"

Perdita waited anxiously while Mrs. Fitzmorris fixed pearl eardrops at her lobes, and fastened a matching lavaliere at her throat. While she'd dressed, Perdita had learned only that Mrs. Fitzmorris was a young widow and resided quietly in Bath.

"You may look now," the other woman announced. "I do hope you'll be pleased," she said with the assurance of one who believed her taste was unerring.

Perdita rose from the low chair and turned toward the mirror—and saw an elegant stranger looking back at her.

She could find no fault with the outfit of fawn merino heavily trimmed with black cording, beneath which were embroidered garments so fine that she had been afraid her rough hands would snag the fabric.

The color of the dress made her skin seem creamier, her cheeks rosier, and her eyes brighter. Mrs. Fitzmorris had dressed Perdita's dark hair in a soft knot at the crown, and teased masses of ringlets to fall on either side. It changed her appearance dramatically.

So this is Miss Hexham, Perdita thought. *So elegant and proper. I wonder what her . . . what* my *Christian name might be? Surely something formal and grand. Augusta? God forbid, Hortense?*

She smiled feebly at her unspoken jest, and saw the young lady in the looking glass smile back warmly. It was difficult to reconcile her reflection with her sense of self.

Mrs. Fitzmorris cocked her head. "Ravenall judged your figure accurately."

Perdita flushed. It was true. The outfit was exactly right, except for the kid slippers, which were a trifle large. They'd stuffed the toes with bits of silver tissue paper.

"If you've preened enough, Miss Hexham? We mustn't keep Lord Ravenall waiting," her companion said in her astringent way. "Here is your bonnet. No, no!" she chided. "You are not a kitchen maid on her way to market. Do not tie the strings under your chin but beneath one ear, like this. Ah, that is better. Now, turn as I do."

Perdita swirled in front of the mirror, and watched the soft fabric flow around her. Any last qualms over her decision died then: she was warm, fed, and clothed in the height of fashion. And she was safe.

Hadn't Lord Ravenall given her his word?

She held her arms as her companion did, and tilted her head at the same aloof angle. Mrs. Fitzmorris watched Perdita closely. "You're a quick study, I'll grant you that. You've a natural talent for mimicry. It will stand you in good stead."

Picking up her reticule, she handed Perdita a pair of elegant tan kid gloves. "Put these on."

"But we are only going down to the parlor. I don't need gloves."

Mrs. Fitzmorris fixed her with a steely eye. "You must trust me to be the judge of what is acceptable in a young lady of quality! You will wear them at all times in public, even while eating."

Perdita's jaw dropped. "But . . . how *silly*! They'll become soiled."

"Don't be impertinent! There are many things of which you are ignorant, Miss Hexham, and you must learn to trust me. Gloves will hide the roughness of your hands. For another, they are *de rigueur*. No lady would consider herself dressed without them. If you fail in your attempt to storm society, it will be on your head, not because I have not instructed you in the things every young lady must know."

She slipped her own smooth white hands into a fresh pair of dove-colored gloves. "Are you ready, Miss Hexham?"

Although there were butterflies dancing inside her, Perdita felt a spark of mischief, too. When she answered, her tones were round and clear—and a very good imitation of the other woman's voice and manner. "Yes, Mrs. Fitzmorris," she said grandly, "I believe that I am, indeed!"

Her companion smiled coolly and opened the door. "A parrot can do as well, Miss Hexham."

Feeling more than a little deflated, Perdita followed her out of the room and down to their private parlor. The hem of her skirt whispered along the staircase behind her, and she felt like a princess. A very nervous princess. As her slippers touched the last step, Perdita's heart beat as though it would burst.

The moment of truth was at hand.

Mrs. Fitzmorris nodded at the door, and Perdita turned the polished handle. Ravenall was sprawled in a chair before the fire, a glass of brandy on the table beside him. He glanced up casually when the door opened, then abruptly rose to his feet. It had taken him a few seconds to recognize his protegé.

Even the way she held her head and carried herself was different, as if she'd slipped into a new skin instead of a change of garments. He knew then that he'd made the right decision: she was a born actress.

And she was stunning.

He made her a sweeping bow. "Your servant, Miss Hexham."

She almost bobbed him a curtsy, as if she were still a serving girl at the Stag and Crown. Instead she inclined her head, as Mrs. Fitzmorris had coached her to do, swept back her skirts and bent her knees in the proper gesture of respect from a young lady to one of the great earls of the land.

Ravenall's eyebrows lifted. He smiled past Perdita to where her companion stood in the shadows, beside the closed door. Perdita noticed the intimacy beneath their words, the secret way they seemed to exchange signals.

"My compliments, Fanny. You've accomplished a minor miracle."

Mrs. Fitzmorris smiled thinly. "It was an easy enough task. Miss Hexham is a beauty, and will no doubt become all the rage once she appears on the London scene."

The table was set for a late luncheon and steaming dishes awaited them beneath polished covers. Perdita's mouth watered. So much food! Again!

Mrs. Fitzmorris crossed the room, and Ravenall pulled the chairs away from the table for the ladies. "Pray be seated."

That was Perdita's first obstacle. She couldn't manage her skirts. Curved chair legs and her own slender legs tangled in the fabric. The too-large slippers added to the problem, and she pitched forward. She would have fallen, if not for Ravenall's strong hand on her arm.

"There is more work to being a lady than I realized," Perdita sighed.

Ravenall quelled her with a look. "Miss Hexham of Hexham Court was born a lady. You would do well to remember it. I won't always be at your side to remind you of your lapses!"

Mrs. Fitzmorris was chagrined. "I should have had her practice while we were still in the bedchamber. Watch me, Miss Hexham, and do as I do."

With a graceful motion of her hand, she swept her skirts aside and took her chair. Perdita's imitation was not nearly as skilled, but at least it was partially successful. She got it on the second try.

Ravenall lifted his eyebrows. "You are an apt pupil, Miss Hexham."

She felt a flush rise up in her cheeks. "I only hope I may learn all my lessons as easily."

The meal was slightly strained. Neither Perdita nor Ravenall could forget the incident of the fallen screen earlier that morning. She could scarcely meet his eyes, while he couldn't seem to tear his gaze from her. Perdita was ravenous, and wanted to fall on the thick roast beef and fricassee of chicken, but restrained herself. Instead she watched Mrs. Fitzmorris, and imitated her every move. The fork was held just so in her companion's dainty hand, the other resting elegantly in her lap. Perdita didn't think she'd ever acquire the knack of carrying on light conversation at the same time. She turned her attention to the excellent food and made short work of it.

She was about to clean her plate when Mrs. Fitzmorris cleared her throat. "A lady," she said icily, "always leaves something on her plate."

Perdita was aghast. "A waste of good food!"

"Nevertheless, my dear girl . . ."

Sighing, Perdita set down her fork. Ravenall laughed at her. "There are a good many rules of society which you will find irksome. That will surely be the least of them."

"I have gone to bed hungry too many times—"

He stopped her with a gesture. "*Miss Hexham,*" he said coolly, "has never gone to bed hungry in her life."

She met his intent gaze. "I understand you, my lord."

"Excellent. Now that you are finished, will you take a stroll with me? The sun is warm, and there is a fine walk along the cliffs."

Perdita wiped her gloves carefully. "I suppose so."

Mrs. Fitzmorris leaned forward. *"I should be pleased to walk with you, Lord Ravenall."*

Perdita gritted her teeth. She took a deep breath. "I should be pleased to walk with you, Lord Ravenall."

He gave her a smile so dazzling it made her giddy.

"Good girl." He bowed to Mrs. Fitzmorris. "Fanny, you have worked a miracle!"

Ravenall offered Perdita his arm, and she placed her gloved fingers on it, very aware of the masculine strength beneath the fabric of his coat.

It was a fine afternoon and several others were promenading along the well-trod paths lined with seashells. Two young women passed by with an older companion. All three quickly averted their eyes from Ravenall's scarred countenance.

Perdita was angry on his behalf, but he gave the appearance of not having noticed. She followed his lead. He escorted her some distance from the George. "There is something I wish to show to you, Miss Hexham."

Once they were away from the shelter of the inn, the wind was strong. It whipped at her fashionable skirts, and it took her a few yards to get the hang of walking in them in so stiff a breeze. She put a hand to her bonnet.

Ravenall scanned the sky. "The Channel will be choppy today," he said as he led her up a gentle slope of grass.

They crested it, and Perdita found herself gazing breathlessly out over the wide, silvery stretch of water that separated England from France. She was glad that her hand was nestled in the crook of Ravenall's arm. The ground at her feet fell off suddenly in sheer cliffs to the sea. Another few steps and she would have set foot on nothing but air.

The scene was wild and beautiful. Combing waves ran up the sandy shore in the green coves far below, and a ship rode the swells beyond the frothy breakers. In her days on Dartmoor she had sometimes glimpsed the sea from the top of Giant's Tor, a faded line of blue on the far horizon. To see the vastness of it stretching away until it merged with the cloudless azure horizon robbed her of speech.

"Well?" Ravenall said finally.

"It is astounding. I have never been this close to the sea before," she murmured.

"No," he said sharply, "you are wrong. Look to your right."

She turned and saw what the edge of her parasol had hidden: a charming town interspersed with treed hillsides, sloping down to a harbor sheltered by the crook of a seawall. Dozens of vessels of all sizes and colors bobbed on the blue water like a flock of seabirds, most with their sails tightly furled.

"Why, there must be hundreds of them!" she exclaimed. "I have never seen the like!"

"You are in error, Miss Hexham." A small smile of private amusement lit Ravenall's eyes. "This entire scene is familiar to you."

She sent him a questioning look. "That," he went on, "is the town of Lyme Regis you see spread out below, and that harbor and seawall are known as The Cobb. Your parents hired a house just outside Lyme Regis. It is there that you were staying when your nurse carried you off. In the next few days you will grow to know it quite well."

The wind caught at the brim of her bonnet playfully once again, but she ignored it. Something about the scene was intensely familiar. Perdita concentrated. Images unfolded: a towering stone wall with tiny steps set into its steep sides; the lap of tiny wavelets edged with lacy foam. Half of a dull black seashell which, when turned over, revealed a smooth side as sleek and shimmery as gray satin.

As quickly as they'd come, they faded. Perdita fought to hold on to them. Were they scenes from a book? A vaguely recalled dream?

Or were they bits of true memory?

She looked at Ravenall, her eyes shining. "I . . . I think I remember something of it now."

He smiled wryly. "I am sure you do."

His eyes grew opaque as he frowned down at her. She felt as if a shutter had been thrown closed. "Why do you look at me so strangely, my lord?"

"Was I doing so? Forgive me. I wasn't aware of it," Ravenall said. "We haven't much time. Listen well: for the past seven years you have lived a retired life with two elderly maiden ladies. Sisters, by the name of Trewethey. You were brought to them by your nursemaid, who had been in service there. Recent illness had erased your memory. Your garments, although muddy and ripped, were of the finest quality. The nurse—Agnes Redd was her name, by the by—claimed that you were an orphan, gently bred, but penniless and without a soul in the world to take you in and offer you a roof over your head."

The quantity of information he threw at her made her head reel. Perdita tried to absorb it. "And where is this nursemaid now?"

"Do not interrupt." He regarded her steadily. "Most conveniently for our purposes, Agnes Redd vanished, never to be seen again. Miss Trewethy and Miss Abigail Trewethy took you in and raised you as their own."

"Generous of them!" Perdita exclaimed. "Do you think this story will hold water?"

"Don't be pert! It isn't becoming."

"Forgive me, my lord." She glanced down, flushing. "It is just that I am so overwhelmed."

"You need not be. Only do as I say, and all will go well."

Perdita watched a bird seem to fly straight into the cliff below them. She realized it must have its nest on one of the precarious ledges. Her own future seemed to be built out of sticks and thin air, as well.

"What of the two spinsters? I suppose they have conveniently vanished, also?"

She expected him to be displeased, but Ravenall smiled. "I see you've gone before me. Alas, the two sisters died peacefully—and recently—within days of one another. The cottage was put up to be sold—and my cousin Andrew Waverly came to see if it would suit him. You can see the hand of fate at work," he said dryly.

More like the mind of Lord Ravenall, she thought. *And what a thorough and inventive one it is!*

His cynical smile widened. She flushed, aware that he knew exactly what she was thinking.

Ravenall continued smoothly. "My story is soon told: when he saw the mark on your wrist and heard your history, he realized the connection, and wrote at once to me. And that, my dear Miss Hexham, is how you came to be traveling with Mrs. Fitzmorris, on your eventual way to Ravenall Castle!"

Perdita's thoughts were racing. "Will his story be believed?"

The question startled Ravenall. He stared at her a moment, then laughed softly. "Waverly is a gentleman of unimpeachable reputation. His credibility is unquestioned. And with my acknowledgment of you as my ward, no one will dare to say otherwise."

Perdita sighed. He was right, of course. No one would challenge the Earl of Ravenall. Certainly not she.

Ravenall stopped and took her chin in his hand. "You are tired and perhaps a little disheartened by having to take in so much, in so short a time. You must learn to rejoice in your good fortune," he admonished her, "and remember to hold your head up high. You are, after all, Miss Hexham of Hexham Court! That is not a small thing."

Guilt rendered her mute. Perdita felt her color rise beneath Ravenall's regard. When she had grasped at this chance, her only thought had been of escaping the greed and cruelty of Mrs. Croggins, and a chilling future.

There had been no time to really consider the matter, to even begin to grasp the difficulty of the task before her. Her skin grew clammy with fatigue and anxiety. What if she were found out as an imposter? What would happen to her then?

She had returned kindness with deceit. That was surely a sin of major proportions. *But,* a small voice inside her said, *there truly was no choice. And what is the real harm in it?*

Ravenall frowned at her continued silence. "Do you have second thoughts? It is too late. You have embarked on a journey of discovery, and the only way from here is forward."

"I understand, my lord. But it is a path I never thought to travel. I am woefully ignorant of how to go about it."

He gave her hand a light squeeze. "You have already taken the first steps. Even your pattern of speech has changed. I doubt that 'woefully ignorant' is something you had much call to say to anyone at the Stag and Crown."

Perdita laughed. "No, although I did *think* it on occasion."

"Only on occasion? From what Andrew and Danes told me of the landlady there, I find your restraint commendable."

His sally surprised her into laughter. It took a moment for

the rest of it to sink in. "Then you have no recall of the events following your injury?"

"Only isolated recollections," he replied curtly, "like something from an evil dream. I have no wish to delve deeper."

It is an odd coincidence, she decided, *that I am trying so hard to remember my past, and Lord Ravenall is trying to forget.*

They walked a little way along the cliffs, with the sea breeze fresh off the water. "I've noticed how you watched Mrs. Fitzmorris at breakfast, and adopted her mannerisms. You will do well to use her as your model in the weeks ahead."

"Yes. She is every inch the fine lady."

Once again that spark of wry humor showed in his eyes. "She will instruct you in everything you need to know. You must learn it all, until it is second nature. Do you understand me?"

She did. Unless she was found out, she would step into another young woman's identity, assume an entirely different way of life. The self she knew would vanish like mist on the moors, as if it had never been.

She would be absorbed.

Squaring her shoulders, Perdita met him gaze for gaze. "Yes, my lord. There is no turning back from this moment. The past is gone, and there is only the present and the future."

He gave her a smile of encouragement. It warmed his harsh face, and made her heart skip a beat.

"Good girl! We'll see this through yet."

A seabird cried overhead, and they paused to watch it skim through the air, and swoop over the cliffs and down toward the cresting waves. She was glad of the diversion. Being so close to him, feeling the strength of his arm beneath her hand, made it difficult for her to concentrate. They stood in companionable silence, watching the whitecaps hurl themselves against The Cobb.

Gradually she became aware that his gaze rested on her profile, not on the restless waves. A flush rose up from her throat. *What is he thinking? Who does he see when he looks at me?*

The world at large might accept her as Miss Hexham, of Hexham Court. She suspected that no matter how elegantly she spoke and dressed, he would always think of her as the poor wretch from the Stag and Crown, in an overlarge and mended dress.

"We should turn back, Miss Hexham," he said at last.

She slanted a look up at him from beneath her angled parasol. "May I know my Christian name, sir?"

"Of course. It is Pauline. However, I believe it would be wise to continue with the one you already claim. We shall say it was given you as a pet name. That way you are less likely to slip up. And," he added, "it suits the story."

So, there will still be a little something of me left, after all! Tears stung her eyes. "Thank you, my lord."

At his signal a man who had been standing some distance away joined them. She recognized him by his russet hair, and green eyes in a deeply tanned face. The man called Jack. She'd seen him in groom's garb on the moors, then at the inn, and now dressed in the height of fashion.

At the present he wore a dark green jacket, buckskin riding breeches, and top boots. An onyx ring was on one finger, a gold seal fob hung from the chain of his watch, and he had the assured walk of a gentleman. All of which meant he was not a servant at all.

"You've met before, but haven't been properly introduced," Ravenall said. "Let me make Mr. Malone known to you, Miss Hexham. He is an old friend of mine, from the West Indies."

Jack bowed. "Your servant, Miss Hexham."

Ravenall turned to Perdita. "I am leaving you and Fanny—Mrs. Fitzmorris—under his protection."

He saw the startlement in her eyes. "I assure you that Jack isn't in the habit of climbing in and out of inn windows or helping me to spirit young girls away in the dark hours of the night. You can trust him with anything you value, including your life. There is no better man I know."

She felt a catch of panic in her chest. "I thought that you were our escort, and that London was our destination."

He frowned. "I see there has been a misunderstanding: I go to London, Miss Hexham. *You*, however, will remain at the George for some time while Mrs. Fitzmorris tutors you in how you should go on."

Her chin lifted in that stubborn way he was starting to know. "I do not wish to remain at this inn, splendid as it is, my lord. I wish to go to London."

"How unfortunate for you," he said. "Your wishes do not come into it." She recoiled at the sting in his words. Ravenall's face softened a little. "Credit me with some intelligence, as I do you. There is no way that you could pass as a gently bred lady, without studying how a lady conducts herself more thoroughly. How she moves, and speaks, and passes her time."

She bit her lip. "Can I not do that in London?"

"Under the watchful eye of the *ton*? I think not!" Ravenall touched her cheek. "You must learn to dance and to ride. You must polish your speech, and memorize French phrases—"

"French!"

Laughing at her dismay, he continued without losing a beat: ". . . to curtsy and flirt behind your fan, and give impertinent gentlemen the set-downs they deserve."

"I think," she said with a cool look, "that I would like to learn that last one, most especially."

Jack, who had been listening in silence, gave a bark of laughter. "She's got you there!"

"Yes, an excellent setdown," Ravenall said admiringly.

He paused, considering. "I think that should be your style, you know: a bold, quick retort, barbed with humor. Then people will assume it is one of your clever remarks, when you say something . . . ah . . ."

"Stupid?" Perdita offered.

"That would be far too harsh a word." The light danced off the water, glinting in the blue depths of his eyes. "Let us say, *ill-considered.*"

A reluctant smile teased the corners of her mouth. "An excellent setdown, my lord."

"I thought so." He took her gloved hand in his. "Come, let us not quarrel. You must spend some time in the 'schoolroom,' if you mean to make a go of this."

She was still unwilling to be left behind. Her face was pale in the sunshine, and her mouth trembled. Ravenall took her other hand, and pressed them both firmly.

"It will not be so bad." Again that hard blue stare raked her face. "Courage, Perdita," he said in a voice so low only she could hear. "You will carry it off splendidly."

He stepped back, still holding one hand, and executed a low bow over it. "*Au revoir, Miss Hexham.*" Without warning he leaned down and kissed her cheek. Perdita knew this moment was etched forever in her mind. She would remember this day, this wild cliff path as long as she lived.

And she would remember Lord Ravenall looking down at her so gravely with the breeze ruffling his dark locks and his blue eyes as dark as a twilit sky.

Ravenall squeezed her hand, then turned and made his way toward the cliff's edge. She watched, unmoving, as he went down the path to the bay until he vanished from view.

And now, she thought, *I must do the same.*

"Are you ready, Miss Hexham?"

She turned to the man beside her. His background still puzzled her. She had first thought him a groom, then a gentleman, and now she wasn't sure of anything—except that Lord Ravenall had told her she might trust him.

"As ready as I will ever be, sir."

Mr. Malone offered her his arm. "Ravenall never fails in anything he tries, you know."

"Never?"

Jack thought of Véronique. "Well, once. But he was young and in love, and very foolish as young men in love tend to be. The world has knocked some sense into him since then."

"Perhaps you won't credit it, but I think I am a little relieved to know that, Mr. Malone."

A smile curved her lips. If she could face Ravenall, and imagine that he had been very foolish—once upon a time— she wouldn't feel quite so intimidated by him.

She realized that Mr. Malone had been speaking to her.

"Forgive me," she said, recovering quickly. "I was not attending to what you were saying."

"A blow to my manly pride!" But he looked concerned. "You've been through a good deal in the past few hours. Perhaps we should return to the George. Mrs. Fitzmorris will be wondering where you are."

"Who *is* Mrs. Fitzmorris?" Perdita blurted.

Jack lifted an eyebrow. *So,* he thought, *that's the way the land lies. How like Ravenall not to explain! What the devil is he up to?*

Aloud he said: "She is a widow of impeccable lineage, and could move in the first circles if she chose. She and Ravenall are very close friends."

"Oh. I see." Perdita's face fell. *His mistress. I should have guessed.*

"He thought it best if no one was brought into this except those absolutely essential to the success of the venture."

Perdita digested this news. She'd wondered why a fine lady such as Mrs. Fitzmorris would be drawn into the earl's scheme and jaunt about the countryside by moonlight. Now it made sense.

"It seems that Lord Ravenall has us all dancing to his piping!"

"Aye, he does. Once he sets out on an adventure, there is no turning back. No matter," he added, "what squalls may blow or where the wind might take him."

"Ruthless, in fact!"

Jack considered that. "Some call him so. I would rather say he is determined."

Perdita realized they were almost at the door. With her gloved hand on her companion's arm, she walked beside him daintily, as Mrs. Fitzmorris had shown her how to do—and though she felt like a fool mincing along instead of walking at her normal brisk pace, she held her head high and kept the wind from snatching her parasol. Whatever had happened in the past was gone: it was the future that mattered now.

She would grasp at the straw Lord Ravenall had given her. Like the miller's daughter in the tale of Rumpelstiltskin, she must take that straw and spin it into gold.

By the time they reached the door, Perdita had made the first uneasy transition in her own mind: she was no longer a poor scullery maid at an obscure country inn—she was Pauline Hexham, heiress of Hexham Court.

And, for good or for ill, the ward of the Earl of Ravenall.

Twelve

Outside the fashionable Bond Street club, the street lamps glowed softly and the sound of carriage wheels on pavement were becoming infrequent. The clock struck, marking the lateness of the hour.

"It is the most amazing thing," Andrew Waverly said to the other members of the club gathered round. "There I was in Somerset, intent on examining a house that was for hire, when I stumbled upon the long-missing heiress."

He accepted another glass of wine from the waiter, and turned the stem between his finger. He wasn't used to prevarication—indeed was very uncomfortable with it—but he would do anything to help his cousin save Ravenall Castle from its creditors.

The other gentlemen listened with emotions ranging from curiosity to intense interest. London was thin of company, and the news of the discovery of a beautiful and wealthy heiress had caused a stir.

Mr. Kirkston raised one eyebrow. "Did you recognize the girl at once, Waverly?"

"No, sir, although I knew Pauline Hexham's sad history."

Old Lord Padden nodded. "I remember it well. The little girl had been abducted by a servant, and was presumed to be dead when no trace of either was ever found."

Andrew turned the stem of his wine glass.

"The searchers expected the nursemaid had taken the girl to London. They looked in the wrong direction." He had their full attention as he spun his story.

Young Lord Stanhope sighed when Andrew was finished.

"A terrible thing. But why did the nurse abduct the girl in the first place?"

"She was extremely attached to the child. After Miss Hexham's parents died, there was talk among the servants that the nurse would be let go, and the girl sent away to boarding school. Evidently this unbalanced her mind. Fearing that she would be separated forever from her orphaned charge, the nursemaid fled with the child."

"Remarkable," someone murmured.

"Poppycock!" Calvin Bridgeforth sauntered up in time to hear it all. Bridgeforth shook his head. "Surely," he drawled, "there is more than one Miss Hexham in England, my dear boy."

A warm flush rose up Andrew's cheeks. "But not, I think, more than one with the mark of the Hexhams on her wrist!"

"What?"

"As clear as if it had been branded there," Andrew vowed. That got Bridgeforth's full attention. "The devil you say!"

Andrew colored, tipped back his glass and took a healthy swallow. "She bears a strong resemblance to her late mother, and the stories match up like two halves of a coin. Even Ravenall is convinced of it."

Lord Stanhope followed the conversation with interest. He was a viscount, young and pleasant-looking, in a rabbity sort of way, with a fine air of address and no fortune at all to recommend him. While he wasn't hanging out for a rich wife, marriage to an heiress would certainly improve his fortunes.

"I say, is she pretty, Waverly?"

Bridgeforth looked down at him through his quizzing glass. "Of course she is, Stanhope. It is well known that *all* heiresses are not only pretty, but ravishingly beautiful."

There was general laughter at his sally. Even Andrew joined in. "So the saying goes. However, Miss Hexham is truly lovely. A dainty thing, with hair like a blackbird's wing, and the most amazing violet eyes it has ever been my pleasure to see."

"Is she in town? Will she be presented at court?" Stanhope asked eagerly. "I hope to meet this paragon as soon as you can introduce me."

"She is not in town," a cool voice said from behind him.

"She is on her way to Ravenall Castle to make the acquaintance of my grandmother."

Ravenall sauntered into the room. "You will meet her when she is presented, Stanhope. However, you may be sure I'll warn her about you before she so much as steps foot in London."

"Unhandsome of you." Stanhope grinned unabashedly. "I was sure you'd want to welcome me into the bosom of your family, Ravenall."

"Were you, indeed? Then I can only suppose you've dipped into the claret a little too freely this evening."

"Alas, no," Stanhope said with a mock sigh. "Although, after your cruel dismissal of my pretensions, I may reconsider the matter."

Calvin Bridgeforth leaned against the mantelpiece. "Then you mean to play the role of guardian very strictly."

Ravenall showed his teeth. "I mean to guard Miss Hexham well. She hasn't been about in society. I won't let her throw herself away upon some gazetted fortune hunter, or," he added pointedly, "some smooth-talking coxcomb, whose tailor makes him."

"I see." Bridgeforth's gaze rested on Andrew. "Perhaps you've already picked out a bridegroom for her. Young Waverly would be ideal. You could keep all that wealth in the family, so to speak!"

Andrew flushed darkly. "When the time comes, I will choose my own bride."

Ravenall turned his back to Bridgeforth and set his glass down. "Do you know," he said smoothly, "I am afraid I may have to resign from this club. They are letting anyone in these days."

The air grew still and tense. Stanhope looked down at his newspaper and Andrew forced himself to keep silent. Bridgeforth was white with anger, but he reined it in.

"You are determined to quarrel with me, Ravenall. I will not play your game."

The earl moved away from his cousin and regarded Bridgeforth steadily. "No, I didn't think you would. But it is a game of your own making." He lowered his voice dangerously. "I warn you now: do not push me too far."

Bridgeforth spun on his heel and exited the salon. The smile was gone from Lord Stanhope's pleasant face. "By God, the man was trying to force you into calling him out!"

"He is too cowardly to do it himself," Ravenall said. "He knows I would be the victor—and he the victim."

"Are you so sure of that, Justin?" Andrew was still pale. "I've heard he's a capital shot, and a good swordsman."

"You wound me, cousin, really you do." The corners of Ravenall's mouth turned up. "I assure you I am much better than he, at both."

Stanhope frowned. "I do not understand why he seems to hate you so."

Ravenall shrugged. "It's no secret. Calvin Bridgeforth and I were both suitors for the hand of the same woman. I won." He brooded a moment. "A Pyrrhic victory, as it turned out. Do you know, it is the only time that Bridgeforth has ever come out the better, in any of our dealings?"

"Good God, Véronique . . . ?" Andrew blurted. A hot flush flooded his cheeks.

Ravenall's smile was strained. "Just so."

He nodded to the others and moved away. A waiter materialized beside Andrew. He set down his empty glass on the silver tray and followed Ravenall. "Forgive me . . . I . . . I didn't know! I didn't mean to revive unhappy memories in such a fashion!"

"Dismiss it from your mind as I have dismissed her from mine." Ravenall's face grew remote. "Véronique! A woman of extraordinary charm and beauty."

A cool smile played over his mouth. "She, also, made the mistake of underestimating me."

"Good Morning, miss. I've brought your tray up early."

Perdita opened her eyes slowly. The maid had opened the heavy draperies while she'd slept, and dawn light slanted across the foot of her bed.

After the maid propped up the pillows and set the tray across Perdita's lap, she dropped a curtsy and left. Perdita fell back against the soft pillows in delight.

Every morning it was the same: she awakened to this beautiful room at the George, this sheer luxury, and was afraid that she was still dreaming beneath the eaves of the Stag and

Crown. Then, when the reality of it all sank in, she was almost overwhelmed by it.

The past three weeks had been intense. She felt as if she'd been swept up by a whirlwind. They'd taken many enjoyable outings—carriage rides down the steeply sloping Broad Street to the Marine Parade, and walks down narrow lanes and through the grassy paths of Langmoor Gardens. They had tea overlooking The Cobb, visited various shops along the parade, and purchased books, ribbons, and tins of sweets.

There had been excursions with Jack Malone to sites of interest, like Buddle Bridge, in the center of the old smuggler's district, and the place where Mary Anning, decades before, had discovered the ancient bones of gigantic dragonlike beasts.

The flat, spiraled fossil shell he'd found and presented to her was tucked away in her jewelry chest, beside a necklet of coral and her precious brooch with the blue stone. Perdita imagined that stone was like the fossil shell, holding within its indigo heart all the locked secrets to her past.

Being a young lady of fashion, however, hadn't been all pleasant walks and tea cakes. From dawn to dusk, Perdita had been playing backward pupil to Mrs. Fitzmorris's strict headmistress.

There was so much that she had never given any thought to: how to walk, how to sit, and how to stand, how to speak—and when to remain silent. How to address servants, how to address one's peers, and how to address one's betters. Even such a seemingly simple thing as the proper way to hold her hands folded in her lap, required much practice.

Perdita gave a fleeting thought to that vanished child whose name and identity she had taken. *I am so sorry. I wish that I knew what really happened to you. And I pray that you will forgive me, for doing what I must to save myself.*

The connecting door opened, and Mrs. Fitzmorris came through, already dressed for travel in an outfit of green wool trimmed with military frogging and smart brass buttons. She looked very young, very pretty and dauntingly sophisticated. She also looked very annoyed. Perdita wondered if she'd been quarreling with Jack Malone again. They couldn't seem to be in the same room without rubbing one another the wrong way.

"Good morning," she said briskly. "I trust you slept well?"

Perdita hesitated only a fraction. "Very well, indeed, Mrs. Fitzmorris. And you?"

She received a nod of acknowledgment. "You did that splendidly." She moved restlessly about the room, making sure that nothing had been missed when Perdita's things were packed up the previous evening.

"I have been thinking the matter over, and decided that you must call me Fanny," Mrs. Fitzmorris said abruptly. "And I shall call you Perdita, if you please. We shall be forever in each other's company, and it would be deemed odd in the circumstances, if we were not seen to be on greater terms of intimacy with one another."

Perdita let out a sigh of relief. "I should like that very much . . . Fanny."

Fanny smiled, and looked much less severe. "Good. I'd advise you to come down for a hearty breakfast when you are dressed. I've just received a note from Mr. Malone, and we will be setting forth within the hour." Her eyes were bright with excitement. "I am so anxious to see Ravenall again."

Perdita choked on her hot chocolate. *I would be, too, if I were the earl's mistress,* she thought. She set her china cup back in its saucer with a little rattle.

Over the past week, Perdita had seen many examples of the strain between her companion and Lord Ravenall's friend. True, Jack Malone had a wry sense of humor, and loved to tweak the widow's sensibilities with it. As for her part, Mrs. Fitzmorris—*no, Fanny!* Perdita reminded herself—was unfailingly polite and depressingly cool to him. It made her very uncomfortable.

She nibbled at her toast. "Lord Ravenall told me that Mr. Malone is the finest man he knows."

She was rewarded with a frosty blue gaze. "Lord Ravenall is also entitled to form *his* own opinions! Finish your toast and chocolate. We've a busy morning ahead of us. Oh, I have something for you. It arrived at the George only this morning with a note from Lord Ravenall."

She went out and came back shortly, with a blue leather box, about the size of a thick book. She set it on the edge of the tray. "Here you are! I have the maid finishing my last-minute packing. I'll send her in to you the moment she's done."

Finishing her chocolate, Perdita set aside the tray and took the box. There was a raised circle in the center and the entwined initials *PH*. Her fingers trembled a bit as she undid the snaps that held it closed, and lifted the lid.

There was a folded note inside:

I found this among your mother's things in storage, and thought that you should like to have it. R.

Perdita put the note aside. The leather box was lined inside with blue moiré taffeta, and a set of brushes and a comb, fashioned of carved ivory, was nestled in fitted compartments. Flowers and butterflies and heavy scrollwork decorated them, with the same initials. It was terribly poignant to see them there, to know that perhaps they had last been used on the day that the girl had vanished.

She picked the brush up gingerly. The warm ivory was as smooth as satin against her skin. Perdita thought of Pauline Hexham's nurse, or perhaps her mother, running the brush through the missing girl's hair. As she did, she could almost feel the tug of the bristles through her own thick locks, the gentle scrape of the comb against her temples. It seemed so real, her scalp prickled.

Sadness overwhelmed her. None of them knew what would happen in time. *But then, not a one of us do!*

Replacing the brush in its fitted place, she closed the lid and fastened it. She wished that Ravenall had never sent it to her.

Jack Malone was waiting for them in the private parlor. "I've already broken my fast," he told them, "and I'll see your trunks and valises safely stowed. I'd advise you to tuck into your food, ladies. It will be many hours before you see the castle and a hot meal set before you again."

Fanny purposely picked at the food she selected, but Perdita eagerly did as he advised. Eggs, rashers of bacon, thick slices of country ham all vanished before her onslaught.

She realized that the widow was eyeing her balefully. "But I have left a portion untouched on my plate, as you instructed me."

"After consuming enough to keep a regiment on the move,

during a forced march! You must learn to curb your voracious appetite, Miss Hexham. It is unseemly."

"Do you think so, Mrs. Fitzmorris?" Jack took another slice of roast beef from the platter. "For myself, I prefer to see a woman enjoy the bounty God gave us, rather than push it about her dish as if she'd been served mealworm stew."

Fanny set her fork down so swiftly it clinked against her plate. "That is disgusting. Furthermore, there is no such thing as mealworm stew."

A twinkle lit the Irishman's eyes. "Do you think so? Perhaps you should ask Lord Ravenall. It is not his favorite dish, nor mine. But I assure you we've both tasted it. More than once."

The widow glared at him frostily. He rose, unfolding his lanky form and bowed. "If you will excuse me, ladies? I'll settle with the landlord, make sure the luggage is secured, and return to escort you to the carriage."

When he left, silence reigned in the private parlor until Perdita could stand it no longer. "He would not make such jokes if you were not so disapproving."

Fanny's shoulders were rigid with indignation. "If there is any one of the three of us who is *not* in need of etiquette lessons, Miss Hexham, I believe that I may safely say that *I* am that person."

Perdita stole another slice of ham from the platter. "I find him amusing, and unfailingly kind," she said, wielding her knife and fork with gusto. "What is there about him that makes you dislike him so?"

"By his own accounts, he is a vagabond and an adventurer. Indeed, I have always suspected that he was to blame for Justin's exile to the West Indies. I will say no more on the subject."

Perdita was curious. "Mr. Malone said that he and Lord Ravenall have sailed round the world together."

"So they did." Fanny sighed and collected herself with an effort. "I very much fear that, at heart, they are two of a kind."

Then, Perdita thought guiltily, *there are three of us!*

Jack drove the open carriage with Perdita and Fanny beside him, parasols raised against the sun. Their luggage—including all the purchases they had made for Perdita's wardrobe in town—had already gone on ahead. She didn't know why she needed half so many, or where she hoped to wear them.

Once away from the George, Jack didn't take the route that led inland, but drove them along the cliffs, with a fine view. The wind was fresh and clean and the English Channel an incredible periwinkle blue, fading to deepest sapphire in the distance. Sunbeams danced on its surface, bright as a mermaid's treasure of gold and silver coins.

Eventually their route turned inland, and they followed an obscure lane that wended its way down to the sea. A sleek vessel rode the waves just inside the cove, as graceful in her element as a bird in air. Perdita was enchanted. She shaded her eyes with her hand against the dazzle as they came out at the base of the cliffs. The track ended at a beach of fine white sand.

"Ah, I see he kept his word," Fanny murmured.

Perdita turned her head and her heart gave a little lurch. Lord Ravenall was there on the strand beside a dinghy. Even with his body in profile she recognized him.

He moved with smooth athletic grace, and she felt a flush rise up her cheeks, as she remembered the sinewy contours of his naked limbs as he'd lain so still beneath the sheets after his accident. It came back to her vividly: the candlelight outlining the sculpted muscles of his wide chest and shoulders as she'd bathed away his fever in the long vigils of the night. The long, tapering lines of his back beneath her work-worn hands.

The heat and scent of him.

He strode over to her while Fanny directed the removal of some bandboxes. His face was bronzed by sun and wind and his eyes were bluer than she remembered.

The memories that assaulted her were so potent, Perdita was sure he could read it in her eyes. She had to fight to keep from averting her face.

Ravenall's eyes were hard and appraising. "Good morning, Miss Hexham. You don't look very pleased to see me."

Her blush deepened. "I didn't expect to see you, my lord. I thought you still in London."

"My business there is completed. For now."

"I am glad."

Ravenall's eyes narrowed. Her heart skipped a beat, but it was too late to retract her words.

"If not for you," she amended, "I should still be cleaning pots and slopping hogs on Dartmoor."

"No, you would not! You would be living at Rosemont Cottage, and mourning the two spinsters who raised you," he said severely.

Perdita sighed. It was the first slip she'd made in days, but a major one.

Ravenall looked down at her, taking in her trim figure in the navy and white nautical outfit with its row of small brass buttons. Her wide violet eyes sparkled in the clear light, and her skin was as perfect as a rose petal. *A little beauty, in fact! If she plays her part well, she will take London by storm.*

The story he'd concocted of the "discovery" of Miss Hexham had already made the rounds of the fashionable drawing rooms, and the first part of her transformation was complete, thanks to Fanny. The rest of Perdita's education would be in his hands. Originally, he'd deemed it an onerous task. At the moment he was rather looking forward to it.

"Mrs. Fitzmorris has done a marvelous job in creating the surface illusion of a young lady of quality," he said. "If anything betrays you it will be a lapse in conversation such you just let slip."

"I will remember, my lord." She turned her face to the vessel riding at anchor with the swells. There was nothing else in sight. "Why were we brought here, my lord?"

He glanced out to the vessel riding the waves beyond the clear green waters of the cove. His features seemed softer, younger, as he looked out to sea.

"I've come to escort you aboard the *Raven*. It's a fine day for sailing!"

"I have never been aboard a ship before."

Ravenall smiled. "Not a ship, Miss Hexham. A yacht."

"I will learn," she said earnestly.

He touched her cheek. "You'll do very well, my dear."

She felt her senses swim with sensations that were new to her. She feared him just a little, yet longed for his company, and desperately hoped for his approval. But his nearness confused her thoughts and the fluttering responses of her body added to it.

He was her rescuer, but could dash her down as easily as he had raised her up in the world. Her fate, quite literally, was in his hands. Perdita could not be totally at ease with it.

Jack and Fanny joined them. Malone shook hands with Ravenall. "Everything is right and tight. I'll say Godspeed, and be on my way, then."

"Very well. I'll expect you at the castle by month's end."

"I've no wish to intrude on your hospitality, my lord."

Ravenall's jaw tightened. "Then I'll have to come fetch you by the scruff of your collar and drag you back willy-nilly. My grandmother has expressed a great desire to make your acquaintance."

The other man grinned. "And so she will, God save her. I'll be putting up in the neighborhood, my lord, and will pay a call upon the dowager countess at the earliest opportunity!"

Fanny looked startled. "You do not accompany us, Mr. Malone?"

Jack swept them a bow. "His lordship has business for me elsewhere. This is, alas, where I must take my leave of you, ladies. May fortune smile upon you, Miss Hexham." The look he gave Fanny was more constrained. Another bow. "Until we meet again, madam."

"Thank you for your escort, Mr. Malone," she replied coolly. There was a slight pause. "I look forward to seeing you at Ravenall."

To Perdita's surprise, he flushed beneath his tan. "Do you, indeed?"

There was faint color in the young widow's cheeks. "Lord Ravenall will take it very unkindly, you know, if you do not avail yourself of his invitation."

The corners of Jack's mouth turned wry. "Ah, yes. I mustn't offend the earl," he said abruptly, and gave Ravenall a deep, mocking bow.

"Be damned to you, Jack," Ravenall said with a careless laugh. "Enough of this, or we'll lose the tide."

The two men moved away toward the carriage. When Jack drove off, Perdita sighed. "I wish he might have come with us now," she said wistfully.

"Have you formed a *tendre* for Mr. Malone?" Fanny asked sternly. "It will not do, you know!"

Perdita was startled. "Whatever do you mean?"

"He's a handsome fellow, I must allow, but quite beneath your touch. He hasn't a feather to fly with. You must seek far higher for a husband, Miss Hexham. I cannot advise you to throw yourself away on a penniless adventurer, charming rogue though he may be."

Perdita slanted a look at her companion. "From vagabond adventurer to charming rogue, all in the course of one morning."

"I may not approve of Mr. Malone," Fanny said coolly, "however, I am not blind. I can see the appeal he would have to a young and inexperienced girl. But if you think Ravenall will let you throw your cap over the windmill for Jack Malone, you're mistaken, indeed. He would make you a poor husband."

"I assure you, a husband is the furthest thing from my mind!"

"Really?" The light blue eyes regarded Perdita steadily. "Has no one captured your heart yet?"

Perdita could feel herself blushing rosily. "It still beats within my breast, unclaimed."

Her companion adjusted her bonnet. "Then that is all right. You still have much to see of the world, my dear Miss Hexham. Your life to this point has not been easy. It would be no wonder if you decide to enjoy it before settling down."

Ravenall returned and rowed them out to where the *Raven* rested at anchor. The yacht was much larger than it had appeared from the strand, and she rode the waves proudly. Brass fittings winked in the sunshine, and the waves threw dancing water lights against the sleek white hull.

"Oh, beautiful!" Perdita said beneath her breath.

"Isn't she?" Ravenall pulled on the oars, and she could see the muscles of his arms and shoulders bunching beneath his jacket.

"Look," Mrs. Fitzmorris cried out. "An osprey!"

The shadow of the bird streaked over them. "A happy omen for our short voyage," Ravenall said. "Our family associates them with good fortune. There is a legend that as long as the osprey nests on the turret above the battlements, the castle will never fall."

Perdita watched the bird until it became a tiny speck, disappeared against the bright blue sky. She hoped the good fortune would extend itself to her.

Once aboard the yacht, Ravenall and Fanny moved a little apart from her, and talked in low tones as the crew went about their business.

The sails unfurled in a rustle and snap of canvas, and the wind filled them. The *Raven* weighed anchor and moved swiftly out to sea. The great cliffs shrank and blurred with distance. They passed The Cobb, where dozens of vessels bobbed on the waves. Soon they, and the neat wooded town of Lyme Regis, vanished altogether. There was nothing but the creak of wood, the hum of the wind, and the soothing hiss of the hull through the water.

The rest of the world had ceased to exist.

Perdita was fascinated. To her, this skimming across the sea was more magical than her transformation from scullery maid to aspiring debutante. The vast stretch of water was even more amazing viewed from the yacht, than from the cliffs. Although the complete opposite of Dartmoor's high, rocky fastness, there was the same sense of wildness and power to its liquid rhythms. In the brilliant light, it glittered like shattered glass.

Fanny joined her and Perdita looked up. By the green-tinged pallor of her companion's face, and the desperate way her gloved hands clenched the rail, Fanny took little joy in sailing.

"You are ill. Let me help you go below and—"

"No!" the widow said between clenched teeth.

"But surely—"

"Believe me when I say that my only hope is staying above-decks in the fresh air as long as possible, and clinging like a barnacle to this rail."

"You dislike sailing intensely, and I think that you don't like me very well, either," Perdita ventured. "Why have you put yourself to such discomfort on my behalf?"

"I don't know you well enough to either like or dislike you," her companion said, raising one delicate hand to her brow. Her skin looked clammy. "However, your speech is far too bold for a girl who has supposedly not been out in Society!"

Perdita eyed her companion straightly. "All our conversations have been this way, Fanny. You know everything there is to know about me. In return I have learned only how to address the servants, the various degrees of respect—or lack of it—in a lady's bows and curtsies, and which topics I must avoid at all costs."

"This is one of those topics!"

Lifting her chin, Perdita fixed her violet gaze on the woman's face. "And you still haven't answered my question. That seems far more rude to me than my 'speaking boldly,' as you put it."

Fanny struggled with an angry retort. Good breeding won out. "For myself, I have no desire to re-enter Society, nor am I at all eager to sponsor a young woman whose reappearance in the polite world is as liable to spark scandal as it is interest. I am doing this for Justin," she said. "For Lord Ravenall."

Perdita looked out over the water. "You must care for him very much."

"I do." The widow turned to her with a sharp look in her pinched face. "But that is another question you should not ask of someone who is almost a stranger to you. Which," she added in a shaky voice, "is something a true lady should know instinctively."

Despair blossomed in Perdita's bosom.

She could look the part and hopefully act the part, but it was not a world in which she was used to move. Every day she'd struggled through newspapers filled with unfamiliar words and bewildering names and places which she had to memorize and discuss during dinner. Thus far the "discussions" hadn't been a roaring success. The specter of disaster loomed large.

"I don't understand why I have to go to London," Perdita said quietly. "I have thought it over. It would be much easier to conduct myself properly if I didn't have to face that hurdle. I would be perfectly happy to live a retired life, snug and secure at Hexham Court."

"It is every female's duty to marry advantageously and produce children," Fanny said bitterly.

Perdita's ears pricked up. "You sound as though you are quoting someone."

The widow eyed her sharply. "It is accepted knowledge among ladies of our class."

"I have been rude again. Forgive me." Perdita's eyes flashed with frustration. "I seem to lack the ability to make polite conversation. I am either too bold, or too uninformed in my opinion."

Fanny's face softened. For the first time she looked. at her young companion as if she were a person, and not a project undertaken unwillingly.

"You must learn not to blurt out the first thing that enters your head. If the conversation turns to matters where you are ignorant," she advised, "you must flutter your eyelashes and say that you 'know nothing of such things, and leave them to wiser heads' than yours."

Perdita arched a brow. "Good God! I would rather be taken for a fool!"

"Nonsense. It will serve you well in almost any occasion. The men, of course, will be flattered, and the women will think you very well brought up. A female of fashion must never be taken for a bluestocking. That would be quite fatal to your chances!"

"No one could possibly make that mistake," Perdita said with conviction.

Fanny smiled shakily. There was more mettle in her young charge than she'd imagined, and a lively if unchallenged intelligence.

"We'll have you up to the rig well before you make your debut. You must remember that most young ladies of your station will be every bit as uninformed about Acts of Parliament and foreign affairs as you. *I* certainly was at your age. My head was filled with nothing but ball gowns and dance cards."

That was the closest thing to a confidence she'd shared.

"You cannot be much older than I," Perdita replied.

"I am eight-and-twenty," her companion said quietly. "My father married me almost out of the schoolroom to Mr. Fitzmorris, when I was sixteen. I was forced to grow up quickly."

From the tone of her remarks, Perdita gathered the marriage had not been a happy one. She wondered if that was part of the reason for the young widow's cool demeanor, or if she had always been aloof and remote.

The yacht rose on a sudden swell, and Fanny bit her lip. "I believe I shall go below and take a medicinal draught. Pray that I sleep until we make land-fall!" With an abrupt little movement, she turned and walked back toward the stern. Perdita watched her pick her way past the neat coils of rope as gingerly as if they were serpents.

For the first time she felt sympathy and a common bond with her companion. She had imagined that Fanny's life had been an easy one, all the bumps smoothed out by position and breeding. Perdita realized that she had been wrong: beneath Fanny's elegantly invincible façade, lay both passion and pain.

She sighed, realizing once more how little she knew of the people who surrounded her. Unlike Sukey and Mrs. Croggins, who chattered and scolded like magpies, and who never had a thought they failed to utter aloud, Lord Ravenall and Fanny were reserved. Even secretive.

The earl could be both cool and distant, and yet Perdita sensed restless emotions beneath his controlled surface. Depths as complex and compelling, as powerful as the sea itself.

She shook her head. *It is too splendid a day, too great a thrill to be sailing swiftly through the waves, to brood about either one of them.* Instead she cleared her mind of all thought, and watched the seabirds swoop and dart like silver arrows, over the ultramarine sea.

She took a chair that was placed for her, and whiled away the hours with a blanket over her knees and *Mrs. Cotterley's Etiquette for Young Ladies* open on her lap, unread.

As far as the eye could see, the water shimmered like a jeweled mosaic in every shade of blue and silver, green and gold. It paved the way to Ravenall Castle: journey's end—but the beginning of her new life.

Her stomach clenched. She wished again that Jack Malone had come aboard the yacht. She liked him very much. He was neither so grand nor so intimidating as Lord Ravenall—and never once in the past days, by word or glance, had he given so much as a hint that he remembered a certain ragged serving wench from the Stag and Crown, called "Polly."

She gave a start when a voice sounded at her shoulder: "A penny for your thoughts, Miss Hexham."

She hadn't heard Ravenall come up behind her. The breeze shifted, and she caught his masculine scent and subtle cologne. She would recognize him by it, even in the dark. Her heart sped up in double time, as it always did when he was near.

"I beg your pardon," she said. "I was just thinking of Mr. Malone."

His brows knit in a scowl. "If you are thinking of him as a possible husband, my dear girl," he said silkily, "let me warn you that I expect you to make a match far higher."

First Fanny, and now Ravenall. She tipped her chin. "You would not give your consent, even though he is your friend?"

"*Especially* because he is my friend!"

"I see." She flushed with humiliation.

"No," he said, "you don't."

She let that pass. "Mr. Malone told me that you have sailed the seven seas, my lord. What places you must have seen! What adventures you must have had!"

"Indeed." His smile cooled. "But not all of them were wonderful, Miss Hexham." His next words were a shock. "We will make land at Raven's Head within the hour. You will be able to see it soon."

He saw that she was nervous, and entertained her with anecdotes about his grandmother, the dowager Countess of Ravenall, and her beloved gardens, and his childhood escapades when he summered there. With him at her side, exerting all his charm, she wished the voyage would never end.

Suddenly his eyes flashed and he smiled, and directed her gaze toward the horizon. "Look, Miss Hexham! Do you see that dark line on the horizon? It's Raven's Head. And there, if I am not mistaken," Ravenall said in an entirely different voice, "is the ubiquitous Lieutenant Nutting. Damn his impertinence!"

He went to the rail and, taking a brass spyglass from inside his coat, he held it up to his eye. Light flashed along its length as Perdita joined him. A sailing vessel came into view, sleek and fast, and flying the British flag.

Ravenall scowled. "What the devil does he want?"

It wasn't many minutes before they found out. The other craft hove to beside them. A boat was lowered and a man in the uniform of the Inland Revenue was rowed over to the *Raven.* Ravenall gave the sign to let him board.

"Well met, my lord. I've been wanting to have a word with you." He bowed.

Ravenall smiled, although he didn't quite meet his eyes. "Miss Hexham, may I present Lieutenant Nutting? You may find him out upon the water at any time, scouring the coves and headlands for pirates."

The lieutenant smiled. "There have been no pirates hereabouts in over a hundred years," he said dryly. "They are far too afraid of the local smugglers."

"How disappointing," Perdita said.

Ravenall showed his impatience. "You're chasing a chimera, Nutting. The 'gentlemen' haven't been abroad in these waters since before I was born. And," he added, "you're a long way from your usual haunts."

"I go where my duty takes me. There have been reports of strange lights off Ravenhead. I wondered if any rumors of it had reached your ears."

Ravenall's eyes glittered coldly. "Surely I am the last person of whom you should ask that question." He turned his face and the lieutenant gasped when he saw the mass of scar tissue that marred the earl's cheek. "As you can see, I have had far weightier matters on my mind."

The lieutenant bowed stiffly, like a toy soldier. "Of course. I had heard of your accident, my lord, and am glad to see you in such fine fettle. I will take my leave of you. Good day to you, my lord. Your servant, Miss Hexham."

When he was gone, Perdita was curious. There seemed to have been more going on beneath the words the two men had exchanged.

"What was that all about?"

Ravenall's mouth tightened. "About Nutting's hunger for advancement. He's hoping to break some of the free traders, who bring in goods from France."

"Did he suppose that you had the hold filled with smuggled brandy?" she said indignantly.

Ravenall laughed. "No, Miss Hexham. I believe he only wanted a closer look at you."

The wind caught a strand of her hair, tugging it loose from her bonnet. He caught it and tucked it back. "I cannot say I blame him," he said softly. "You are very beautiful."

As his fingers brushed her cheek, their eyes locked. Her world narrowed down to the moment. To him.

"What is it, Miss Hexham?" he asked. Ravenall took her firm chin in his hand. "Are you afraid of me?"

"Not in the least!"

I am afraid of myself. Of how I feel when you look down at me like this. When your skin touches mine. I am afraid of

*the fire that leaps between us, and where it might lead. I am
afraid that one day you will discover that I have deceived you,
and that when you learn of my hoax, that you will hate me
for it!*

Perdita couldn't say any of it aloud. "How green the waves
are over there," she said for diversion.

Ravenall stepped back. "We're nearing the shallows. There
are unsafe waters ahead."

Somehow, Perdita thought it wasn't just the sea he was
referring to. She felt the heat of his warm touch burning her
skin, as if she'd taken too much sun.

For a moment his eyes searched hers, his expression completely unreadable. She was so aware of him, she imagined
she could feel the thick hair that curled against his strong neck,
the roughness of his cheek beneath her palm. *He dazzles me,*
she thought, *like sunlight off the waves.*

"You will spend a considerable amount of time at Ravenall," he said at last. "I do hope you will learn to love it, Miss
Hexham."

"Thank you, my lord. If it is your wish, I shall try my best
to do so."

"Dutiful of you," he said shortly.

They turned their faces toward the distant smudge of land,
and watched it grow larger, clearer, with the yacht's swift
approach. Perdita could make out two villages, one beneath
the rocky summit, the other perched just above the bay. Their
streets were so steeply pitched, the whitewashed houses with
their gold slate roofs seemed to dangle from the side of the
cliffs like fobs on a watch chain.

"Ravenhead and Ravensea," her companion told her. "Like
the earls of Ravenall, they took their names from the shape of
the headland itself."

Perdita shaded her eyes against the glare. "I don't . . . Oh,
yes! Now I can see why."

In profile, the jutting thrusts of two cliffs gave the illusion
of a raven's head, frowning out to sea. As they drew nearer
she noticed that most of the cottages faced the sea; but there
were several built with blank walls overlooking the bay. Not
so much as a tiny window broke their façades. Perdita inquired
about them.

Ravenall was pleased. "So you noticed that, did you? I

learned the story at my grandfather's knee. And now, I shall tell it to you.

" 'Once upon a time,' as they say, the village of Ravensea was the haunt of smugglers. One night they found a man, severely injured and seemingly unconscious, at the foot of the cliff. He'd fallen from the path above. The tide was coming in, and they might have left him to be swept away; but one of the lads recognized the son of the first earl, who had befriended 'the gentlemen,' on a previous occasion."

"Out of the goodness of his heart, no doubt."

A twinkle of amusement lit his eyes. "Truth to tell, there were several kegs of fine brandy in the castle cellars and silks in my lady's wardrobe that had come from France, courtesy of 'the gentlemen.' "

Perdita nodded, remembering nights at the Stag and Crown, when the sounds of muffled hooves were heard in the stable-yard, and footsteps belowstairs when the inn was dark and all lay abed. Sukey had whispered that the landlady used her cellars to store smuggled goods.

"Did they harm him, my lord?"

"They might have killed him, had he let them know he was stunned but still aware. Instead, they put him over a packhorse and delivered him right to the castle gates."

"That was an act of great courage on their part. Or perhaps foolhardiness," she said. "Were they recognized?"

"Evidently. Several months later they were apprehended and brought before the local magistrate—who happened to be Lord Ravenall's eldest son—the very same man whose life they'd saved that fateful night."

"A quandary to puzzle Solomon!"

A smile played over his lips. "Indeed. By law he should have ordered them to be hanged, but gratitude demanded something more. In those days the aristocracy had great power to act as they thought fit within their jurisdiction. My ancestor pardoned the prisoners, on the condition that the smugglers take a vow then and there, that they would henceforth turn their backs upon the sea."

Perdita saw the glint in his eyes and clapped her hands together. "How clever of them. They built their houses facing inland to comply with the literal terms of their vow. And I imagine they continued at their, ah, trade?"

Ravenall's small smile flashed to a white grin against his sun-bronzed skin. "You've a quick wit, Miss Hexham. Let us just say that they were never caught at it again."

She looked across the bay at the backwards houses, and smiled. "I am glad of it. Thank you for telling me the story, my lord."

His smile faded abruptly. "It's only one of many I'll be telling you in the days ahead, Miss Hexham," he said a little stiffly.

Perdita turned her head to face the bow again. At first the castle was only a vast jumble of massive stone towers and turrets against the cloud-flecked sky. As they drew nearer she saw tall windows reflecting the sunshine, and peaked roofs of the local gold-colored slate. It looked like something from a picture book.

Her heart was up in her throat. She said a quick prayer for courage.

Perdita realized that the air had grown noticeably cooler. Heavy clouds had scudded in, muffling the sky in thick gray wool.

A call from one of the crew members, a creak of wood and shifting of sails, and the *Raven* was pointed homeward. The castle's walls and towers loomed dark and ominous in the altered light, the shining windows were now dull and black. *It still looks like something from a fairy tale,* Perdita thought in alarm.

One written by the Brothers Grimm.

A chill rippled through her, and she wrapped her shawl around herself more tightly.

Thirteen

"Here you are, safe on land once more, Miss Hexham."

Perdita took Lord Ravenall's extended hand, and stepped out of the dinghy, and on to the sandy, shell-strewn cove. Fanny had preceded her, and stood with her back to the sea, staring up at the sheer dark wall of granite looming overhead.

The castle, built of the same stone, seemed to grow out of the rock itself.

"How in heaven's name do we get up to it from here?" Perdita asked.

"There is a cliff path." Ravenall lifted his hand, indicating the precipitous track that led from the cove to the top of the precipice.

"Oh! The same one from which the first earl's son fell, before he was rescued by the free traders?" She eyed it dubiously.

Fanny shaded her eyes. "He is teasing you. I declare the only view of the sea I will ever cherish again is one from a considerable distance!"

Laughing, Ravenall guided them around a tumble of broken granite, where centuries of high tides had undercut the cliff base. In the distance an open carriage stood at the top of a wide set of steps hewn from the heavy granite, complete with a groom in black and silver livery.

Perdita lowered her lashes and went over the history he'd given her. She had lived quietly with the two spinsters, who had raised her as if she were their younger sister, dividing her time among their flowers, their books, and their beloved pets.

"Two dogs, Lady and Berenice; two cats, Whiskerkins and Boots; two birds, Rajah and Mina," Perdita whispered beneath her breath.

Ravenall raised an eyebrow. "And which one bit you on the arm?"

"Neither. It was old Mr. Grimes's puppy who bit me—on the ankle."

Fanny joined in the game. "And how far a stroll was it to town?"

That particular question had never been broached before. Perdita laughed suddenly. "Why, too far to walk, ma'am!"

Lord Ravenall sent her an approving glance. "I'm sure you must miss Rosemont, Miss Hexham," he said in a slightly louder voice. Perdita guessed at once that he was speaking for the benefit of the groom upon the box. "I hope the charms of Ravenall may distract you from your sad memories."

"I will do my best, my lord."

He favored her with a dry smile. "I believe, if you set your mind to it, that you will prove equal to the task."

At first Perdita had been annoyed by all the things she was supposed to know. There seemed no reason to memorize such trivial details as the name of the cook's son, who had gone to sea, or the direction that Rosemont faced.

"Who will ever ask?" she'd demanded.

"Perhaps no one," her preceptress had explained. "But you will eventually begin to feel that it is all completely true. And that, Miss Hexham, is of the essence."

And so, Perdita had imagined her room at Rosemont, and where she had set her ivory brushes on the bureau. She had pictured the river, and the wide spot where the swans swam every day. She knew there was a cracked hearthstone in the kitchen, that the housekeeper was a cheery woman named Mrs. Wills, and Breen, the aged gardener, was mad for growing mangel-wurzels in the kitchen garden, and creeping roses on the sunny, sheltered terrace.

It sounded so cozy and homey now, confronted as she was by the looming presence of Ravenall Castle, that Perdita wished she were safe at the fictitious Rosemont Cottage this very moment. The prospect of meeting Ravenall's grandmother, the dowager Countess of Ravenall, filled her with trepidation.

Ravenall leaned forward. "Why are you frowning so, Miss Hexham?"

"I am so anxious," she confessed, "that I'm afraid I will

trip when I'm introduced to Lady Ravenall, or say the wrong thing. I have never met a countess before, of course. Is she . . . is she very grand?"

Fanny exchanged a speaking look with Lord Ravenall. "Not at all," he said soothingly. "Have you been imagining her in my image? Proud and disdainful, with steely eyes and a spine to match?"

"Something very like, my lord."

A spark danced in his blue eyes. "Unhandsome of you, Miss Hexham! You were supposed to deny that you see me in such an unflattering light."

"I shall make a note of it for future reference, my lord." She folded her hands demurely in her lap.

"You've a sweet voice and a sharp tongue," he said, not at all disapprovingly. "Let me reassure you regarding my grandmother. She is every inch the noblewoman, but there is nothing of the imperious grande dame about her. Although there may be days on end when she ignores you completely."

Perdita was startled. "I beg your pardon?"

"The countess is a noted biographer," Fanny said, with a stern look at Lord Ravenall, "and has spent her widowhood here, retired from the world. Currently, she is compiling a history of the Ravenalls."

Ravenall was unrepentant. "My grandmother has made the top two floors of the east tower into her own apartments, and often takes her meals within her suite. Chances are she may become so wrapped up in her writing about the thatch-gallows who founded the family that she will forget your existence for days on end."

"I only hope I'll be so fortunate!"

"I doubt Miss Evans will feel fortunate," Fanny murmured. "Poor, shy creature that she is! She must find life very dull at the castle, I fear."

"Harriet Evans is a distant connection on my father's side," Ravenall explained. "The family is cursed with them. You cannot ride through the countryside without seeing sturdy farm lads and blacksmiths' apprentices who bear the Ravenall features. Harriet is fortunate to have escaped that fate at least!"

Fanny sighed. "I see you are full of jokes today, my lord. Poor Harriet," she told Perdita, "acts as companion to the dowager countess and assists her in her research."

"That's true," Ravenall said. "Although why you call her 'poor Harriet' and waste your pity on her is more than I can fathom. Miss Evans seems quite happy with her lot in life. Certainly she is happier since she came to join my household than she was living under her stepmother's rule at Faversham."

The look Fanny gave him surprised Perdita. "Ah, Justin," the widow said, shaking her head. "As experienced as you are in the world, and yet you don't have a clue as to what tumult goes on within a woman's breast!"

He went white. "You must be right: Véronique hurled the same accusation at me, on more than one occasion." He clamped his white lips together and looked away.

Fanny gave a small cry of dismay. "I was not thinking of your wife, Justin. Pray, forgive me!"

"We will not speak of it—or of her—again," he said stiffly.

Perdita's heart plummeted so rapidly she almost fainted. *Wife?*

Her world shattered, then pieced itself back together in another shape. There were gaps in it now, and sharp, cutting edges. It had never occurred to her that Ravenall was married.

They'd reached the carriage. "I'll join you later," Ravenall said as he handed them into it, "after I've seen to the disposal of the luggage."

Soon the vehicle was winding its way up to the castle. Perdita was silent, staggered by what she'd just learned. In all her imaginings she had never once pictured Ravenall with a wife.

She was still pondering it when the road merged with a graveled avenue that wound through sweeping parkland. The castle rose in the distance, far more impressive and even more intimidating than it had appeared from the sea. There was nothing to soften the impact of all that massed stone, those heavy, machiolated ramparts. Flanked by its great towers, the gray bulk of the keep rose like a clenched fist against the darkening sky.

Perdita felt overwhelmed. God only knew what awaited her inside those thick walls! Not even the revelation of a newer wing, with tall arched windows and terraced gardens, comforted her.

Biting her lip, she gazed straight ahead at the unyielding mass of granite. The carriage rolled beneath the wide stone

gate, carved with the Ravenall arms, and pulled up inside the
castle's courtyard.

At one side was an arch that led to the stableyard, and the
far end was pierced by long windows set in stone traceries,
and wide worn steps leading to a massive doorway.

Perdita's heart fluttered. The history of the castle could be
traced back for generations, solid as that great oak door. Her
own was blank as glass and fogged with lies. An involuntary
tremor shook her.

Fanny took Perdita's gloved hand in hers and gave it a little
squeeze. "It will go more easily than you expect," she said
softly.

"I would feel less anxious if the countess knew everything.
I pray God that I don't expose myself in some unthinking
manner!"

"Lady Ravenall is far less likely to notice a lapse than the
servants." She smiled. "They, of course, will take any blunders
on your part as one of those eccentricities to which the aristocracy are prone."

"And what of Miss Evans?"

"There you must be a bit more careful. You will likely see
her only at dinner, and she is too self-effacing to put herself
forward by questioning you in detail. But for all her vagueness
and retiring ways, she is shrewd, and a very noticing sort of
person."

The carriage had rolled to a stop before the door. Its stout
wood was banded with iron and studded with intricate bosses.
The grain of the ancient door had darkened and mellowed with
time, and the edges were rounded by centuries of wind and
rain, and the touch of human hands.

Perdita shrank back against the squabs. "Fanny, this is a
mad scheme," she whispered. "You will wish yourself well
out of it."

"One thing you should know: once Ravenall is determined
to accomplish something, there is nothing that will be allowed
to stand in his way."

Perdita felt a tiny shiver run up her back. "I don't doubt
that in the least."

The widow kept her gaze fixed on Perdita. There was pity
in it, and staunch determination. "It is futile to resist him, you
know, once he has the bit between his teeth. But that is not

my entire reason for taking part in his plan, Miss Hexham."

She smoothed her gloves over her hands. "Life is not always easy for women of our station. My other object in joining this masquerade is to restore you to your rightful place in society without the least hint of scandal attached to your name. You, at least, shall marry when and where you choose. That is my vow to you!"

"You are very kind," Perdita said in a low voice.

Tears of shame stung her eyes and clung to her lashes. She was a rank imposter, and had stolen a dead girl's name. So many people had already been drawn into her increasingly intricate tapestry of deceit. So many more must follow, or it would all be for naught. Perdita straightened her shoulders. From this moment on, everything she said and did would be a lie. A lie that she must convince herself was the truth.

There was no other way.

The steps were let down, the carriage door was flung open, and there was no time for more. Two footmen stood on either side to hand the ladies out. Fanny was first. Perdita alighted behind her and was trying not to gape at the splendid façade, the glittering windows framed in carved stone.

On the top step, a tall woman in severe black bombazine, wearing a heavy chatelaine about her waist, waited beside an ancient, very dignified butler. Fanny took Perdita's hand and guided her up the stairs. The housekeeper beamed and curtsied, and the butler bowed.

"Welcome home to Ravenall, Miss Fanny! I should say, Mrs. Fitzmorris!"

"Thank you, Burton. I have been away far too long. It is good to be back!"

They'd reached the top of the stone stairs, and the housekeeper stepped forward to greet them. She was wreathed in smiles.

"Good afternoon, Mrs. Overland," Fanny said smoothly. "You see that I have brought Miss Hexham with me. As you have no doubt been informed, she will be making her home at Ravenall."

"Everything is in readiness, Miss Fanny. I've put you in your usual chambers in the new wing, and Miss Hexham in the Blue Suite." She eyed Perdita with warmth and a good deal of barely concealed curiosity.

"I hope Lady Ravenall is in good health?"

"Oh, blooming, Miss Fanny. Her ladyship is in her apartments, happily at work on her latest manuscript with Miss Evans. She asked me to bid you welcome, and looks forward to seeing you and Miss Hexham in the drawing room before dinner."

Perdita hoped her sigh of relief wasn't too noticeable. The dreaded meeting was postponed.

They went up the steps, with the housekeeper leading the way through a vast dim hall hung with shields and antlers, and into the bright drawing room where tea and iced cakes awaited them. Perdita had never been in a chamber so large, or so fine. She hovered just inside the door, stunned by the splendor before her.

The chamber was high-ceilinged, the walls covered in yellow silk with tasseled draperies embroidered in an intricate black and gold design. Gilded mirrors hung above the mantels at the far ends of the long room, and there were rows of portraits and landscapes in heavy gold frames. Lacquered tables and chairs and settees were placed in inviting arrangements on a colorful Oriental carpet.

Fanny admired a porcelain vase set in solitary splendor on a pedestal. "This is new to me. I have always loved the proportions of this drawing room. In a room less grand, these lovely antiques and furnishings would be overwhelmed."

Perdita gazed at the inlaid cabinets and satin-covered sofas, the polished tables, chairs, and screens. *It certainly overwhelms me!*

The housekeeper bustled out. When they were alone, Perdita expressed her surprise at the servants' familiarity. "I couldn't help but notice that both Burton and Mrs. Overland addressed you as Miss Fanny."

"Oh, Burton has known me since I was in leading strings. I ran tame here in my childhood." A soft smile lifted the corners of her mouth. "My father's estate marched with Ravenall lands. Justin and I grew up like sister and brother—squabbles included."

"Oh! I thought—" Perdita broke off, aware of how infelicitous it would be to tell her companion that she had thought Fanny was Ravenall's mistress.

The other woman raised her eyebrows. "I see that Justin didn't explain anything. How like him!"

"That he did not." Perdita hesitated. "I wasn't even aware that he had a wife!"

Fanny's eyes and voice were flat. "Véronique is dead."

Perdita's eyes went wide. "But . . . she must have been young! How did she die?" The question was wrenched from her.

Fanny took her arm in a surprisingly hard grip. "You heard what Ravenall said. We will not speak of her. Ever!"

Which, of course, instilled in Perdita's chest a burning desire to know everything there was to know about the mysterious Véronique.

After finishing their refreshments, Fanny rang for the housekeeper. "If you will be kind enough to escort Miss Hexham to her chambers, I have some instructions for Burton from Lord Ravenall regarding the luggage." She floated toward the hall while the housekeeper led Perdita toward the curving staircase.

Perdita was too tired and overwhelmed to take in much of the hall, except for the great table in the center and the massive iron chandelier above. She had an impression of great age, enhanced by the suit of armor that guarded the foot of the stairs, and the stone treads worn down in their centers. As she mounted the steps, her hand glided along the rail that topped the intricately carved balustrades, rubbed to satin smoothness by generations of hands.

At the top of the stairs two corridors branched off, one leading to the older part of the edifice that was the actual castle. Not much could be seen but shadows, and the arch of a window with leaded glass.

Mrs. Overland led Perdita through a vaulted archway into a gracious newer wing. They were in a long and spacious gallery that ended in a high window. Sunbeams struck the lusters hanging from the wall sconces, spraying rainbows over the white damask-covered walls.

The words of an old tune ran through Perdita's mind: *"I dreamt that I dwelt in marble halls, with vassals and serfs by my side . . ."*

For surely this was a dream: soft carpets, glowing with color; cabinets of curios; chairs covered in silk tapestry; and

tables inlaid with ivory. At intervals busts of alabaster were
set into arched niches, and she had glimpses of classic faces
and noble profiles.

"And here are your chambers, Miss Hexham," the housekeeper said, throwing open a door to a cozy sitting room that
overlooked the terraced gardens and a reflecting pool. "I hope
you will find everything to your liking."

How could I not? Perdita thought, looking around in
delight.

It was a bright, cheerful room, filled with dainty furnishings
upholstered in dark blue velvet. The wainscoting was white,
and papered above with narrow stripes in pale blue and white.
The mantelpiece was white, with a gilded mirror above,
flanked by shaded sconces, and the draperies at the long windows were done in the same pale blue looped back with scalloped swags.

The bedroom beyond was in deeper, richer shades of the
same hues, the high bed hung with sapphire draperies corded
in gold. Here was luxury such as she'd never imagined!

"Your dressing room is just beyond," Mrs. Overland announced, opening yet another door. Perdita peeked in at the
hip bath, the gilded screen, and the other accoutrements. A
young maid in a crisp uniform entered with a can of steaming
water for the washbasin.

"This is Nettie," the housekeeper said. "She will be waiting
upon you, until someone more suitable is found. I will leave
you to freshen up."

Nettie dipped a shy curtsy, relieved Perdita of her hat and
stood waiting for her orders. Perdita smiled, but inside she felt
very wobbly. A week ago she had been a servant: who was
she now, that this pleasant young girl should bow to her so
anxiously, and try to please?

An imposter, her conscience reminded sternly. *A mere serving girl, who thought that her ability to read and write would
see her through an ambitious scheme, that her need to escape
her dreary lot at the Stag and Crown by any means excused
her actions.*

She had deceived Lord Ravenall, by not telling him her
mark was actually a burn scar; she had taken advantage of
Fanny's kindness.

And she would do it all again, in a minute!

Letting the maid assist her out of her traveling clothes, which Nettie held reverently, she slipped into a peignoir of fine lawn, edged with points of lace. Perdita had never seen it before. Obviously, Lord Ravenall had seen to its delivery: she wondered what other surprises lay in store behind the doors of the mirrored armoire, and in the drawers of the beautifully carved chiffonier.

"Is there anything else you require, miss?"

"Thank you, Nettie. I shall ring when I need you."

Perdita spun around slowly, trying to take it all in. Elegant gowns, warm beds, delicious foods to tempt her appetite. A room all to herself, which was larger than the taproom and private parlor at the Stag and Crown combined, and more lovely than anything she had envisioned, even in her dreams.

When she went to bathe her face and hands in the china basin, she found the water scented with lavender and bergamot. It was suddenly all too much. Spreading her arms wide, she whirled around again, then started spinning faster and faster, until she was giddy with joy.

One emotion led to another, and they swept over her with soul-wracking power. It was as if an invisible dam had broken. She was inundated with them: fear, relief, shame—and over all, a profound gratitude to Lord Ravenall.

Sobs shook her slender frame. For so long she'd been forced to swallow her pride and anger, to hide her sense of isolation and terrible loneliness, that trying to hold them back now would have been like trying to bottle up the sea.

She finally collapsed in a heap on the bed, laughing and weeping by turns, until she fell into an exhausted sleep.

. . . She was rambling through that vast, dim house that haunted her nights, desperately opening door after door. It was growing darker by the minute. Somewhere a clock ticked, like the beating of a heart.

She found nothing but cold, empty rooms with shuttered windows. In the distance there was the sound of women's voices and muffled weeping. It frightened her dreadfully—and yet, somewhere ahead, she knew was the promise of light and warmth, color and gaiety and safety. If she could only find her way!

Cocking her head, she listened. Soft strains of music lured

*her through the twilit chambers toward tall double doors.
Light poured like liquid gold beneath the heavy panels. A sudden knowledge came over her, a certainty, that just beyond
them was everything she had ever wanted, or hoped for.*

Perdita pushed the doors open eagerly.

*The ballroom was alight with candles and the gleam of
satin and jewels. Relief and joy poured through her. She found
herself in the center of the dance floor, and the skirts of her
cream silk gown rustled like summer leaves. People were staring, moving away to leave her in a circle of open space. Inside
she fought a terrible panic: she didn't know the steps of the
dance.*

*Someone took her hand in a warm grasp. Perdita looked
up. Intense blue eyes smiled down into hers and her heart gave
a leap. "Lord Ravenall!"*

*Her breath caught in her chest. How handsome he was, all
traces of his hideous scar vanished, his face looking younger.
Almost carefree. "Are you happy, Perdita?" he asked as he
led her out.*

*"Happier than I ever thought possible, my lord. And I owe
it all to you. I can never thank you enough."*

*"Oh, but you can!" he assured her, and drew her close
against him.*

"Take me away," she begged Ravenall.

*"Is that what you really want?" His blue, blue eyes burned
into hers. There was tenderness in them, and need.*

*Her heart sped up and he lowered his head, and she raised
her face for his kiss. His features blurred and shifted. To her
horror, Perdita saw that his face was melting, peeling away
like a mask of wax.*

*As the globs slithered free, other features were revealed. It
was Sam Bailey who loomed over her, his eyes burning with
hellish light, and it was Sam's hand that held hers, his arm
that encircled her waist.*

*Bits of bogweed clung to his garments. Tatters of flesh hung
from his body and skull to show the bone beneath. Only his
eyes were alive inside the bony sockets. The ivoried teeth
grinned wide.*

*"Little fool! Didn't you know me for what I am?" He threw
back his head and laughed.*

She tried to pull away but he only drew her closer. "Don't move!" he warned, in a vicious whisper. "I have you in my power. Dead or alive, my dear Miss Hexham, it doesn't matter to me. You see, either way, I win . . ."

She tried to scream, but her throat had closed up. All around her the men and women danced while she fought for her very life. Couldn't anyone see what was happening to her?

She struggled and struggled, until finally she broke free. A thick mist rose and blotted out the moorland. She was running, running down a dim corridor, the only sounds her own echoing footsteps.

Pushing the last door open, she found the way blocked. Someone had bricked up the opening. There was no escape.

Before she could whirl around a skeletal hand caught her, gripping her shoulder cruelly. She was spun violently around and gasped in shock, to face Sam Bailey.

"You cannot run from me, Miss Hexham. It is far too late for that."

Stark terror held her rooted in place . . .

Perdita awakened with a start. She was sick with fright, trembling violently. Her breathing slowed as she took in her surroundings. *I am at Ravenall Castle,* she reassured herself, *and I am safe now.*

As she rose from the bed, the effects of the nightmare lingered. Although the face had been Sam Bailey's, the voice had surely been Lord Ravenall's.

She knew then that the dream was a warning, and her feeling of safety no more than an illusion.

Fourteen

Perdita poured water from the pitcher into the painted china basin, and splashed her face with it. She had no idea how long she'd slept atop the coverlet. Long enough for the water to grow cold, at any rate. She reached for the bellpull and rang for Nettie.

The maid bustled in, cheerful as a sunrise. "La! miss, and I wondered if you would sleep right through till morning."

"I cannot believe that I fell asleep!"

"It was my lord's orders to let you rest undisturbed. Is there any particular gown you wish to put on, miss?"

She flung open the armoire, and Perdita stared at the array of colors and textures: rose, wood violet, and the soft purple-pink of foxglove; spring-leaf green, winter's dark holly, and glowing primrose-yellow; the blues of a summer's sky, and the white wool of clouds; the silken shimmer of moth wings in moonlight.

Every gown was lovely, but she didn't have any idea of what was suitable for a day at Ravenall Castle. "Which do you think is most becoming?"

Nettie's cheeks pinked with pleasure. "They are all so beautiful, miss. If I had to choose, it would be either the plum with the pink ribbons and scalloped neck—or this."

She opened the other side of the armoire and removed a smart afternoon dress in the subtle, deep amber of honey in the comb.

"That is the one," Perdita said, hiding her awe.

When she was gowned in it, the warm color and the froths of lace at throat and wrists brought out the contrast between her black hair and fair skin. Her eyes shone with delight.She stroked her hand over the softly draping fabric, taking enormous pleasure in the smooth flow of it beneath her palm.

Her hands were no longer chapped, but she remembered how humiliated she had been when she'd put on her first lovely dress at the George, and felt her work-roughened skin catch the delicate threads. How she'd had to hold herself back from devouring every last crumb on her plate.

The girl that she had been seemed to have vanished completely, replaced by the elegant creature in the looking glass.

"Miss?"

Perdita jumped. She'd been so rapt in the vision reflected in the mirror that she had forgotten Nettie's very presence.

She took her seat at the dressing table and tried not to look as if she'd never seen the crystal perfume bottles before. The maid dressed her hair high, fixed with two tortoiseshell combs. A string of amber beads and matching earrings, produced from a velvet box in a drawer, completed her ensemble.

She felt a moment of panic. She was like an ant that had stepped into honey, trapped in all the sweetness this new life promised. And Perdita knew that she would do anything to keep from going back.

"Your shawl, miss."

Rising carefully, Perdita let Nettie drape an ivory shawl about her shoulders. The addition made her look more mature, and increased her confidence. *Another layer in the disguise*, she thought.

"I am ready."

Perdita followed Nettie out of the room, and along a positive maze of corridors. On the way she memorized landmarks: the tall blue and white vase on the left where the first corridor branched; the portrait of the young woman with two spaniels at the next turning, where she must go right; a cabinet of particolored woods, filled with curiosities. Then they came through an archway and she found herself at the head of the stairs.

She left Nettie and descended to the lower level, just as a familiar figure stepped into the hall. It was Ravenall's valet, whom she hadn't seen since the Stag and Crown. Heat rushed to her cheeks. *"Mr. Danes!"*

The valet eyed her with calm detachment. "And you are Miss Hexham, I presume? Welcome to Ravenall, miss."

She stepped forward shyly and lowered her voice. "Do you not recognize me?"

"I have seen the miniature of you and your late mother, which his lordship has in his possession; however, you have greatly changed since then," he said coolly.

Perdita heard the warning in the valet's voice, but she thought that she saw the gleam of conspiracy in his eye, before his expression went bland.

She understood. As far as the world was to know, this was their first and only meeting. The hours they had shared keeping watch over Ravenall at the Stag and Crown must forever be denied. She nodded a little sadly, and floated off to the drawing room in her elegant amber velvet gown, feeling quite forlorn.

Danes watched her retreating form with concern. He was no fool, and knew more of what was going on than anyone at the castle, except Lord Ravenall. And he guessed even more than his master suspected.

A footman threw open the door and Perdita entered the drawing room quietly.

Looking about for Fanny, she spied a figure standing before one of the terrace windows, and gave a tiny squeak of dismay.

"Lord Ravenall! I didn't expect to find you here."

Ravenall turned, one eyebrow lifted. "Really? And yet this is my home, you know."

She stiffened. "You always seem to put me at a disadvantage, my lord."

"For pointing out the obvious? How unhandsome of you, Miss Hexham. I am not an ogre."

"No, my lord." His cool formality unsettled her. *So,* Perdita told herself sternly, *the masquerade has truly begun.*

"Pray be seated," he said, "while I ring for refreshments. I'm sure you're feeling peckish, and we've a good deal of business to conduct this afternoon."

At his summons, the butler appeared with lemonade, which she had never tasted before, and a plate of delicacies that made Perdita's mouth water. She nibbled at the food, too nervous to eat after all. Ravenall discussed the weather, proposed a drive the following day, and complimented her on her gown.

"Really, my dear Miss Hexham," he said at last, "you must make some effort to keep the conversation going!"

"You instructed me to speak as little as possible," she reminded him, "and only upon subjects of which I have some knowledge."

"In public," Ravenall rejoined. He strolled over to her chair and looked down at her. "But we are private now."

Once again she was aware of that same tension in the air that had blossomed that night at the Stag and Crown. She felt excited and frightened, but most of all, confused. *What is he thinking? What does he see when he looks at me?*

Ravenall assessed her, as if she were one of the exquisite jade carvings on the mantelpiece. In the amber gown, with her hair dressed so becomingly, she had taken him by surprise. In fact, she had almost taken his breath away. And those eyes! Thickly lashed, and darker than violets. She'd create a sensation in London, all right. The thought no longer pleased him.

"Like any other rare jewel, you are displayed to best advantage in the proper setting," he said softly. "I'd known you were very pretty. What I hadn't realized, Miss Hexham, is that you are truly beautiful."

She didn't know how to answer him. The silence lengthened, and this time he made no effort to break it. His eyes, so deep and penetrating a blue, dazzled her witless. Then he turned away so abruptly, she felt as if the sun had gone behind a cloud.

The door opened behind her and she jumped, almost oversetting her glass. Burton entered and announced a visitor: "Mr. Clements, my lord."

Perdita looked up to see a handsome man with thick, dark hair, dressed in breeches and top boots. The snowy cravat at the neck of his green coat was as neat as the rest of him, and added to his distinction.

The newcomer looked taken aback to find her present. "My apologies, my lord. Burton didn't explain that you had a visitor. I will take my leave and return another time."

"Your timing," Ravenall said, "is excellent. And it is Miss Hexham, here, who is the cause of my sending for you."

Clements stared. "Miss *Hexham!*"

Ravenall crooked an eyebrow. "Miss Hexham, of Hexham Court."

"Your ward?" The agent was confounded.

"Exactly so. Did you doubt that I would find her?" Ravenall favored him with one of his cool smiles. "I am ever a man of my word, Clements. You'd do well to remember that."

He made the introductions. Perdita extended her hand and Clements bowed low over it. "Your servant, Miss Hexham."

She responded prettily, and Ravenall gave her a look of approval. "Pray be seated, Clements. We have much ground to cover." He lifted a crystal decanter. "But first, I think a little brandy is in order."

"Indeed, my lord." Clements took the glass that the earl handed him, gathering his thoughts. He realized, belatedly, that he was staring. "You must forgive my surprise. I will drink your health, Miss Hexham."

Ravenall raised his glass to her. "Mr. Clements read law at Oxford; however, like his father before him, he serves as agent to the Ravenall lands, as well as being my solicitor. I believe you could do no better, Miss Hexham, than to put your own affairs into his hands."

Perdita folded her hands. "You will know best, my lord."

The agent flushed and looked greatly pleased. "I will be happy to do anything in my power, Miss Hexham."

"Excellent." Ravenall took the chair across from Clements. "I have several commissions for you. The first order of the day is to make arrangements to hand over to my ward any of the jewelry left to her by her parents' estates. Secondly, Miss Hexham requires a lady's maid. Young, but experienced, and with a good sense of fashion. I would be grateful if you would interview the candidates and narrow them down to one or two."

"I would much prefer to keep Nettie!" Perdita said.

"As you please."

Clements couldn't seem to take his eyes off Perdita. "I still cannot believe that Miss Hexham has been found after all these years!"

Perdita realized she must add something to the conversation. Something convincing. "Had I known my true history, sir," she said tartly, "I should not have been 'missing' for so long a time."

Clements flushed and shifted uncomfortably. "No, of course not. I beg you will forgive my awkwardness in expressing myself."

Ravenall watched it all with a slight smile. "Let me tell you the series of coincidences that led to this happy reunion."

He spun the tale so smoothly that Perdita had to marvel. ". . . and the results you see before you! The missing heiress is found."

"Why, it is an amazing story. Almost like a work of fiction," Clements exclaimed.

"I have noted the resemblance myself," Ravenall replied.

Perdita smiled. He was testing her, preparing her for the challenges she might receive in society.

The agent leaned forward. "I cannot credit that no one realized the connection all this time. Surely inquiries were made?"

"Miss Trewethy and her sister had no reason to disbelieve my nurse's story. They lived a retired life, sir, and did not go about in society. They were perfectly content as I was, among our books and gardens."

"But now," Ravenall interjected, "everything must necessarily change, Miss Hexham. You will, under my guidance, take your rightful place in the polite world. I have no doubt of you being declared the success of the Season. Indeed, I expect to receive so many offers for your hand that I shall have to hire a secretary to weed through the aspirants."

This was new and intimidating. Perdita pushed down the panic she felt. Everything was moving far too quickly for her peace of mind.

"You will have your joke, Lord Ravenall."

"Your modesty is charming," Ravenall said. "However, you are both beautiful and a substantial heiress. Although you may be pleased to remain single at the moment, you will meet many very eligible young gentlemen, who will try and convince you otherwise. One of them is sure to succeed."

Perdita felt herself blushing. It was true: marriage was now an option. One she hadn't truly considered. She raised her eyes to Ravenall. "Must I marry, my lord?"

He laughed aloud. "There is no need to sound so piteous. You are wealthy in your own right, Miss Hexham. You may marry when—and *if*—you choose."

"On the whole," she said, "I believe that I would rather not!"

"Either way," he replied, "that leads us to the third order of business. You must have a will, Miss Hexham."

"A will?" The thought had never occurred to her. "I am

young and strong, my lord. Surely there is no need."

Ravenall gave her one of his enigmatic looks. "Unfortunately, accidents happen all the time, Miss Hexham. Else I would still be captain of a sailing ship, and not an earl!"

Perdita wished she'd been better prepared for this. If marriage was something she'd never considered, neither was disposing of a fortune.

Ravenall leaned back in his chair. "I am right, Clements, am I not? Everything is left to Miss Hexham, outright. Nothing is entailed or otherwise bound up?"

"Not in the least. When she comes into her majority, Miss Hexham will have full say in the way her great fortune is spent."

Perdita went as white as she had formerly been rosy. She looked up at him from under her lashes. "You have called me an heiress, my lord, but I never heard the word 'fortune' spoken in that regard. Is it so very large?"

Clements cleared his throat. "It is indeed. There are holdings in various countries, investments in funds, lands and estates in England and in the West Indies."

She listened in stunned silence. Ravenall and the other gentleman went on for some minutes.

Perdita shook her head. "I know nothing of wills and estates. Nor of how to leave them. You must think me very foolish. I should, of course, wish to put my affairs in order. Perhaps . . . perhaps I might provide for a foundling home and school for young girls?"

Ravenall stared at her. "Admirable of you, Miss Hexham. But not exactly usual."

Twisting her hands in her lap, she sighed and turned to Clements. "Perhaps you can advise me, sir."

"It would be usual," the agent told her gravely, "to leave your personal possessions distributed among your friends. Since you have no family, however, the bulk of the estate should properly be left to your guardian—the Earl of Ravenall."

Her eyes opened wide in astonishment. "Look at this room, this castle! He cannot have any need of it!"

A frown knit Clements's brow, but Ravenall's voice was bland. "My dear girl, this is a shockingly expensive place to maintain!"

She hadn't thought of that. Perdita shrugged. "I would still wish to establish a foundling home. However I should inform you that I intend to lead a long—and shockingly expensive—life."

"Is that so? Then I hope you may get your wish, Miss Hexham." The look he slanted her way was unreadable. His lips curved in an enigmatic smile. "I sincerely hope you may. In fact, I would advise you to undertake every method you might to insure it."

Perdita was aware of Mr. Clements watching them. "You should not joke of such matters, my lord. You will upset Miss Hexham."

"It was not intended as a jest! I know too well how fragile life is. If Miss Hexham is wise, she will seize it with both hands. But it is always well to be prepared."

Clements rubbed his chin. "According to the law, Miss Hexham, you must have reached your majority before you are entitled to make out a will; however, if you would let me draft a list of your suggestions for bequests, I am certain that Lord Ravenall would honor it."

She frowned a little. "What happens to the bulk of my estate if I should not survive to see that day?"

The agent spread his hands. "It devolves entirely to Lord Ravenall, as your guardian."

They spent the next hour discussing particulars and Clements agreed to write up Perdita's wishes informally. The clock whirred and chimed the half hour.

Ravenall uncrossed his long legs. "My grandmother will have my head for tying you up with business all afternoon, Miss Hexham. It is almost time to dress for dinner."

Turning away, he rang for the butler. "I hope you'll stay to dine with us, Clements? We keep country hours, as you know."

"I would be honored, my lord. However, I'm not dressed for the occasion."

Dinner was sure to be an ordeal, but not quite as horrid a one as Perdita anticipated, now that Mr. Clements had been invited to stay.

"I am sure that my cousin Waverly will have something to fit you. The two of you are much of a size."

Perdita brightened. "Mr. Waverly will be here to dine?"

"He arrived a short time before you came down."

The agent was convinced to stay, and looked rather pleased about it in the end. When Clements was gone, Ravenall favored Perdita with a piercing look. "If I'd known my cousin's arrival would send you into raptures of delight, Miss Hexham, I would have told you sooner."

"Oh, dear. Should I not have said anything?"

"Not at all. I am glad to know that Andrew's presence here puts you in such a sunny mood. He is on leave of absence and will be staying at Ravenall."

"I didn't know," she said stiffly. "There was no occasion for us to discuss such matters."

"He spent several days in your company. What *did* you discuss?"

She couldn't gauge his mood, but it didn't seem pleasant. "I was far too busy to indulge in idle conversations. Nor did I have much to discuss," she snapped, "so gay and interesting as my life had been!"

He bowed. *"Touché!"*

"I beg your pardon?"

"A fencing term. A direct hit, Miss Hexham. You have wounded me with your quick wit."

Perdita hated it when he talked to her in that way. It made her feel ignorant and vulnerable.

He eyed her narrowly. "However, that was a slip, you know. One that could sabotage everything. A short time ago you claimed that your time at Rosemont was happy and fulfilled. You must not be so careless in company."

"I understand you," she said in a mortified voice. If she couldn't watch her tongue for an afternoon, how would she manage it for an entire London Season?

But Ravenall was still watching her with a frown between his brows. She lifted her chin. "Mostly," she said icily, "Mr. Waverly spoke of you."

"Good God! My condolences, Miss Hexham."

"He said nothing but good."

Ravenall laughed, his dark mood changing as quickly as it had come. "I am gratified to hear it."

"He, no doubt, has never been caught up in one of your elaborate schemes, and then left to fend for himself!"

Her flare of anger didn't singe a hair on his head. "I wondered if you would throw that up to me," Ravenall said coolly. "Acquit me of carelessness. I knew you were in very good hands with Fanny to guide you, and Jack Malone to protect you both. As for my schemes, he is immersed in this one! But we will speak no more of such matters. Do you understand?"

"I do not know how you come to be related to such a gentleman as Mr. Waverly," she said stiffly. "His manners are always pleasing."

"Our grandfathers were brothers. No doubt he inherited the best of the Waverly blood, while I inherited the worst of it."

He held out his hand to her. "Let us cry friends, Miss Hexham."

His fingers closed over hers. Perdita was startled by the jolt that went through her as his skin met hers. She felt it from the crown of her head, to the soles of her feet. She tried to draw back a little, but he held her hand in an iron grip.

"Why do you blush and pull away?" Ravenall asked quietly. "Do you not wish a more cordial relationship between us?"

Her breath hitched in her chest. She wanted it very much, indeed.

"I cannot force your good will," he said slowly, "but I do wish you would learn to trust me."

It is myself I do not trust, she said silently. "I must go up and dress for dinner," she said aloud.

Ravenall released her. As he did so, he caught a glimpse of his ruined face in the mirror. It still came as a shock.

"Don't show your revulsion of me in public, if it is at all possible," Ravenall told her. He reached for the bell cord. "I'll have someone show you up to your room so you may change for dinner."

"I know the way. I learn quickly, my lord."

"Yes," he said, frowning down at her. "You do."

He watched her leave the room and stood staring at the door long after the footman had pulled it closed. Fate had handed him a golden opportunity, and he'd seized it. He'd thought, in his hubris, that he could control it. Bend Perdita's will like soft metal, to any shape he wished. He saw now that he'd been extremely foolish.

There was steel in his prodigy. It showed in the lift of her stubborn chin and the depths of her violet eyes. She had

strength and some resiliency, yes. But he feared that if he tried
to bend her to his will too forcefully, she might break.

And that, he thought, *could cause injury to both of us.*

Cursing softly beneath his breath, he followed her out of
the drawing room.

Fifteen

"Charming!" Lady Ravenall said, as Perdita entered the drawing room and paused just inside. The countess was a small woman with enormous presence, and must have been a beauty in her youth. She was seated on a brocade scttee, her blue eyes bright with curiosity. "Come here, girl, and let me have a good look at you!"

Perdita did as she was bid, dipping a low curtsy. Her rose-colored gown rustled softly. She was relieved not to trip over the hem and make a fool of herself. This was her first, real test, and she dreaded it.

Dinner at Ravenall Castle required long gloves, a necklet of pearls, and pearl and garnet eardrops that pinched Perdita's lobes uncomfortably. The corset, however, was the worst of it. Her waist was so pulled in, her breasts so confined, she felt they would pop out of the low bodice if she so much as sneezed. From the look on the faces of Andrew Waverly and Mr. Clements, she imagined they thought the same. Lord Ravenall gave no indication that he'd noticed at all.

But he had. The moment the doors had opened to admit her, he'd been aware of her in every cell of his body. Only years of practice in hiding his true feelings masked them now. She was incredible. That rose-petal skin, those long-lashed eyes, those incredible shoulders and perfect bosom! From the way both Andrew and Clements looked, she'd had the same effect upon them.

Devil take it! She is liable to have any number of suitors for her hand coming round after her first appearance on the London scene. Ravenall frowned. That threw his timetable forward by quite a margin, and he didn't like having his hand forced. *There is nothing for it,* he decided reluctantly. *I will have to make my move sooner than I'd planned.*

Perdita was glad that she had a fine, fringed shawl she might pull a little closer. Nettie had removed it from a drawer, where it was packed in silver tissue. "You look a picture, miss," she said. "Every eye will turn to you tonight."

Which was exactly what Perdita hadn't wanted. "I don't suppose that instead of this scarf, you have a cloak of invisibility I might wrap around myself?" she'd asked. "Like the one the gallant soldier wears in the story of the Twelve Dancing Princesses?"

"Now there's a tale I haven't heard, miss," the maid had chuckled. "You must tell it to me sometime, if you will. But why would you want to be invisible, so pretty as you are? Especially with three handsome gentlemen at dinner?"

At the moment Perdita wished she could vanish, but it was no use. She must get through the long evening as best she could.

She rose from her bow, aware of Lady Ravenall's intense scrutiny. Smiling despite her inner fears, she surveyed the dowager Countess of Ravenall in return. Her hostess was nothing like she'd imagined. In her mind's eye she'd pictured an austere recluse, stern and disapproving.

Lady Ravenall was tiny, silver-haired, and as ethereal as a sprite. In the immense drawing room she looked like a dressmaker's doll. But beneath her fairylike exterior, Perdita sensed a core of steel.

The dowager countess tipped her head to the side. "You have the look of your mother. A pity that she did not live to see you grown."

Perdita's coolness deserted her. She didn't know what to say. Any step she took was likely to land her in quicksand. "I . . . I didn't realize that she was known to you, my lady."

"We will not talk of sad things on such a happy occasion," the countess said lightly. "Well, Miss Hexham, do you see a resemblance between my grandson and myself?"

That took Perdita aback. "Only in your mutual charm and air of authority," she said at last.

"Hah! I like you. You're not mealymouthed like some of the younger generation."

She patted the loveseat beside her and Perdita swept aside her skirts and took her place there. "I'm of an older and lustier generation," Lady Ravenall told her. "We spoke our minds.

None of this skittering around subjects in the mistaken notion of civility, as happens these days. I have no tolerance for fools, and none at all for hypocrites."

"Then I shall exert myself to be neither," Perdita replied.

Immediately she felt a pang of guilt. Presenting herself to Lady Ravenall under false pretenses certainly fell under both categories.

The dowager countess took Perdita's hands in hers. "I think I shall enjoy your company very much, my dear. Welcome to Ravenall."

"You are most kind, ma'am."

The countess inclined her head. "I believe a lady must cultivate all the virtues. However, I do not let them interfere with my work. You will perhaps think me less kind when Miss Evans and I retire to my study, and abandon you to Fanny and my scapegrace grandson for days on end."

"You must not forget me, ma'am," Andrew Waverly said with a laugh. "I have promised to do my best to keep Miss Hexham entertained."

Ravenall leaned against the mantelpiece, watching Perdita and listening to the byplay. She was terrified. He could see it in the wideness of her pupils and the quick rise and fall of her breasts. However, he sincerely doubted that anyone else could tell. His eyes were cynical.

She has missed her calling, that one! With her beauty and ability to blend into whatever background she finds herself thrust, she might have been an actress of renown. A consort of kings.

A pity she will have to make do as a mere heiress!

Although he stood some distance from her across the drawing room, Perdita was intensely aware of him, and noticed when he turned and walked away. His presence was a constant distraction to her, like a pin pricking her skin. She could not ignore him for a moment.

She was almost sorry dinner was to be informal. The dowager countess had advised her that since they were only seven, they would take the meal in the parlor the family used on everyday occasions.

"I refuse to sit at one end, like a bird on a perch, and shout down to the other," Lady Ravenall said. "It is much more enjoyable to dine *en famille,* and all join in the conversation. Ah, Harriet! Come and meet our guest."

Perdita smiled at the mousy companion and found herself skewered by a set of intelligent gray eyes. Her greeting was so subdued it was almost inaudible.

The table in the state dining room, so Nettie had told her, sat sixty easily, but was only used when there were grand house parties. While the many courses and unfamiliar forks and spoons would have proved daunting, Perdita rather thought she would have preferred it. It might have been safer to be seated so far apart from the others that it was impossible to carry on a conversation in any depth. The dining parlor proved to be a comfortable room with a table that could hold no more than ten comfortably.

With Lord Ravenall on one side, and Andrew Waverly on the other, Perdita managed to get through the meal relatively unscathed. She was so on edge, and so intent on not making a fool of herself before the countess, that afterward she couldn't remember any of the succulent dishes offered in any of the courses.

Miss Evans was a quiet young woman in a plain blue gown, with fair hair plaited atop her head in a manner long gone out of fashion. Perdita couldn't judge her age, but thought she could be no more than four-and-twenty. The spinster hid behind her thick spectacles, and uttered little more than "yes" and "no" when direct questions were asked of her, but her eyes seemed to make note of everything.

Lady Ravenall directed the conversation skillfully. Unfortunately for Perdita, she had very little knowledge of any of the topics that were broached. The fatal moment came when Mr. Clements made a comment about the Foreign Office, and turned to her:

". . . don't you agree Miss Hexham?"

She stared at him blankly. She knew nothing of the Foreign Office. Or the Home Office. Or any office. They were words in the newspapers she had read, and everything else was gone from her mind, but sheer horror at her ignorance.

She was about to commit a terrible social gaffe. What was it that Fanny had told her to say in just such a situation?

Taking a deep breath, Perdita fluttered her eyelashes and repeated the magic phrase: "I am afraid that I know nothing of such things, Mr. Clements, and must leave them to wiser heads than mine."

It worked like a charm. Mr. Clements was flattered, and smiled at her warmly.

"You must forgive me, Miss Hexham. I forget that not everyone is as interested in the topic of colonization as I."

"Let us speak of matters closer to home," Ravenall interposed. "Tell us, Miss Hexham, your impression of Ravenall Castle."

Perdita was still flustered. "I think," she said, uttering the first thing that popped into her head, "that it is very large!"

Everyone laughed at that, as if she'd made a great joke. Ravenall's eyes met hers, and she saw the glint of approval there. Her heart sped up and she felt a little breathless, as if she'd climbed to the top of Giant's Tor, and was looking down the dizzying heights.

But I know nothing of Giant's Tor or Dartmoor, she told herself sternly. As Lord Ravenall had reminded her repeatedly, she would not convince anyone else unless she first convinced herself. It was becoming easier.

She heaved an audible sigh of relief when the last course was removed by the hovering footmen, and the ladies withdrew to the drawing room. Lady Ravenall settled herself on a sofa, with Harriet Evans nearby at her embroidery frame. Fanny took the opposite chair.

Perdita sat at a little distance, so she might watch the countess and Fanny, and learn by their example. She was suddenly aware of Miss Evans watching her, while she pretended to thread her needle. Glancing up quickly, Perdita was astonished to find herself the subject of a cold, hard stare.

Then the spinster smiled at her, and Perdita thought that perhaps she'd only imagined it, or the light reflecting off Miss Evans's spectacles had created the effect. *After all, why would she have any reason to dislike me? She knows nothing of me!*

Folding her hands in her lap, as she'd been taught, Perdita listened to the talk, and watched Harriet's deft needle flicker in and out in the lamplight. The countess directed a question about their voyage aboard the *Raven.* Perdita answered and tried not to fidget: the evening stretched before her, like a steep, uphill climb, pitted with conversational bogs and boulders.

She was thankful that the gentlemen didn't linger long over their port and cigars. It was less than half an hour before the doors opened to admit the three men. Andrew and Clements took chairs near the countess, but Ravenall came to Perdita's side.

"You handled your response to Clements very well," he said, as he leaned over Perdita's chair.

"Do you think so? I felt like a fool!"

"There is no reason why you should. You must remember that most young ladies of your station will be every bit as uninformed about Acts of Parliament and foreign affairs as you."

She looked up at him gratefully. "They could not be less!"

Mr. Clements joined them, and another catastrophe loomed.

"Do you play, Miss Hexham? I am very fond of music," he added, "and the pianoforte at Ravenall has a most wonderful tone."

"Alas, I have no talent for it!" she said truthfully.

"But you must sing! Your voice is so very musical."

Perdita glanced over in panic at Lord Ravenall, who glowered back.

"Yes," Fanny announced into the sudden silence. "Miss Hexham sings, and very prettily. You needn't be shy. Miss Evans will accompany you. She is quite accomplished."

The countess's companion flushed a deep shade of crimson. ". . . so kind," she muttered disjointedly, and hurried over to riffle through the music. But the look she shot Perdita was flinty.

Perdita was appalled at the situation. She sent Ravenall a look of veiled panic. He merely smiled and brought the branch of candles over to the pianoforte.

Fanny intercepted their looks and stepped into the breach. "Perhaps you might favor us with that old country air I heard you sing only this morning, as you were dressing your hair?"

"I would be happy to oblige you."

"And I, to turn the pages of the music." Clements rose and followed her.

"I doubt there will be any need, sir," Perdita answered hastily. "It is called 'When I Am Gone,' and is not very well known."

Miss Evans looked up, her spectacles winking blindly in

the candlelight. "Oh, but I do know the tune! A Border air. Indeed, I may have it here somewhere among my sheets of music."

Ravenall scowled. Clements looked like a schoolboy in the throes of calf-love. *Does he think I'm blind?* He folded his arms across his chest. *I'll be having a word with him before he leaves.*

Perdita hoped Harriet wouldn't find the music, but the other woman gave a sound of triumph. "Here it is! Can you sing in this key, Miss Hexham?"

It seemed to Perdita that the most innocent statements had traps. Keys, to her, were something with which to unlock cupboards. She sent Fanny an imploring look.

This time it was Andrew to the rescue. "Let Miss Evans try a few notes," he suggested, "and you shall decide which suits your voice best."

The spinster played several keys, and the two young women decided on the midrange. After a few moments of whispered conversation, Miss Evans struck a cord, and Perdita nodded.

Ravenall watched her closely. How she conducted herself now would give him some idea of what was to come. Thus far she'd shown a great facility for mimicry. And for lying.

And, God in heaven, she was beautiful. More so than earlier, with her ivory skin and those stunning violet eyes glowing in the candlelight.

That could bring complications. One of them was the hot surge of desire in his loins. He ground his teeth. *Devil take it! If only she were homely, I wouldn't find myself in such a cursed intolerable position.*

"Do you mean that, Justin?" a low voice murmured.

Ravenall realized he'd spoken aloud, and cursed softly: Andrew stood at his elbow, staring.

"Surely," his cousin said, "you would have done exactly the same thing in restoring Miss Hexham to her proper place, if she were as ugly as a toad! After all, she *is* Miss Hexham of Hexham Court."

"Yes," Ravenall snapped. "She is indeed Miss Hexham. For good, or for ill."

Or any mixture of both.

He smiled tightly. He was glad now that he hadn't taken

Andrew into his full confidence. His cousin had a kind heart, and trusting disposition. Some people thought him gullible, but Ravenall didn't: it was just that Andrew couldn't convince himself that people were as truly wicked as the earl knew them to be.

Perdita closed her eyes, and she looked so vulnerable and tender that he was amazed. She was exquisite. A diamond of the first water. Whatever her background, she looked to belong in this drawing room, as she never had at the Stag and Crown.

Perhaps, Ravenall mused, he wasn't quite as clever as he'd thought. The plan had been simple enough. He'd provide her with clothing and jewels and a roof over her head. She, in turn, would provide him with the means to further his own ends.

This growing physical attraction to her was a danger, and must be handled carefully.

His eyes narrowed. In retrospect he knew the attraction had been there from the very beginning. And on both sides. He could tell she was affected by the way her eyes were drawn to his, and the quick flush that rose beneath her porcelain skin. By the way she looked hurriedly away, and the trembling of her hands whenever he took them in his.

Even with her ability to play her role so well, that was one thing she couldn't hide. Not from him.

Suddenly he was caught up in a need so hot and uncontrolled, the drawing room and everyone in it vanished. Everyone but Perdita. For a moment he imagined her stripped of her fine silks and naked in his bed, with her dark hair tumbling over her shoulders. Imagined his hands upon her lovely breasts, the touch of his mouth against her lips. The hardness of his body covering hers as he stroked and caressed her.

He struggled to banish the images, the burning desire, and won by sheer force of will. Ravenall's jaw squared. He would not play the fool and risk everything. There was too much at stake.

Then he saw Clements lean down and whisper something to Perdita. Anger flared out of all proportion. Was his agent as smitten as he acted—or did he think that he might snare himself an heiress?

Andrew leaned toward him. "They make a pretty picture, do they not?"

"Remind me to drop a word in Clements's ear," Ravenall said with quiet menace, "and inform him that Miss Hexham is far above his touch!"

Andrew's brows rose. "I was referring to the two young ladies, one so dark and the other so fair. Surely you don't think Clements is dangling after your ward? Why, he scarcely knows Miss Hexham."

"No," Ravenall snapped, "but I assure you that he knows everything there is to know of her fortune!"

"I cannot think it of him," Andrew chided.

"Her fortune is enough to tempt most men," Ravenall said in a low tone. "Only you, cousin, are unworldly enough that you haven't tried to fix your interest with her."

Andrew laughed. "We shouldn't suit."

"Hush," Lady Ravenall called across to them, as Harriet straightened on the piano bench. "Miss Hexham is about to sing."

The music began, and Perdita waited for her cue. She was aware of Ravenall watching her, and very nervous. She couldn't remember ever being the center of so much attention, certainly not by a countess and several gentlemen, and one of them an earl!

Then she saw that Andrew Waverly and Mr. Clements were both smiling at her encouragingly. Perdita took a deep breath and closed her eyes. When she opened them, she fixed her gaze on a painting on the far side of the room and began. The old words and melody flowed out of her, free and light as air.

As Miss Evans's clever fingers rippled over the keys, unlocking the music, Perdita's voice soared like a lark.

> *And who will comb your pretty fair hair,*
> *When I am gone, when I am gone.*
> *And who will shoe your bonny little feet,*
> *When I am dead and gone . . .*

The plaintive notes pierced Ravenall like arrows. Her voice was untrained, but sweet and pure and true. It sent shivers up his spine, but not because of that.

No, it was the outpouring of memories that suddenly assaulted him: the dim room, a wooden chair. An unfamiliar bed, covered with fine sheets with the Haycross ducal crest embroidered on the pillowcase. A soothing, gentle hand upon his back.

Upon his *naked* back.

Ravenall stared at Perdita and cursed beneath his breath.

The night was well advanced, and Ravenall lay awake in his high tester bed. Ever since visiting the ravine, he'd begun to remember more. Tonight it was fresh and immediate and raw. The incident played over and over like the refrain of a song:

The open moor towering off to his left, with the craggy granite of Giant's Tor thrusting high into the peerless blue sky. The distant thunder that had actually been the echo of a gunshot.

And then, again and again, he relived the helpless horror of being caught and dragged by the runaway team, his sudden release when the carriage plunged down the ravine, and he went plummeting down after.

Cursing, he rolled over on his side. Many a time before he'd faced danger and near death; but not one of those haunted him like that long, spiraling fall down into the clearing.

For weeks there had been nothing between setting out from Haycross and his waking up at the Stag and Crown but muddied shadows, like a badly rendered drawing in pen and ink. Tonight, since hearing Perdita sing, everything had come back. He remembered the room at the Stag and Crown, and the tiny window that looked out over the rolling moors, the crack on the plastered ceiling. He remembered the sound of rain on the roof overhead, and the smell of cooking from the kitchen belowstairs. The scent of ale. Remembered pain and frustration, and Danes attempting to feed him custard.

Most of all he remembered Perdita.

Not just isolated glimpses of her face and the mark upon her wrist, but a hundred other things. The images fleshed out, took on color and texture. He saw her sitting in the chair by the bedside, the light from the fire and a single, shielded taper casting a golden glow on her fair skin. Reading quietly, the dark wings of her raven hair shimmering like black satin as she turned the pages.

Sponging the sweat from his face, while he lay there wracked with agony. Her gentle hands combing his hair, bathing his fevered body with a cool cloth.

He thought of her as she was then, pretty in her dark blue homespun, with her hair tied back with a scrap of blue ribbon. As she had been tonight, beautiful . . . desirable . . . in her rose silk gown, with the pearl and garnet eardrops enhancing the lovely line of her throat, the necklet of pearls accentuating the creamy whiteness of her skin.

The mantel clock struck three, and he rose in darkness and dressed without calling his valet. Ravenall left his chambers, not by the door to the wide corridor beyond, but through a winding staircase concealed inside the wall.

There was no moon, only a million stars overhead, shining down between the swiftly moving clouds, to shower the night with their brilliance. The landscape was dark in contrast, but he knew every inch of the way he traveled, following the murmur of the sea on the rocks below. At the cliff's edge, he stopped and braced his legs.

The cove below was black as death. He couldn't make out the rocks, only the glitter of spray as starlight caught the crashing waves. Far out to sea the restless water blended into the sky, until he couldn't tell where one ended and the other began.

Were those stars on the horizon, or the subdued lanterns of the free traders, making for their hidden coves with booty? Despite his words to Lieutenant Nutting, Ravenall knew the gentlemen still plied these waters. A small light—warmer in color, brief as a firefly's glow—shone one of the eastern headlands. It came and went so swiftly he wasn't sure if he'd seen it at all; but since before his grandfather's time, the inlets and coves of the West Country had been the haunts of smugglers.

A smile touched his lips. The very brandy he'd offered his guests at dinner had been brought over from France by "the gentlemen" for his grandfather. Some said the fourth earl had even led them in their adventures.

He wouldn't be at all surprised if it were true: *We are a reckless bunch, we Ravenalls.*

He and Jack had tried their hand at smuggling of another kind in their younger days, when Jack had first come to train his uncle's horses at Ravenall Castle. That had led to a series of disasters.

As he turned back, the wind picked up, ruffling Ravenall's thick hair. He was as restless as the combing waves and scudding clouds. He was halfway back when Perdita's window came into view. Light shone through a crack in the draperies, where they hadn't been drawn tight.

So, she is awake, too.

He felt his heart speed up. Was she sitting up with a book, as she'd done while she watched over him by night? Or was she watching the shadows flicker on the ceiling, thinking . . . perhaps of him?

She would be wearing one of the embroidered lawn gowns he'd ordered for her, so fine you could easily see your hand through it. Or her lush body, glowing like a pearl through the filmy fabric. Her limbs, smooth as alabaster. Her breasts, high and firm, and rosy-tipped.

The quickening in his loins reminded him that he was a fool. Ravenall closed his eyes. That only made it worse. He could picture her in his bed, her thick dark hair spilling like silk over her naked shoulders, feel it against his bare chest, exquisitely erotic as he slid his length over hers. Imagine the softness, the warmth of her mouth as it opened to his, the edge of her sharp little teeth grazing his lip. Feel the satiny smoothness of her skin beneath his caressing hands, and the quiver of quickening passion in her body.

A shudder racked his body. Ravenall clenched his fists. If he'd been the first earl, a robber baron who seduced every pretty maid he'd ever laid eyes on, he would have bedded her that first night.

And who would stop you now? the dark voice of desire whispered. *Are you not master here?*

"I am a civilized man," he said aloud. But the wind laughed and snatched away his words.

No, it whispered. *There is a wildness in your blood and it calls to the same in her . . . and you are a passionate man who has denied himself too long.*

What if, it said, *you mounted those terrace steps to the second balcony, and knocked upon her door? She would open it—to you!*

It was true, and he knew it. She was so innocent, despite the tawdry inn where she'd lived, that she *would* open the door to him. She was naïve enough to think that no harm could come to her in a gentleman's house.

The voice of temptation whispered seductively inside his

head. He knew that her nature was so deeply passionate beneath that thin façade, that a kiss, a touch, and she would respond as lightly, as eagerly, as the *Raven* did beneath his guiding hand.

Need curled through him like smoke. Like flame. To be the man who brought her over the threshold into the fullness of womanhood was a thought so tempting it almost overwhelmed him. Ravenall fought it.

He wanted her so desperately that if he were a lesser man, it would have been both their undoing.

He stared up at that faint candleglow, while the sea sighed in the darkness. Other men in his position might not show so much restraint. It certainly would be an easy thing to seduce her and force her into marriage. But she was the wild card in this high-stakes game he was playing. There was too much at risk. One wrong move and his house of cards, built so carefully out of guile and half-truths, hope and fear and bald-faced lies, would collapse.

He knew what he must do, much as he regretted it.

The wind off the water was keen, and he shivered suddenly. He almost wished he'd never heard of the Druids' Oak, the Stag and Crown Inn—or a ravishing, violet-eyed girl who called herself "Perdita."

I am the one who is lost, he thought bitterly. *Cast adrift in a storm, with waves so towering, it will be a miracle if I can bring myself about.* The ramparts of the main castle stood out amidst the star-pricked sky. He was conscious of the weight of generations of proud Ravenall history. *I cannot throw everything away because a beautiful woman sets my blood on fire.*

Ravenall turned away from the new wing, and that single, tantalizing sliver of golden light that marked Perdita's bedroom window. Melding with the shadows, he went back inside the castle by the secret way he'd left.

Sixteen

It has been three weeks today since I came to Ravenall Castle.

Perdita stood at her bedroom window and looked out past the balcony balustrade. It still seemed like a marvelous dream.

The view was all warm sunlight and deep blue sky dotted with gold-edged clouds. Autumn was at its height, and would soon begin to fade. It filled her with restlessness.

Nettie finished putting away her discarded robe. "Will you be wanting anything more, miss?"

"No, Nettie. I shall ring for you if I require anything."

The words tripped lightly off her tongue. It amazed her that she fitted into her adopted life as if she were born to it. As the days passed, she tried, very hard, to convince herself that she had been. If not to such splendor as Ravenall Castle, surely to the gentle life.

She persuaded herself that her skin had known the textures of fine lawn and velvet, her eyes the subtle gleam of silver, the glint of crystal, and her ears the feel of pearls and the jeweled sounds of music.

It was a strange existence—pampered, given not only the elegancies of life, but the luxuries—and yet she never felt completely secure and safe. Disaster awaited in the most innocent of conversations, the wrong turn of phrase. A moment's forgetfulness.

As she put her hand on the window curtain, the the small amethyst ring on her right hand glowed deep in the filtered afternoon light. It was one of the pieces of jewelry Lord Ravenall had given her from among Pauline Hexham's inherited belongings, and she no longer felt guilty seeing it there. It had become as familiar to her as morning chocolate, or down-filled pillows.

As Lord Ravenall's eyes, watching her without seeming to do so.

Perdita could not be in the same room with him without being acutely aware of it; as if they were tied together by invisible links, which swayed minutely when either of them moved. She knew, even if her face was averted, when he was gazing at hers. She could tell when he left the room if her back was turned. He was neither approving, nor disapproving that she could tell. Merely . . . watching.

After many days in his company, she knew very little about him. Andrew Waverly, like Mr. Clements, seemed to be an open book, expressing amiable interest in all manner of topics. Lord Ravenall was a fond grandson to the countess, a trusted friend and advisor to Andrew and Fanny. A considerate employer to his staff.

It is only with me that he is so aloof, she thought.

There was something mysterious about him, something untamed and wild beneath the sophisticated exterior. She sensed a dark side to him, beneath the polished charm. A brooding stranger inside the man who took her for afternoon drives and sat beside her at table every night at dinner.

There was always that sense of dangerous currents flowing beneath the surface, sweeping her along on the strong tide of his will. It frightened and attracted her, in equal measures.

There were other currents beneath the seeming pleasantness of life at the castle. It was only she who seemed to have more time on her hands than was good for her. Lady Ravenall and Harriet were busy with the Ravenall history. Fanny was often abstracted—oddly restless and jumpy, and too busy making plans for a dinner party the following week for other activities.

Ravenall would cloister himself away in the old tower where he had his private office, and return looking short-tempered and drained. Other times he took the *Raven* out, sometimes alone, sometimes with Andrew. He never invited her to sail with him as she had hoped.

Andrew, however, spent a good deal of his time in the drawing room and gardens. Lately Perdita had begun to suspect that he lingered about the place in hopes of exchanging a few words with Harriet. Surely if he were interested in courting her, neither Ravenall nor his grandmother would have any objections.

She was about to turn away when something stopped her. He was out there, looking up at her window. She could *feel* it.

Scanning the formal garden and the broad lawn, Perdita saw nothing but the late blooming flowers beneath a soft azure sky. The season lasted far longer here than on Dartmoor's wind-swept heights. The sun was brilliant and shadows of clouds moved over the land, giving a golden, shifting quality to the picture framed by her. She focused on a line of distant trees, and spied a rider on a coal-black horse.

He sat so still that the dark color of his riding clothes and the animal's sleek hide blended into the background. He lifted his face toward the castle's new wing. *Watching.* It was too far to make out his features, but a tiny thrill shuddered through her.

Why? she asked silently. *What is it that you want of me?*

A cloud passed overhead, its shadow sweeping over the ground in a visible manifestation of the uneasiness that rippled through her.

Then he was gone.

"Would you care to have your fortune told?" Andrew asked. He'd driven Perdita, Fanny and Harriet down to Ravensea where they shopped for gloves and took tea at a tiny shop in the high street. "The woman who runs the shop will read the cards or your tea leaves, if you like."

Harriet flushed. "I should like that."

Fanny was less thrilled by the idea, and Perdita not at all. She wasn't sure if she believed in such things, but it was better not to risk the chance of being exposed as an impostor. Andrew seemed as eager as Harriet, and signaled the woman. She was very respectable in a black bombazine dress with a simple jet brooch at her throat and her graying hair knotted atop her head.

"You remember Mrs. Hever, Fanny. She was in service at the castle until she married one of the local sailors."

Fanny greeted Ravenall's former parlormaid with a fair semblance of pleasure. "How do you go on, Mrs. Hever?"

"Quite tolerably, Miss Fanny." She took the chair that Andrew held out for her and reached into her pocket.

"We really should be getting back," Perdita said quickly. "We've already lingered too long."

Mrs. Heever smiled. "It won't take me long, miss. Young ladies always want to know the same thing: 'Is there a husband in my future?' Well, I shall tell you now."

Removing the curiously decorated cards from her lap, she shuffled them a few times, then dealt one out, face down, to each of the women. "This is the foundation," she said matter-of-factly. Another series of cards went around. "This is the present." The last of three were dealt out next. "And here," she said as if she were serving tea biscuits, "is what lies ahead, for good or ill."

Now that the cards were there, Perdita couldn't bear not to know what they predicted. She bit her lip.

"I shall do Miss Fanny first, as I have known her since she was a babe in arms." She flipped the first card up. "The King of Swords. This is your husband that was." She turned the second. The pasteboard showed a woman sitting by her window. "Nine of Coins. You ache for what you lack, but will not leave your safe surroundings to find it."

Fanny's lips were pale as the third card was turned face up. "Ah," Mrs. Hever exclaimed. "Here he is, your Knight of Cups. A dashing warrior with dreams as big as the sky. A risk-taker, this one, who dares much. He rides up and offers you his cup of wine, filled to overflowing—but whether you will accept it or not is up to you."

"What will happen if I do?" Fanny said breathlessly. "Will I be happy?"

Mrs. Hever smiled at her. "That is something only you can decide."

Now it was Harriet's turn. Mrs. Hever frowned at the first one. "The Five of Cups. A loss, but with something left over. That is your foundation." She turned the second. "The Four of Wands. Happiness and a happy life are within your reach." Harriet's eyes shone. The woman picked up the last card. "The Chariot."

"But what does that mean?" Harriet asked.

"Different things at different times. Here it is events moving very swiftly, possibly beyond your control. Use great care and you will arrive safely at your chosen destiny."

Finally it was Perdita's turn. She waited anxiously, won-

dering what would be revealed. The first card showed a young
man about to walk off a cliff. "That doesn't look promising!"

"The Fool is blessed," Mrs. Hever told her. "Perhaps he
might tumble off the cliff—or he may walk on air. You are a
dreamer, miss. Perhaps you can make your dreams come true.
The next will tell me more." She flipped the second card up.
"The Magician. An interesting man, mysterious and masterful.
Does he deceive himself as well as others? He may produce
something out of nothing—or it may be all illusion."

Perdita looked at the card, and for a few unnerving seconds,
saw Ravenall's face so clearly that she gasped. Mrs. Hever
had gone on. She stiffened when she saw the last card, and
her hand swept it off the table with the others. They fell onto
the floor. "Ah, the cards don't wish to be read further," she
said, and started to gather them up.

But Perdita had seen her card. She knelt and picked it up
from among the others. "This is the one."

Fanny gave a little cry of alarm. "The Tower!"

Perdita stared at the card showing a stone tower being destroyed by lightning, two tiny figures hurling down to the
rocks below. "This is an ill omen!"

"It is not always bad," Mrs. Hever said slowly, as she gathered up the others. "It can mean upheaval or even destruction,
yes. But keep this in mind. The old must be torn down before
something new can be built upon an existing foundation."

"I hope you may be right," Perdita said quietly. Andrew
offered the traditional silver coins to the tea shop owner, but
she waved them away. "I'll not take them from you, Mr. Andrew, nor the ladies."

Gathering up their things, they left the shop and walked
along the quay. An uneasiness had fallen over the group and
Perdita knew it was because of her fortune. She wished she'd
followed her first instinct and refused.

The got into the open carriage with Andrew, and the groom
swung up behind. No one spoke until Perdita glanced up at
the cliffs. High off to the right, beyond Ravenall Castle, arches
of delicate stone stood out against the dark cliffs. "Pray, what
is that ruin?"

Fanny lifted her head. "The Monk's Chapel. We used to
play there as children."

"It makes a pleasant excursion," Andrew said. "Perhaps we

can plan a picnic there before the weather turns. You'd find it interesting. There are the remains of the small dark cells where the monks lived, in contrast to the beautiful stonework of the Lady Chapel they built above the sea. Some claim it is haunted." He turned to Perdita. "If you like, we can drive there later this afternoon. We might persuade Ravenall to accompany us."

A shiver passed through Perdita like a cold wind. "Perhaps another time. I believe I have had enough of superstition for one day."

Perdita was the last to arrive at the breakfast table the following morning. The conversation stopped the moment she entered the breakfast parlor. Fanny stirred her tea, Andrew looked self-conscious, Miss Evans busied herself with putting marmalade on her toast, and Ravenall sat back in his chair, watching her entrance with aloof appreciation. Only the dowager greeted her naturally.

"I hope you slept well, Miss Hexham?"

They have been discussing me, Perdita thought, with a tingle of embarrassment. "Very well, Lady Ravenall. What a glorious day!" she said quickly, as she filled her plate from the sideboard, and slipped into the one remaining empty place at table.

The dowager glanced out the window. "Don't be fooled, child. There is rain on the way, and plenty of it."

"Yes, but not for several hours," Ravenall said. "It will blow over by evening."

He was dressed in a blue coat and tight buckskin breeches with elegant top boots. Perdita thought he had never looked to more advantage. It made her feel awkward and tongue-tied.

He set down his cup. "Will you drive out with me, Miss Hexham? I thought I'd show you something of the estate."

She looked up eagerly, wondering what the proper reply should be. She sent a speaking glance at the countess. "If you do not have other plans, my lady . . ."

"Not in the least. It's a fine day for a drive," Lady Ravenall told her. "You need not think you are deserting us, my dear. I have been down to breakfast more these past weeks than I have in months! Not that it hasn't been most enjoyable," she added hastily. "However, Harriet and I have much to accomplish!"

Miss Evans, Perdita noted, did not seem particularly enthusiastic about it.

Ravenall laughed. "What my grandmother is trying to say so delicately, Miss Hexham, is that she is yearning to retire to her apartments and her manuscript."

"Yes, Lord Ravenall informed me that you were working on a history of the Ravenalls," Perdita replied.

The earl nodded. "My grandmother has three loves: they are the castle, her manuscripts, and—"

"My grandson!"

He bowed. "How edifying! I was going to say, your gardens."

"Naughty of you, Justin." The dowager's delphinium-blue eyes sparkled. "And I would have you know, I count you first among my blessings."

Ravenall bowed again. "I shall have to put my hat back on, madam, before my head grows too large for it!"

Everyone laughed, even Miss Evans. She looked younger and rather pretty with her cheeks suffused with color. After they'd breakfasted, Perdita ran upstairs in a merry mood, to change out of her striped morning dress into something more suitable. Ravenall and the countess lingered at the table.

"You have done a marvelous job of putting Miss Hexham at her ease," he said.

"I have taken more than one wounded bird beneath my wing," Lady Ravenall said, eyeing her grandson. "I do my best to see them mended before I let them fly off again. I do not always succeed in my intentions. Sometimes a bone sets ill."

Ravenall drew his gloves through his hands, frowning. "I have recovered well enough from my tumble, I assure you."

"I wasn't referring to your recent accident," she said gently. "I was thinking of that young boy who spent his summers with me many years ago. The one who kept his suffering to himself, no matter how deeply he was wounded."

"That boy grew up," he said stiffly. "He is no longer in need of someone to bind up his scrapes and ease his heart."

Lady Ravenall shook her head. "You are wrong, my darling one. But I won't fuss at you." She cocked her head. "Just remember, I am neither as old nor as vague as I might appear at times."

He touched her cheek. "You are as young as the dawn, and the quickest-witted woman I know."

She searched his face. "Flatterer! I only wish that it were true."

"It is." He took her hand and kissed it. "And I love you more than anyone in the entire world."

She laughed. "Charming rogue! You are trying to divert me. I will say only one more thing, Justin: I shall be exceedingly happy on the day you love *another* woman more!"

Perdita found Nettie waiting in her chamber. "I am going for a drive with Lord Ravenall."

"Yes, miss. His lordship sent word. I've laid the green velvet out for you. It's only just come from London."

A lovely ensemble was set out on the spread, along with a pair of slender boots. Perdita was glad of Nettie's help in unbuttoning all the small glass buttons on her morning dress, and getting into the snug outfit, with its tight-fitted bodice and smart matching hat. The emerald shade was very becoming, but she wasn't sure if she liked the matching boots.

"These boots are very high."

"Yes, miss." Nettie eyed them. She was very taken with her new young mistress, and delighted to be staying on as her lady's maid. "There is a black pair, miss, but I thought these more suitable."

"I am sure you are right."

As she dressed, Perdita kept thinking how strange it was to have Nettie at her beck and call. How nice—and how uncomfortable, at the same time. A tiny frown formed between her brows.

"If you were not in service at the castle, Nettie," she said suddenly, "what would you wish to do?"

The girl looked up at her, puzzled. "I have always wanted to be taken on at the castle, miss. Ever since I can recall. My older sister was taken on by Mrs. Furlong, down at the Hall. She's content enough there, for all the squire's wife isn't so free with her castoffs as she could wish; but me, I've always hoped for better."

Perdita looked deep into the girl's brown eyes. "Are you happy here, Nettie?"

"Oh, yes, miss! I have a warm bed and plenty to eat, and coins to jingle when I go into the village." And a suitor in Charles, the youngest of the footmen. "I could not ask for more."

It was true that she seemed satisfied with her lot. Perdita pursued her own train of thought. "Have you never thought of going beyond the village? Of going off to London, or . . . or learning to read and write?"

Nettie was horrified. "Oh, no, miss! I'm not saying I wouldn't like to visit London once, but I'm a country girl, born and bred. And what have I to do with reading and writing? It would only give me airs above my station, so my mother says."

She shook her head determinedly. "It's better to be happy with what you have. Wanting more always leads to trouble."

"Perhaps you're right," Perdita said quietly. "I only wish I could share your philosophy. I am afraid that I always want something more, something that is out of my reach."

The maid laughed. "But you're of The Quality, my lady."

Perdita laughed. "Are you saying that excuses every odd kick in my gallop?"

"No, miss."

Nettie's flush belied her words. It was true that The Quality had their odd ways, but it wasn't her place to say so. She perched the fetching hat, with its curving feather, atop Perdita's head. "Only that you and I are as different as chalk from cheese. It is only to be expected that a young lady would strive higher! And you an heiress, as they say."

Perdita gazed at her reflection in the looking glass. *Am I so different?* She didn't think so. Except in her aspirations. Perhaps that was something born in her blood. The well-dressed girl in the mirror looked back at her, seeming so assured and serene. There was nothing of the inner Perdita visible there, quaking in her boots.

She wondered how she achieved such outward calm, when inside her emotions were churning. Was Nettie right? *Was* she Quality?

While Perdita wondered, another image flashed through her mind. The room tilted. Faded. She saw an oval mirror, in a gilt frame. A woman in a silk gown the color of daffodils, with a pair of golden combs holding back her upswept curls. And the face of a young girl in the silvered glass. A girl with wide violet-blue eyes, and jetty hair tied back with a pink ribbon.

Other impressions thronged her mind. The scent of roses. The sound of the twill gown as the woman turned and posed before the mirror. The vision shimmered and threatened to break apart. If she held very still, Perdita thought, she could keep it intact . . .

"Miss? Are you feeling unwell? You've gone very white!"

The other room, the oval gilt mirror vanished, along with the woman and the dark-haired child. Perdita's hands were shaking. For just a moment it seemed as if she could tear away the veil that hid her past; but it was as gone as yesterday. And yet that image had been so clear!

Then she knew why. Realization and disappointment surged through her like cross-currents in the cove at Ravensea. In summer the windows of Moor Cottage were open to the little garden of climbing roses. Their spicy scent had filled the house. And the gilt frame that had appeared in her mind's eye had not held a mirror, but the portrait of Miss Barnstable's mother that had hung in the dear lady's sitting room.

Perdita could have wept with disappointment. She forced herself to take a deep, shuddering breath. "I am quite well, Nettie. Merely a little excited. I must not keep his lordship waiting." She paused. "Would you change places with me if you could?"

"Lord, no, miss. As a girl I liked to pretend I was Maid Marian, hiding out from the wicked Sheriff of Nottingham with bold Robin Hood and his Merry Men." The maid dimpled. "But that doesn't mean I would really like to live out in the woods, you know. I know the difference between pretend and real life, miss. I am content with mine."

Glancing back at her reflection in the mirror, Perdita eyed the fashionable stranger looking back at her. She looked serene and poised, but inside she was a knot of jangled nerves, a hopeless tangle of false memories and wishful thinking.

"I wish I could be as certain of it as you, Nettie," she said softly.

*   *   *

Ravenall scrutnized her as she paused on the last step. From the neat boots on her feet, to the pert military-style hat set at a becoming angle on her dark hair, she was perfect.

"Ravishing, Miss Hexham. I have no doubt you will create a sensation when you wear that in town. Perhaps I should send a warning notice into the papers, before you make your first appearance in the park."

She blushed deeply at his joke. "Perhaps that would be wise, sir. Fanny tells me that once I've taken London by storm, I may do anything I like—as long as my behavior doesn't frighten the horses in the street!"

"Yes, that's an old saying," he replied. "Don't take it too literally, however. If you call too much of the wrong attention to yourself, my girl, you'll have to answer to me!"

The carriage was waiting in the front court when they went out. She could smell the changing weather on the air. She'd hoped to have a view of the sea, but he took them inland, up into the gentle swells of heath that reminded her so much of Dartmoor.

"How have your lessons gone this past week?"

"Very well, my lord." She gave him a rueful look. "I know the oyster spoon from the fish fork, can list the kings and queens of England in order, and am committed to memorizing whole pages of Hexham family bloodlines from *DeBrett's Peerage*."

"Good Lord!"

Perdita sighed. "Exactly. At first I was eager to see London. But now I realize there is so much to learn, and I fear I'll never master it all before we go to town. I am coming to dread it! Could I not remain at Ravenall, my lord?"

Reaching over, he placed his gloved hand over hers. "Courage. You don't have to learn it all, not at once. If you listen much, and say little, except polite pleasantries, you can brush through it. With so many chatterboxes trying to impress the *ton*, your quietness will make you seem self-assured."

She gave him an imploring look. "Fanny said perhaps we needn't go to town after Christmas. The height of the Season doesn't begin until everyone returns from the country after Easter Week. *Months* away!"

Ravenall shook his head. "You'll need as much time to

accustom yourself as possible, before the Season begins in full swing."

They drove away, and he amused her with tidbits of gossip from London, choosing just the ones to make her laugh and feel at ease. "Now you are being absurd!" she exclaimed at one particular story. "I cannot believe that Lord Nedham rode his horse into Lady Montenegro's drawing room!"

"God's truth," Ravenall replied. "After the animal was removed, Lady Montenegro told the *ton* that the horse had far better manners than Nedham, and was more welcome to visit again than he."

A peal of laughter rewarded him. Perdita was much more relaxed in his company if he kept the conversation to light matters.

She smoothed her gloves over her fingers. She liked Ravenall very much when he set himself to please her, as he was doing now. They drove off the main road and along a straight track while he beguiled the time away.

"We'll leave the carriage here," Ravenall announced suddenly, reining in.

She looked around, startled. There was nothing to be seen but twisted trees on one hand, and the cliffs and glistening turquoise sea on the other.

Then a familiar redheaded man rode up from a path beyond, leading a pretty gray mare. Perdita beamed.

"Mr. Malone!"

"Your servant, Miss Hexham." He swept off his hat and bowed. "I told you we should meet again, and soon!"

"Well, I am very glad of it." She was aware of the sharp look Ravenall sent her. "What a pretty little mare," she said hurriedly.

"I am glad you approve," Ravenall told her. "She is yours."

"Mine! But I do not ride!"

Ravenall fixed Perdita with one of his grim smiles. "Ah, but you will, Miss Hexham. You will."

"You are wrong, my lord." She shook her head. "Nothing will induce me to get upon that creature's back. I would only fall off."

"Nonsense!"

But he saw the quiver of her soft lips, and the very real

apprehension in her eyes. He lowered his voice. "I would never let that happen."

It was hard to resist him in that cajoling mood. Not when his eyes were bluer than a midnight sky, and his smile so warm. "It would be a shame to soil your stylish outfit—such a fetching riding habit, with such lovely little boots."

She looked down at her ensemble with brass buttons on green velvet, and the matching boots: she'd wondered why the boots were so high.

"I thought a habit was something one *did*. And I didn't know this outfit was for riding a *horse*. I thought it was for *sitting*. In," she added with a darkling look, "a comfortable carriage. That creature does not look at all comfortable, in any sense of the word."

Laughing, Ravenall held out his gloved hand to her. "You must consider this another area of your education that must be thoroughly explored. It is something every delicately nurtured female must attempt, if she entertains any pretensions of becoming fashionable."

Perdita let him hand her down from the carriage, but pulled back when he tried to lead her closer to the mare. Ravenall and his friend exchanged a look.

"She's a beauty, she is," Malone said, rubbing the horse's muzzle. "And as sweet a goer as I've ever seen. Her name is Alanna, and I chose her particularly for you. Come and meet her."

She let Ravenall guide her closer, but was extremely leery. Up close the mare's coat shone like gray satin. She turned her head to watch Perdita, and whickered softly.

"You see," Ravenall told her. "She likes you."

"I like her, too," Perdita answered. "When both my feet are on the ground."

"When we go to London for the Season, I expect you to go riding in the Row with me on fine mornings. You will look superb!"

The mare tossed her mane. Perdita panicked. "I can't. I won't."

The mare, sensing her fear, grew suddenly restive. As she snorted and pawed the ground, Perdita flung a hand up to her forehead. The world seemed to tilt and spin. A scene flashed through her mind: a horse rearing, the rending of wood. A sudden flood of fear.

Ravenall gripped her shoulders. "I didn't expect such a lack of courage from you," he said sharply.

"It is not that," she said in a stifled voice. "Merely a sudden touch of dizzyness. I am over it."

He scrutinized her for a few seconds. "Forgive me, I was too forceful. I should not expect you to attempt the things I take for granted, without giving you time to prepare yourself. I love to ride almost as much as I love to sail, and hoped that you might feel the same. There is lovely countryside to explore."

Ravenall clasped her hand between his. "I will not ask you to ride, Miss Hexham, only to try."

She lifted her wide violet eyes to his, but didn't answer. "You have been up to the mark on everything thus far," he said. "If you will not do it for yourself, then I must ask you to do it for me!"

That hit her in a vulnerable spot. He had given her a name, a home. She had given him nothing in return. She lifted her face to his. "Very well. I will learn to ride if you wish it, my lord, but I cannot promise to enjoy it!"

He laughed. "Only try."

"There is no mounting block."

"I'll take care of that."

Ravenall caught her around the waist. He was so close, she might have leaned her cheek against his coat. The temptation was there, and she almost gave in to it. Confused, she looked up at Ravenall, wondering if he'd noticed.

Their gazes locked, and she felt as if the air had been knocked out of her. Perdita couldn't have torn hers away if she'd tried. She was falling into the indigo depths of his eyes, and only his support kept her knees from buckling.

Something similar was happening to Ravenall, but stronger. The urge to sweep her into his arms and kiss her senseless was overpowering.

Jack coughed softly, and Ravenall thanked God there was a third party present. *Devil take it! What magic does she wield over me, to make me so forget myself?*

He was a man used to being in command of others, and of

himself. Ravenall frowned. He'd have to be very careful. One wrong step, and he'd ruin everything.

"Up you go, Miss Hexham!" With a smooth movement, he lifted her slender frame, and tossed her lightly into the saddle.

She was caught unawares. One moment her feet were on solid ground, the next she was on the mare's back. But those few, brief seconds when she had been held weightless in the air, supported only by Ravenall's strong arms, had left Perdita speechless.

He'd lifted her as if she'd been a feather. She wasn't entirely sure if she liked the sensation of being helpless and out of control of the matter, while he was fully in command. But it had certainly been interesting. Her breath came a little quicker, and she almost overbalanced.

"Easy, now." Ravenall was there to steady her. Waiting until she was settled, he stepped away and nodded to the other man. "I'll take your mount, Jack, and ride beside Miss Hexham, while you lead the mare."

The horse whickered softly and danced sideways. Perdita had no choice but to hang on. "Don't be afraid of Alanna," he told Perdita. "I assure you that her disposition is far better than mine."

She bit back a hot retort. Instead she pressed her lips together so tightly they were blanched. It was alarming to be so far off the ground and at the mercy of an animal so large and energetic.

"Good girl!"

She pretended not to hear him, and Ravenall laughed softly. "Your stubbornness will see you through the worst of it."

The lady's saddle was awkward, and she wasn't sure how to sit upright, and how to manage her suddenly unwieldy skirt. Ravenall swept the green velvet over his arm, and he fanned it out on the horse's flank, then made sure her boots were secure in the stirrups.

With a smile of encouragement, Ravenall left her and mounted the other horse. It was a magnificent animal, black as coal, and so huge it made the mare seem insignificant. Perdita swallowed. Its rider looked equally magnificent, as he wheeled the horse and rode up beside her. The muscles of his back and thighs showed to great advantage.

She'd seen him naked, of course. Not all of him, but

enough to pique her imagination. A flush rose from her breasts to her face, as she remembered the strong curve of his back, the . . .

She saw Jack watching her, and looked hastily away.

"Are you ready, Miss Hexham?"

"As much as I will ever be!"

Grimly determined, she kept her seat the first few steps by sheer willpower. Then she realized that Ravenall was beside her, ready to lean down and swoop her up at the slightest sign of disaster. His eyes met hers in a mutual smile.

Perdita, still remembering his body beneath the monogrammed sheets, was the first to look away.

"Start the lesson. Let's not waste any more time," he said abruptly.

Jack raised his eyebrows. "Remember," he said lightly, "it's best to have a light hand on the reins."

"I don't know what you mean," Perdita said worriedly.

"Ah, but his lordship does!"

Ravenall gave his friend a withering glance. "I don't need you to remind me of it."

The Irishman laughed. "Don't you now?"

"Curse you, Jack, I don't need lessons from you."

"No, but Miss Hexham does. We'd best get on with it. There's a storm brewing out at sea."

Perdita lifted her head. The sky above was still blue, but with a hazy, metallic cast. "There isn't a cloud to be seen!"

"No," Ravenall responded, "but Jack's right. I can smell it on the wind."

While he rode the black horse at a walk beside her, the other led Perdita's mare by her bridle. To her surprise, once she was up on the elegant creature's back, Perdita found it a little frightening, but it was even more exhilarating to be so high above the ground. To feel the warmth and strength of the dainty mare moving beneath her.

She didn't, however, know if she liked it.

They made a slow circle around the heath, while she fought to keep her balance. Ravenall kept a hawk's eye on her, ready to grasp the reins at the slightest misstep. By the time they'd circled the dell again, Perdita had gotten the hang of staying upright in the saddle. She doubted she could keep it up if the mare went any faster.

"It would be far easier if I could sit astride like you," she pointed out.

"Now that," Ravenall said, "would put an end to your ambitions faster than tying your garter in public."

Perdita laughed, and pretended to hold her nose up in the air. "My ambitions are small. And that, my lord, is surely not a fitting phrase to use in the presence of a delicately nurtured female. Even one who 'entertains pretentions of becoming fashionable.' "

His quick smile made her heart give a leap. "No. It was excessively vulgar of me. And that," he said, "was another good setdown. I am lucky you are on horseback, or you would no doubt have boxed my ears!"

She turned her head and gave him a pert smile. "No. That would be excessively vulgar in *me*."

He favored her with a bow. "Touché. Once again, you have bested me, Miss Hexham."

"I don't," Perdita said, "imagine that that happens often."

His smile turned wry. "Not particularly. Are you ready to take the reins, Miss Hexham?"

"No, my lord. Perhaps another time."

She realized what she'd said after the words were already out. She'd committed herself to another riding lesson.

"Tomorrow, then. At the same hour," he said.

Perdita bit her lip. She'd won the skirmish, but he'd won the battle. But then, he'd had more practice.

When the lesson ended, she was glad. The anticipation of having him lift her down, of being so very close to him, was so great she was almost giddy with it. Instead he dismounted and let Jack assist her. Perdita's disappointment was keen.

Later, as they rode back to the castle together, he seemed preoccupied. His handling of the ribbons was masterful, but she sensed his thoughts were far away. *From the crease between his brows, they must be unpleasant!*

As if he'd read her mind, Ravenall turned his head. It unnerved her. Perdita flushed and looked down. He was like a flame, she thought: close and it warmed her; too close, and it might burn. She ran her gloved finger over the mark on her wrist.

But then, look where this little burn has led me!

She rubbed her gloved fingers over the smooth scar.

They crossed a low bridge over a dark stream that rushed eagerly on its way to meet the sea. At last the castle came into view, stark and splendid. It rose up gray, against a grayer sky, defying the elements as it had for centuries.

The air became cool and the light shifted. She pulled the lap rug over her lap, and looked up. Clouds were closing in rapidly. All color was leached from the sky, and the battlements of Ravenall Castle stood out sharply, like one of the pen-and-ink drawings that Perdita had seen within its walls. Lightning spiked across the sky behind the castle's towers, reminding her of Mrs. Hever's fortune-telling.

The riding lesson had been a risk, but it was nothing compared to the one she'd taken when she'd run off with Lord Ravenall. And nothing at all compared to what was yet to come. There was so much more to learn than she had ever dreamed, and and Perdita found it increasingly daunting.

As they made their way past a copse of trees and turned in between the high, iron gates, thunder echoed. The fitful breeze fought the brim of her bonnet. She lifted a gloved hand to hold it. Such a short time ago she hadn't a bonnet to her name, or warm gloves to match a splendid riding habit. She must learn to accept her good fortune.

Wind whipped the avenue of trees that led through the wooded park, until they ascended once more in the open. The carriage bowled along through the swirling ground mists, until it seemed the horses trod on clouds.

As the atmosphere changed, her mood became increasingly fanciful. Ravenall Castle rose up on the headland, like an apparition in a fairy tale. It seemed entirely possible that it might dissolve before her eyes, become nothing more than a denser patch in the rising fog.

Lightning suddenly shot across the sky.

"Don't worry," Ravenall assured her. "We'll be home long before the rains come down."

Thunder rumbled distantly, but Perdita knotted her hands in her lap, and glanced at his profile. As if aware of her notice, he turned his face a little away. But it wasn't his scarred cheek that held her attention—indeed she rarely noticed it anymore—it was the words he'd spoken.

Home! How lovely that sounds!

Her spirits lifted immediately. As they went up the long avenue to the castle she smiled and told herself that she had never been so happy.

So happy that it almost made her afraid.

Seventeen

The first incident happened only a week later.

Perdita's day began innocently, with her riding lessons. She usually rode with Ravenall, although occasionally she and Fanny went out with one of the grooms. She rode well enough to venture out from the stableyard without embarrassing herself, and had come to look forward to the daily outings.

She descended the stairs after changing out of her riding habit to find Ravenall alone in the drawing room. "Where is Fanny?"

"Conferring with my grandmother and Miss Evans on the dinner party that will be given to introduce you to the neighborhood."

Her heart sank. "Will it be a very grand affair?"

"No more than twenty or thirty," he said casually. "Fanny thought you would be more easy with a small party. Afterward the older members of the company will likely set up at cards, and there will be some simple country dances in the hall. I hope you won't dislike it."

"No," she said unconvincingly. "I shall like it above all things. I am sure it will be a most gratifying evening."

Ravenall laughed. "You are quickly learning the value of the polite lie, Miss Hexham. You must only practice your conviction."

"It is just that I am afraid I'll make a horrid mistake. Especially when Lady Haycross comes to stay at the castle." Perdita was terrified of meeting Ravenall's sister.

"Are you imagining her as some grand peeress, full of her own consequence? Disabuse yourself of the notion. While she can be elegant and witty, she is still a sad romp."

"But she is married to Lord Haycross!" And that was another fear. She prayed that the duke had paid no heed to the tavern wench he'd seen so briefly in Ravenall's room, after the carriage accident.

Once again Ravenall seemed to read her mind. "The duke is of the old school. I doubt he'd recognize any of his servants other than his valet, if he passed them in the street. You will like Daisey," he told her, "and I have no doubt she'll take you under her wing and sponsor your London debut."

"But a duchess!" Perdita stammered. "What shall I say to her?"

"Knowing my sister, very little! *She* will do all the talking."

She could tell that there was real fondness beneath his rallying words. "That relieves my mind considerably!"

"Good. Daisey will soon put you at your ease. My sister knows all the latest on-dits, and is a fashionable hostess. If you listen to her, you'll learn a good deal. Her tongue runs on wheels, but she has a shrewd head on her young shoulders. Except perhaps," he murmured, recalling the episode of the wagered diamond earrings "where the Haycross family heirlooms are concerned."

Perdita hadn't heard the last bit. She was too busy with her own worries.

How can I possibly be at ease with the Duchess of Haycross! Every time I look at her, I will remember climbing atop Mrs. Croggins's best chair to stare across the valley to the lights of Haycross Manor. And then I will remember what I can conveniently forget for hours at a time: that everything she will think I am, is a lie.

"Cheer up," Ravenall said. "I have something for you." He turned to an ebony table and retrieved something.

"A gift, Miss Hexham." He handed her a slim packet. "This came down from London while we were out riding. It is something I promised you, in what now seems to have been a very long time ago."

Perdita unwrapped it carefully. "Oh! You remembered!" she exclaimed, her face shining.

"I gave you my word."

She held his gift carefully. It was a slender volume entitled *West Country Tales*, the book she'd left behind when she'd fled the Stag and Crown with him by night. She'd mentioned it only once to him. Of course, this was not her own battered copy, foxed and water-stained from the leaking eaves. Its binding and gold stamped letters were pristine.

He took her hand. "I'm sorry it couldn't be the original. But even if I were able to retrieve it without comment by some miracle, it is better that nothing is left to trace your path backwards from the castle to Dartmoor."

She nodded, so choked up with emotion she could scarcely speak. Her violet eyes sparkled with unshed tears. "I thank you, my lord. You could not have given me anything I would like more! I will cherish it as I did the other."

Ravenall regarded her with amusement. He'd presented her with trunks of beautiful gowns, an assortment of necklaces and earbobs, and a very elegant and expensive horse to hack about the countryside. None of it had provoked such a delighted response.

Raising her hands to his lips, he kissed her fingers. "I hope that you may, in time, come to cherish the giver, as well."

She smiled at him tremulously, and moved a little closer. She hadn't meant to do it. But the moment her body brushed against his, the electricity sprang between them, like lightning between sky and earth. That moment at the George, when the screen had fallen to reveal her in the bath, rose up between them until the air shimmered with it.

Perdita felt every bit as naked as she had been then. The difference was, that if they were in the same situation now, she would have wanted him to keep on looking at her. To cross the room to her and—

With a small groan Ravenall let go of her hands and cupped her face between his. *"You little witch,"* he whispered, as if he'd read her thoughts. Her breath caught in her throat, and his was ragged.

Ravenall fought the hot flare of desire, but was losing ground rapidly. The vision of her standing in the copper tub at the George, with water beading like crystals on her milky skin, had been branded in his brain. So many nights he had lain awake, remembering. Those perfect breasts, that slim waist, those slender legs. *So beautiful!*

And now, so warm and willing.

He wanted to make love to her. To be the first to teach her, to know her. To feel her body arch with ecstasy against his.

To do all the things that would bring her alive to her womanhood and the pleasures of love.

Her nearness fogged his brain, disrupting his thoughts until they were overwhelmed with desire. "Shall we put an end to this farce?" he said fiercely.

His hands came down roughly to her shoulders and she swayed toward him. His mouth was only inches away from hers. Perdita had every expectation that she would be pulled against his chest, that his firm mouth would be on her own lips. She raised her face to him, wanting to be swept into his arms and crushed against him. To be kissed until everything else vanished but the two of them.

Ravenall stepped back with a quick movement and moved away. She felt as if she'd been slapped.

Then she saw that Burton had opened the door to admit Andrew and Mr. Clements. The butler was impassive, but Andrew flushed to the roots of his hair. Ravenall's agent gave an awkward bow.

"I beg pardon, my lord, for intruding!"

"Nonsense," Ravenall said coolly. "I was merely having a talk with my ward." His eyes met his cousin's. "Miss Hexham is nervous about meeting Daisey."

Andrew grinned. "Lord, is that all? From the looks on your faces I'd thought that you'd quarreled."

He made his bow to Perdita. "You needn't worry. Daisey will set you at ease within minutes. She's a great gun!" He sent a laughing look over to Ravenall. "Do you remember the day we went to the Monks' Chapel, and she got her head caught between the stonework? Lord, that was a job to get her loose again."

The earl raised his eyebrows. "What a harum-scarum opinion you will give everyone of my sister! She is a great lady now, Miss Hexham, and well aware of the dignity of her position. At the time Andrew mentions, however, Daisey was only five or six years of age, and had followed us out along the cliff path to the ruins."

"You must go there sometime," Andrew told Perdita. "Before the weather changes, and it gets too hazardous. There is the ruin of an ancient chapel, and five or six caves half bricked up with stone, where the monks lived in the early medieval times. Druids were said to have worshipped there long before the dawn of Christianity. It's quite picturesque."

"I should like to do so," she replied, grateful for the diversion.

Perdita excused herself as quickly as she could without making an issue of it, and went up to her room. Nettie was gone, for which she was thankful. She stood at the window looking out, but saw nothing of the view. Her eyes were still filled with the vision of Ravenall gazing down at her with such passionate intensity her bones had felt liquid.

They still did. In fact, she was shaking with reaction and thwarted desire. In that moment, Perdita realized, with terrible clarity, that she had fallen into a dangerous snare woven from her sensual attraction to Ravenall.

Worse yet, that she had fallen deeply, hopelessly, in love with him.

Perdita was restless, but didn't dare go down until she knew that Ravenall had ridden off toward Ravensea with Andrew. She watched as he rode away, until he was completely out of sight.

For the past few days she'd been reading the romantic novels that Fanny loved, including several that were considered far too racy for an unmarried girl. A gently bred young lady might not know what happened after the villain took the beautiful but unfortunate prisoner away to his bedchamber, or the heroic warrior prince rescued the brave (but suddenly fainting) heroine and swept her off to his island home—but she did.

Oh, yes.

And it didn't end with a closed door, or a coy series of dots upon a page.

For the past two hours Perdita had been thinking of that night she'd accidentally come across the two lovers behind the inn. Of what it would be like to be naked in Ravenall's strong arms, feeling her breasts against his hard chest, the touch of his hands over her smooth, white limbs.

Her body and mind both burned for him. She wanted to feel his weight upon her, pressing her into the soft grass while the stars spun overhead. She wanted to know the heat of his kiss, with their breaths mingling. The silky feel of his mouth upon her aching breasts. The sweet, sharp piercing of their joining, and the swift thrust of his loins.

Her blood was on fire.

She groaned and crossed her hands over her breasts, wishing they were his. Closed her eyes and imagined him touching her, arousing her. Felt his breath against her cheek, his hand against her flesh. The hot rush of blood to her loins—

The door opened and Nettie peeped in. Perdita felt the blood drain from her cheeks.

"Are you ill, miss? You're white as snow. I thought I heard you moan."

"I . . . I have the headache!"

"Let me help you out of that dress and into your wrapper. I'll fetch you one of Dr. Holcum's pastilles and some lavender water to bathe your temples—"

"No!" Perdita recovered herself. "It's fresh air that I want. I'll take my shawl and go out for brisk walk. It will clear my head."

"If you're sure, miss?"

Perdita was adamant. "I'll be back in plenty of time to dress for dinner."

"Very well, miss. Oh, Mrs. Fitzmorris was looking for you earlier, but Burton told her you'd come up to your room, and she didn't wish to disturb you."

"I'll look in on her before I go." And perhaps convince Fanny to take a walk with her. That would help to clear away all thoughts of Lord Ravenall.

She glanced at the pile of books on the table beside her sofa. There were an interesting selection, as different as the people who had selected them. *Thaddeus of Warsaw,* an historical novel, and Southey's *Life of Nelson,* recommended by the Lady Ravenall. There was also Fanny's favorite, Sir Walter Scott's *Marmion*, and *West Country Tales,* which Ravenall had procured for her.

The majority were too cumbersome to carry on a long walk, and she didn't want to risk losing the one Ravenall had given her. Instead Perdita picked up a slender ivory morocco and stamped gold volume of Coleridge's *Kubla Khan*, which Andrew had taken down from one of the shelves, and tucked it safely away inside her deep pocket.

She discovered Fanny in the Yellow Parlor, sharpening a quill with an ivory-handled pen knife. Light from the window turned her fair hair to beaten gold.

"It's too fine an afternoon to stay indoors," Perdita announced. "Will you come for a walk with me? I mean to visit the old chapel and some monks' cells along the cliff walk."

Fanny looked up from her task. "Another time, perhaps. I promised Lady Ravenall that I would make out the invitations to her dinner party."

Since her arrival at the castle as Perdita's companion, Fanny had also been drafted into the role of unofficial social secretary, a task at which she proved very adept.

Perdita wouldn't be put off. "You've been cooped up for far too long. We needn't make a long visit."

The other woman shook her head. "This will take me the rest of the afternoon. And don't forget that Lord and Lady Haycross are due to arrive on Wednesday. There is still so much to be done! Why don't you ask one of the others?"

"Andrew has gone off on an errand, and Ravenall is closeted in the estate room poring over ledgers."

Fanny dipped her pen into the crystal inkwell. "I thought Andrew was expecting Mr. Malone to come by."

"I saw them earlier, going along the corridor to the old wing together, but Burton said they have gone to Ravensea to visit friends."

"I cannot conceive of any friends that either of them have in Ravensea." She set down the pen and made a sound of annoyance as ink spattered one of the thick cream envelopes she'd already addressed.

A small smile played over Perdita's mouth. "I think I heard a tavern mentioned somewhere in the conversation."

"Some waterfront thieves' hang-out, no doubt. Mr. Malone should know better than to draw Andrew into his escapades!"

"From what I heard, it was the other way around." Perdita's suspicions were aroused. "Have you quarreled with Mr. Malone?"

Fanny looked down at the invitation list. Her color was heightened. "I do not care enough about his opinions to quarrel with him about anything."

She went back to carefully inscribing names, and Perdita looked longingly out the open window. The air was fresh, the sun warm, and the invitation to be out-of-doors too enticing to resist. "Very well, if I cannot persuade you, I will go alone."

"Take a groom with you." Fanny glanced up. "I almost

forgot." She waved her hand at a large volume on the table in the window embrasure. "When you return, you might wish to peruse this book which Ravenall came across in the library. He thought you would be interested." Perdita glanced down. *The Illustrated Guide to Noble Houses of Great Britain.* "Is the castle in it?"

"Naturally. And Haycross Manor, where Ravenall's brother-in-law has his country seat. Part of Haycross is even older than the castle. It's not really a manor any longer, but a very grand house."

"So I have heard." *And seen from a distance,* Perdita thought. "I will look through the book tonight after dinner." *Then, if I make any mistaken references to Haycross Manor, it will seem to have come from the guidebook. That is surely what Ravenall had in mind.*

When she went out through the long windows and past the boxwood maze, Perdita could feel the change in the air, the poignant waning of autumn. She imagined how cozy it must be at Ravenall in the wintry months, tucked inside the thick walls with leaping fires and blazing lights, while outside the storms howled beyond the windows.

And I should infinitely prefer curling up with a book to attending all the fashionably overcrowded London parties that Ravenall and Fanny keep dangling before me, as if they were bits of cheese to a starving mouse!

As far as London was concerned, Perdita could only see two benefits to removing to town after Christmas: she would be so busy she couldn't dwell on her attraction to Lord Ravenall—and it would be much more difficult to find themselves alone together.

A brisk walk brought her around to the south side of the castle, where the ancient walls loomed over her. She took the paved path through the shrubbery, as Andrew had advised, and went right where it forked. It was less than a quarter hour along the high cliff path. It wound down the sheer cliff, eventually turning into steps hewn from the living rock.

Perdita hesitated. The way was certainly steep. She could see the waves frothing against the base of the cliff, although their roar was muted at this height. Then she spied the broken walls of the Monks' Chapel, with the single empty window framing the sea, and was impelled to go on.

She noticed as she went along that there were crystals growing in pockets along the rock face of the granite cliff. Tiny darts of light winked from them as they caught the sun.

Perdita put out her hand and clutched the rock, as a wave of vertigo came over her. Cold sweat broke out on her forehead. If she hadn't been almost all the way down to the chapel, she would have turned back the first moment she was able.

She steadied herself and made her way to the jutting chapel ledge.

It proved worth the effort. Perdita came out on a grassy slope, with a huddle of dark little stone rooms, no larger than five feet on a side, built against the cliff's face. But it was the chapel's ruined arches and elegant traceries against the cloudless blue sky that were both beautiful and heartwrenchingly melancholy. She wondered at the little colony of medieval monks who had lived there, spending their lives in prayer while perched on the very edge of infinity.

Miss Evans, with her love of everything Gothic, would certainly approve of the atmosphere here, she thought.

Perdita wandered around happily. Once she thought she heard a woman's voice, but decided it was only the cry of the gulls.

The roof of the exquisite chapel was open to the sky, and the walls covered with green moss. It was enchanting. Where the altar stone had once stood, was a hawthorn bush, and beyond it a view of the headland. She remembered the legend that Joseph of Arimathea had visited the British Isles to bring the Holy Grail to Glastonbury, and plunged his hawthorn stave into the ground, that it had taken root, and that every hawthorn in the country had sprung from the old pilgrim's staff.

There was an air of magic about the setting. Vague feelings stirred in the depths of her memory, but proved as elusive as mist. She was aware though that in such a place as this, anything might happen.

Any wish might come true.

The paving stones of the ancient floor, some with cryptic symbols carved upon their surfaces, were two-thirds intact. There were herbs and perennial flowers growing up around the foundations, and some had seeded themselves into the cracks in the stone floor. Wild vines grew up and over the walls.

Perdita sat on the stone bench built out from the wall at the back of the chapel and opened the book with Coleridge's hypnotic poem:

> In Xanadu did Kubla Khan
> A stately pleasure dome decree:
> Where Alph, the sacred river, ran
> Through caverns measureless to man
> Down to a sunless sea.

The music of the words drew her in. As she was savoring them, something skittered down from above. Perdita tilted her head and looked up at the steep stairs leading down from the cliff walk to the chapel.

"Is that you after all, Fanny?"

There was no reply, and Perdita turned back to her book, only to find it had slipped off her lap to one side. "Oh!" She rose hastily and leaned down to retrieve it.

Two things happened at once: a shadow fell over her, and the air was rent by a terrible groan, as if the ancient stones themselves cried out in pain. A shower of rocks and debris fell from the upper wall behind her. A glancing blow to her shoulder sent Perdita sprawling. She found herself on her stomach, with nothing beneath her face but thin blue air, and the rocks and waves so far below.

She turned on her side, shaking violently, and saw that the back wall had collapsed. The stone bench where she'd been sitting was buried beneath it. If the book hadn't fallen from her lap, she would be dead.

Her shoulder ached abominably, and she was sick with reaction. She heard a shout from the upper cliff path.

"I say, miss, are you injured?"

It belonged to a funny little man with keen hazel eyes, a bald head, and a full white beard. He wore a rusty black jacket over homespun trews.

"Just . . . just badly shaken, I think."

"Don't move! I'll be down as quick as a wink."

Although he was bowlegged as a postboy, he moved with an agility that belied his age. Little pellets of rock rained down, but the rubble didn't shift. Perdita sat up with his help. She was covered with fine dust and bits of dirt and moss.

"I am Mr. Grigg," he told her, "an antiquarian. And you, my dear, are a very lucky young woman!"

"I was sitting on the stone bench," she murmured dazedly.

"The *coffin* shelf, you mean. Very unlucky, that."

"Evidently!" another voice said from atop the cliff.

Perdita looked up dazedly through her pain. "My lord!"

Ravenall came skittering down the path at full tilt, eyes blazing. "Yes, Miss Hexham, it is I—and not in good time, it seems." He knelt down beside her and clasped her hands in his. "What has happened here?"

"I was reading quietly. I heard a terrible groaning, and the wall collapsed."

"I believe someone has been excavating here," Mr. Grigg pronounced, shading his eyes. "If you look closely, you can see the mark of a pry bar on the rocks."

"Nonsense!" Ravenall exclaimed. He helped Perdita to her feet and held her against his side. "It is only where two stones grated upon one another."

"Well," Mr. Grigg said, scratching his long white beard. "If you look even closer, you can see the pry bar lying there in the bushes!"

Ravenall's face went white. "Sir, I will be forever in your debt if you go to the castle at once. Tell them that Miss Hexham has been injured and to send for the doctor. I'll carry her back."

"How'll you get the young lady up those steep steps?" Mr. Grigg asked. "Don't look as how it's possible to me."

Perdita could have sworn she heard Ravenall's teeth grind. "Leave it to me, sir. Please do as I have asked."

Those keen green eyes met the flashing blue ones. "Very well, my lord. If you're sure you'll bring Miss Hexham back safely."

"The word of a Ravenall!"

"Aye, and that's good enough for me." With a tip of his hat, Mr. Grigg hurried off, his short legs pumping as he went up the precipitous stairs.

"Let me see what the damage is," Ravenall said, unbuttoning the top buttons of her dress. His hands were infinitely patient and tender as he worked the fabric away to expose her white shoulder.

This is like a bad dream, Perdita thought muzzily. He was doing exactly what she wished he would do, but not at all under the right circumstances.

She gave a sharp cry when he pushed against her arm. "Not broken, I think. But it must be attended to as soon as possible."

The world was blurred by her pain, and Perdita put her head against Ravenall's shoulder. "How will you get me up?"

He touched her cheek. "Believe, my dear, that I am sincerely sorry this is necessary." There was real regret in his voice.

His hand brushed across her throat and he leaned down. He grabbed her shoulder hard, and blinding pain jagged through her like lightning. She felt herself falling, spinning down and down and down, with a scream trapped in her throat.

Then all the world went black.

Eighteen

Perdita drifted on a river of warm air. She didn't know where she was or why. Gentle hands bound up her shoulder in a silk sling.

"A very unfortunate incident, my lord," an unfamiliar voice said softly, "but she will soon be none the worse for wear. Miss Hexham was a very lucky young lady, and your quick thinking in resetting the dislocation of her shoulder surely saved her from more serious injury."

Perdita heard their voices but they seemed to come from a great distance. Someone pressed a bitter liquid to her lips, and she drank.

It was Fanny's voice, speaking in low, urgent tones, that wakened her.

"How could you be so careless, Justin!"

"Do you think I haven't gone over it again and again in my mind? It was he who spotted the pry bar, Fanny. Despite his age, the old man has eyes like a hawk."

"You must manage him with great care, then."

"Be a little less busy in my affairs," Ravenall said sharply. "I know how to handle the Mr. Griggs of the world. The pry bar—yes, and shovel too—were there because the wall above the chapel was in need of repair."

"And he believed you?"

"Of course."

"Hush, for the love of God. You'll awaken her!"

But Perdita was no longer interested in the conversation. She had succumbed to the sleeping draught, and drifted happily away.

Perdita fought up through layers of nightmare. The kitchen of the Stag and Crown. Sam Bailey chasing her across the stark moors. An empty ballroom, with a thousand gold stars painted on the vast ceiling and great brass chandeliers. Blue silk-covered walls with a hundred doors, and no way out . . .

Bits and pieces of conversation played like music in her head. She tried to sort them out. She remembered then. She'd been inside the old Monks' Chapel when the wall had given way. Ravenall had carried her to safety somehow. It all seemed so real.

"Someone tried to kill me," she said softly.

"Good heavens, miss, you'll never say so!"

Perdita's eyes flew open. The sun was well up, and Nettie had brought her a tray with toast and milk.

"You've been dreaming, you have," the maid said, setting down the tray on the night table. "Mumbling all sorts of outlandish things about scrubbing floors! La, I laughed to hear it, miss! I've laid out your white dress with the cherry ribbons because the Duchess of Haycross will be arriving today; but you're to stay abed until Dr. Ash comes by."

"Pooh! I'm fine." Perdita sat up, frowning. The threads of dreams still clung to her, but she wondered if she'd given anything away by talking in her disturbed sleep.

"I was having nightmares. They seemed very real!" She could hear the voice quite clearly if she concentrated: *"Did you think he would have the audacity to suspect the Earl of Ravenall of attempted murder?"*

The maid positioned the tray over her knees. "They always seem so at the time, even when there are strange things in them, like flying contraptions and dragons."

Nettie was still chuckling as she arranged the pillows behind her mistress's back. "Someone trying to kill you! Why, that's an odd one, all right. Why on earth would anyone wish to harm you, miss?"

"I don't know," Perdita replied. *But if there's any truth to it, I intend to find out!* Perhaps it had been a dream after all. Even as she spread jam on her toast the snippets of conversation were fading, until only an uneasy shadow remained.

Perdita was resting on the sofa in her sitting room when the Duchess of Haycross arrived. Ravenall's sister arrived almost immediately after Dr. Ash's visit, and hurried up at once to Perdita.

Her visitor was a vision in sapphire with a bonnet to match, trimmed with a bunch of plumes in three shades of blue.

"What a fortunate thing that Ravenall was nearby," the Duchess of Haycross exclaimed, perching on the settee at the foot of Perdita's bed. "What splendid adventures you seem to have, Miss Hexham. I declare I am quite envious of you, now that I am a stolid matron."

Since this was so opposite of the fact, Perdita burst out laughing. This charming blond creature, all blue eyes and golden ringlets, was as lovely and dainty as a fairy. "You really are a duchess?" she blurted.

"Oh, yes! But I am Haycross's second wife, you know. Eustacia, the fifth duchess, died in childbirth—so you see, I am a step-mama, as well."

"Oh! You are so young to have such a charge."

Daisey gave her charming laugh. "Did you picture them still in leading strings? My step-daughters are all grown and married, with hopeful families of their own, so I have all the advantages of commanding their fond respect, without having had any of the responsibility of raising them!"

"Then you have no children of your own?"

A shadow passed over the duchess's pretty face. "It has only been two years," she said wistfully. "There is still time to give my lord an heir."

Perdita realized at once that she had erred. "Forgive me. I should not have asked." Once again she'd trespassed and uttered what Fanny termed "the sort of questions a lady never asks."

"I do not count it, so you should not, either." Daisey shrugged daintily. "As old as I am, I have still been known to be shockingly indiscreet, myself."

"Why, you cannot have more than a year or two on me, Lady Haycross."

"I am two-and-twenty," Daisey replied, as if it were a vast age. She undid the strings of her bonnet and threw it on the edge of the bed. "I can't think why I bought this now. Of course, I did think it was rather fetching at the time."

"It is truly lovely," Perdita said, bewildered by the leap in subject matter.

"So I thought, as well. But Ravenall says it is far too matronly, and of course that ruined it for me, completely. Fifty guineas thrown away!" the young duchess exclaimed. "But I daresay I can use the feathers on another bonnet, or perhaps with a ballgown and my sapphire hair clips. Do you think that would serve?"

She didn't really expect an answer, which was just as well, for Perdita's mouth hung open in amazement. *Fifty guineas for a bonnet!* She couldn't believe that anyone could be so extravagant.

Daisey eyed their reflections in the dressing table mirror. "How fortunate that you are dark and I am fair. We shall set one another off quite splendidly, you know. I predict that you will be declared an accredited beauty, Miss Hexham, and be the envy of all the other girls making their come-out. Oh, what fun it will be to plan the ball we shall give in your honor at Haycross House." She lowered her voice. "The Prince Regent will doubtless attend!"

Perdita's head was whirling. It was exactly like being in one of those dreams where things kept changing, and nothing at all turned out the way she might expect. She found Ravenall's sister fascinating and alarming in equal measures. And the Prince Regent! *I cannot pull it off,* she thought, daunted by the prospect. *I will be totally undone!*

Daisey saw her error. She smiled and put her hand over Perdita's. "Oh, my runaway tongue! I've frightened you half to death."

Her dimples deepened. "You may think I do not feel for your position, Miss Hexham. Indeed I do. My father's lineage was impeccable, but his pockets were all to let. When Haycross chose to pay his addresses to me I was all in a muddle. To go almost from the schoolroom to become a peeress of the realm was a great shock, you know. But I soon learned my way about—just as you will."

"I hope you may be right, Lady Haycross."

"Oh, have no fears on that head. And you must call me Daisey," she announced with another swift conversational tack. "After all, we shall be sisters when you wed my brother."

Perdita blushed deeply. "I have no plans to marry your brother, Lady Haycross. I do not know where you came by that idea!"

Daisey cocked her head. "I thought it was Ravenall told me. Perhaps I am mistaken."

"You most certainly are," Perdita said. "I have no intention of marrying anyone, least of all Lord Ravenall!"

The duchess rose and shook out her crumpled skirts. "How famous," she said. "It is always best to keep a man on tenterhooks. But you cannot fool me. I can tell that you are not indifferent to Justin, by that fire in your eye."

She shook her head, making her curls bounce prettily. "People meeting me for the first time often underestimate me, because of the way I rattle on; however, anyone who knows me will tell you that I am awake on every suit."

Daisey picked her hat with the waving plumes up from the bed and eyed it askance. "Perhaps I should offer this to Miss Evans; however, I doubt she would wear such a frivolous confection. I know! I will give it to Fanny. It is the very thing for a dashing young widow. It might even attract some gentleman's eye. Her late husband lost his fortune through bad investments, and put a period to his life. It caused a very great scandal."

"What?" Perdita was stunned. "I am sorry to hear of it." *No wonder she is so bitter.*

"She was desperately in love with a dashing young regimental officer. Imagine, to be married against her will to another, only to have him take his own life and leave her destitute!"

Perdita was distressed. "I didn't know. I thought her to be a lady of means."

"She hasn't a feather to fly with! But a comment Justin made earlier leads me to believe he has something up his sleeve. 'I have plans for Fanny,' he told me, 'so you may rest easy.' And do you know, Justin is very determined and inventive. When he gives his word he always manages to come through."

"I don't doubt it."

Daisey leaned down and kissed Perdita's cheek. "How alive the castle seems, now that you and Fanny have come to live here. I am so glad of it! Later, if you feel more the thing, come to my chambers and I shall show you the latest fashions from Madame Fancot. You must buy all your dresses from her, and no one else!"

The duchess swept out of the room, leaving Perdita torn between laughter and chagrin.

*   *   *

Later that afternoon, while the duchess was resting, Perdita spent some time in the drawing room with the others. The dowager countess and Miss Evans were going over lists for the projected dinner party while Andrew entertained Perdita with stories of his travels abroad.

"I should like to visit Rome, of course, but most particularly Venice, now that Napoleon is vanquished."

Miss Evans looked up with shy eagerness. "He called it 'Europe's Drawing Room.' Is it very beautiful, Mr. Waverly? Like the painting of the Grand Canal that hangs in the reception area outside the ballroom?"

"Indeed it is, and more. Perhaps one day you will see *La Serenissima* in person."

Miss Evans smiled wanly and made no reply. It was clear that she felt such a journey was well beyond her limited means. Perdita bit her lip. *Harriet works to earn her bread, pleasant as her surroundings might be. And I have merely stolen mine!*

Perdita smiled across at her. "I have a great desire to see Venice myself, Miss Evans. If I should go, perhaps you would care to accompany me, if Lady Ravenall can spare you?"

The other woman stared at her blankly, her small face pinched and white. "Do you mean to go there on your honeymoon, Miss Hexham?"

Perdita went rigid. "Since I have neither a fiancé nor a husband, I have no plans to honeymoon anywhere at present!"

Fanny provided an interruption, arriving with a handful of envelopes on a silver tray. "Burton just received the mail. These all look to be acceptances to your dinner party, Lady Ravenall."

The dowager was elegant in a gown of pink silk with quantities of lace at her throat. She looked up from the list before her. "If you please, my dear Fanny, open them for me. My hands feel all knotted today. There will be rain tonight."

She waited until the envelopes were slit, then took them out herself. "Well, then, it seems that my places at table will be filled. General Galsworth. Lady Lennox will be here with her daughter Isabel. Ah! and a Mr. Malone. I do not know him, but my grandson speaks most highly of him. I believe they met in their travels."

Both Perdita and Fanny looked up in astonishment, but they didn't dare glance. A rosy flush flooded the widow's cheeks. She bit her lip and looked away.

The dowager consulted her list again, and made a series of ticks down the paper with her pen. "Fourteen to sit down to dinner, and the rest to come afterward for refreshments and dancing. Both Lieutenant Nutting and Calvin Bridgeforth accept as well."

"Good God," Andrew exclaimed. "What on earth persuaded you to invite them? Especially Bridgeforth?"

The dowager sent a sharp look at her grandnephew. "I did not know that I needed your permission before planning my guest lists!"

"I beg pardon!" Andrew's face flamed.

Lady Ravenall's blue eyes looked very much like her grandson's. "The Coast Guard and Inland Revenue officers may not be favorites among the villagers, given Ravensea's long history. However, if Ravenall has no objection, I cannot see what difference it makes to you. Lieutenant Nutting is the son of old friends, in addition to being assigned to patrol the coastline."

She continued in a milder tone. "As for Calvin Bridgeforth, he is, after all, a member of this branch of the family, and his estate is not ten miles from here. It would be thought extremely odd of me to leave him out of my arrangements."

She smiled warmly at Perdita. "I particularly wish to make him known to you." She smiled at Perdita. "He was a friend of your father's, you know."

Ravenall entered the drawing room just then. Andrew exchanged a look with him. It seemed to Perdita that neither had a liking for the man. Some imp of perversity invaded her.

"If Mr. Bridgeforth was a friend to my father, then of course I shall look forward to making his acquaintance."

Ravenall leaned against the mantelpiece. "Then I am glad I followed my instincts where he is concerned."

Daisey intervened to smooth over the disturbance. "I'd forgotten about that painting of Venice which you mentioned earlier, Harriet. It is attributed to Canaletto. Would you care to see it?"

The countess looked amused. "I believe that she has seen it before, many years ago. When you were a child of eight or

nine, Miss Hexham, Mr. Bridgeforth came to pay a call, and
brought your parents to visit with him. Oh, dear. I must be
getting old, indeed! I had forgotten all about it until just now."

Perdita colored. "I have no recollection of it, my lady."

Perdita hadn't been in the old wing of the house at all, but
when they went through a pair of tall doors, she stopped in
her tracks. It was very familiar to her: the long, dim corridor,
the rows of closed doors. Even the pattern of the inlaid stone
floors. She had seen it a hundred times in her dreams. Gooseflesh rose on her arms.

The others had gathered in the antechamber, to admire the
Venetian painting, and a large landscape of the castle, painted
in an earlier era. She heard Ravenall come up beside her.

"What is it?" He took her arm. "You are white as an oyster."

"I . . . I know this place." Nervous excitement filled her.
"Those doors on the left—they lead to a small parlor. Those
on the right to a ballroom paneled in gold, with a minstrel's
gallery above. There are views of the sea on both sides, and
the ceiling is painted with gilt stars in the pattern of the constellations . . ."

Daisey turned to stare at her. "How marvelous! You do
remember!"

Andrew threw the doors open, and it was exactly as she'd
described. Perdita was dizzy. Could it be true? By some fantastic coincidence, could she truly be the missing heiress?

She walked about the ballroom in a haze. Ravenall watched
her with an odd look upon his face. She was so absorbed in
trying to reconcile her wild hopes with reality, that she almost
collided with him.

Andrew looked up at the ceiling. "There is Orion. Yes, and
Andromeda. I used to come here as a boy to memorize them,
and amaze my friends when I went home and showed them
the night sky."

Daisey laughed, and regarded Perdita. "How clever of you!
And how curious that you remember this chamber, and have
no other recollections of the castle."

"It is not mysterious at all," Ravenall said cryptically. "As
you'll see when we return to the drawing room."

He wouldn't say more, and they had to be satisfied with
that. Perdita was puzzled. She sensed a coldness in him that

had not been there before. He went at once to the table where she'd been sitting, and opened the pages of *The Illustrated Guide to the Noble Houses of Great Britain.*

He pointed to one of the colored engravings inserted between the bound pages.

"Here it is, Miss Hexham." He read the words beneath it. " 'The ballroom at Ravenall Castle is unique and much admired, situated as it is on a promontory, giving views to the sea on either hand. The walnut minstrel's gallery and the azure ceiling, filled with gold-leafed stars, are thought to have been part of the original medieval structure, although it has been much renovated over the generations.' "

Perdita looked down at the hand-tinted picture in dismay. It was true. One plate showed the long corridor with a glimpse of a parlor through open doors. The other was a long view of the ballroom, showing the sprinkle of constellations across the ceiling.

Her disappointment was severe. Tears stung her eyes. For a few, blissful moments she had imagined that she belonged in this aristocratic company. That she had been a beloved child with a place in the world . . . that she had found it at last.

She couldn't recall Miss Barnstable having any books so valuable as this. Perhaps she'd seen the engravings elsewhere once upon a time. Perhaps what she had long considered a true memory in her dreams was nothing more than a distortion. A mirage.

Or perhaps she had glimpsed the engravings earlier, while her mind had been occupied with the conversation about the party, and she'd tangled it all up with her vague memories of the recurring dream.

"Well, Miss Hexham? What do you think?"

She tried to smile but it went awry. "It is a very good likeness of the ballroom," Perdita answered, and turned away.

Ravenall followed her to the settee. "Do not try to force your memories," he said. "It will only prove futile and frustrating. If you are meant to remember, it will come in its own good time."

There was warmth in his eyes and smile. She smiled back at him gratefully and wondered why she had imagined that she'd displeased him.

He paused and lowered his voice. "Do not try to be too

clever. It might rebound. Someone in the know—such as myself—is sure to catch you out."

Mr. Clements was announced while they were still gathered together. "I came down from London a day early. I didn't realize I would be intruding on a family party."

"Nonsense!" Ravenall said. "You need not stand on ceremony with us. You have run tame here since we both were in short pants."

The dowager added her welcome, and in the end Clements agreed to join them for dinner again. He expressed his gratification with a pretty speech, and Perdita could see how at ease he was at Ravenall.

He was a well set-up man and good-looking. *Although,* she amended to herself, *not as handsome as Lord Ravenall.* She noticed then how Clements's gaze met Ravenall's, and slid past the earl's ruined cheek as if embarrassed. She was surprised: it had been a long time since she'd ceased to pay any heed to it.

After greeting the dowager and Fanny, he made his bow to Perdita. "I need not ask how you are, Miss Hexham. You look in high bloom, with roses in your cheeks! The air at Ravenall must agree with you."

"Then you cannot have heard!" Daisey exclaimed. "Miss Hexham went alone to see the Monks' Chapel last week, and a wall of the ruins almost came down upon her."

"Good God!" He frowned. "It almost seems as if there is a curse upon the place, so many accidents as there have been recently."

"The fault is mine," Ravenall said coolly. "Had I come back immediately after I ascended to my uncle's dignities, the repairs to the estate would have been well in hand."

There was an awkward pause. The clock struck, shattering the solemn mood, and Fanny exclaimed at the hour. There was no time for more, and the ladies went upstairs to change for dinner.

An hour later Daisey stopped by Perdita's room on her way down. Despite the country hours they kept, everyone dressed as elegantly as if they were in town. The duchess was splendid in figured ivory satin trimmed with gold ribbons, and a necklet of diamonds made to resemble stars.

She eyed Perdita approvingly. "I like the way your hair is arranged." She nodded at Nettie. "Most becoming!"

Nettie beamed with happiness. She had been afraid that the duchess would think her not smart enough to have the dressing of Miss Hexham. To receive such a compliment from Lady Haycross was something, indeed.

Daisey crossed the carpet to where Perdita stood beside the cheval glass. "You look lovely!"

"Do you think so? Indeed, I was thinking that this is not at all the thing."

Perdita dismissed Nettie with a smile, and surveyed her image in the glass. She was wearing a new gown of tissue silk with a foam of lace ruffle around the shoulders, and cut so low she was afraid to draw a deep breath.

"It shows your charms off to perfection," Daisey told her. "And I am considered a great judge of such things. If Ravenall has not already popped the question, this outfit will pull it out of him! No, don't tug at it so," she chided. "The dress is made to show off your bosom. Only dowds and old maids wear their necklines high. And of course, only a married lady may wear them as low as *I* do."

"We will both catch our deaths," Perdita protested, but the duchess had turned her attention to accessories.

"Let me see . . ." She rummaged around among the trinkets in Perdita's jewel box. "Too bright," she said, rejecting an enameled necklace. "I think this one." She held up a simple necklace of moonstones, with a lavaliere depending from it.

She clasped it about Perdita's neck and stood back. "Ah, yes. Stunning! It is always imperative to call attention to one's best features!"

Since the lavaliere hung in the cleft of Perdita's breasts, it was clear what features the duchess had in mind. "But the neckline does quite enough on its own!" Perdita protested.

When they went below, the men were waiting in the drawing room, impressive in their evening dress. Fanny looked particularly pretty in deep bronze taffeta that changed to green as she moved. Lady Ravenall was resplendent in cerulean-blue, lavished with lace, but Perdita felt a pang when she saw Harriet in an outmoded gown of pink muslin. The color ill-suited her, and it was cut far too narrow in the skirts. A thin chain with a garnet cluster was her only adornment.

Perdita felt overdressed and selfish. It seemed unfair that she should have boxes delivered almost every day from fashionable dressmakers and a chest full of baubles, while Lady Ravenall's companion had so little. She determined that she'd go through the wardrobes with Nettie and find something that might suit the other girl.

"It will be much duller going tomorrow," Ravenall warned her, "when we shall be formal."

The thought of conversing only with the gentlemen on either side of her in turn, for heaven knew how many courses, was daunting. Perdita knew it would be far too easy to make some terrible slipup.

The duchess had reassured her. "You needn't be too concerned. Although my rank takes precedence, you are the guest of honor, and you'll be seated beside Ravenall, with General Galsworth on the other side. His only interests are military ones and his stable of racehorses." Her dimples showed. "All you need do is nod and look interested, and try to not fall asleep in the soup."

"Daisey, you let your vivaciousness carry you too far," the dowager chided, but her eyes sparkled.

Between Mr. Clements's presence and Daisey's gossip, dinner was a lively affair, and they got through it without a hitch. The closest call came when Perdita almost spilled her wine glass, but it was righted without damage. Fanny smiled across at her. *Those lessons you hated so have paid off,* her eyes said.

As the ladies waited in the drawing room for the men to join them afterward, Perdita tugged at the neckline of her dress again. Fortunately, Daisey didn't notice.

The duchess and the dowager countess were having an animated conversation, Harriet Evans was helping Fanny sort through embroidery floss, and Perdita had escaped to a corner of the drawing room. She was idly glancing through *The Illustrated Guide to the Noble Houses of Great Britain* when the men finished their port and joined the ladies.

The moment Ravenall entered he drew her eye. His gaze caught hers, and he made his way down the room toward her, looking so very handsome in his evening dress, and she found her heart beating so fast it felt as if it would jump up her throat. "If ever there was a speaking look, Miss Hexham, that was one. I take it you wish to have a private word with me?"

"No! Yes. Well . . . Lady Haycross made a very strange statement to me earlier, my lord. She is under the impression that there is an understanding between us. And Miss Evans suspects me of planning a honeymoon abroad."

Ravenall slanted an unreadable look down at her. "Are you making me an offer of marriage, my dear? I must tell you that it is not at all the thing."

She felt the rush of hot blood to her face. "I wish you would be serious."

"I am. Do you know, you look like a bonbon in a frilled paper, in that frothy white gown. Very becoming!"

Perdita was aware that the top of the ruffle was now so low it came just above the tips of her breasts. It might be the latest fashion, but she felt vulnerable and exposed. She could feel the moonstone nestled snugly in her cleavage, and wanted to rip it from her neck.

Ravenall leaned over her chair. She hoped he was looking at the engraving of Chatsworth, and not anything else.

"You haven't addressed the subject, my lord," she said hurriedly.

"The subject of our marriage?"

She looked up in shock. He continued smoothly: "There is nothing to discuss. You, my dear Miss Hexham, have expressed your unwillingness to enter the married state. And I am not the sort of guardian who would marry his wealthy ward out of hand before she is even of age—even if the circumstances were different!"

Ravenall bowed and walked away.

Perdita felt as if she'd been slapped. His cool words had reminded her of the past that she was trying so deperately to leave behind. No matter how fine her gowns and jewels, to him she would always be the scullery girl he had rescued from a ramshackle inn on the edge of Dartmoor.

Pleading a headache, she went up to her room at the earliest possible moment. Nettie was surprised to see her so soon. As she undressed, Perdita looked at the beautiful gown she'd worn. From now on the lacy confection would be relegated to the back of her wardrobe, a reminder of her humiliation.

Nineteen

"Will you go for a sail with me?"

Perdita looked up to find Ravenall standing at the parlor door. It was a fine day, perhaps one of the last warm ones of the season. The other ladies had all gone up for a beauty rest before the evening's festivities.

She shook her head. "I must decline, my lord. Perhaps Andrew will accompany you."

"He is nowhere to be found. And I believe I owe you an apology for my comments last night." Ravenall gave her one of his dazzling smiles. "I have a picnic hamper filled with wine and your favorite delicacies to show my sincerity. Come for a sail so I can know that you forgive me."

Just as she was about to refuse again, she caught a glimpse of movement from beyond the window. Andrew and Harriet Evans, standing side by side. From the frown between his eyes, and the impassioned look on her face, there was a much closer degree of intimacy between the two than Perdita would have guessed in her wildest dreams. They seemed to be caught in mid-argument, but suddenly Andrew clasped Harriet's hand in his, and raised it to his lips. She broke away, went a few feet, and collapsed on a bench. Andrew hurried to her side and knelt beside her.

"Well, Miss Hexham?"

Perdita jumped at Ravenall's voice. She realized his position in the doorway didn't allow him to have the same view of the garden as she. "I . . . I should like that! Only let me fetch my things."

She almost fled the room, with Ravenall behind her. For some reason she didn't think that he would condone a romantic relationship between his cousin and his grandmother's shy companion.

In her opinion it would be a wonderful match.

No sooner had she reached the top step than she remembered she had left a bracelet on the desk. It had been digging into her wrist and she'd removed it. Since Daisey had given it to her as a welcome gift, she felt it would be rude to leave it there.

As she came to the head of the grand staircase, Perdita looked down at the splendor of the Great Hall below. Two figures stood in the shadows of a massive carved cupboard, heads together: it seemed she was destined to intrude on Andrew and Harriet wherever she went.

Then she realized it was Fanny and Lord Ravenall, and stepped hastily back. Not, however, before she saw him tip Fanny's face up to his and smile down at her.

Jealousy hit Perdita like a hammer blow.

How silly I am. After all, they have known one another since the cradle!

Perdita gave herself a little shake. *I am being foolish beyond permission.* She blamed it on the lurid novels she'd been reading when she was supposed to be improving her mind. Whatever skeletons lurked in the castle's dungeons, she was sure that an unnatural relationship between Fanny and Ravenall was not one of them.

She was about to step forward once more when suddenly Ravenall put his arms about Fanny and pulled her tight against his shoulder.

Perdita gave a little gasp of shock, and they looked up quickly. Whirling about, she retreated down the corridor.

By the time she reached the sanctuary of her own bedchamber, Perdita had a better grip on her emotions. Nettie was spreading a tailored yellow dress and matching jacket out on the bed. She looked up as Perdita entered.

"His lordship said as how he would be taking you on a picnic this afternoon, miss. I hope you'll find this suitable."

Perdita bit her lip. "Please convey my excuses to his lordship. I have the headache."

"I'll fetch some lavender water to bathe your temples, miss."

"No! I . . . I thank you. I only wish to lie down in a darkened room until dinnertime."

Despite Nettie's persistence in wanting to bring her a half-dozen assorted remedies, from headache powders to cooled tea, Perdita managed to shoo her from the room. The headache she'd pretended to have was becoming real.

Nettie entered quietly and stood wringing her hands. "Begging your pardon, miss, but his lordship says as how you're to dress and come out for a sail with him, or he'll fetch you himself."

"Let him, then. Bolt the door, Nettie!"

It opened while the maid stared at her, mouth agape. Ravenall stood on the threshold. His voice was as harsh as his face. "Shall Nettie dress you, Miss Hexham, or shall I?"

Perdita's anger was replaced with the certain knowledge that he meant exactly what he'd said. "If you leave us," she said with an effort at dignity, "I shall be ready presently."

"See that you are."

The door closed and he went out. The maid rolled her eyes. "I've never seen his lordship in such an odd humor."

"He is," Perdita said, "a man of many moods!"

She changed into the sailing dress, certain that she wouldn't enjoy one minute of the excursion.

He was waiting for her at the foot of the staircase. "Very fetching," he commented. "Did you choose that outfit, or did Fanny? I believe that yellow is one of your best colors."

Perdita lifted her chin. "I have no talent for small talk, my lord."

"Then you should cultivate it, by all means. It helps to bridge the social awkwardness that might arise. However, we will speak of other matters. Why did you run back along the corridor earlier?" he asked calmly.

Perdita flushed. She didn't know how to respond.

Ravenall tipped her chin in his hand and gazed down at her steadily. "A word to the wise, Miss Hexham. Do not jump to conclusions. Nor is it generally advisable to put the worse possible construction on anything you may see or hear. It does not do you credit. Fanny is like a sister to me."

"I saw you take Fanny in your arms, in a most unbrotherly way."

His eyes darkened. "You saw me offering comfort to a lady whom I hold in great affection, and who was laboring under great distress. I will say no more on the matter. Nor should you."

Holding out his arm, he tucked her hand in the crook of it and led her through the drawing room and down the steps to the next terrace. Perdita didn't know what to think. The ways of The Quality were very odd, to her notion: one second he was scolding her, the next acting as if nothing at all had happened.

She decided to do the same. There seemed to be some good sense behind the unspoken rules of etiquette after all.

They took a walk through the gardens and down a steep flagged cliff path to the cove below. They rounded a tumble of sea-sculpted granite, and there was a small sailboat, tied up at the end of a short stone jetty. A picnic basket was tucked beneath the seat.

"The *Adventurer*," he told her. "I've had her since I was a boy of sixteen."

Perdita eyed it doubtfully. "It's beautiful."

"Not an *it*, my dear, but a *she*. All water-going vessels are female, you know."

"I didn't. Why do you suppose it is so?"

"Perhaps," he suggested lightly, "because they respond so well to a man's touch."

Perdita flushed and turned her head away. "If I had said such a thing, you would have told me that it was excessively vulgar."

"It is." He grinned unabashedly. "However, you should have pretended not to understand me."

She slanted a look from beneath her lashes. "I believe that you make up these rules and change them from minute to minute, in hopes of driving me mad."

Ravenall only laughed.

Within minutes they had weighed anchor and moved away from the shore. The water in close was green as an emerald, the spray of wave on rock like diamonds in the sun. Soon they were out beyond the cove, where the small, white-hulled vessel swooped like a gull over waves that were now a brilliant blue.

Perdita stood near the bow with the warm sun and cool wind on her face. It was exhilarating to move so swiftly and silently, with only the creak of wood and the rush of water, the sharp cries of the birds.

Everything looked vastly different from here. At first she

couldn't tell where the rocks ended and Ravenall Castle began. The stone of one blended into the other. The base of the cliffs was riddled with deep crevices and shallow caves. She could see why the free traders had used Ravensea as their base. It would take weeks for Lieutenant Nutting and his men to search them all.

The sailboat skimmed over the waves like a sunbeam until the castle was no more than a silhouette against the sky. She slanted a look at Ravenall without turning her head. He stood, feet braced apart and hands on the tiller. He was magnificent. And he was dangerous to her peace of mind.

She was intensely attracted to him, yet she continually misjudged him. If his tongue was sometimes sharp, he had shown her nothing but kindness in his actions.

But at the back of her mind tiny doubts shifted like shadows.

Ravenall dropped anchor and took in the sail. "Are you feeling peckish? Pull out the hamper, Miss Hexham. Let's see what delicacies Mrs. Overland has put up for us."

She slid it out and he took the place across from her while they rocked at anchor. The sea was alive with motion, but when he turned to her with one of his blinding white smiles, everything went still. Even, for a moment, her heart. Then it sped up again, as swift and wild as the feelings that coursed through her.

Perdita smiled back at him, and his face went grave. The wind whipped her bonnet loose and Ravenall caught it with one bronzed hand before it could be blown away. His other hand touched her hair, tucking in the shining strand that had come free.

As his fingers brushed her ear a shiver ran up her spine and the backs of her arms. It was followed by a flow of warmth that began in the pit of her stomach and spread through her limbs. "Don't!" she gasped.

Ravenall's thumb grazed her lower lip. It was a slow, seductive movement, calculated to elicit a response. He watched her eyes widen and darken, saw the flush that rose from her graceful throat to color her cheeks. His eyes held hers, questioning. Daring her to pretend that she didn't feel the same hum in her blood, the same dark stirrings that touching her had roused in him.

She trembled. When he looked at her like that, eyes hot and lips curved in that small, intriguing smile, the rest of the world dropped away. There was nothing but the two of them in the sunlight, and all the possibilities of what might happen next quivering in the air.

It was too intense. She broke eye contact first. "I find I haven't much appetite after all."

"Really? It is just the opposite with me. Should we find a pleasant cove and take our meal there? Or would you like to go on?"

"Keep going," she said. "Go on forever." They sailed along the coast in silence.

He regarded her wistful face with a tender smile. "There are squalls brewing out at sea. Can you smell them on the wind? I can. I'm afraid we must go back to reality soon, my dear. We have had a pleasant little excursion, but now it must end."

She never knew quite how it happened. As she strained for a better view, the boat heeled sharply, and something buffeted her shoulder. There was no time for the pain to register. One moment she was looking out over the water, and the next she was in it.

The waters closed over her head in eerie silence. Her skirts weighed her down, but she struggled and broke the surface. There was nothing but waves and sky as far as her eye could see. Her throat closed in panic. She couldn't utter a single cry.

Then Perdita heard distant shouts. A hand caught her roughly by the nape of her dress, another beneath her arm, and she was hauled like a flapping fish over the side of the vessel. It was so low in the water she thought the vessel would be swamped. A few seconds later she lay on the boards, gasping and choking as Ravenall supported her shoulders.

He pulled a flask from his coat and forced fiery liquid between her lips. "Swallow. All of it!" He ignored her weak protests. "Silly fool," he said. "Don't you know better than to try and stand in a sailboat?"

"But I didn't . . ." She sputtered and broke off as another fit of coughing racked her.

"You certainly did."

She was shivering with cold and reaction, and her bruised shoulder ached abominably.

"Better that than your head," Ravenall said scathingly. He pulled an oilskin packet to him, and removed a blanket. "Wrap this around yourself. I'll weigh anchor and get you back to the castle. And don't move!"

A few minutes later they were skimming back toward the cove. Light winked off bright metal. "What was that?" Her lips were so numb the words came out clumsily.

"The good lieutenant is watching through his spyglass."

Perdita saw the masts in the distance and recognized Lieutenant Nutting's cutter. "How humiliating!"

"Do you think so, Miss Hexham?" Ravenall's face was grim. "I should rather say it is fortunate."

"I cannot agree with you!"

He shaded his eyes and set the rudder. "You would feel differently if we had both been swept into the sea. The villagers might not take kindly to the good lieutenant, but he has rescued more than a few fishermen from the deep."

She had no answer for that, and was shivering too badly to care. Ravenall maneuvered in to the jetty and hauled her, dripping, from the sailboat. Perdita's teeth were chattering. She looked down at her hands and was astonished to find her fingernails blue with cold.

"You'll never make it up the cliff stairs in that soggy mass," Ravenall said. She wondered, rather hazily, if he meant her to remove her clothes. She didn't think she could. It didn't matter, because now she was becoming suddenly warmer. And very sleepy.

Ravenall looked at her and muttered a curse. Drawing her out of the wind, he pulled off the damp blanket, and yanked at the buttons of her gown. The navy glass beads popped like shelled peas, as he loosened her sleeves and tugged her bodice down.

She sagged against him, too exhausted to protest. At least the bone-rattling click of her teeth had ceased. In fact, she no longer felt the cold at all. A warm lethargy crept over her, dulling her thoughts.

When he had her stripped to her shift, Ravenall wrapped the blanket around her once more, and swept her up in his arms. Perdita was aware of the heat radiating from his chest and strong arms. Of the effects of the brandy curling like fog through her body.

She slumped against him as he carried her over the sand and up the crunching shingle. One moment the sky was bright overhead, and then they were in the dark. She could hear his footsteps echoing hollowly and the sounds of his breathing. Somewhere water dripped close by. They seemed to be going up a steep incline at first, then steps.

"Where are we?" Her own voice was as sluggish as her thoughts.

"Save your energies. I'll have you snug in your bed in a winking."

After what seemed like interminable minutes, he stopped and shifted her weight against his shoulder. She could smell his cologne. A very nice cologne, she thought muzzily.

There came a low, scraping rumble, and then they were back in the light. It was dimmer, and she realized they were inside a stone-walled room. A coat of arms was carved into the overmantle of an empty fireplace, and sun came thinly through casement windows, set with thick rondelles of clear glass. He set her down but kept her supported in the circle of his arm.

They came out into a stone-flagged corridor and she realized they were inside the old part of the castle. A short time later Ravenall opened a stout door, and Perdita half-walked, half-stumbled out into the Great Hall. Fanny was just coming in from a walk.

"Good heavens, what has happened? You are both sopping wet!"

"Miss Hexham fell overboard." A smile flickered over his features. "You may say that I joined her there, with great reluctance. Fortunately for us both, our adventure ended well."

Fanny turned to the housekeeper, who had come in response to her sharp tugs on the bell. "Mrs. Overland, send up hot water and warming pans to Miss Hexham's chamber, at once."

"Yes, madam. I'll do the same for his lordship. Burton! Where is Danes? Has he returned from his trip to the village? Oh, the poor, dear lambs. Do go up, Miss Hexham, before you catch your death."

Nettie was aghast when she saw her mistress. She pulled a chair up to the fire and threw a warm quilt around Perdita's shoulder. "La, miss, we must get you out of those wet garments!"

Perdita shook her head. "I'll wait until the hot water is brought up, thank you." The fact was that she had more interest in the other two people in the room. Ravenall looked harassed, and there was an arrested look on Fanny's face. "Two accidents in so short a time!"

"Yes. She was in shock. I had to take the old way up from the cove."

"You went through the caverns? *Oh, Justin! Was that wise?*"

Perdita realized they didn't know she could hear them. The hard surface of the cheval glass seemed to bounce back their words.

Ravenall hesitated. "I had no choice. Nutting was watching," he said slowly.

"Good heavens! How much did he see?"

"I don't know." Ravenall ran his finger along his scarred cheek. "Quite enough, I imagine."

Twenty

"What do you think?"

Perdita turned around for Fanny to see the gown she'd chosen to wear for the dinner party.

White or black were all the mode, and she'd selected a gown the modiste had described as "the color of moonlight on snow," which exactly captured its shimmery essence.

Like the dress she'd worn the previous evening, it was cut low both front and back, but this one was more sophisticated. She only wished that she were old enough to wear diamonds with it. There were two suites of the precious stones locked up in her dressing case and it seemed a shame they were deemed unsuitable for a debutante.

She turned the other way and her skirts brushed a side table. They almost swept off an exquisite porcelain shepherdess in panniered skirts. Perdita caught the figurine but sent a silver picture frame crashing to the carpet.

"I am jumpy as a cat."

"You've lost weight since your fitting," Fanny said. "Your maid can quickly take it in at the waist."

Perdita agreed. Her figure was more slender than when she'd arrived because nerves had dulled her appetite the past few weeks. Another pound or two, Nettie had warned, and it would have to be taken in at all the seams. She'd memorized the guest list and the brief background information she'd gleaned from Fanny and the dowager.

At least there would be quite a few familiar faces. Lady Lennox and her daughter Isabel had paid a call, and she'd met General Galsworth while riding out with Ravenall one afternoon.

"It will be good to see Mr. Malone again," she said.

There was no reply from her companion. Glancing in the

mirror, she saw that Fanny was busy examining the ring on her right hand, as if it were the most important thing in the world.

"Why don't you like him, Fanny?"

"I am not immune to his charm," the other woman said stiffly. "It's his way of life that I condemn."

"Good heavens, how can you disapprove? He sailed with Ravenall, he said. Surely there could be nothing wrong in that. He seems a perfect gentleman."

Fanny's smile was off-kilter. "So he does. I have reason to fear, however, that he is a member of 'the gentlemen.'"

That arrested Perdita's attention. The term was one the villagers used for the smugglers, who carried on an active business all up and down the coast. It was Lieutenant Nutting's job to try and put an end to it, a thankless task. Smuggling, Andrew had told her, vied with fishing for providing the local income.

"A free trader, you mean," she said slowly. She was astonished. "Surely Ravenall would not invite him here if he suspected him of that?"

Fanny rose and brushed her skirts in place. "Sometime, when there is no one else in earshot, you must ask Justin why he came to be exiled to the West Indies by his father." She bit her lip. "I place the fault entirely at Jack Malone's doorstep!"

The two women had grown easier in each other's company, but there was still a distance that neither crossed: Fanny from a natural reserve, and Perdita from dread of the hazards such intimacy might create. If feats of derring-do were the coin of men's friendships, exchange of confidences were the female currency. She was socially bankrupt.

Daisey came rustling in and they let the matter drop. Like Fanny, she'd chosen black for her gown, as more suitable to a married lady. It made her fair skin glow, but her eyes looked wistful.

"I do wish Haycross could have come down to Ravenall. I miss him dreadfully." She held out a string of crystals and pearls interspersed with amethyst clusters, and a matching set of earbobs. "I found these taking up room in my jewel chest, and never wear them. Far too pretty to be hidden away, but I haven't the coloring for them. I thought perhaps they would suit you better, Miss Hexham."

Perdita smiled. What a graceful way Daisey had of giving her a gift, yet making it seem as if it were Perdita who was bestowing the favor.

"They are beautiful, Daisey, and the very thing for this gown. Thank you most sincerely." As soon as she was decked out in the garnets, they went down to the drawing room together.

Oliver Clements was there, talking to Andrew, while Ravenall sat beside the dowager. Miss Evans sat a little apart, looking wistful in her same "best" pink gown.

The moment the agent saw the ladies enter, he rose. "Three goddesses! What a vision in loveliness. I predict that you will have all the gentlemen at your feet!"

"As long as they stay there," Ravenall murmured. He picked up an Indian brass ornament and turned it over. Carriage wheels sounded in the drive, and he set it down. "Our guests begin to arrive."

He gave Perdita a quick glance of encouragement and she held her head high. Jack Malone was the first to arrive, and he made an elegant bow to the dowager, regaling her with edited stories of his adventures abroad with Ravenall and the time they had saved themselves from a superstitious villain, by predicting an annual meteor shower.

"There is one tonight, in fact. If the weather holds, perhaps you would care to view it from the comfort of the terrace, Lady Ravenall?"

The dowager thanked him prettily and declined. "I am far too close to heaven at my age to enjoy anticipating it, Mr. Malone. I shall be at the whist table, with General Galsworth and the Eddingtons. However, I encourage you to take the others out to view the falling stars."

The drawing room soon began to fill, and Perdita found herself separated from anyone she knew. A deep voice greeted her and she turned.

The newcomer was tall and exceedingly elegant, with a quizzical gleam in his hazel-blue eyes. "Ravenall informed me his ward had come to live with him, Miss Hexham. He neglected to say that you were so beautiful."

He took her hand in his and gazed into her eyes soulfully.

"Sweet Venus! Only tell me that he hasn't managed to win your heart away, and that my hopes are not dashed forever!"

She laughed and tried, unsuccessfully, to reclaim her hand. "Lady Haycross warned me there would be several outrageous flirts among the company. I see, sir, that she has the gift of understatement."

For a moment the gentleman was taken aback. He watched as the sudden color flamed in her cheeks. Then he laughed, too. "Ah, I see you are an original. Do not guard your tongue with me. I enjoy a female with wit and boldness."

Andrew Waverly came to the rescue. "Good evening, Calvin. I see the press of people was too great for you to seek out your host or hostess."

Ravenall came up on the other side of her. She felt like a princess with two knights to fend off the dragon. Although she wasn't entirely sure she wished them to fend Mr. Bridgeforth off at all.

The other man released Perdita's hand with a mocking bow. "Your reactions puzzle me, cousin. Am I poaching on your preserve?"

"No. I am only doing my duty as guardian. Go make up to one of the other ladies, Bridgeforth. I want a private word with my ward."

Ravenall drew Perdita off through a connecting door to a small parlor. Only one branch of candles had been lit. "What the *devil* do you think you are doing, letting that fellow maul you in such a fashion?"

She was angry and humiliated. "*I?* I did nothing, my lord, to encourage him!"

"Your behavior shows a severe want of judgment. If you think letting him treat you like one of the muslin company—in my own drawing room!—is nothing, then you are no more fit to be in polite society than a—"

Her violet eyes sparkled with wrath. "Than a serving wench at a tawdry tavern?"

His fingers dug into her arm. "You mistake my meaning," he said stiffly. "Be careful what you say," he warned, "and what you do. Bridgeforth may look to be in the first stare of elegance, but he has a hard reputation among his fellows."

"Indeed? Daisey doesn't like him, either, but *she* says he is eminently eligible."

Ravenall wanted to shake her. His mouth grew grim. "He's a rogue with little more than charming manners and a modest estate to recommend him. At the rate he gambles, he'll be all to pieces in six months. There are far better matches to be made in London by an heiress such as yourself. I am sure you can set your sights higher if you've a mind to it."

"Oh, indeed. Perhaps one of the royal dukes," she said, in a fury. "I am told that there are one or two who are highly susceptible to the charms of dashing females."

Ravenall was not amused. "If your ambitions run so high, Miss Hexham, perhaps we should not wait until after Christmas to go to London. I wouldn't want you to miss your chance. At any moment those elderly fellows might be snatched up by some title-seeking adventuress—if not first by their Maker!"

"Surely you didn't take my remark seriously?"

"No," he said, by now as angry as she. "But if it were in your power, I believe you might try!"

Her cheeks burned as though she'd been slapped. "Your remark, my lord, was uncalled for."

"Was it?" Ravenall leaned down and spoke close to her ear. "Be careful what you're about, my dear. If you aim too high you may fall instead, and sink yourself beyond reproach!"

"Then perhaps you would prefer that I allay myself with one of the stableboys," she hissed. "Someone you deem more suitable to my former station in life."

His fingers caught her wrist and held it. "This is your first true test. Hold your tongue, Miss Hexham, or your temper is like to be your undoing."

Perdita unclamped his fingers. "And yours, my lord. As to whom I marry and when, once I come of age, you will have nothing to say in the matter."

"Indeed," he said in a low, harsh voice. "But until then, Miss Hexham, you will march to my tune. Now go back and join the others, and try not to create a scandal by flirting like a Covent Garden flower girl with every man in the room!"

Back stiff, she turned and walked away, so angry she was trembling. She took a chair near where Andrew and Miss Evans were listening to General Galsworth's account of the Battle of Waterloo. By the glazed look in their eyes it seemed they had heard the tale before.

Dinner was announced and the company processed in according to rank. As she waited for her escort, Bridgeforth leaned over. " 'And the animals went in two by two,' eh, Miss Hexham?"

She tried to look shocked. "I was not thinking that!"

"Oh, yes. You were." His smile was both mocking and humorous. She wasn't sure if she liked him, but he was certainly interesting.

The dining parlor was splendid with all the lamps lit, and crystal and fine china ranged up and down the polished table. Perdita was surprised to see Fanny seated beside Jack Malone. Perhaps that was too mild a word for her feeling, since it was Fanny herself who had made up the seating arrangements. As for Harriet and Andrew, they were seated on the same side of the table, and therefore couldn't even exchange glances.

The meal was not the ordeal Perdita had feared. She'd avoided any serious mishaps by watching Fanny's and Lady Ravenall's every move, and when it was time to turn her attention to the general, he did all the talking, just as she'd been told he would do.

As course after delicious course was removed, she picked daintily at *boeuf en croûte,* quail with sage, artichokes *à la française,* and the splendid assortment of aspics and jellies. She remembered a time when she had lived on bread crusts and meat drippings and thanked Providence for the change in her estate. Although she only sipped at her wine, it still went to her head, and by the time the ladies left the dining room, she felt heated and just a little dizzy.

The weather being unusually sultry, it was decided to forgo the dancing, and set up some tables for cards, and round games for the diversion of the younger guests. Harriet and Fanny were assigned the task of selecting them.

"There is a lotto game in this cupboard," Harriet told her. "I cannot reach the top shelf—if you would be so kind, Miss Hexham?"

Perdita stretched up on tiptoe and pulled at the edge of the brocade box that held the mother-of-pearl fish. At first it wouldn't budge. She gave a little jump in her satin slippers, and the brocade box tipped down. So did everything else on the shelf. A stamped tin hit the door with a clatter and its lid went spinning away. Bits and pieces of black rained down on the two of them.

"Oh, it is the charcoal Andrew made for my drawing lessons!"

Harriet looked down in horror. Her pink gown was streaked with black from bodice to hem. She brushed at it in horror, which only made the stains spread, and when she raised her hands to her cheeks, they left dark patches on her face, as well.

Perdita saw that her companion was in tears. "It was my fault. So clumsy! Don't be distressed! We're much the same size. Let's go up to my chamber and clean up. Nettie will help us change into something suitable from among my wardrobe."

Harriet shook her head. "Really, Miss Hexham—"

"Perdita, if you please. Now come along. I'll signal to Fanny. Ah, she's seen us. If we hurry, we can be back before the gentlemen have finished their cigars."

Leading the other girl out the doors at the far end of the drawing room, Perdita guided her to her own chambers and rang for her maid. Nettie came through the connecting door.

"La! Miss Perdita, whatever have you been up to? And Miss Evans, as well! Oh, your pretty pink dress is quite spoiled!"

"Never mind that now." Perdita took the wet cloth her maid handed her and wiped her hands. It would take more than water to rid herself of the powdery, greasy charcoal. "Have some hot water sent up and lay out my yellow dress with the tiny gold beads. Miss Evans will put on the white gown I wore yesterday, if you have had it cleaned?"

"Oh, yes, miss. I brushed it myself and hung it up to air." She glanced shyly at Harriet. "It will suit Miss Evans to perfection!"

Despite the other girl's mild objections, everything went as Perdita ordered. It took longer than anticipated, but eventually she was gowned in layers of yellow tulle spangled with tiny gold beads, while Harriet was transformed into a vision of classical elegance, in the white taffeta Perdita had worn the day before.

"You must wear these amethysts, as well. Oh, they are the very stone for you, my dear Harriet." Perdita looked through one of her jewelry trays and came up with a dainty necklet of beaded gold with a carved amber cameo. A pair of plain gold earrings finished off her new look.

"We look none the worse for wear." She turned to Harriet, her eyes sparkling. "Do you know, that gown does not suit me nearly as well as it does you. I cannot think why I ever thought it did. I am sure it makes me look insipid. Perhaps you will be kind enough to take it, Harriet."

I didn't pull that off quite so well as Daisey would have done. Still, the effect was what she'd aimed for. The other girl stuttered and stammered in mingled dismay and delight and finally accepted the gown and a shawl of Norwich silk. *Just let Andrew get a look at her now,* Perdita thought happily, *and he'll be completely bowled over. If he does not declare for her I'll be amazed.*

They arrived back in the drawing room almost an hour after they'd slipped away, to find it deserted. Except for those playing at cards in the adjoining parlor, the rest had gone out to view the falling stars.

Ravenall was standing on the first terrace, waiting for them. He lifted his eyebrows, complimented both on their appearance, and sent Perdita a speaking look. Whatever it was that she had done, it displeased him greatly. She cast her mind back over the dinner itself, and tried to recall any gaffe she might have committed.

As Andrew came up to escort Harriet to the lower terrace where the others were congregated just then, it appeared there was no way Perdita could avoid the lecture that was evidently in store for her.

"I hope you are happy," he said by way of introduction.

"I am enjoying myself immensely," she said. And it was true. She never felt more alive than when she was butting heads with Ravenall.

"You know I was not referring to that. We must have a little talk, Miss Hexham."

"I dislike it when you say that in such severe tones," Perdita told him. "It usually means I am in for a scolding. What have I done now?"

"Come with me, Miss Hexham." He held out his hand and drew her along a walkway of crushed stone that wound through the gardens, and seated her on a bench. She heard the "oohs" and "ahhs" of the others, as a series of bright flashes streaked through the skies.

"We are missing the heavenly show, my lord."

He scowled down at her. The night had leached all color from their garments, making them a study in black and white.

"Don't try to distract me, my dear girl. I didn't cut my eyeteeth yesterday. You are playing the matchmaker between my cousin and Miss Evans and you've decked her out like an heiress. I will thank you not to encourage that alliance," he said shortly. "It won't do."

"So I was right, it is to be a scold!" She knotted her fingers together in her lap, the way Fanny had taught her. "Why is that? Harriet is a most superior sort of girl. They seem to have much in common."

"Too much in common. They are both poor as church mice. If either of them had a farthing to their name, the match would be unobjectionable."

Perdita frowned. "Andrew hopes to make a name for himself in the diplomatic service. Harriet has a good deal of intelligence and gentle, pleasing manners. I believe that she would be a credit to him."

"She would also be a debt!" Ravenall put his foot up on the bench and leaned his arm across his knee. "He will never offer for her, you know."

"I don't believe you!"

"Think, Miss Hexham. Harriet is the only daughter of an impecunious country parson, with two young brothers ready to go away to school! As for Andrew, he is a gentleman, and will adhere to his code. He has obligations of his own. He must marry a girl with more to offer than an informed mind and your good wishes!"

She was disappointed in him. "I am sorry to learn you're so ambitious, my lord. I thought your first wish would be for your cousin's happiness."

"And so it is." He gestured impatiently. "Andrew's property produces a very small income. His duty to his sisters, however, is very great. They live very modestly in Bath, with their great-aunt. He must support them now and provide their marriage settlements—or condemn them to a life of spinsterhood and penury."

She looked up sharply. "Then . . . you are saying he hasn't

enough income to support a wife and his sisters, as well?"

"Certainly he does not! Especially if there would be children born of such a marriage, Miss Hexham."

"I didn't know . . . didn't realize!" Perdita was dashed. She thought everyone who wore fine clothes, and visited grand manors, and hired carriages, was wealthy. Certainly in comparison to what she'd had so short a time ago, they were.

"Oh, it is so unfair! They *love* one another! I am sure of it."

He gave her one of his disconcerting glances. "How long do you think that love would last, in the face of poverty and mutual resentment? In time his wife—no matter how loving at the start—would come to grudge every bite of food for their mouths or clothes for their backs, as coming at the expense of her own children. So you see it is the very devil of a coil."

She lifted her face to him. "That need not happen. I believe that love can endure under the worst of circumstances."

"Do you? How charming." Ravenall smiled cynically. "I shall ask you that question again in a year or two, my dear girl, and we'll see if your answer has changed."

"You do not believe in love," she accused.

"You wrong me. My sister and Lord Haycross were an arranged match. It is often the case in our circle. My father felt they were suited in rank and temperament, although there was the disparity in age."

Ravenall shook his head, remembering. "I was away at the time, or I should have raised a strong objection to Daisey being married off to a man old enough to be her father—which would have been a great pity! She went to the altar harboring grave doubts, but in the end, it turned into a love match. I have never known a more happy couple."

Perdita pounced on that. "You are contradicting yourself, then. A marriage that seems unsuitable may be blessed with love."

"You forget that older, wiser heads prevailed. Haycross is rich as Croesus. The warmest man in England, they say, and indeed, the settlement upon my sister is generous in the extreme."

His mouth turned down. "My parents were another story. A love match that they thought would stay afloat on the seas of passion. Alas, that was all they shared. Their relationship foundered on the rocks of financial straits before their first anniversary. It sank without a trace shortly after my sister was born."

She listened quietly, watching the shadows of the past flicker across his countenance. His eyes gleamed dark as a stormy sea.

"My parents could not stand to be in the same house, much less the same room! We were raised amid strife and discord, Miss Hexham, and I can tell you there is nothing worse than love gone awry. It turns savage, and destroys everything that was good."

His jaw tightened. *God knows, I am an expert on the subject.* "There is no more to be said. You may give your gowns to Harriet if you like; but I will squash any efforts on your part to bring the two of them together."

He led her down to where the servants had placed gilded chairs from the ballroom along the terrace, so they might enjoy the show of stars. After seeing her safe with Jack Malone, he left them and managed to remove Andrew from Harriet's side by some means.

Perdita responded to Jack's comments rather mechanically. Her mind was busy, turning over the problem of Andrew and Harriet. Ravenall's opposition to the romance only made her more determined to assist it.

There must be a way!

She decided there was nothing for it but to speak to them. Slipping through the stargazers, she went down the steps to the third terrace, where she'd last seen them walking with Lady Lennox and her son, the Honorable Eddie.

She hadn't gone a half-dozen yards when Mr. Clements intercepted her. "A few of the ladies have already gone inside, since the air is growing chill. Would you care to return to the drawing room?"

"I have my shawl, sir. I am not so dainty that a cool breeze will carry me off with the lung fever," she laughed. *After all, I have slept in an unheated eavespace with a roof so in need of repair, I once found my blanket dusted with snow!*

Clements chatted with her easily as she realized they'd come out on the south lawn when they strolled past the fountain. Stone dolphins spurted streams of silver in the moonlight and it fell back in the enormous carved basin like drops of liquid pearl. They crossed the fountain court and passed beyond into the shrubbery.

A few dry leaves skittered down the marble steps behind them, blown from the trees. She saw him glance back, to see if they were followed. "Are you expecting my guardian to come leaping out with a fiery sword?"

"He didn't seem pleased to see you go off to one side with Mr. Bridgeforth earlier." Mr. Clements tugged at his shirt collar. "Forgive me for being so forward . . . but his lordship became so incensed, my first thought was that he reacted with the heat of a jealous lover!"

She looked up at him in surprise. "I cannot believe I heard you correctly."

"Please forgive me, I spoke out of turn."

"No . . . I . . ." She couldn't tell him her astonishment was not at his implied criticism of his patron, but his other words. "Lord Ravenall takes his responsibilities as my guardian seriously," Perdita said. "His interest in me runs no deeper than that."

He looked down at her with concern. "Ah, I wish I were as certain as you."

Perdita's heart beat faster. The last thing she wanted was for Mr. Clements to declare himself. "If you were a betting man, sir, you might safely wager your fortune on it. At times he seems to scarcely tolerate me!"

His answer startled her: "It is more pleasant, but certainly not mandatory, that there be anything more than tolerance between husband and wife, in a marriage of convenience."

She stopped and looked up at him. In the moonlight his face was limned with concern. "I do not know what you are saying."

"My dear Miss Hexham! Only think! You are thrown into his company by circumstances," Clements said, suddenly taking her hand in his. "I have nothing to say against Lord Ravenall. Indeed, I am beholden to him . . ."

"That is very true!"

A groan of anguish was wrenched from him. "The Ravenall name is old and distinguished. But he would not be the first man to feather his nest by marrying his wealthy ward."

Perdita was so stunned she almost laughed aloud. "I don't believe there is any chance of Lord Ravenall's needing my inheritance to settle his accounts. Even less so," she said, "of his wanting to wed me!"

Clements took her other hand in his, drawing her closer against her will. "I wish with all my heart that I could believe that. Forgive my plain speaking, Miss Hexham! But I am in agony. I can hold it in no longer. My dear Miss Hexham! For these past few weeks that we have known one another, I have come to cherish your friendship most highly. Indeed, to prize it above all things. I cannot sleep . . . I cannot think!"

A shadow came between them and the moon. "Evidently not, Clements, or you wouldn't be out here making a cake of yourself with my ward!"

Perdita looked up to see Ravenall looming over them. His jaw was set, and his eyes shone like black ice in the reflected starlight.

"My lord!"

Ravenall caught the other man by the collar. "You had better say 'My God!' and hope that your prayers will be answered. What the devil do you think you're doing, Clements!"

"I . . . uh, I asked Miss Hexham to take a stroll upon the terrace with me, my lord. To . . . to enjoy the cool breeze and the fine view of the heavens."

"Did you, by God? And may I ask, my good fool, why you thought such an invitation to my ward was appropriate? Or," he said dangerously, "*permitted?*"

Perdita tried to intervene. "I thought—"

"Spare me your excuses, Miss Hexham, whatever they are. You are a young lady, inexperienced in the world—and Mr. Clements is a gentleman, and should know better!"

"My lord," the other man said with great dignity. "My regard for Miss Hexham is boundless. I meant no harm—"

"Then you should not have taken her away from the others to walk with you unchaperoned, in the dark. Tongues are already wagging." Ravenall's voice was low and menacing. "Rejoin the other guests, if you please. I wish to speak with my ward privately. And," he said quietly, "I will speak to *you* later!"

"Miss Hexham—"

"It is all right, sir," Perdita said stiffly. "Please! I, also, have something I wish to say to Lord Ravenall—in private."

With a bow, Clements retreated. As he mounted the steps

to the lower terrace, there was an angry silence. She waited until he vanished from view.

"How *dare* you—" she began, but was swiftly cut off.

"First Bridgeforth, and now Clements! What the *devil* do you think you were doing down here alone with him in the shrubbery—and in a dress that is ready to fall off your bosom?"

Perdita's eyes sparkled with anger. She hadn't had time to have Nettie take it in. "Merely enjoying the night air, my lord! Since Mr. Clements is a guest at the castle, I didn't think you could have any objections."

"Think again! A young, unmarried lady of breeding does not put herself into such a situation in the first place."

She was furious out of all reason. "But then, you can hardly expect it of *me,* can you?"

"You don't know what I think of you," he said in a harsh voice.

Without warning, he pulled her into his arms. She stepped on the hem of her dress and felt the top give, and didn't care. His mouth came down on hers so swiftly she didn't have time to protest. One moment she was staring up at his rigid face, the next she was hard against his chest, while his embrace threatened to break her ribs. His mouth was hot on hers, fierce and passionate. She knew then that she had wanted this to happen, almost from the first.

Anger and fear dissolved into triumph. Into hunger so great it ravaged her senses. She twined her arms around his neck and kissed him back with all the passion that welled up inside her. Her lips softened beneath his, yielding. He groaned and reached up to touch her face. Instead his hand came up and brushed her bare breast.

He was right about this gown, she thought dazedly. Then she was mindless with shock and pleasure as his long fingers splayed over her skin, and his hard palm cupped her breast. Warmth curled through her, became heat that robbed her of breath. Of any thought of resistance.

She wanted this.

Ravenall's breath drew in with a hiss. The moment his fingers stroked her satin-smooth flesh he was lost. Her heart fluttered beneath his touch, and he felt her quiver. Oh, she was hot and passionate as he'd known she'd be.

As he feared she'd be.

The fire that burned between them was fierce and uncontrolled. It had nothing to do with a girl from the wilds of Dartmoor and the Earl of Ravenall. It was far more elemental. A call of like to like. A searing communion of man and woman, a mingling of primal passions beyond any hope of reason.

Her mouth opened to his and he plunged in, tasting her as if she were a rare and precious wine. Her fingers twined in his thick hair. Her breasts ached for him. To feel the roughness of his cheek against her tender skin, the heat of his mouth upon them. She was melting with longing. Flowing into him like a river tumbling down to its inevitable joining with the sea.

Suddenly he pulled away, and the cool wind blew over her exposed breasts. Her nipples tingled with it. With need. She clutched at his lapels to keep her shaky limbs from collapsing beneath her.

His mind was reeling. He wished he'd never followed her out of the house. He wished they were anywhere but here, with a houseful of guests a few hundred yards away. He wished they were up in his room, naked together on the big tester bed, with firelight glazing the lush curves of her body.

Ravenall cursed softly, and pulled the deep bodice ruffle up to cover her. "Oh, you little witch! What Gypsy spell did you put on me, to make me lose all sense of honor?"

Perdita felt as if he'd struck her. *How dare he blame me!* She lifted her hand and slapped him, hard. "It was not I who began this, my lord," she said with an angry sob. "But it is I who shall end it!"

"I didn't mean . . ." he started; but she was already gone.

She ran from the shrubbery, almost tripping in her haste. *How dare he treat me like a common doxy!* She bit her lip and willed back tears. *How dare he kiss me, and touch me—and then stop!*

She didn't know which outraged her more.

It was several minutes before she realized she'd come the wrong way. She broke out of the darkness and found herself standing high above the sea. Perdita watched for several minutes as streaks of light fell from the sky, while their reflections glimmered in the waves. Once she was calmer, she retraced her steps.

Oh, please! she prayed silently, as she went past the dolphin fountain again. *Let this long evening end soon!*

Her plea was answered before she even reached the steps leading up to the terrace. There was a small cry, and then a dark shape came hurtling down at her without warning.

Perdita pressed against the balustrade as the shape thudded to the ground beside her, just missing the marble edge of the lowest tread.

What had looked dark and menacing against the stars was now a pitiful heap of crumpled white taffeta and twisted limbs.

"Harriet!"

She knelt beside the girl and tried to find a pulse.

Twenty-one

The doctor arrived and most of the guests departed. "If I may," Lieutenant Nutting said to Fanny, "I shall come by tomorrow to inquire after Miss Evans."

"Of course. I only hope we will have good news to give you."

Nutting made a smart bow to the ladies and went off. There was nothing for Perdita to do once Dr. Ash was there to examine Harriet, but go to the drawing room and wait with the others. The dowager countess, Mrs. Overland, and Nettie had shooed her out, and Fanny, too.

The room, so cheerful only a short time ago, was filled with gloom. Andrew's hands shook as he poured out his third glass of brandy.

"I shall always blame myself," he said bitterly. "I should never have let her stray from my side."

"My dear Waverly," Oliver Clements said, "you cannot have prevented her from tripping over her unlaced sandal."

Jack spoke quietly from his chair in the shadows. "I don't believe that is how the event occurred. You see, Miss Evans was sitting on the balustrade at the top of the stairs, tying her sandal ribbon, when she came to fall."

A silence fell over the room. "That cannot be," Fanny said at last. "It's a good five feet from there to the top of the stairs."

"My point, exactly."

Something stirred through the room, but no one cared to give it a name. Perdita drifted over to Andrew as he lifted the decanter again. "Do you think you should?" she asked softly. "She may awaken and ask for you."

"By God, you're right." He set the heavy crystal down, and ran his hands through his disordered hair. "What shall I do if she doesn't wake up?"

"You must not think that way! Remember how badly hurt Ravenall was when you brought him to the inn—"

She broke off, realizing that Mr. Bridgeforth had wandered in from the terrace where he'd been blowing a cloud. The smell of cigar clung to his jacket. "Will you take a turn about the room with me, Miss Hexham?"

Andrew glowered, but she put her hand on Bridgeforth's arm and let him promenade her down the length of the drawing room.

"Ravenall seems to have recovered well from his accident," he said smoothly. "He is either very determined, or very lucky."

"I believe he must be both. Except for the mark on his cheek, sir, there is no other sign that it affected him."

"I felicitate him on his good fortune. I imagine that young Waverly was on pins and needles while Ravenall recuperated."

"Yes. There is an abiding affection between the two cousins."

Bridgeforth raised his elegant brows and smiled. "I was referring to the possibility of Andrew Waverly becoming an earl."

She gave him a sharp look. "I do not understand you, sir."

"Three almost fatal accidents within few days of each other—yes, and then there was the affair of the castle rampart giving way during his inspection," Bridgeforth announced. "It was a very near thing, you know. And one cannot forget Ravenall's unfortunate carriage accident. And Waverly waiting in line to the title!"

Perdita rapidly revised her opinion of her companion. "You do him great wrong, sir. There is no harm in Mr. Waverly, and his fondness for his cousin is very real."

He smiled down on her almost pityingly. "It's impossible to tell what anyone might do, given the proper temptation," he said in his polished, insinuating voice. "Everyone can be bought, my dear Miss Hexham. It is only discovering what their price may be. For some it's wealth, for others, status. Or merely the love of a woman."

Sukey had said much the same thing to her once, and Perdita had hotly denied it. But that was before Ravenall had come into her life, dangling impossible dreams before her like jewels on a chain.

Sukey was right. I did her an injustice. It seems that I did have my own price, after all.

Did Andrew?

She sat a little apart from the others once Bridgeforth and Jack had taken their leave. Andrew was terribly broken up over Harriet's fall. Could a man who loved a woman so deeply be capable of the things that Bridgeforth was suggesting?

She didn't think so. He was too kind and good and unassuming.

He was also, her evil genius noted, too poor to afford a wife. At least that was what Ravenall had told her. Was it the truth?

She drifted across the room and took a seat on the sofa beside him. "Forgive me for speaking so boldly, but it is plain to me that you are head over heels with Harriet. Is there an understanding between you?"

He stared stonily down at his feet. "I will not be offering for Miss Evans's hand in marriage."

"Surely I am not mistaken in your feelings for one another!"

"I love her dearly," he said in a flat voice. "But it cannot be. It was wrong of me to have encouraged the attachment between us. It is beyond my current means to afford a wife and family."

"Can't you go to Ravenall? Is there nothing he can do to assist you?"

"Good God, no! He is as—" Andrew stopped himself in the nick of time. "Believe me when I say he is no position to come to my aid."

"Then he is less the man I thought him," she said.

Andrew fisted his hands. "If she recovers, I will go away. It is the right thing to do." He buried his face in his hands. "Oh, God! She must recover!"

The clock struck half past twelve. Fanny rose and walked agitatedly about the room. "Where is Ravenall?" she asked suddenly. "He has been gone this hour and more."

"He left with Mr. Malone," Perdita said. "I saw them go down across the lawn together."

A sound came from the doorway. They looked up to find Dr. Ash there. Three faces watched his anxiously. "She will recover," he said heartily. "She has already come to her senses, but her head is clanging like a bell. The only other damage is to her wrist, which I believe has sustained a negligible fracture."

"Thank heaven! May we go up to her?"

"It would be best if you did not. I have given her a strong sleeping draught. Mrs. Overland and Nettie will spell one another through the night. In the morning, if she feels up to it, you may visit her with my blessing."

With a bow and a promise to return the following day, he left them. Perdita turned to Andrew, her face radiant with relief. She and Fanny were alone in an empty room.

A cold draft swirled through the open terrace window.

The events of the evening had upset Perdita terribly. If Harriet hadn't paused at the foot of the stairs, the poor girl might even now be lying dead. That had shaken everyone; but even earlier Perdita had been aware of a growing tension among the members of the house party. A gathering of invisible storm clouds. It had put her every instinct on the alert.

She bit her lip. Coming so close upon her own misadventure, Harriet's fall seemed suspicious. She began to wonder if it had been an accident at all. It made no sense. Who would attack her or sweet, shy Harriet? And why?

She shook off her misgivings as an attack of nerves.

Harriet Evans might have been killed, but if there was any good to come of it, it was Andrew's reaction. He hadn't been able to keep his feelings for Lady Ravenall's companion under wraps any longer. *Perhaps they would make a match of it yet.*

Perdita paced her bedchamber restlessly. The stillness of the house was oppressive. Outside she could hear the wind's sighing rush through the treetops. Suddenly she could not bear to be inside with her agitated thoughts. Opening the door to the upper terrace, she went out into the night. The breeze, although stronger, was still warm, and ruffled her gown about her ankles playfully.

Clouds were sweeping in, but there was still one clear patch. Inside it, the crescent moon seemed to hang from a single bright star, like a diamond brooch pinned to the velvet sky. Perdita moved to the marble balustrade and leaned against it, watching until even that was gone. Darkness rushed in to fill the void.

She unplaited her hair and let the wind stream through it. She was filled with strange, unnamed longings. With a deep ache, an emptiness that cried out to be filled. Holding her arms out, she threw her head back and whirled around and around until her gown spun out around her calves, dancing to the pagan rhythms of her blood.

A sound startled her, and she almost pitched headlong down the stairs. Instantly she was caught up by a strong arm, and held against a man's chest.

"What the devil do you think you're doing out here?" Ravenall rasped in her ear.

She clutched at him for balance, and his other arm wound around her. He was in his shirtsleeves and he smelled of brandy and cigars. She was aware of her nakedness beneath her sheer gown, and the overwhelming heat of his body. It poured through hers, and ignited a glow deep in the pit of her stomach.

For a moment their hearts beat together. She felt the pounding of his against her breasts, heard the ragged intake of his breath.

She felt him wanting her. Absorbed his need through her skin as if it were the air she needed to breathe. Her body swayed against his.

Ravenall grabbed her wrists, and held them prisoner. "Don't," he whispered. "You are playing with fire."

She knew that he desired her. Knew then, with lightning-struck clarity, that she must be the one to take the first step. She wanted him to kiss her, to sweep her up in his arms and carry her into the bedroom. Place her on the bed and strip her gossamer gown away. Initiate her into the secrets of womanhood. She gave a tiny moan of longing.

He released her so abruptly she almost stumbled. "Go to your virginal bed, Miss Hexham. And lock the door so I am not tempted to follow you!"

She stood fast, looking up at him in the dimness. There was such raw desire in his face it made her tremble. "And if I will not?"

"Then I shall make you." He swooped her up off her feet and carried her to the open door and inside.

The wind closed the door softly behind them. A shudder

ran through Ravenall's body. He set her down, but held her close within the circle of his arms.

The firelight gilded his high cheekbones, the scarred cheek that she longed to soothe with her fingertips, his strong nose and firm, sensual mouth. His eyes smoldered an intense blue, and she saw his face was filmed with sweat.

Perdita knew that the night's events had tipped him off balance, stripped away all the carefully built façade. Her courage wavered only a split second. This was the moment she had dreamed of, the moment that she had thought would never come to be.

He looked dangerous and savage and she wanted him to take her in his arms and do with her what he willed. She smiled and touched her fingers to his mouth. He grasped her hand and kissed her fingertips. His voice was so low she could scarcely hear him: "Tonight, when I thought it was you lying there at the foot of the stairs, my heart stopped."

Then he pulled her into his arms and kissed her roughly. His hands pressed her against him, so close that the two layers of fabric between them might have been air. Perdita melted into his embrace, while his mouth ravaged hers. "I couldn't have borne to see you like that, my darling."

His hands moved possessively over her body, and she arched to meet them. He was so passionate and wild it made her head spin with delight. And yet she had always guessed that he would be this way. Ardent. Demanding. She responded in kind, his match in every way.

Her arms wound around his neck while he tangled his fingers in her cloud of long, Gypsy hair. He kissed her eyes, her temples, the vulnerable spot beneath her jaw. She trembled in his arms, and felt her blood go molten. Hot and dark, it coursed through her veins. Nothing existed but this moment, and the heat that consumed them.

Flame to flame, they burned against one another. She realized her sheer gown was gone, pooled at her ankles. She wondered if it had melted from her body by the sheer heat of their desire.

Ravenall lifted her in his arms again, and carried her to the bed. They tumbled onto the mattress together in a tangle of limbs and need. His shirt was gone, and she found her mouth against his bare chest. She pressed kisses against his skin, her tongue darting out to taste him. It was an instinctive act, and it drove all reason out of him.

He was mad with desire. He had wanted this moment from the first time he'd seen her. He knew it now. Perhaps had always known it. Everything since then had led to this end, the two of them naked in the firelight.

Shadows dipped and wavered. The lights slid over her up-thrust breasts, the graceful curves of her waist and hips, and slender legs. His hands followed the supple contours. He wanted to know every inch of her. To let his mouth explore, his tongue taste, his hands caress, until she begged for mercy. And then he would take her further, deeper, into the pleasures of love, until she shuddered in his arms in the ecstasy of release.

She was so beautiful, so innocent yet wanton in her first arousal, that it made his blood pound in his ears. It was all he could do to keep from taking her then. He caressed her breasts, held them in his hands as if they were doves, then bent his head and brought his mouth to one.

Perdita was lost. There was nothing in all the world but Ravenall and the things he was doing to her. She had never guessed at the deep well of sensuality within herself, or the joy and abandon of it. The way her body molded to his, the strength of his thighs as he moved over her, the brush of her breasts against the crisp hairs of his chest, were exquisite. She was half-mad with wanting him. Wherever he led her, she would follow.

His mouth caught the tip of her breast, tugged until she writhed beneath him with the pleasure of it. His hands were sure, seductive, as they slid over her rib cage, along the softness of her belly and silken thighs. She gave a tiny cry when he touched her intimately, and he went still. She moved her hips against his hands, and sighed when his fingers slipped between them. Surprise lasted only an instant. Then the flame inside her burst wide, consuming her.

She arched against him, time and again, while he whispered encouragement. She lay panting beside him, her rosy mouth open as she tried to quiet the racing of her heart. There was to be no respite for her. He began again, this time more slowly. She knew he was watching her reactions, ready to retreat at her slightest signal.

She shifted beneath his questing hand. She felt swollen with love for him, and ached for more. He soothed her impatience with promises, and more exquisite delight. Her body trembled as she welcomed him. When his dark head brushed down between her breasts, pressing hot kisses on her soft skin, she wound her fingers in his hair. When he moved low and spread her thighs she held her breath in an agony of anticipation.

His breath was warm against her, his mouth inches away. Then he cupped her buttocks and lifted her hips to meet his most intimate kiss. Her body trembled and she welcomed him. She felt her body seem to expand, like a flower unfurling. Her hips rocketed upward as she flew through a rush of heat and light. When it was over, she lay cradled in his arms.

"I never knew . . ." she whispered. "Never dreamed . . ." Perdita took a deep breath. "Can you do that . . . again?"

Ravenall cupped her breast in one hand, and kissed her mouth. "My darling, we haven't yet begun!"

He worshipped her body from head to toe, tantalized every inch of her until her hands clutched at the sheets and she writhed beneath him. Only when he'd urged her to fever pitch, did he go the next step. She gasped at the first touch, the fullness of him between her legs. The sudden, sharp pain that was lost in pure pleasure as he entered her. The heat of his loins, the masculine strength of him, astonished her. So did the reaction of her body. They moved together as if they had always lain like this. Locked in each other's arms. The gathering speed and power of his thrusts made her greedy for more. She raised up to meet each one, caught up in the primal glory of their joining. What she'd felt before was nothing to this.

He lifted her against him and thrust deeper, harder. Their bodies were slicked with sweat in the firelight, but it was the internal heat that drove them. Then she was swept away by such intense sensations she thought that she might die of pleasure. His magnificent body bucked, bowed back, and suddenly there was new warmth inside her. Then his mouth was on hers, devouring it with kisses.

It was only afterward, when he lay atop her, breathing hard, that she waited for the words that never came. Words of endearment. Pledges of love.

She felt a hollowness inside her when he rolled away, but

was comforted when he drew her into his embrace. They lay side by side, until she drifted off to sleep.

Ravenall lay awake in the firelight, listening to the wind in the trees, and cursing his loss of control. But she had been there in the night, eager and willing, and so had he. A set of circumstances that would have inevitable complications.

Long after she lay asleep at his side, one hand curled up beneath her chin, he stroked her hair, her silken skin. It was too late for regrets, he knew. One moment of carelessness, of giving in to hot desire, and his plans were in disarray. She was his opposite and his equal in passion, and he knew that he could never get his fill of her.

That made her the most dangerous woman he had ever known.

The thought aroused him. He rubbed his thumb across the tip of her breast, watched the tender nipple come erect. Although her eyes were closed, he knew the exact moment when she awakened. He slid his hand down the soft curve of her belly, into the silky curls, and felt the warm honey of her on his fingers. His body responded eagerly.

Need flooded through him, forcing back the tinge of despair. Dawn would come soon, and with it everything must change. He had made a terrible mistake, and he felt it deeply. This night's work would only end in regret.

Ravenall looked down at Perdita, with her eyelashes casting shadows on her cheek. The damage was already done. There was no going back. If he could take back these last few hours, he hoped that he would have the courage to do so. But if he were a betting man, he wouldn't take the wager.

He touched her hair, tangled his fingers in the long, gleaming strands. The night was not half gone. In these last few hours, he must put the past and future aside, live only in the now.

He kissed her ivory shoulder. She sighed and moved her legs apart, but still her eyes were closed. Ravenall smiled. So, she liked to play games. Well, so did he.

He teased his hand lower, felt the quickening in his blood, the languid sensuality of her body as she moved to his touch. She was everything he'd imagined she could be: wildly responsive, passionate and abandoned. Willing to take and to give. He lowered his mouth to her breast and let the heat wash over him again.

If this one night was all he would ever have of her, he would damned well make the best of it.

The sound of thunder woke Perdita. Her eyes flew open. Then she saw Ravenall beside her, and smiled. A lock of his hair was tumbled over his brow. Her love for him was so warm and real, the very room seemed to glow with the heat of it. Then she realized that he was dressed. She trembled. Had he meant to steal away without a word to her?

Thunder rumbled again, much closer at hand. Ravenall leaned on one elbow and turned to look at the windows. It wasn't their passion that had turned the dim light from blue to red. The glare lit the night sky beyond her windows, flashing through the chinks in the curtains.

Ravenall threw back the covers and went to the windows giving on the terrace. "Hell and damnation!"

"What is it?" She knelt on the bed, holding the bedsheet before her like a shield.

"A distress signal. There is a vessel sinking off the headland. We'll have to man the lifeboat crew."

He opened the door and the wind blew into the room, raising gooseflesh on her bare back. Over its sounds, she could hear small cries, like the shrieks of distant gulls. It made her blood run cold.

Ravenall went out through the terrace doors, and Perdita slipped on her wrapper and followed him out to the terrace. The wind tugged at her long locks, and blew them across her face and throat. Her thin garment whipped against her ankles.

She tipped her head as another rocket burst up, shattering the night with sound and light. "Must you go?"

There was no answer. When she turned around, Ravenall had vanished.

Perdita was afraid. Usually she could not hear the sea from this spot, but tonight it was clear, a restless crash and boom of breakers against the rocks. She imagined the ship drawn ever closer to their teeth, heard the splintering of wood on stone. Envisioned Ravenall in the lifeboat, rowing with his men, in a suicidal attempt to save the floundering sailors.

She said a swift prayer for those imperiled on the waters,

and one for herself, as well. "Bring him safely back to me," she whispered.

The wind snatched her words away and hurled them straight into the sea.

Twenty-two

Bathing in cold water from the pitcher, she dressed with trembling hands, hid the evidence of their lovemaking, and then went down to the drawing room. Every light was ablaze and Burton stood at the window, with Fanny beside him. He held a brass spyglass to his eye.

The drawing room provided a sweeping view of the bay and the waters below the headland. Another rocket lit the waves. The waves seemed made of blood.

"Can you see them?" she asked.

The butler and Fanny both jumped. "Perdita! What are you doing up at this hour?"

"I couldn't sleep. I saw the signal flares."

"The lifeboat has reached the vessel," Burton told her, "but it is going down. The sea is in a cruel way this night. One lifeboat overturned, but there are three men clinging to it. The other lifeboat is heading to their rescue."

Danes, Ravenall's valet, joined them. He also had a spyglass. It was even more powerful. " 'Tis my lord," he said quietly.

Perdita waited for agonizing minutes, wanting to snatch the spyglass from his hands. Burton gave a shout. "They have got the last man up and over the gunwales. They'll be coming in!"

Fanny rang the bellpull, and two sleepy footmen came hurrying in. "Thomas, bring hot tea and brandy to the library in sufficient quantities. Charles, make sure there are warm blankets and that the fire is high."

They bowed and hurried off. She turned to Perdita. "Go up to bed, my dear. There is no need in your being exhausted."

"Indeed, you are wrong. I have much experience in nursing those chance travelers . . . er, people who have suffered from exposure to the elements. I can be of great assistance to you."

Fanny sized up her determination. "Very well. With Mrs. Overland and Nettie out of the picture, I shall be glad of your assistance."

"Shall we ring for one of the other maids?"

There was a slight pause. "No," Fanny said hurriedly. "We can handle it among ourselves. Most of the men will be taken in down at the village, in order to get them warm and dry as soon as possible. It is only the members of our own household that will come up to Ravenall. If they are able."

Soon everything was in readiness. The library fire was so hot Perdita found herself sweating, as she instructed the footmen where to place the warm blankets on the leather couches. "They will strip beneath the blankets," Fanny said, "with Charles and Thomas helping. Burton will oversee it. Once they are in warm, dry clothes, our part will begin."

A wagon came up the drive from the village, and disgorged six men: two stablelads and one of the footmen were the first down. Ravenall and Andrew followed. The last wore a knitted jersey and a cap pulled low. It didn't take Fanny's gasp to tell Perdita it was Jack Malone.

They shambled inside, their bodies numb from cold. Andrew looked the worst of the lot. His skin was so pale and sallow it might have been parchment with two burned holes for eyes.

Ravenall refused to let Burton attend to him. "See to Mr. Waverly."

"But your lordship is drenched."

"Sea spray and the water we shipped, merely. But Waverly took a bad dunking. As soon as he is changed, we'll take him up to his room. Meanwhile, I must have a word with Lady Ravenall."

He went out into the corridor, holding the door open for Perdita. "You're very angry," she said.

"Yes, by God, I am! The young fool! He might have been killed!"

"You cannot blame him for going out with the lifeboat," she said in amazement.

"He wasn't in the lifeboat," Ravenall growled, pulling her along the corridor. "Go back to bed. This business is none of yours."

"I cannot leave Fanny to deal with this alone."

"You can and will, or I'll see you locked in your chamber."

It was almost dawn when Lieutenant Nutting arrived at the house. Ravenall met him in his private study. "A bad night, Nutting. Were there any souls lost?"

"None aboard my cutter." He eyed Ravenall steadily. "One of the smugglers was, however. We fished him out with a gaff. I believe him to be from the village of Ravensea. The villagers denied it, and no one claimed the poor lad's body."

"What will you do with the body?"

"I had thought of leaving it hanging from the boat hoist in the village; but I thought it might distress the women to see such a grisly sight. The gaff went through him."

Ravenall's mouth tightened. "If no one steps forth, he must be given a proper burial. You may send the bill to me."

"Very much the lord of the castle!" Nutting said. "I heard you are quite the hero, Lord Ravenall. They say you pulled three men from the brine yourself tonight."

"Every fellow who mans a lifeboat is a hero, Nutting. There were many out there besides myself. We rescued those who went out in the first lifeboat and capsized."

"Then you saw nothing of the smugglers, bringing brandy from France to our shores? It was a shot from our cutter that sank their vessel."

Ravenall's eyes glittered darkly. "And did they escape you?"

"Tonight fortune was on their side," Nutting told him. He sent the earl a hard glance. "The next time I will be luckier. You know that this area has been a stronghold for free traders for hundreds of years. It is only in the last few weeks that we have begun closing in on them. Set the warning abroad, my lord. And any man, no matter how high his standing, will be placed under my arrest."

"But of course," Ravenall said. "It is your duty to the Crown to stop the smuggling."

"You may be sure that I will!"

It was almost noon before Perdita awakened. She sat up in bed, and remembered what had happened amid the rumpled sheets. Wrapping her arms around her shoulders, she hugged herself in sheer happiness.

She was in love. And she was loved.

The only reason Ravenall had been so abrupt was his concern for the men who'd manned the life boats. He hadn't meant to be so harsh with her.

There was no sense in ringing for Nettie, who was either asleep or caring for Harriet. Perdita hummed a lilting song as she slipped into a daydress of old rose trimmed with violets. It was one of Ravenall's favorites, and brought out the color of her eyes.

Before going downstairs, she stopped by the invalid's room just as Lady Ravenall was leaving. "She is doing well, but it was quite a shock to her system. I know you will not tire her."

"No, indeed, ma'am." Perdita scrutinized the countess. There were dark circles beneath her eyes, and she looked every bit her age in the noonday light. "You are not in good frame, either, I think."

"Only a little pulled by all the sorry events. I shall have a little rest, I think."

Perdita watched her until the turn in the corridor hid her hostess from sight.

She knocked and was admitted to a cheerful yellow room. Harriet was propped up on the pillows, awake but pale, taking sips of sugared tea that Nettie resolutely forced upon her. She smiled wanly when Perdita took the chair at the bedside and asked after her health.

"I may be up and about tomorrow, Dr. Ash said, but he recommends I do nothing strenuous for the next few days." She twisted her hands. "I am afraid I have torn the hem of your beautiful dress, but Nettie assures me it can be mended."

"I only hope your head can be mended as easily." A sudden thought smote her. "I am taller by an inch, and I noticed the dress was a trifle long on you. I hope it was not the hem which tripped you!"

The other girl looked away. "No, I did not trip." She hesitated and sent a glance to make sure that Nettie was out of earshot. "Perhaps the knock to my head has addled my wits. I don't remember quite perfectly . . . but oh! Miss Hexham. I was *pushed*!"

"What? Who would do such a thing?"

Harriet blushed. "I don't mean to say it was done intentionally. There was a crush of people at the head of the steps. I was standing with my back to them. The next thing I knew there was a blow to my back, and I was falling! If the person who jostled me only realized the consequences, think how he or she must have felt."

"Do not speak any more of this now," Perdita said. She could tell the recollection was upsetting the other girl. "Rest and drink your tea. Shall I bring you up a book to read?"

"No, thank you. My head aches abominably."

"Then I won't tease you any longer. I'll stop by later, if I may?"

"Please do."

Perdita went down to the drawing room shyly hoping to find Ravenall there, but it was empty. Perhaps he was in his study, where he often spent an hour or two each day. She wanted very much to see him, to reassure herself of his regard. To have him hold her in his arms and kiss her again, until she was breathless and banish all her foolish fears.

His study was in the older part of the building, and one of the footmen gave her directions. It wasn't until she reached the door that she recognized it. This was the room they'd come through from the cavern below the castle. There was the Ravenall coat of arms in the stained-glass window and over the plastered front of the chimney breast. But where was the door?

The dark wainscoting presented an unblemished front, and try as she might, Perdita could find no sign of the door or a secret latch. She did locate a hidden storage closet, but there was no exit into the caverns from it. Disappointed on both fronts, she started back to the newer wing.

Somehow she got lost, and came out near the Music Room. Daisey and Fanny stood in the alcove outside it, and she saw that the duchess was in great distress.

"What is it! What is wrong?"

Daisey turned to her with a crumpled piece of notepaper in her hand. "My husband writes to me that my brother has put our family home up for sale! I cannot believe Justin means to dispose of The Priory and not a word of it to me. It has been in the possession of Waverlys for three hundred years! But Mr. Clements has confirmed it."

Fanny sent her a sharp look. "Perhaps he feels that the castle is all he needs. You know how deep his love is for Ravenall."

"But to sell The Priory! To see strangers living there! Oh, no. I cannot bear the thought of it."

"It is his to dispose of, you know," Fanny said lightly. "I'm sure in time you will become used to it."

Although Fanny tried to calm her, the duchess was still agitated. "Never! Oh, I cannot believe he would do such a thing!" she said again, with tears in her eyes.

Perdita stepped in. "If you feel so strongly about it, perhaps he will listen to you. He might let it to a family rather than sell it outright. You must talk to him before you become more upset."

Daisey wiped her eyes and blew her nose in a dainty handkerchief. "I intend to do so immediately!"

"Well, you cannot." Fanny bit her lip. "That is what I came in search of you to say. Justin has gone up to London with Mr. Clements. They left at dawn."

Perdita was struck dumb. *Gone to London? Without so much as a word to her, after all that had happened between them last night?*

The duchess stared at her. "London! What maggot has he got in his brain now?"

"Indeed, I do not know. Burton said he left no written messages for anyone."

They started back along the corridor, wondering what had called Ravenall away, and Perdita fell a step behind them. Her emotions were in complete turmoil. He had made love to her and then gone away, leaving not so much as a note.

Common sense asserted itself. It must be urgent indeed if he hadn't taken leave of the others. Surely he would write to her from London.

For the next week she waited eagerly for the post to be delivered. A letter came for Andrew, and a short note to Daisey, sending his apologies and explaining he would not be back at the castle before her departure on Thursday. Another came for Fanny a day later.

There was nothing for Perdita at all.

After Daisey left for Devon the place seemed empty and sad. Everyone seemed unsettled. Harriet came down and reclined on the sofa to read and play at draughts with Fanny, but Andrew was scarce. He spent a good deal of time alone in the billiard room, racking the balls and breaking them in angry silence, and there was the smell of brandy on his breath far too early in the day. Perdita tried to find out what he knew, to no avail.

Jack Malone came to dine twice, Calvin Bridgeforth and General Galsworth to play at cards with Fanny and the dowager, and there were morning callers, as well. But to Perdita the castle was a different place without Ravenall's darkly commanding presence. Every day she waited for word from him, to no avail.

And every night she cried herself to sleep.

Another week passed slowly, without Ravenall's return. He sent a brief note to his grandmother, explaining that circumstances had detained him indefinitely, and that he would likely not see them until later in the month.

Perdita felt the ache inside her turn to emptiness. Then anger came, scalding and bitter. She only hoped in time it would become complete indifference, but the wounds were so fresh she despaired of them healing anytime soon.

She was certain that she knew why he'd left. She'd thought their lovemaking would seal the bond between them, but it had only served as a wedge. Her actions that night had satisfied his desire, but they given him a disgust of her. She had proved to him, beyond any doubt, that she was no better than a common tavern whore.

She stared out the window of the breakfast room. *And once I thought myself so far above poor Sukey. The only difference between us is the inheritance that I have stolen, and the lies that I have told. At least she was more honest about it.*

It was a very lowering thought.

Perdita wrapped a warm shawl around her and went out to the terrace. The gardens were almost out of bloom, with only a few autumn flowers to lend color to them. She paced up and down the stone flags, restless and unhappy.

At least the round of dinners and dancing parties in the neighborhood had helped to pass the time, although she didn't enjoy them much. Following Fanny's example, however, she put on a smiling front, and put herself out to be a charming guest. It was more fatiguing than she had ever imagined.

The mindless activities kept her from dwelling on anything

for long, and the preparations for their going up to London were under way. Fanny began showing her pattern books and talking of rides in the Row and shopping in Bond Street.

For the first time Perdita was eager to go to London. Anything to escape the castle and the man who had won her heart and then callously betrayed her. Even though he would be at the mansion in town, they need not spend much time in the same room. The thought was cold comfort.

"I will not show him that I care a whit!" she said beneath her breath.

"I beg your pardon?"

She hadn't realized that Harriet had come out to the terrace. "Oh, there you are. I wanted to show you a . . . a hat that Lady Haycross gave me, which I thought would suit you better."

She'd gone through her wardrobe with Nettie ruthlessly, selecting anything that she thought might be suitable for Harriet without making her feel like a charity case. The other girl accepted the castoffs warmly, and they continued in their unspoken conspiracy to make Andrew declare himself. Thus far the plan had not been a success.

Harriet retired for a nap and Perdita decided to ride. She dressed in her habit and had Alanna brought round from the stables. The pretty mare pranced daintily and whickered in welcome when she saw her mistress.

Once she was swung up into the saddle, Perdita dismissed the groom. "I am safe enough on Ravenall lands."

The young man swallowed and his Adam's apple bobbed. "Begging your pardon, miss, but his lordship wouldn't like it."

Her smile was wry. "His lordship is not here."

Without another word she wheeled Alanna about, and they left the courtyard in a brisk trot. Once well away, she let the horse have her head, and they enjoyed a splendid gallop across the parklands. She loved to ride and wondered that she had ever feared it.

Eventually they ended up near the cliff walk. Since the episode of the falling wall, Perdita had avoided the Monks' Chapel. Something drew her there today.

Leaving Alanna in the shade of a tree, she walked to the edge of the sheer drop. Perdita paused at the top of the path leading down to the lonely cluster of monks' cells and the chapel. The arched window was still standing, framing a breathtaking view. She hesitated only a moment before descending.

All the debris had been cleared and stacked neatly to one side, revealing another stone wall behind it. The blocks were huge, irregular and fitted together so well she doubted a knife blade would go between the joints. They must predate the chapel by hundreds of years.

There were several strange scratches in one. She leaned down. "Why, they are runes." She had seen some of the ancient writings on the tors, along with engraved circles and spirals and horned animals. Another was in English, although the spelling was odd. She traced the letters with her fingertip, translating them as she went.

Their message was simple and touching: *For Those in Peril on the Sea, O Lord Have Mercie.*

As she turned back toward the empty arch of the window, something caught her eye skimming on the sea perilously near the base of the distant cliffs. She hoped the intrepid sailor would benefit from the prayer, as the vessel swerved between two thrusting rocks. Suddenly she recognized the vessel. It was Ravenall's small sailboat, *Adventurer.*

No one but Ravenall himself ever sailed it. And he was in London.

Surely if he'd returned he would have come to me!

As she was craning her neck for a better look it vanished from view. A sound made her turn, heart leaping to her throat. The walls still stood around her, but she was no longer alone. Calvin Bridgeforth bowed from above.

"A lovely day for exploring, Miss Hexham. But I cannot help but feel that you are a little foolish in tempting fate twice in the same way."

There was something menacing in his words and she eyed him warily. "I didn't know you were still in the neighborhood, sir."

Bridgeforth came lithely down the steep steps. "I have some unfinished business." He smiled warmly. "Some of it with you."

She stepped back and bumped against the side wall. His smile widened at her reaction and he leaned against the stone bench where the coffins of long-dead monks once rested for their requiem.

"Let me be frank, Miss Hexham. I offended you when I cast hints that Waverly might be behind the attacks on Lord Ravenall," Bridgeforth said. "Of course, you were right in your assumptions, and I was wrong. I have made discreet inquiries. It is not young Andrew whom you have to fear. He is badly dipped himself. He would certainly not want to be saddled with Ravenall Castle, when the estate is foundering on the brink of ruin."

Perdita frowned. "I do not understand you."

"Shall I take the gloves off, Miss Hexham? Very well. Ravenall is on the rocks. His properties are encumbered and he is unable to pay off the mortgages on others. Bad mismanagement on his part. Or"—he cocked his head—"more likely gaming. It was the late earl's fatal tendency, you know."

He sent her a dazzling smile. "You were a windfall for Ravenall. If not for your sudden appearance, Ravenall would surely have lost the castle by now."

She stared at him. "What do I have to do with Lord Ravenall's finances?"

He raised his brows. "Oh, dear. Have I spoken out of turn? But how could I be expected to know you weren't aware of it?"

His languid insinuations made her want to scream with frustration. "Aware of what, Mr. Bridgeforth?" she said through clenched teeth.

"That Ravenall has control of your fortune until you are twenty-one. It is your estates he is using to bolster his finances. He has already sold off what he can of his family holdings in order to keep above hatches."

She had a horrible sinking feeling at the pit of her stomach. "You are referring to The Priory?"

"Yes. You are better informed than I realized. The Priory has been the seat of the Waverlys for hundreds of years. I would never part with my own estate of Canfield Park. I can only imagine what great desperation would cause Ravenall to rid himself of it."

Her quick mind was leaping ahead. "How long have his affairs been in such bad shape?"

"A good six months and more, from the rumors now surfacing."

Her heart sank like a stone. She realized what a fool she

had been. What a pawn in Ravenall's schemes. The view over the sea became more watery because of the sting of tears in her eyes. "Then the search for Mi . . . for me was not motivated by any wish to restore me to my rightful place in the world?"

Her traitorous tongue stumbled over her lies.

Bridgeforth gave a sharp laugh. "More to restore Lord Ravenall to his, my poor child."

The blood drained from her face. She thought for a moment that she might faint. Bridgeforth was all solicitousness.

"I see my revelations have proved a shock. How maladroit of me, my dear Miss Hexham. I am desolate! Ravenall is a dashing figure, quite like the hero of a romance. No doubt you thought he set out to find you out of the goodness of his heart."

"Either way, the outcome is the same," she said stiffly.

"It is the final outcome that concerns me," he murmured. "There have been several untoward incidents concerning you, my dear. First the falling wall here, then your little dip in the brine. Oh, yes. Lieutenant Nutting entertained us with that story when Clements and I were watching the meteor shower."

"I don't wish to think about that night. It started so well, and ended so badly."

"It might have ended far worse—for you! Refresh my memory, if you please, but at dinner on the night Miss Evans fell on the terrace, I believe she wore some shade of pink at dinner, and you wore white."

"Yes, that's very true."

"But later, when we were out star-gazing, you were wearing yellow, while she was in white. Or does my memory fail me?"

"You are correct again. I spilled something on our gowns, and we were forced to go up and change." She felt her heart beating harder. "I did not know that you were so interested in fashion, Mr. Bridgeforth."

"Tol-lol!" he said, with an airy gesture. "Most of the time I am not." His eyes met hers and held them. "After all," he said, with telling emphasis, "one dark-haired young lady in a white dress looks very much like another."

She sat stiff and trembling. The same thought, persistent but unexamined, had occurred to her. Perdita fixed him with a level stare. "I think, sir, that you have a motive behind every word you utter. I wonder what it may be in this instance?"

He lifted his quizzing glance and eyed her with approval. "You are very quick, Miss Hexham. My only wish is to put you on your guard. It is my opinion that Miss Evans did not trip at all. She landed too far from where she was standing—a shove or blow sent her out before she tumbled down!"

"Who would do such a thing? I am sure you are mistaken," she lied. "There is as little reason for anyone to harm me as there is to attack Harriet."

"You must not make the common mistake of thinking that everyone who is polite to your face wishes you well."

He let those words sink in. "You are a great heiress, Miss Hexham. You have a rich estate to pass on to your own heirs, if something should happen to you."

"Nonsense! I've set up a will leaving much of my fortune to charity."

His blue eyes were faintly mocking. "Did you, indeed? How odd. Are you aware that, under law, a female who has not attained her majority cannot draw up a valid will?"

She stared at him, stunned. "But it was Lord Ravenall himself who had Mr. Clements come to draft the documents for me." She shook her head. "It makes no sense."

"Unless it was used as a ploy to lull your doubts. I am very sure a moment's reflection will tell you who would inherit your estate if you died before you were old enough to make a valid will."

Perdita bowed her head. "I imagine it would devolve to Lord Ravenall, as my guardian."

Bridgeforth made her a low bow. "A woman of both beauty and superior understanding."

She lifted her chin. "You do not know me well, yet you have gone out of your way to put me in the possession of these facts, sir. May I ask why?"

"I like you, Miss Hexham. You're clever and lovely and have spirit. In many ways, you remind me of Ravenall's late wife. I knew her in the West Indies, many years ago." He tilted his head like a malevolent bird. "She came to a tragic end, you know."

The chill off the water seemed to settle in Perdita's bones. "Véronique. I have heard of her." She clasped her gloved hands together tightly. "No one speaks of her: it is not allowed. Will you tell me what happened to her, Mr. Bridgeforth?"

He gave her a little bow of apology. "As I was not present when she died, I cannot really say."

"Except that she came to a tragic end! I do not believe your protestations, sir. Surely you must know something of what was said at the time."

His face became grave. "It was generally believed that Ravenall murdered her."

For a moment Perdita thought she'd gone deaf. All the sound was sucked out of the world. The roar of the sea, the cries of the birds—everything was gone in the hot rushing of blood in her head. She sat down abruptly on the coffin bench. The cold flowed out of the stone and into her, lodging around her heart.

"I cannot believe such a thing of him," she said at last.

"Can't you?" Bridgeforth murmured softly. "Perhaps it is all too much to take in, Miss Hexham. But take care that he does not exert his wiles to draw you into his clutches. He will stop at nothing to get your fortune by one means or another."

By the stricken look on her face he learned that his guess was right: Ravenall had been making up to the girl. Not that he blamed him one bit.

"I will leave you alone with your thoughts, Miss Hexham. But I would advise you not to remain alone too long . . ."

As he sauntered away she held her head high, but inside she was shaking.

Bridgeforth turned back when he reached the very top of the cliff, and surveyed the forlorn little figure he'd left behind.

He was satisfied that his poisoned darts had gone home.

Since the day Justin was born, he has been a thorn in my side. And now I have paid him back. She will never marry him now, and he will never salvage his estates.

Bridgeforth smiled to himself. Each man had his talents. His own particular genius was for sowing discord.

A small vice, he told himself, *but highly entertaining.*

Perdita mounted her mare and rode her hard across the open parkland, trying to outrun the terrible things that Calvin Bridgeforth had told her. The wind was up and the sun westering when she retraced her way back to the castle.

Ravenall had returned.

She saw his luggage being unloaded from his carriage, and

was filled with dismay. After handing Alanna over to a groom, she hurried up to her room, hoping she wouldn't meet Ravenall on the way.

There was little chance of that. He locked himself away with Andrew in the study for hours, only sending out for more wine and sandwiches, and sent word that neither of them would dine at home that night.

As she was dressing for dinner, she saw the two men ride off together on horseback. Something strange was afoot.

The ladies of the house dined with only Oliver Clements for company. He seemed delighted with his feminine audience and the good food. Since he was alone, he didn't linger over his port. When he joined the ladies in the drawing room, it wasn't difficult for Perdita to get him off to one side for a few minutes while the countess was talking to Fanny.

"Is it true," she asked, "that the will I made is invalid, since I am not of age?"

He colored and looked very chagrined. "I cannot deceive you. It is true."

"Then why did we go through that charade?"

"My dear Miss Hexham, I am employed by the Earl of Ravenall. How could I refuse him such an innocuous request?"

"Yes, I see."

But she didn't. "Has my lord asked you to sell off any of . . . the Hexham inheritance?"

Clements paled. "I don't know if we should be having this discussion, Miss Hexham. Your affairs are in the hands of your guardian."

"But you are his agent. And since the Hexham estate is mine in its entirety, I feel certain you must have some obligation to me to speak truth!"

He considered that a minute or two. "It would be best if you spoke to your guardian yourself. However, I will tell you that he has asked me to look into the sum that Hexham Court might command, if it were to be sold."

She was furious, and it took all her best manners to hide it from the others until after the tea tray was brought in, and Clements took his leave. Before going upstairs, Perdita dashed off a quick note for Ravenall, requesting to see him at his earliest convenience. She gave it to Burton to deliver to Danes, and almost immediately regretted sending it. She'd wanted a confrontation—he might think she had something completely different in mind. Even his skilled lovemaking, she thought wrathfully, had been nothing more than a way to further his schemes. What a fool he must think her!

As she was unbuttoning her cuffs, one of the servants delivered a message. Ravenall had returned, and would see her in his study in ten minutes' time.

"I'll ring for you when I return, Nettie." She rebuttoned her cuffs and went to his study, wishing she'd waited until morning to send her note. Her throat was dry.

He'd sent for her as curtly as if she were a servant.

Which, of course, in his mind I am. Polly from the Stag and Crown!

By the time she reached his study, she had worked herself up to a fine pitch. He was sprawled back in a leather chair behind the desk, with a glass of brandy in his hand. Something sparked in his eyes when he saw her, but his voice was as cool as ever.

"You are looking well, Miss Hexham. It seems my absence has agreed with you."

"Indeed it has, my lord! Did you expect to return and find me wan and wasted?"

His mouth firmed. "You are impertinent! It does not suit you."

"And you are a thief! You intend to sell off my estates, using my wealth to keep yourself above the hatches!"

"Such a very vulgar expression sits ill on a young lady's lips," he said with icy reserve. His own had blanched white. "You have been busy while I was away. May I ask where you have heard this tale?"

"From more than one source, my lord. Do you deny the truth of it? That you have control over my fortune until my twenty-first birthday—and that you mean to sell off my properties, and divert my funds to pay off your creditors?"

"Where did you hear this?"

"From Mr. Bridgeforth."

"Pah! He is an envious creature. You would be wise not to listen to his venomous spewings."

"When I spoke with Mr. Clements tonight, he only confirmed my worst fears."

"I see. Not content to discuss me with Bridgeforth, you then interviewed my employee! What else did these gentlemen have to say about my character?"

"Far more than I am sure you wished them to divulge!" Her violet eyes looked almost black in the lamplight. "That you have mismanaged your estates and are on the brink of ruin. That you will likely bankrupt my estates as well and leave me penniless."

Her voice broke on an angry sob. "You are a liar and a villain through and through. I know know why you seduced me—so that no one else would have me, and you could control my fortune as long as possible!"

"How dare you speak to me that way! If not for me, you would be gutting chickens and fending off the advances of any man with enough coins to tempt Mrs. Croggins. I have given you more than you have ever had in your life!"

"No, my lord," she said frostily. "You have merely restored it to me."

"Have I, *Miss Hexham*?"

She stopped short. Ravenall took her wrist and held it out where they could both see it. "The mark of the Hexhams," he said savagely. "And you dare call *me* a liar!"

"What . . . what do you mean?"

"This!" He smiled icily, and rubbed his thumb over the burn mark on her wrist. Then he touched his own face. "You see, if there is one thing I know, 'Miss Hexham,' it is *scars!*"

For a space of several beats she could hear the blood drum in her ears. There was no use pretending. "How long have you known?"

"From that first night when I made you my proposal—and you accepted. How did you come by this burn?"

"A wafer iron," she said in a small voice.

He released her hand, and she sat down abruptly on the chair behind her. It didn't make sense to her at first. "But . . . why? You knew me for an impostor, yet you continued this masquerade, even drawing the others into it! Fanny and Jack and Andrew. Even Daisey!"

"Acquit me of that! They all sincerely believe you to be the missing heiress. You and I are the only ones who know the truth."

"I see," she said slowly. "And the truth is that everything Mr. Bridgeforth said was on the mark. You had no wish to

restore an orphaned heiress to her station in life. You made
me part of your plan so that you might use Pauline Hexham's
fortune to your own advantage. And that is the only reason
you embarked upon this mad scheme."

Her disillusionment was devastating.

"I did not do it for myself, but to save Ravenall. I inherited
a title and a mountain of debts, and grasped at the chance to
extend my credit that fate put into my eager hands. But I have
never touched Pauline Hexham's inheritance! *Your* motives
are not so innocent."

"I was in fear of my life for Sam Bailey and could only
think of escape! I knew I was stealing a dead girl's inheritance,
but I was fighting for my life!"

His eyes were hidden beneath his heavy lids. "Do you mean
to expose me?"

"I don't know what to do."

Ravenall frowned down at her. "In the eyes of the world,
you are Miss Hexham. You must continue on in your adopted
role. It becomes you, you know! You will be a great success
in London, and find a man worthy of winning your heart."

She shook her head. "I will remain Miss Hexham, my lord,
only as long as it takes to pack a few things. I will find a
position in Ravensea if need be, but I will not continue this
farce any longer."

Ravenall was furious. "That will never happen, my dear.
You will stay under my protection!"

Her back straightened. "*Your protection?* You have tricked
me with lies and then ruined me into the bargain. What will
you do to me if I try and leave? Pry a rock wall atop me?
Push me off a sailboat or down a flight of stairs?"

His eyes glittered. "What are you saying, Miss Hexham?
That I made attempts on your life?"

"The facts speak for themselves. As Pauline Hexham, I
have a great deal of money. And it all comes to you if I should
die."

He moved so quickly she had no time to escape. Ravenall
reached out and clasped her by the wrists. His voice was icy.
"Why do you speak of dying, my dear? You are young and
in good health."

She tried to pull away. *"So was Véronique!"*

The instant the words were out of her mouth she knew

she'd gone too far. His face was dark with rage. "What do you know of my late and unlamented wife?"

"There are some who say you murdered her!"

There. It was out in the open. Ravenall's voice was low, his eyes dangerous. "And what do you say, Perdita? You who have lain in my arms and explored the erotic pleasures with me. Do you think I could love a woman—and then murder her? Can you really believe that I would harm you in such a way?"

She wanted to hurt him, but she couldn't lie. Perdita shook her head. "No," she sighed. "I cannot."

He gave her a mocking bow. "I am gratified." He let her go and strode across to the mantel. "I will reward your faith in me with the truth. I did not kill Véronique. She would have deserved it if I had!"

Perdita gasped and he went on. "She was false and cruel and destructive. A woman without morals. I will tell you what I have told no one else, and only this once. I was young, dazzled, and foolishly in love. She was not. She married me because her lover was married, and she needed the protection of a man. You see, when we exchanged our vows she suspected she was carrying his child. Eventually we separated, and they continued their affair. They ran off together, but when she told him she was carrying his child, he abandoned her. He told her she must rid herself of the baby, and sent her to a woman who was versed in such matters."

Ravenall paced the room, lost in the pain of his recollections. "She came back to me and begged me to take her in. She worked herself into a towering rage when I refused, but I was adamant." His face was haggard in the light. "Then she began to hemorrhage. It was one of the most horrifying things I have ever seen!

"I carried her up to the bed we had once shared and sent for the doctor. As it turned out, she was not with child at all. It was a chancre eating at her diseased womb. For weeks she lay ill. She could not bear the pain, the knowledge that it would continue and grow worse. One evening Véronique picked up the dagger I used as a letter opener, and plunged it into her heart."

"But why were *you* blamed?"

His mouth was cynical. "She was of the Roman faith, and

could not be buried in hallowed ground as a suicide. Her family pleaded with me to hide the circumstances of her death. I did—reported it to the authorities as a tragic accident—and the consequences of my chivalry have haunted me ever since! I was branded a murderer by innuendo and gossip. How can a man fight what is never brought out into the open? It is like fighting shadows—exhausting and fruitless. I will go to my grave with her death credited to my account!"

He looked tired and broken, and Perdita's eyes were filled with tears. "But that is unthinkable! There must be some way to set the record straight!"

He shook his head and his shoulders straightened. "I can never restore the lustre to my reputation—but, by God, I can and shall restore Ravenall to its former glory!"

He rounded on her. "I swear by all that is holy, that I have not borrowed so much as a shilling from the Hexham estates. And, by God, I never shall!"

"Then how will you save yourself? And Ravenall Castle?"

"By any other means necessary. Go to bed. Your fortune is secure—*Miss Hexham*."

He went out and left her standing there, all alone.

The next seven days were a terrible strain on all. The countess was busy finishing the last stages of her history of Ravenall Castle. Ravenall scarcely put in an appearance, Andrew was on edge, and Harriet nervy. Fanny jumped at every sound. Dinners were an ordeal.

Perdita began to feel that she and the dowager were the only two not completely affected. The only normalcy was provided by their occasional guests, but the country was thin of company. Perdita wished desperately that she could turn back time.

Late one night Perdita was awakened by Nettie on the eighth night. It was well after midnight, she saw as she tried to clear her groggy mind. "What is it? Is someone taken ill?"

"No, miss. It is Mr. Clements. He says that it is urgent that he speak to you at once. Burton has put him in the ladies' parlor."

Dressing quickly, she went down to the parlor. Clements stood beside the fire, his face drawn. "Lord Ravenall is in the devil of a fix," he said, with no preliminaries. "The revenuers are after him. They know that he's been working alongside the free traders these past weeks. He escaped this time, by throwing the contraband overboard. Nutting's gone for a warrant, and will be back."

"Where is Ravenall?" Perdita was shaking.

"Waiting for you to open the door that guards the secret passageway. I don't know where it is, you see, and he cannot make his way safely to shelter any other way. It is his only hope."

"How did they come to discover he was involved?" she asked, clutching at his arm.

"I'm afraid it was something I inadvertently said. I mentioned seeing Ravenall's sailboat vanish at the foot of the cliffs, and they came to their own conclusions."

Perdita remembered seeing the same thing, from the ruins of the Monks' Chapel.

"I am not exactly sure how to open it, but I will take you there at once."

She led him through to the old wing of the castle. The shadows were dark and deep and disorienting at so late an hour. She took a wrong turning in her haste, and they had to retrace their steps.

Clements was agitated. "Please do not waste any more time," he said roughly.

It seemed so out of character for him, that she glanced up sharply. "You ae very loyal to Ravenall," she said.

"Yes. I have loved the castle since I was in leading-strings. My loyalty to the place runs deep."

"I meant to the earl himself," she told him in surprise.

"Of course. However, my first charge must always be the well-being of the estates. It is a sacred charge handed down to me by my father. 'Although we can never claim the castle as our own,' he said to me, 'we shall at least prove ourselves to be great stewards of her care.' Of course, that was before things went bad on the Exchange, when it was thought that Napoleon had defeated Wellington at Waterloo."

"But he did not!"

Clements sighed. "My father had 'borrowed' against the estate to make investments. He meant to pay it all back. He really did. He withdrew the funds at a terrible loss. There was a terrible panic in the city. A mistake, as we learned later when

Wellington triumphed. It was disastrous. My father had no way of paying back what he had taken. He tried desperately to recoup the Ravenall fortunes, but everything he touched turned to dross!"

"How could he hope to keep it secret so long?"

"He was able to hide it from the previous earl quite easily." His lip curled. "As long as the late earl had enough money for his travels and gambling and women, he didn't care. He left everything to my father's discretion. But my father died of an infected foot. It is left to me to restore the family fortunes!"

They turned a corner and were almost at the study. "Has your family always lived in Cornwall?" she asked a little nervously.

"Oh, yes. Since the time of the first Lord Ravenal. Our line goes back to him, and the son he fathered on a local girl. Many times over the centuries our blood has commingled. I am," he said harshly, "as much a Ravenall as anyone beneath this roof!"

Perdita saw him in profile then. The famous Ravenall nose!

And she knew that he had not come to the castle by night on any mission to help Ravenall. She must use her wits to discover his true purpose. "You do not like him," she said encouragingly.

"No. No more than do you." They'd reached the study and entered it. "I knew you were on my side when you began questioning me about his handling of your affairs. And now you must show me where the secret door is, so that I may go through the cavern and open the smuggler's cache to Lieutenant Nutting!"

Her eyes went wide with shock. "You said it was Lord Ravenall you wished to admit."

Clements sent her a conspiratorial smile. "Ah, but I wasn't sure of you. Now that I know you are on my side, I can speak the truth. Before this night is over, Miss Hexham, the earl and his cousin will be in chains. And when they swing from the gallows at Ravensea, I will be there laughing!"

He looked around the study with its ancient windows, the Ravenall crest in the plastered chimney breast. "And when they are in their graves, I will still be here!"

She knew then without a doubt that he was mad. Her danger was acute. "How will you hope to restore the funds your father stole—ah, *borrowed*—after all this?"

Clements raised her hand and brought it to his lips. Perdita's skin crawled. "After you and I are married," he said calmly, "we shall sell off everything possible and purchase the castle when it goes upon the auction block to pay off the accrued debts. You will not care if I do so?"

"Oh . . . oh, of course not. The castle *must* be saved."

Her heart was racing but her thoughts kept pace. She must lead him on as long as possible. "You are so good," he said. "My angel!"

Inside she was shaking like a blancmange, but her voice sounded calm, if just a little breathless. "You may sell off anything you wish. My entire fortune, if need be."

Leaning forward, Clements pressed his wet mouth against hers. "It is very fortunate that Ravenall survived the accidents I engineered to the balustrade and his carriage, or we should never have met one another!"

He pulled back and smiled down at her, his eyes glittering. "We cannot be earl and countess, of course, but I promise you this, my dear. You shall be lady of the castle," he told her, "and I—I shall at last be the master of Ravenall!"

Perdita's blood congealed in her veins. She was all alone in the old part of the castle with a man who was three parts insane. A man who admitted he'd attempted murder as easily as if he were commenting upon the weather.

"I don't understand why you tried to rid yourself of me— that was you, was it not, who knocked the stone wall down and later tripped Miss Evans?"

"Oh, my darling. I am so sorry for that. I didn't love you then as I do now. And Ravenall proved so very hard to eliminate! I thought only that if I had your estate to liquidate, I might bring the Ravenall fortunes about. It had become an obsession to me! Poor Miss Evans. I felt quite guilty over her mishap. She hasn't had a happy life," he said.

Perdita couldn't believe her ears. He was a confused mix of guilt and apology and arrogance. *Mad as a hatter! I must escape and warn Ravenall! But how?*

Clements was still babbling. "I was attracted to you from the first, but in these past few weeks, with Ravenall away, we have spent so much time together in each other's company.

And that is when I truly fell in love with you. Tell me you will forgive me, dear heart?"

Her smile was a rictus of fear. "Oh, yes. After all, you did it because you were trying to save the castle."

His hand cupped her cheek. "Oh, my darling, you do understand! But now you must show me to the secret passage. Lieutenant Nutting is waiting in the cove, and the tide will be coming in very soon."

She thought desperately for some way to escape from him. Then it came to her in a flash. "This way!"

Perdita slid her hand along the wainscoting until she felt the tiny lever hidden behind the trim. She pulled it and the door swung open. Relief surged like a tide. Perfect!

"Hurry," she cried, urging him to go through the opening.

The moment he did, she closed the secret panel. There was a moment of utter silence, then a shout of surprise. There were no secret stairs there, only stacks of strong boxes and oilskins. Clements cursed as he tried to pound his way out of the hidden storage closet. The stout oak held. He could throw himself against it until kingdom come, and it would never give.

Taking up her candle once more, she ran off in search of help. She made her way along the dim corridor and found Andrew asleep in his room. He woke fast enough when Perdita told him what she had done to Clements.

Andrew cursed. "They said it was for tomorrow! Damn him, this is Ravenall's doing. He went in my place. Where is Ravenall now?"

Perdita swallowed. "Mr. Clements claims that Ravenall is out with the free traders."

"Is he, by God? After threatening me with great bodily harm if I should ever dare sail with them again? Why in God's name would he do something so foolhardy?

She was near weeping. "Out of pride! To save Ravenall from ruin! Clements and his father played fast and loose with the estate income in the late earl's time, then tried to cover it up."

Andrew shook his head. "No. He did it to save me. He surely persuaded them to tell me the wrong night. Damn his eyes! Everything hinges on it." He touched her arm. "I learned two weeks ago that things were in bad oar, but not that they were at a standstill. I thought he might apply to you for a loan, with his estate as collateral. It is frequently done. But he told me he'd rather see Ravenall in ruins and himself with it, than touch so much as a farthing of your fortune."

Her guilt was terrible. "We must warn him that Nutting is waiting in the cove. That is one favor which that murderous madman gave to us."

"Ravenall and Jack are too cagey to fall for that trick. They'll have taken the other way in." Andrew cursed beneath his breath. "It's high tide. If they're not careful, instead of shooting through the cavern opening they'll smash into the cliffs."

He dressed hastily while she waited in the corridor. Soon they were traipsing back toward the old wing of the castle. "Why did you call Clements a murderer?"

"He was behind all the accidents! Everything! When Ravenall became suspicious that the accounts had been tampered with, Clements loosened one of the battlements. It was ironic that he almost went over himself, and Ravenall saved him!"

"I would not have thought it of Mr. Clements," he said, shocked. "He seemed such a gentleman. It is hard to believe."

"Not when you know the details. And," she said grimly, "it was Clements himself who shot at Ravenall upon the moor, causing his dreadful accident!"

"Is that true? I had suspected Bridgeforth, myself! I owe that snake-tongued court-card an apology."

She digested this. "Although I cannot like Mr. Bridgeforth, I believe him to be a mischief-maker, but no more than that."

The further implications of what she'd just revealed hit him. "Damn him to hell, then it was Clements who pushed Harriet down the stairs?"

"Yes. Thinking she was me."

"I'll wring his damned neck with my own two hands!"

They left the cellars through a hidden door, and found themselves in a tunnel hewn from living rock. The sound of the sea grew loud, magnified by the walls.

Such guilt washed over her that she couldn't speak. She had no doubt it was her accusations that had goaded Ravenall into this folly. Her pride and his had led to this.

Just ahead dark water swirled and a battered rowboat was tied up inside the cavern. Two burly men struggled forward, half-carrying a third. She cried out when she realized it was Ravenall. His face was white and still.

"We didn't dare use the flares," one said. "The boat's capsized. He's taken in a lot of water, but he's alive. Don't know about the rest, but Malone's gone out with the lifeboat. He'll bring them back around the headland."

So, Perdita thought, *Fanny was right. Jack is one of 'the gentlemen' after all.* "He's near froze from being under so long. Where do you mean to hide him?"

Andrew hesitated. "We can't take him to his chamber. When they are thwarted of their prey at the cove, Nutting and his men will seek a warrant and come to the castle."

"Take him to mine," Perdita commanded.

The men stared at her. "Take him up to my room, strip off the wet clothes and boots, and hide them in Lady Ravenall's room. Not even Nutting would dare enter her chambers. Leave the rest to me!"

She followed the sailors up through the caverns to the cellar, then mounted the servants' stair to the bedroom wing. "Oh, Ravenall, you fool! It wasn't worth the risk," she said beneath her breath.

Andrew heard her as she followed them inside the chamber. "It will be, if he lives. He's made his fortune all over again." His smile wavered. "And mine. He knew I'd gotten entangled with 'the gentlemen' and tried to stop me at first. The next I knew he was in charge of the whole enterprise, God help him!"

She watched as they carried Ravenall in, with Danes hurrying after. The look on the valet's face was so bleak her heart turned over. She would have wept, if there was time.

There wasn't. Already they could hear sounds of a carriage rattling full tilt up the drive. "Oh, hurry!" she pleaded.

"You'll be leaving, miss," Danes said.

"No, I won't. Stoke up the fire, Andrew."

She turned to the men. "Put him in the bed. I'll turn my head if you like." For all the good that would do. "Andrew, fetch one of his lordship's nightrobes."

Danes appeared at her shoulder, holding a red silk dressing gown. He coughed softly. "His lordship has no nightrobes, Miss Hexham; however, he does wear this."

"Excellent. You are a man of quick action, Mr. Danes."

She tossed it on the floor.

"Very well," she said, once Ravenall was beneath the bed-covers. "You may go. And my thanks go with you!"

She issued stern orders to Andrew: "Keep them occupied as long as you can. Offer them brandy . . . not the French, of course! Stall them as long as possible."

Then she told Burton what she wanted him to do. "But, miss . . . !"

"There is no time to waste. Go!"

When the door was closed behind her, Perdita took Ravenall's dressing gown and flung it over a chair. She blew out all the candles but a branch on the mantel, then stripped off her own gown. It was a lovely gown, and it gave her a pang to do it, but she gritted her teeth and ripped it down the front. Not satisfied, she threw it on the floor in a rumpled heap beside the bed. Then she unbound her plait, shook out her long hair, and climbed into the bed with Ravenall.

He was so cold against her bare skin that her heart sank. Then she felt the slow rise and fall of his chest, felt his light breath ruffling her hair. She covered him with her own warmth, feeling it seep into his body.

Dear God, let him awaken!

"Open your eyes," she begged him, clasping his cold hands in hers. "Oh, my love, you must not die!"

He moaned, and flung an arm over his head. Still he didn't awaken.

Her ears pricked up. There were voices. Loud voices coming along the corridor. She didn't know what to do. And then she did. Really, the solution was quite simple.

The voices were outside her door now.

Burton's, raised in indignant protest, came through the heavy wood door. "This is Miss Hexham's suite, Lieutenant Nutting. You cannot mean to burst in there!"

"I've a warrant in my hand. Stand aside, man, and let me see what you are hiding!"

The door swung open and the lieutenant entered without a by-your-leave. He took three paces into the room, and stopped dead. Lord Ravenall lay spread-eagled in the bed, with Miss Hexham beside him. A decanter of brandy and a glass on the night table glittered in the light from the branch of candles on the mantel.

Perdita lay on her back with her cheek resting against Ravenall's wide chest. Her dark hair fell around her like a cloak, and the corner of the sheet provided some modesty. Still, there was enough silky white thigh and rosy-tipped breast revealed between the firelight and lamplight to give Nutting fevered dreams for years to come.

The officer gasped and Perdita lifted her head, with a startled little cry.

Nutting gulped at the unexpected sight before him, then wheeled around on his heel, and marched out the door. His face, so red a moment earlier, was grayer than a corpse.

"My God! I didn't see . . . uh, know . . . I was profoundly mistaken," he said in a queer, high-pitched voice. He turned to the officer beside him.

"What are you gawking at, Yancey?"

"N-nothing, sir! Didn't see a thing. Couldn't, you know. You blocked the doorway!"

The lieutenant fixed the other man with a gimlet eye. "Exactly! You didn't see what . . . didn't see . . . what *I* didn't see! And," he added, "if it ever comes to my ears that you let loose one word of anything that occurred here tonight, I'll have you scrubbing barnacles for the rest of your days!"

"Aye, aye, sir!"

Nutting swallowed. "The smugglers are half-way to France by now. We'd best be on our way, or there will be the devil to pay!"

Burton, his face as expressionless as before, moved them down along the corridor with the skill of a border collie heading two witless sheep. "Perhaps you would care for some refreshment, gentlemen?"

"No, damn . . . er, thank you!"

Nutting could still see Perdita in his mind's eye, lovely and alluring in her nakedness. Visions of demotions danced in the lieutenant's head. Dreams of glory faded like mist on the horizon. Nightmares of Lord Ravenall with a pair of dueling pistols in his hands reared up like a rogue wave at sea.

"M-my apologies for rousing the household," he stammered. "A dreadful mistake! We'll be on our way, then. I won't be bothering his lordship again. No need to show us out, Burton!"

Aware that he was babbling like a madman, Lieutenant

Nutting moved to the head of the stairs with his men, and beat a hasty retreat.

The butler followed them down, slowly and with great dignity.

When they were gone, Danes crept out of the doorway on the other side of the corridor. He frowned at Nettie, who stood gaping at Perdita's door.

"Miss Hexham is a great lady!" he said, shaking his head. "A very great lady."

Nettie clasped her hands on her bosom. "Yes, indeed. Such a one as will make a great countess! It was a happy day when his lordship brought Miss Hexham here."

The matter settled to their mutual satisfaction, they smiled conspiratorially and went about their business. No doubt Miss Hexham and his lordship would summon them, if they required anything.

Separately, of course.

Twenty-three

Perdita lay gasping against Ravenall's shoulder. He was warm now, his body burning her cool skin like a hot coal. The tension, the exertion, and the eroticism of the past few minutes had taken their toll. When she got her breath back, she started to roll away.

"Oh, no you don't!" Ravenall's arms wound round her, holding her close. "You can't start something like that, my love, and not finish it!"

"How long have you been awake?"

"Long enough to enjoy the situation!"

She struggled against him, but every wiggle brought the sensitive tips of her breasts into contact with the hairs on his chest. "I suppose it is no use fighting the inevitable."

"None at all."

"You wondered why I was so cold to you. You were in danger, my love. It broke my heart to do it, but I couldn't let Clements see how things stood with us. Will you forgive me?"

"Yes. I understand now. You never went to London. You were here, hiding and protecting me. And keeping Andrew from compromising himself."

He stroked the hair back from her forehead and looked into her eyes. "You've ruined your reputation, you know. There's nothing for it now but to marry me."

Perdita sighed. "I suppose so. It is a terrible punishment for doing a good deed, but I see no other way out of this sorry predicament!"

"You little jade, you're laughing at me!" He pulled her face down to his and kissed her long and slow.

"How long were you really awake?" she said suspiciously.

Ravenall laughed, and she realized he'd never sounded so

carefree before. "Oh, from somewhere between nibbling on my ear, to uh—"

"Oh!" She punched his arm lightly. "What a fraud!"

He rolled over in the bed, turning their positions so that he was atop her. "I had to see how you meant to sacrifice yourself on my behalf. Would you care to do it again?" He nuzzled her throat. "This time, without the pretense?"

"I believe I would, my lord."

They made love with all the pent-up energy coursing through them. The first time was hot and fierce, exactly as they both wanted. The second time was slow and lazy. He kissed her from head to toe, stopping to enjoy all the wonderful places in between.

The wantonness of their lovemaking astounded them both. Perdita abandoned herself to it, lunging to meet him until her loins throbbed with heat. This time it was she who was in control, Ravenall who lost it. It was his voice crying out hoarsely, his eyes that were closed to savor every sense: her scent, her touch, the inner warmth of her enclosing him.

When it was over, they lay side by side, wrapped in each other's arms, waiting for the dawn. The room was filled with pink light when he rolled over and kissed her mouth. Her arms wound around him tightly. His bruised ribs hurt like the very devil, but he didn't care. She was his. Now and forever.

Perdita turned pensive. "I still cannot believe that Mr. Clements was such a villain. But you guessed his secret."

"It was he who tried to kill me, first with the faulty balustrade—which ironically almost cost him his own life. Then by shooting my horses when I was up on Dartmoor. He knew that if I found out how his father had raped the estate, and how he'd gambled trying to make up the losses, he would be ruined. He tried to blame it all on my uncle instead."

"I don't understand how getting rid of you would have saved him."

"He would have the winding up of my estate, and would have found a way to shift the blame to my shoulders. Then you came on the scene, and he shifted his tactics. I proved too hard to kill; but if he could dispose of you, he would have all the Hexham monies to funnel into Ravenall, and then hide his machinations under mountains of papers."

"And then I proved hard to kill!"

"As I failed you, my darling. I should have moved against him long before the night of the party, but I wanted to gather more evidence. I would never have done so had I known he was a danger to you."

"What will happen to him?"

Ravenall sighed. "By now he'll have discovered the second latch inside the closet, and have made his escape via the caverns. Tonight he will wait and worry and pace the floor of his cottage. Jack and I will pay a call on him quite early. He will, of course, be expecting it. He will listen quietly while I lay out the case against him, and the measures I have taken. Shortly afterward I imagine he will take a walk along the cliff with his dogs and his shotgun. And he will not return."

Perdita shivered. "I can almost feel it in my heart to be sorry for him."

"Do not waste your sympathy on him," Ravenall said fiercely. "He had none for you!"

He kissed her hand and smiled. "I shall save all mine for Lieutenant Nutting. He'll never recover from seeing you naked in my arms tonight." He brushed the hair back tenderly from her forehead. "Nor will I."

She laughed and snuggled her face against Ravenall's shoulder. "Poor man, he was so very shocked! And," she said, "he doesn't even know the half of it!"

He laughed softly, and caressed her. "I doubt that you do, either, my dearest love."

Perdita smiled. "Then I believe that is something I should very much like to learn!"

Epilogue

So many things happened in that autumn that the villagers of Ravencliff and Ravensea talked of it for years to come.

The first was the sad affair of Mr. Clements, who had been agent to the Earl of Ravenall, just as his father had been before him. It was hushed up, but rumors circulated that his untimely death was not an accident.

Some blamed the ghost of Black Roger, the old smuggler who was said to haunt the caves below the castle. Mr. Grigg, an antiquarian who was visiting in the area, when he stumbled across Clements's body, said he'd seen the gunshot wound with his own eyes. The Earl of Ravenall and the dowager countess attended the solemn occasion when he was laid to rest beside his father. There were no other mourners.

The second happening was much more pleasant and involved the sudden reassignment of Lieutenant Nutting to the rugged coasts far north, near the Scottish border. This news was received in the area with general jubilation.

The prosperity of the villagers rose sharply following his transfer.

The most exciting occurrences were centered around the castle itself.

While repairing the foundations—so it was officially said—an enormous cache of gold was discovered, allegedly hidden by the second earl in his heyday.

If any of the locals had their doubts as to the truth of this windfall, they kept them under their caps. Just as they kept their smuggling gold hidden beneath their hearths.

Shortly after the amazing treasure was found, Mr. Waverly and Miss Harriet Evans tied the knot in the chapel at Ravenall. They planned to take up residence at The Priory, Mr. Waverly's estate outside Ravencliff, following their honeymoon in

Venice. The house and grounds were a wedding gift from Lord
Ravenall. His young sisters, who had been living with relatives
in Bath, were expected to join them upon their return. The
local gentry were pleased that The Priory remained in the
Waverly line. So was Daisey, Duchess of Haycross.

Last and best of all, the Earl of Ravenall and his young
ward, Miss Hexham, were married by special license with the
bishop presiding. The location of the happy couple's honeymoon was not divulged.

Sun sparkled from the crystals beneath the mighty oak, as
Ravenall reached down inside the roots. His hand closed on
the small object nestled in the hollow. Odd that he hadn't seen
it before.

Or perhaps not.

Over time he'd come to believe in the magical properties
of the Wishing Tree. Hadn't it given him what he'd wished
for so desperately?

Rising, he turned to his bride. "It's here."

He held out his hand and Perdita looked at the small object
lying in his bronzed palm: a heart-shaped locket, with a tiny
diamond in the center of an engraved, six-pointed star.

"So it was all real!"

She'd awakened beside her husband this morning at Haycross Manor, which Daisey and Haycross had lent to them for
the first part of their honeymoon. Ravenall had been asleep,
his beloved face on the pillow beside hers, while she floated
on the hazy edge between sleeping and waking.

Perhaps it was a dream—or perhaps it was a memory—but
she'd had a sort of vision. In it she'd been very small, and
she'd lost a locket here, in this very clearing. One that her
father had given her on her birthday.

She didn't remember either her father or the birthday in
question, only the fact of the gift, and its loss.

In the dream she'd been surrounded by glowing spears of
light. In reality the giant quartz crystals shimmered in the sun,
breaking the light into dancing rainbows. They were smaller
than she'd expected, no more than two or three feet long at
the largest. In her mind they had been enormous, hovering
over her like angels of light.

"I am afraid to open it," she whispered. She was trembling from head to toe.

"Then you needn't," Ravenall told her gently.

His long fingers stroked her cheek, cupped the side of her face tenderly. "I love you as you are. For yourself alone. I need no proof of anything but your love for me, my darling—and that you give me every moment of the day."

She smiled mistily up at him. "I don't know what to do."

He swept her into his arms, the locket tight in his fist, and kissed her sweet mouth. Her heart and his beat to the same rhythm. When he lifted his head there was a question in his eyes. "Shall I put it back, unopened?"

Perdita shook her head. "We have come this far. If we leave now I will always be tormented by wondering."

"The decision must be yours, my love."

"What if it is empty? Or shows another face?"

His dark blue eyes reflected light, like a summer sea. "It doesn't matter." Lifting her hands, he kissed her fingers, where the sapphires in her wedding ring flashed bluer than his eyes. "I will still love you to the depth and breadth of my soul."

A shiver shook her. "Very well."

Taking the locket from him, Perdita closed her fingers tightly over the small bauble. It was warm from his touch, and that gave her courage. She inserted her nail in the slot, and opened the locket. The delicate halves folded out like butterfly wings. One side held a picture of a beautiful woman, the other of a handsome man.

Eyes brimming, Perdita showed it to Ravenall. He smiled, but didn't appear at all surprised. The woman was the same as the one in the miniature that Daisey had shown to him months ago. And Perdita had her father's determined chin. The resemblance was uncanny.

"Your parents," he acknowledged softly. "You may not have your memories back, but at least you have had your history restored you."

"My mama and papa," she said wonderingly. "How very young they were. How sad to know their story ended so tragically!"

Her breath caught on a sob, but he pulled her into his arms once more, and kissed away her tears. One kiss led to another.

Love and desire and hope flowed over them in the dappled sunshine, as if they'd received a blessing.

They made love in this magical place where they had each suffered hurt, and now healing. The branches of the great oak sheltered them like a silken canopy, and only the warmest of breezes caressed their naked skin.

He was an ardent lover, teaching her pleasures she had never dreamed existed. Each time was a revelation. And when the glorious moment came, they were dazed and blinded by passion and the sudden blaze of light, as if of a thousand candles. The air glittered, diamond-bright, and they rode its glory together, wrapped in each other's arms.

Later, when they lay contented in each other's arms, they kissed and touched until desire overwhelmed them, and they made love once more. Perdita would have spent the day there, naked in his embrace. The air cooled, the branches danced and the breeze, and Ravenall sighed regretfully. He kissed her eyelids.

"Time to return to the manor, my darling."

"Not yet," she whispered, running her hands over his chest and shoulders. "I don't want to go."

"The *Raven* is anchored at Dartmouth, and leaves with the tide, my love, and Italy is calling. But I promise I shall make love to you in Rome, and Venice, in Florence and on the Isle of Capri. And of course, on the *Raven*. We will lie out on deck beneath the stars, with the sea whispering around us."

"More likely the sailors," she told him, laughing.

"Well, they won't see anything," he said, and joined in. "I'll guard you jealously."

He kept his promise that night, as the yacht swept over the waves.

"There is one thing I've been meaning to ask. Will you tell me what you did with Sam Bailey?"

"Did you suspect me of leaving hs bloodied body in a bog? He was sent round the Horn as an impressed sailor. The ship, unfortunately, was lost in a violent storm."

Something was bothering Perdita as the sea rocked them gently. She was trying to think of what it was, but Ravenall's hand stroked along her hip and thigh, and was so distracting she couldn't concentrate. He pressed a kiss against the small of her back.

"So soft," he murmured against her skin. "Your skin is like ivory satin."

"I'm trying to remember something," she teased. "How can I think with you making love to me?"

Ravenall's hand reached around and cupped her breast in his palm. "My dear wife, why on earth would you even *want* to think of anything, when I'm making love to you?"

"I don't." She shivered as his fingers rubbed the tender peak. Heat shot through her body and she sighed, leaning back against him. As she did, she saw the burn scar on her wrist, and it dawned on her. "Wait! I remember now."

There was laughter in his eyes, as if he'd been waiting for this moment. She bit her underlip. "You said that every member of the family bloodline had the star birthmark somewhere upon their bodies. If I am truly Pauline Hexham, where is mine?"

Ravenall nibbled at her shoulder, then proceeded to kiss and nip his way down her spine. "In a place where no one but I have been privileged to see it, since your nurse bathed you at Hexham Court."

His mouth moved lower over the delicate ivory skin of her back, until it reached the low in the dip of her back. "Right here!"

She turned over and faced him indignantly. "You discovered proof of my identity, and you never said a word about it?"

He turned her gently in his arms, until she was looking up at the ceiling of the yacht's cabin.

"Not until after you rescued me and made a jibbering idiot of Lieutenant Nutting. At that particular moment, Lady Ravenall, I was far more concerned with proving myself as your lover. As I intend to do once more."

Perdita smiled, welcoming him. "I will expect you to do so frequently, my lord."

He took her face between his hands and kissed her until they were both breathless and aching with need. "Never fear, my darling. I shall give you all the proof you require."

The full moon rode high over the ancient landscape of Dartmoor. In the small clearing in the center of a wooded reeve that cleft the moors, a great oak stirred in the starlight. Crys-

tals flashed silver and ebony beneath the massive roots. It was more than mere reflection. They held an inner glow, as if they were filled with dreams and captured moonlight.

Although there was no breeze, the leaves danced and whispered like fairy voices. For centuries blood had been spilled here in sacrifice. Today, for the first time, something new had been added.

Not death, or ritual blood-letting, but the precious gift of love. The promise of flourishing new life. It was an unspoken wish. It didn't matter.

That wish too would be granted.

Fall in love with the spellbinding novels of

MARIANNE WILLMAN

THE MERMAID'S SONG

"It is impossible to resist the lure of THE MERMAID'S SONG.
From beginning to end, this love story, entwined with passion,
intrigue, and mystical charms, held me in its spell."
– Julie Garwood

THE LOST BRIDE

"A beautifully mystical journey of love, loss, and triumph.
Romance gilded with magic shimmers in THE LOST BRIDE.
Marianne Willman once again guides the readers through the
light and shadows of the heart."
—Nora Roberts

THE ENCHANTED MIRROR

Sweeping from the sun-baked sands of Egypt to the glittering
world of London's aristocracy, from the lost treasures of an
ancient land to the forbidden kiss of destined lovers,
THE ENCHANTED MIRROR shimmers with rich history, lush
adventure, and unforgettable romance...

**AVAILABLE WHEREVER BOOKS ARE SOLD
FROM ST. MARTIN'S PAPERBACKS**

WILLMAN 6/99

Haywood Smith

"Haywood Smith delivers intelligent, sensitive historical romance for readers who expect more from the genre."
—*Publishers Weekly*

SHADOWS IN VELVET

Orphan Anne Marie must enter the gilded decadence of the French court as the bride of a mysterious nobleman, only to be shattered by a secret from his past that could embroil them both in a treacherous uprising...

SECRETS IN SATIN

Amid the turmoil of a dying monarch, newly widowed Elizabeth, Countess of Ravenwold, is forced by royal command to marry a man she has hardened her heart to—and is drawn into a dangerous game of intrigue and a passionate contest of wills.

AVAILABLE WHEREVER BOOKS ARE SOLD
FROM ST. MARTIN'S PAPERBACKS

HAYWOOD 11/97

"VERY FEW WRITERS ARE ON PAR WITH DELIA
PARR WHEN IT COMES TO SCRIBING FRESH AND
INTERESTING HISTORICAL ROMANCE."
—Affaire de Coeur

Read all of Delia Parr's wonderful novels:

THE MINISTER'S WIFE

After years of scandal surrounding her illegitimacy, Emilee seems
to have finally found propriety by marrying the town minister.
But soon, Emilee is trapped—wedded to a man who can't fulfill
her passionate longings. When Justin Burke, exiled years ago
because of a shameful family secret, returns to town, an instant
attraction is sparked. But can the two lovers battle the wrath of a
small town—and their own buried wounds—to finally arrive at
happiness?

THE IVORY DUCHESS

Adored by millions, the Ivory Duchess knew fame as an accomplished European pianist—but her heart longed to free from her
tyrannical guardian. When she escaped to America, she found
the love of a lifetime...with the man who was hired to retrieve
her to her captor.

BY FATE'S DESIGN

Happy to live among the gentle Shakers, JoHanna Sims' world is
shattered when she is taken from her quiet community to await
her role as the wife of a stranger. But while she prepares for her
unwanted role, she meets a man who awakens in her a most forbidden and passionate love...

AVAILABLE WHEREVER BOOKS ARE SOLD
FROM ST. MARTIN'S PAPERBACKS

PARR 6/98

KATHLEEN KANE

"[HAS] REMARKABLE TALENT FOR UNUSUAL,
POIGNANT PLOTS AND CAPTIVATING
CHARACTERS."

—Publishers Weekly

The Soul Collector

A spirit whose job it was to usher souls into the afterlife, Zach
had angered the powers that be. Sent to Earth to live as a
human for a month, Zach never expected the beautiful
Rebecca to ignite in him such earthly emotions.

This Time for Keeps

After eight disastrous lives, Tracy Hill is determined to get it
right. But Heaven's "Resettlement Committee" has other
plans—to send her to a 19th century cattle ranch, where a
rugged cowboy makes her wonder if the ninth time is finally
the charm.

Still Close to Heaven

No man stood a ghost of a chance in Rachel Morgan's heart,
for the man she loved was an angel who she hadn't seen in
fifteen years. Jackson Tate has one more chance at heaven—if
he finds a good husband for Rachel ... and makes her forget a
love that he himself still holds dear.

AVAILABLE WHEREVER BOOKS ARE SOLD
FROM ST. MARTIN'S PAPERBACKS

KANE 9/98